WILMETTE PUBLIC LIBRARY
3 1239 00653 1070

D1069268

The Collected Stories of
Robert Silverberg

VOLUME FOUR

Trips
1972-73

The Collected Stories of
Robert Silverberg

VOLUME FOUR

Trips
1972-73

ROBERT SILVERBERG

SUBTERRANEAN PRESS 2009

First Edition

978-1-59606-212-2

Subterranean Press
PO Box 190106
Burton, MI 48519

www.subterraneanpress.com

ACKNOWLEDGMENTS

"In the Group" first appeared in *Eros in Orbit*.

"Getting Across" first appeared in *Future City*.

"Ms. Found in an Abandoned Time Machine" first appeared in *Ten Tomorrows*.

"The Science Fiction Hall of Fame" first appeared in *Infinity*.

"A Sea of Faces" first appeared in *Universe*.

"The Dybbuk of Mazel Tov IV" first appeared in *Wandering Stars*.

"Breckenridge and the Continuum" first appeared in *Showcase*.

"Capricorn Games" first appeared in *The Far Side of Time*.

"Ship-Sister, Star-Sister" first appeared in *Tomorrow's Alternatives*.

"This is the Road" first appeared in *No Mind of Man*.

"Trips" first appeared in *Final Stage*.

"Born with the Dead" first appeared in *Fantasy & Science Fiction*.

"Schwartz Between the Galaxies" first appeared in *Stellar*.

"In the House of Double Minds" first appeared in *Vertex*.

TABLE OF CONTENTS

For Barry Malzberg
Bob Hoskins
Don Pfeil
Edward L. Ferman
Terry Carr
Roger Elwood
Judy-Lynn del Rey
Joseph Elder
Jack Dann

INTRODUCTION

We arrive now at the fourth of these volumes in which I am engaged in bringing together a record of my life in science fiction, my long adventure in this wonderful field of storytelling.

The stories here, all of them written between March of 1972 and November of 1973, mark a critical turning point in my career. Those who know the three earlier volumes have traced my evolution from a capable journeyman, very young and as much concerned with paying the rent as he was to advancing the state of the art, into a serious, dedicated craftsman now seeking to leave his mark on science fiction in some significant way. Throughout the decade of the 1960s I had attempted to grow and evolve within the field of writing I loved—building on the best that went before me, the work of Theodore Sturgeon and James Blish and Cyril Kornbluth and Jack Vance and Philip K. Dick and half a dozen others whose great stories had been beacons beckoning me onward—and then, as I reached my own maturity, now trying to bring science fiction along with me into a new realm of development, hauling it along even farther out of its pulp-magazine origins toward what I regarded as a more resonant and evocative kind of visionary storytelling.

The stories reprinted here were difficult stories for difficult times. As I have already noted in the introduction to Volume III of this series, the years when the stories of Volumes III and IV were written were years in which the traditional values of American society and much of

Western Europe were crumbling, and the science fiction written at that time reflected the dislocations and fragmentations that our society was experiencing. New writers, armed with dazzling new techniques, took up the materials of s-f and did strange new things with it. Older writers, formerly content to produce the safe and simple stuff of previous decades, were reborn with sudden experimental zeal. It was a wild and adventurous time, when we were all improvising our way of life from day to day or even from hour to hour, and the science fiction of that period certainly shows it. Science fiction, which in the United States had been a child of the pulp magazines, turned into a form of avant-garde literature. (It is significant to note that of the fourteen stories in this book, only two appeared in conventional science-fiction magazines, and the rest in anthologies of previously unpublished fiction.)

Did the readers follow me as I proceeded with these experiments? Not many of them, apparently. I did retain some of my audience—four or five of the stories in this book were nominated for Hugo or Nebula awards—but the actual Hugos and Nebulas went elsewhere during this period, with the exception of the Nebula that "Born With the Dead" won for me in 1975. Awards are only an indirect reflection of the state of mind of the readership; but in those years the sales of my books began a sudden steep plunge that told me a great deal more about how the readers felt about the changed tone of my recent work. My perplexity over that, as you will see, was followed by disillusionment and anger, and even the abandonment (temporary, as it turned out) of my career as a professional writer.

These stories, then, reflect the turbulence of their times both in their content and the manner of their telling—and the seven years of silence that separates the last piece in this volume of my *Collected Stories* series from the opening story of the next one demonstrates quite eloquently, I think, the degree of interior turbulence that their creator was experiencing at that time.

Robert Silverberg

IN THE GROUP

In the early part of the 1970s, hard as that may be to believe today, many people living in the Western industrial nations devoted a substantial degree of energy to erotic activity. Historical records indicate that it was a time of vigorous sexual experimentation, the formation of unconventional mating relationships, the use of illicit chemicals to enhance physiological response, and, in general, a whole lot of weird stuff. Many of the people who took part in these things are still alive today and some of them actually remember much of what they were doing back then.

Under the circumstances, it should not be surprising that the editors of thematic science fiction anthologies in that far-off era had the idea of publishing stories that dealt with the future of sex. Two such collections were launched virtually simultaneously in the—ah—seminal year of 1971, and I contributed stories to both of them. The first of them was "Push No More," for a book edited by Thomas N. Scortia called Strange Bedfellows; *I wrote it in November, 1971 and it was included in the third volume of the present series of collections. Then, in March, 1972, I wrote the story reprinted here, "In the Group," for Joseph Elder's* Eros in Orbit. *(It also appeared in* Penthouse Magazine.*) It's one of my favorites among my own stories. I like it for its fast pace, its high-gloss surface, its technological inventiveness, and in particular for the bleakness of its conclusion. Even in the midst of all the fun back then I sensed that old-fashioned emotions might eventually intrude on all the disengaged copulators of that free-swinging era and there was likely to be trouble for some of them somewhere down the line.*

It was a restless time for Murray. He spent the morning sand-trawling on the beach at Acapulco. When it began to seem like lunchtime he popped over to Nairobi for mutton curry at the Three Bells. It wasn't lunchtime in Nairobi, but these days any restaurant worth eating at stayed open around the clock. In late afternoon, subjectivewise, he paused for pastis and water in Marseilles, and toward psychological twilight he buzzed back home to California. His inner clock was set to Pacific Time, so reality corresponded to mood: night was falling, San Francisco glittered like a mound of jewels across the bay. He was going to do Group tonight. He got Kay on the screen and said, "Come down to my place tonight, yes?"

"What for?"

"What else? Group."

She lay in a dewy bower of young redwoods, three hundred miles up the coast from him. Torrents of unbound milk-white hair cascaded over her slender, bare, honey-colored body. A multi-carat glitterstone sparkled fraudulently between her flawless little breasts. Looking at her, he felt his hands tightening into desperate fists, his nails ravaging his palms. He loved her beyond all measure. The intensity of his love overwhelmed and embarrassed him.

"You want to do Group together tonight?" she asked. "You and me?" She didn't sound pleased.

"Why not? Closeness is more fun than apartness."

"Nobody's ever apart in Group. What does mere you-and-me physical proximity matter? It's irrelevant. It's obsolete."

"I miss you."

"You're with me right now," she pointed out.

"I want to touch you. I want to inhale you. I want to taste you."

"Punch for tactile, then. Punch for olfactory. Punch for any input you think you want."

"I"ve got all sensory channels open already," Murray said. "I'm flooded with delicious input. It still isn't the same thing. It isn't enough, Kay."

She rose and walked slowly toward the ocean. His eyes tracked her across the screen. He heard the pounding of the surf.

"I want you right beside me when Group starts tonight," he told her. "Look, if you don't feel like coming here, I'll go to your place."

"You're being boringly persistent."

He winced. "I can't help it. I like being close to you."

"You have a lot of old-fashioned attitudes, Murray." Her voice was so cool. "Are you aware of that?"

"I'm aware that my emotional drives are very strong. That's all. Is that such a sin?" Careful, Murray. A serious error in tactics just then. This whole conversation a huge mistake, most likely. He was running big risks with her by pushing too hard, letting too much of his crazy romanticism reveal itself so early. His obsession with her, his impossible new possessiveness, his weird ego-driven exclusivism. His love. *Yes;* his love. She was absolutely right, of course. He was basically old-fashioned. Wallowing in emotional atavism. You-and-me stuff. I, me, me, mine. This unwillingness to share her fully in Group. As though he had some special claim. He was pure nineteenth century underneath it all. He had only just discovered that, and it had come as a surprise to him. His sick archaic fantasies aside, there was no reason for the two of them to be side by side in the same room during Group, not unless they were the ones who were screwing, and the copulation schedule showed Nate and Serena on tonight's ticket. Drop it, Murray. But he couldn't drop it. He said into her stony silence, "All right, but at least let me set up an inner intersex connection for you and me. So I can feel what you're feeling when Nate and Serena get it on."

"Why this frantic need to reach inside my head?" she asked.

"I love you."

"Of course you do. We all love all of Us. But still, when you try to relate to me one-on-one like this, you injure Group."

"No inner connection, then?"

"No."

"Do you love me?"

A sigh. "I love Us, Murray."

That was likely to be the best he'd get from her this evening. All right. All right. He'd settle for that, if he had to. A crumb here, a crumb there. She smiled, blew him an amiable kiss, broke the contact. He stared moodily at the dead screen. All right. Time to get ready for Group. He turned to the life-size screen on the east wall and keyed in the visuals for preliminary alignment. Right now Group Central was sending its test pattern, stills of all of tonight's couples. Nate and Serena were in the centre, haloed by the glowing nimbus that marked them as this evening's performers. Around the periphery Murray saw images of himself, Kay, Van, JoJo, Nikki, Dirk, Conrad, Finn, Lanelle, and Maria.

Bruce, Klaus, Mindy, and Lois weren't there. Too busy, maybe. Or too tired. Or perhaps they were in the grip of negative unGrouplike vibes just at the moment. You didn't have to do Group every night, if you didn't feel into it. Murray averaged four nights a week. Only the real bulls, like Dirk and Nate, routinely hit seven out of seven. Also JoJo, Lanelle, Nikki—the Very Hot Ladies, he liked to call them.

He opened up the audio. "This is Murray," he announced. "I'm starting to synchronize."

Group Central gave him a sweet unwavering A for calibration. He tuned his receiver to match the note. "You're at four hundred and thirty-two," Group Central said. "Bring your pitch up a little. There. There. Steady. Four hundred and forty, fine." The tones locked perfectly. He was synched in for sound. A little fine tuning on the visuals, next. The test pattern vanished and the screen showed only Nate, naked, a big cocky rockjawed man with a thick mat of curly black hair covering him from thighs to throat. He grinned, bowed, preened. Murray made adjustments until it was all but impossible to distinguish the three-dimensional holographic projection of Nate from the actual Nate, hundreds of miles away in his San Diego bedroom. Murray was fastidious about these adjustments. Any perceptible drop-off in reality approximation dampened the pleasure Group gave him. For some moments he watched Nate striding bouncily back and forth, working off excess energy, fining himself down to performance level; a minor element of distortion crept into the margins of the image, and, cutting in the manual override, Murray fed his own corrections to Central until all was well.

Next came the main brain-wave amplification, delivering data in the emotional sphere: endocrine feeds, neural set, epithelial appercept, erogenous uptake. Diligently Murray keyed in each one. At first he received only a vague undifferentiated blur of formless background cerebration, but then, like intricate figures becoming clear in an elaborate oriental carpet, the specific characteristics of Nate's mental output began to clarify themselves; edginess, eagerness, horniness, alertness, intensity. A sense of Nate's formidable masculine strength came through. At this stage of the evening Murray still had a distinct awareness of himself as an entity independent of Nate, but that would change soon enough.

"Ready," Murray reported. "Holding awaiting Group cut-in."

He had to hold for fifteen intolerable minutes. He was always the quickest to synchronize. Then he had to sit and sweat, hanging on desperately to his balances and lineups while he waited for the others. All around the circuit, the rest of them were still tinkering with their rigs, adjusting them with varying degrees of competence. He thought of Kay. At this moment making frantic adjustments, tuning herself to Serena as he had done to Nate.

"Group cut-in," Central said finally.

Murray closed the last circuits. Into his consciousness poured, in one wild rush, the mingled consciousnesses of Van, Dirk, Conrad, and Finn, hooked into him via Nate, and, less intensely because less directly, the consciousnesses of Kay, Maria, Lanelle, JoJo, and Nikki, funnelled to him by way of their link to Serena. So all twelve of them were in sync. They had attained Group once again. Now the revels could begin.

Now. Nate approaching Serena. The magic moments of foreplay. That buzz of early excitement, that soaring erotic flight, taking everybody upward like a Beethoven adagio, like a solid hit of acid. Nate. Serena. San Diego. Their bedroom a glittering hall of mirrors. Refracted images everywhere. A thousand quivering breasts. Five hundred jutting cocks. Hands, eyes, tongues, thighs. The circular undulating bed, quivering, heaving. Murray, lying cocooned in his maze of sophisticated amplification equipment, receiving inputs at temples and throat and chest and loins, felt his palate growing dry, felt a pounding in his groin. He licked his lips. His hips began, of their own accord, a slow rhythmic thrusting motion. Nate's hands casually traversed the taut globes of Serena's bosom. Caught the rigid nipples between hairy fingers, tweaked them, thumbed them. Murray felt the firm nodules of engorged flesh with his own empty hands. The merger of identities was starting. He was becoming Nate, Nate was flowing into him, and he was all the others too, Van, JoJo, Dirk, Finn, Nikki, all of them, feedbacks oscillating in interpersonal whirlpools all along the line. Kay. He was part of Kay, she of him, both of them parts of Nate and Serena. Inextricably intertwined. What Nate experienced, Murray experienced. What Serena experienced, Kay experienced. When Nate's mouth descended to cover Serena's, Murray's tongue slid forward. And felt the moist tip of Serena's. Flesh against flesh, skin against skin. Serena was throbbing. Why not? Six men tonguing her at once. She was always quick to arouse, anyway. She was begging for it. Not that Nate was in any hurry: screwing was his thing, he always made a grand production out of it. As well he might, with ten close friends riding as passengers on his trip. Give us a show, Nate. Nate obliged. He was going down on her, now. Inhaling. His stubbly cheeks against her satiny thighs. Oh, the busy tongue! Oh, the sighs and gasps! And then she engulfing him reciprocally. Murray hissed in delight. Her cunning little suctions, her jolly slithers and slides: a skilled fellatrice, that woman was. He trembled. He was fully into it, now, sharing every impulse with Nate. *Becoming* Nate. Yes. Serena's beckoning body gaping for him. His waggling wand poised above her. The old magic of Group never diminishing. Nate doing all his tricks, pulling out the stops. When? Now. Now. The thrust. The quick sliding moment of entry. Ah! Ah! *Ah!* Serena simultaneously possessed by Nate, Murray, Van, Dirk, Conrad, Finn. Finn, Conrad, Dirk, Van, Murray, and Nate simultaneously possessing Serena. And, vicariously throbbing in rhythm with Serena: Kay, Maria, Lanelle, JoJo, Nikki. Kay. Kay. Kay. Through the sorcery of the crossover loop Nate was having Kay while he had Serena, Nate was having Kay, Maria, Lanelle, JoJo, Nikki all at once, they were being had by him, a soup of identities, an *olla podrida* of copulations, and as the twelve of them soared toward a shared and multiplied ecstasy Murray did something dumb. He thought of Kay.

He thought of Kay. Kay alone in her redwood bower, Kay with bucking hips and tossing hair and glistening droplets of sweat between her breasts, Kay hissing and shivering in Nate's simulated embrace. Murray tried to reach across to her through the Group loop, tried to find and isolate the discrete thread of self that was Kay, tried to chisel away the ten extraneous identities and transform this coupling into an encounter between himself and her. It was a plain violation of the spirit of Group; it was also impossible to achieve, since she had refused him permission to establish a special inner link between them that evening, and so at the moment she was accessible to him only as one facet of the enhanced and expanded Serena. At best he could grope toward Kay through Serena and touch the tip of her soul, but the contact was cloudy and uncertain. Instantly on to what he was trying to do, she petulantly pushed him away, at the same time submerging herself more fully in Serena's consciousness. Rejected, reeling, he slid off into confusion, sending jarring crosscurrents through the whole Group. Nate loosed a shower of irritation, despite his heroic attempt to remain unperturbed, and pumped his way to climax well ahead of schedule, hauling everyone breathlessly along with him. As the orgasmic frenzy broke loose Murray tried to re-enter the full linkage, but he found himself unhinged, disaffiliated, and mechanically emptied himself without any tremor of pleasure. Then it was over. He lay back, perspiring, feeling soiled, jangled, unsatisfied. After a few moments he uncoupled his equipment and went out for a cold shower.

Kay called half an hour later.

"You crazy bastard," she said. "What were you trying to do?"

He promised not to do it again. She forgave him. He brooded for two days, keeping out of Group. He missed sharing Conrad and JoJo, Klaus and Lois. The third day the Group chart marked him and Kay as that night's performers. He didn't want to let them all share her. It was stronger than ever, this nasty atavistic possessiveness. He didn't have to, of course. Nobody was forced to do Group. He could beg off and continue to sulk, and Dirk or Van or somebody would substitute for him tonight. But Kay wouldn't necessarily pass up her turn. She almost certainly wouldn't. He didn't like the options. If he made it with Kay as per Group schedule, he'd be offering her to all the others. If he stepped aside, she'd do it with someone else. Might as well be the one to take her to bed in that case. Faced with an ugly choice, he decided to stick to the original schedule.

He popped up to her place eight hours early. He found her sprawled on a carpet of redwood needles in a sun-dappled grove, playing with a stack of music cubes. Mozart tinkled in the fragrant air. "Let's go away somewhere tomorrow," he said. "You and me."

"You're still into you-and-me?"

"I'm sorry."

"Where do you want to go?"

He shrugged. "Hawaii. Afghanistan. Poland. Zambia. It doesn't matter. Just to be with you."

"What about Group?"

"They can spare us for a while."

She rolled over, lazily snaffled Mozart into silence, started a cube of Bach. "I'll go," she said. The Goldberg Variations transcribed for glockenspiel. "But only if we take our Group equipment along."

"It means that much to you?"

"Doesn't it to you?"

"I cherish Group," he said. "But it's not all there is to life. I can live without it for a while. I don't need it, Kay. What I need is you."

"That's obscene, Murray."

"No. It isn't obscene."

"It's boring, at any rate."

"I'm sorry you think so," he told her.

"Do you want to drop out of Group?"

I want us both to drop out of Group, he thought, and I want you to live with me. I can't bear to share you any longer, Kay. But he wasn't prepared to move to that level of confrontation. He said, "I want to stay in Group if it's possible, but I'm also interested in extending and developing some one-on-one with you."

"You've already made that excessively clear."

"I love you."

"You've said that before too."

"What do you want, Kay?"

She laughed, rolled over, drew her knees up until they touched her breasts, parted her thighs, opened herself to a stray shaft of sunlight. "I want to enjoy myself," she said.

He started setting up his equipment an hour before sunset. Because he was performing, the calibrations were more delicate than on an ordinary night. Not only did he have to broadcast a full range of control ratios to Central to aid the others in their tuning, he had to achieve a flawless balance of input and output with Kay. He went about his complex tasks morosely, not at all excited by the thought that he and Kay would shortly be making love. It cooled his ardor to know that Nate, Dirk, Van, Finn, Bruce, and Klaus would be having her too. Why did he begrudge it to them so? He didn't know. Such exclusivism, coming out of nowhere, shocked and disgusted him. Yet it wholly controlled him. Maybe I need help, he thought.

Group time, now. Soft sweet ionized fumes drifting through the chamber of Eros. Kay was warm, receptive, passionate. Her eyes sparkled as she reached for him. They had made love five hundred times and she showed no sign of diminished interest. He knew he turned her on. He hoped he turned her on more than anyone else. He caressed her in all his clever ways, and she purred and wriggled and glowed. Her nipples stood tall: no faking that. Yet something was wrong. Not with her, with him. He was aloof, remote. He seemed to be watching the proceedings from a point somewhere outside himself, as though he were just a Group onlooker tonight, badly tuned in, not even as much a part of things as Klaus, Bruce, Finn, Van, Dirk. The awareness that he had an audience affected him for the first time. His technique, which depended more on finesse and grace than on fire and force, became a trap, locking him into a series of passionless arabesques and pirouettes. He was distracted, though he never had been before, by the minute telemetry tapes glued to the side of Kay's neck and the underside of her thigh. He found himself addressing silent messages to the other men. Here, Nate, how do you like that? Grab some haunch, Dirk. Up the old zaboo, Bruce. Uh. Uh. Ah. Oh.

Kay didn't seem to notice anything was amiss. She came three times in the first fifteen minutes. He doubted that he'd ever come at all. He plugged on, in and out, in and out, moving like a mindless piston. A sort of revenge on Group, he realized. You want to share Kay with me, okay, fellows, but this is all you're going to get. This. Oh. Oh. Oh. Now at last he felt the familiar climactic tickle, stepped down to a tenth of its normal intensity. He hardly noticed it when he came.

Kay said afterward, "What about that trip? Are we still going to go away somewhere tomorrow?"

"Let's forget it for the time being," he said.

He popped to Istanbul alone and spent a day in the covered bazaar, buying cheap but intricate trinkets for every woman in Group. At nightfall he popped down to McMurdo Sound, where the merry Antarctic summer was at its height, and spent six hours on the polar ski slopes, coming away with wind-bronzed skin and aching muscles. In the lodge later he met an angular, auburn-haired woman from Portugal and took her to bed. She was very good, in a heartless, mechanically proficient way. Doubtless she thought the same of him. She asked him whether he might be interested in joining her Group, which operated out of Lisbon and Ibiza. "I already have an affiliation," he said. He popped to Addis Ababa after breakfast, checked into the Hilton, slept for a day and a half, and went on to St. Croix for a night of reef-bobbing. When he popped back to California the next day he called Kay at once to learn the news.

"We've been discussing rearranging some of the Group couplings," she said. "Next week, what about you and Lanelle, me and Dirk?"

"Does that mean you're dropping me?"

"No, not at all, silly. But I do think we need variety."

"Group was designed to provide us with all the variety we'd ever want."

"You know what I mean. Besides, you're developing an unhealthy fixation on me as isolated love object."

"Why are you rejecting me?"

"I'm not. I'm trying to help you, Murray."

"I love you," he said.

"Love me in a healthier way, then."

That night it was the turn of Maria and Van. The next, Nikki and Finn. After them, Bruce and Mindy. He tuned in for all three, trying to erode his grief in nightly frenzies of lustful fulfilment. By the third night he was very tired and no less grief-smitten. He took the next night off. Then the schedule came up with the first Murray-Lanelle pairing.

He popped to Hawaii and set up his rig in her sprawling beachfront lanai on Molokai. He had bedded her before, of course. Everyone in Group had bedded everyone else during the preliminary months of compatibility testing. But then they all had settled into more or less regular pair-bonding, and he hadn't approached her since. In the past year the only Group woman he had slept with was Kay. By choice.

"I've always liked you," Lanelle said. She was tall, heavy-breasted, wide-shouldered, with warm brown eyes, yellow hair, skin the color of fine honey. "You're just a little crazy, but I don't mind that. And I love screwing Scorpios."

"I'm a Capricorn."

"Them too," she said. "I love screwing just about every sign. Except Virgos. I can't stand Virgos. Remember, we were supposed to have a Virgo in Group, at the start. I blackballed him."

They swam and surfed for a couple of hours before doing the calibrating. The water was warm but a brisk breeze blew from the east, coming like a gust of bad news out of California. Lanelle nuzzled him playfully and then not so playfully in the water. She had always been an aggressive woman, a swaggerer, a strutter. Her appetites were enormous. Her eyes glistened with desire. "Come on," she said finally, tugging at him. They ran to the house and he began to adjust the equipment. It was still early. He thought of Kay and his soul drooped. What am I doing here? he wondered. He lined up the Group apparatus with nervous hands, making many errors. Lanelle stood behind him, rubbing her breasts against his bare back. He had to ask her to stop. Eventually everything was ready and she hauled him to the spongy floor with her, covering his body with hers. Lanelle always liked to be the one on top. Her tongue probed his mouth and her hands clutched his hips and she pressed herself against him, but although her body was warm and smooth and alive he felt no onset of excitement, not a shred. She put her mouth to him but it was hopeless. He remained limp, dead, unable to function. With everyone tuned in and waiting. "What is it?" she whispered. "What should I do, love?" He closed his eyes and indulged in a fantasy of Kay coupling with Dirk, pure masochism, and it aroused him as far as a sort of half-erect condition, and he slithered into her like a prurient eel. She rocked her way to ecstasy above him. This is garbage, he thought. I'm falling apart. Kay. Kay. Kay.

Then Kay had her night with Dirk. At first Murray thought he would simply skip it. There was no reason, after all, why he had to subject himself to something like that, if he expected it to give him pain. It had never been painful for him in the past when Kay did it with other men, inside Group or not, but since the onset of his jealousies everything was different. In theory the Group couples were interchangeable, one pair serving as proxies for all the rest each night, but theory and practice coincided less and less in Murray's mind these days. Nobody would be surprised or upset if he happened not to want to participate tonight. All during the day, though, he found himself obsessively fantasizing Kay and Dirk, every motion, every sound, the two of them facing each other, smiling, embracing, sinking down onto her bed, entwining, his hands sliding over her slender body, his mouth on her mouth, his chest crushing her small breasts, Dirk entering her, riding her, plunging, driving, coming, Kay coming, then Kay and Dirk arising, going for a cooling swim, returning to the bedroom, facing each other, smiling, beginning again. By late afternoon it had taken place so many times in his fevered imagination that he saw no risk in experiencing the reality of it; at least he could have Kay, if only at one remove, by doing Group tonight. And it might help him to shake off his obsessiveness. But it was worse than he imagined it could be. The sight of Dirk, all bulging muscles and tapering hips, terrified him; Dirk was ready for making love long before the foreplay started, and Murray somehow came to fear that he, not Kay, was going to be the target of that long rigid spear of his. Then Dirk began to caress Kay. With each insinuating touch of his hand it seemed that some vital segment of Murray's relationship with Kay was being obliterated. He was forced to watch Kay through Dirk's eyes, her flushed face, her quivering nostrils, her moist, slack lips, and it killed him. As Dirk drove deep into her, Murray coiled into a miserable fetal ball, one hand clutching his loins, the other clapped across his lips, thumb in his mouth. He couldn't stand it at all. To think that every one of them was having Kay at once. Not only Dirk. Nate, Van, Conrad, Finn, Bruce, Klaus, the whole male Group complement, all of them tuning in tonight for this novel Dirk-Kay pairing. Kay giving herself to all of them gladly, willingly, enthusiastically. He had to escape, now, instantly, even though to drop out of Group communion at this point would unbalance everyone's tuning and set up chaotic eddy currents that might induce nausea or worse in the others. He didn't care. He had to save himself. He screamed and uncoupled his rig.

He waited two days and went to see her. She was at her exercises, floating like a cloud through a dazzling arrangement of metal rings and loops that dangled at constantly varying heights from the ceiling of her solarium. He stood below her, craning his neck. "It isn't any good," he said. "I want us both to withdraw from Group, Kay."

"That was predictable."

"It's killing me. I love you so much I can't bear to share you."

"So loving me means owning me?"

"Let's just drop out for a while. Let's explore the ramifications of one-on-one. A month, two months, six months, Kay. Just until I get this craziness out of my system. Then we can go back in."

"So you admit it's craziness."

"I never denied it." His neck was getting stiff. "Won't you please come down from those rings while we're talking?"

"I can hear you perfectly well from here, Murray."

"Will you drop out of Group and go away with me for a while?"

"No."

"Will you even consider it?"

"No."

"Do you realize that you're addicted to Group?" he asked.

"I don't think that's an accurate evaluation of the situation. But do *you* realize that you're dangerously fixated on me?"

"I realize it."

"What do you propose to do about it?"

"What I'm doing. now," he said. "Coming to you, asking you to do a one-on-one with me."

"Stop it."

"One-on-one was good enough for the human race for thousands of years."

"It was a prison," she said. "It was a trap. We're out of the trap at last. You won't get me back in."

He wanted to pull her down from her rings and shake her. "I *love* you, Kay!"

"You take a funny way of showing it. Trying to limit the range of my experience. Trying to hide me away in a vault somewhere. It won't work."

"Definitely no?"

"Definitely no."

She accelerated her pace, flinging herself recklessly from loop to loop. Her glistening nude form tantalized and infuriated him. He shrugged and turned away, shoulders slumping, head drooping. This was precisely how he had expected her to respond. No surprises. Very well. Very well. He crossed from the solarium into the bedroom and lifted her Group rig from its container. Slowly, methodically, he ripped it apart, bending the frame until it split, cracking the fragile leads, uprooting handfuls of connectors, crumpling the control panel. The instrument was already a ruin by the time Kay came in. "What are you *doing?*" she cried. He splintered the lovely gleaming calibration dials under his heel and kicked the wreckage of the rig toward her. It would take months before a replacement rig could be properly attuned and synchronized. "I had no choice," he told her sadly.

They would have to punish him. That was inevitable. But how? He waited at home, and before long they came to him, all of them, Nate,

Van, Dirk, Conrad, Finn, Bruce, Klaus, Kay, Serena, Maria, JoJo, Lanelle, Nikki, Mindy, Lois, popping in from many quarters of the world, some of them dressed in evening clothes, some of them naked or nearly so, some of them unkempt and sleepy, all of them angry in a cold, tight way. He tried to stare them down. Dirk said, "You must be terribly sick, Murray. We feel sorry for you."

"We really want to help you," said Lanelle.

"We're here to give you therapy," Finn told him.

Murray laughed. "Therapy. I bet. What kind of therapy?"

"To rid you of your exclusivism," Dirk said. "To burn all the trash out of your mind."

"Shock treatment," Finn said.

"Keep away from me!"

"Hold him," Dirk said.

Quickly they surrounded him. Bruce clamped an arm across his chest like an iron bar. Conrad seized his hands and brought his wrists together behind his back. Finn and Dirk pressed up against his sides. He was helpless.

Kay began to remove her clothing. Naked, she lay down on Murray's bed, flexed her knees, opened her thighs. Klaus got on top of her.

"What the hell is this?" Murray asked.

Efficiently but without passion Kay aroused Klaus, and efficiently but without passion he penetrated her. Murray writhed impotently as their bodies moved together. Klaus made no attempt at bringing Kay off. He reached his climax in four or five minutes, grunting once, and rolled away from her, red-faced, sweating. Van took his place between Kay's legs.

"No," Murray said. "Please, no."

Inexorably Van had his turn, quick, impersonal. Nate was next. Murray tried not to watch, but his eyes would not remain closed. A strange smile glittered on Kay's lips as she gave herself to Nate. Nate arose. Finn approached the bed.

"No!" Murray cried, and lashed out in a backward kick that sent Conrad screaming across the room. Murray's hands were free. He twisted and wrenched himself away from Bruce. Dirk and Nate intercepted him as he rushed toward Kay. They seized him and flung him to the floor.

"The therapy isn't working," Nate said.

"Let's skip the rest," said Dirk. "It's no use trying to heal him. He's beyond hope. Let him stand up."

Murray got cautiously to his feet. Dirk said, "By unanimous vote, Murray, we expel you from Group for unGrouplike attitudes and especially for your unGrouplike destruction of Kay's rig. All your Group privileges are canceled." At a signal from Dirk, Nate removed Murray's rig from the container and reduced it to unsalvageable rubble. Dirk said, "Speaking as your friend, Murray, I suggest you think seriously about undergoing a total personality reconstruct. You're in trouble, do you know that? You need a lot of help. You're a mess."

"Is there anything else you want to tell me?" Murray asked.

"Nothing else. Goodbye, Murray."

They started to go out. Dirk, Finn, Nate, Bruce, Conrad, Klaus. Van. JoJo. Nikki. Serena, Maria, Lanelle, Mindy. Lois. Kay was the last to leave. She stood by the door, clutching her clothes in a small crumpled bundle. She seemed entirely unafraid of him. There was a peculiar look of—was it tenderness? pity?—on her face. Softly she said, "I'm sorry it had to come to this, Murray. I feel so unhappy for you. I know that what you did wasn't a hostile act. You did it out of love. You were all wrong, but you were doing it out of love." She walked toward him and kissed him lightly, on the cheek, on the tip of the nose, on the lips. He didn't move. She smiled. She touched his arm. "I'm so sorry," she murmured. "Goodbye, Murray." As she went through the door she looked back and said, "Such a damned shame. I could have loved you, you know? I could really have loved you."

He had told himself that he would wait until they all were gone before he let the tears flow. But when the door had closed behind Kay he discovered his eyes remained dry. He had no tears. He was altogether calm. Numb. Burned out.

After a long while he put on fresh clothing and went out. He popped to London, found that it was raining there, and popped to Prague, where there was something stifling about the atmosphere, and went on to Seoul, where he had barbecued beef and kimchi for dinner. Then he popped to New York. In front of a gallery on Lexington Avenue he picked up a complaisant young girl with long black hair. "Let's go to a hotel," he suggested, and she smiled and nodded. He registered for a six-hour stay. Upstairs, she undressed without waiting for him to ask. Her body was smooth and supple, flat belly, pale skin, high full breasts.

They lay down together and, in silence, without preliminaries, he took her. She was eager and responsive. Kay, he thought. Kay. Kay. You are Kay. A spasm of culmination shook him with unexpected force.

"Do you mind if I smoke?" she said a few minutes later.

"I love you," he said.

"What?"

"I love you."

"You're sweet."

"Come live with me. Please. Please. I'm serious."

"What?"

"Live with me. Marry me."

"What?"

"There's only one thing I ask. No Group stuff. That's all. Otherwise you can do as you please. I'm wealthy. I'll make you happy. I love you."

"You don't even know my name."

"I love you."

"Mister, you must be out of your head."

"Please. Please."

"A lunatic. Unless you're trying to make fun of me."

"I'm perfectly serious, I assure you. Live with me. Be my wife."

"A lunatic," she said. "I'm getting out of here!" She leaped up and looked for her clothes. "Jesus, a madman!"

"No," he said, but she was on her way, not even pausing to get dressed, running helter-skelter from the room, her pink buttocks flashing like beacons as she made her escape. The door slammed. He shook his head. He sat rigid for half an hour, an hour, some long timeless span, thinking of Kay, thinking of Group, wondering what they'd be doing tonight, whose turn it was. At length he rose and put on his clothes and left the hotel. A terrible restlessness assailed him. He popped to Karachi and stayed ten minutes. He popped to Vienna. To Hangchow. He didn't stay. Looking for what? He didn't know. Looking for Kay? Kay didn't exist. Looking. Just looking. Pop. Pop. Pop.

GETTING ACROSS

Now it is a little later in the spring of 1972 and I have finished the complicated process of resettling myself in balmy California after a lifetime spent in the grim urban sprawl of New York City. The indefatigable Roger Elwood, he of the multitudinous original-story science-fiction anthologies, was now compiling one on the theme of the future of cities, and invited me to contribute. With the iron acres of the Northeastern United States still clanging in my memory, I could do nothing else but imagine the future of the city as one vast world-wide Northeastern United States, town after town cheek by jowl. I thought of "Getting Across" as a rite of exorcism from my former existence on the crowded East Coast. Looking back at it now, though, I see that I would very much rather live in the relatively orderly urban dystopia I imagined here than in the chaotic actual New York of today, which worries me because it's only about three thousand miles from the place where I currently make my home, and that doesn't seem like sufficient distance. New York is one of the great cities of the world, but I have grown accustomed to the slower pace and greener environment of California in all these decades of my transplanted life, and I'm no longer fit, it seems, for the New York style of doing things. California has its own problems, ofcourse. And so, too, does the worldwide city I depict in this story.

1.

On the first day of summer my month-wife, Silena Ruiz, filched our district's master program from the Ganfield Hold computer centre and disappeared with it. A guard at the Hold has confessed that she won admittance by seducing him, then gave him a drug. Some say she is in Conning Town now, others have heard rumors that she has been seen in Morton Court, still others maintain her destination was the Mill. I suppose it does not matter where she has gone. What matters is that we are without our program. We have lived without it for eleven days, and things are starting to break down. The heat is abominable, but we must switch every thermostat to manual override before we can use our cooling system; I think we will boil in our skins before the job is done. A malfunction of the scanners that control our refuse compactor has stilled the garbage collectors, which will not go forth unless they have a place to dump what they collect. Since no one knows the proper command to give the compactor, rubbish accumulates, forming pestilential hills on every street, and dense swarms of flies or worse hover over the sprawling mounds. Beginning on the fourth day our police also began to go immobile—who can say why?—and by now all of them stand halted in their tracks. Some are already starting to rust, since the maintenance schedules are out of phase. Word has gone out that we are without protection, and outlanders cross into the district with impunity, molesting our women, stealing our children, raiding our stocks of foodstuffs. In Ganfield Hold platoons of weary sweating technicians toil constantly to replace the missing program, but it might be months, even years, before they are able to devise a new one.

In theory, duplicate programs are stored in several places within the community against just such a calamity. In fact, we have none. The one kept in the district captain's office turned out to be some twenty years obsolete; the one in the care of the soulfather's house had been devoured by rats; the program held in the vaults of the tax collectors appeared to be intact, but when it was placed in the input slot it mysteriously failed to activate the computers. So we are helpless: an entire district, hundreds of thousands of human beings, cut loose to drift on the tides of chance. Silena, Silena, Silena! To disable all of Ganfield, to make our already burdensome lives more difficult, to expose me to the hatred of my neighbors—why, Silena? Why?

People glare at me on the streets. They hold me responsible, in a way, for all this. They point and mutter; in another few days they will be spitting and cursing, and if no relief comes soon they may be throwing stones. Look, I want to shout, she was only my month-wife and she acted entirely on her own. I assure you I had no idea she would do such a thing. And yet they blame me. At the wealthy houses of Morton Court they will dine tonight on babes stolen in Ganfield this day, and I am held accountable.

What will I do? Where can I turn?

I may have to flee. The thought of crossing district lines chills me. Is it the peril of death I fear, or only the loss of all that is familiar? Probably both: I have no hunger for dying and no wish to leave Ganfield. Yet I will go, no matter how difficult it will be to find sanctuary if I get safely across the line. If they continue to hold me tainted by Silena's crime I will have no choice. I think I would rather die at the hands of strangers than perish at those of my own people.

2.

This sweltering night I find myself atop Ganfield Tower, seeking cool breezes and the shelter of darkness. Half the district has had the idea of escaping the heat by coming up here tonight, it seems; to get away from the angry eyes and tightened lips I have climbed to the fifth parapet, where only the bold and the foolish ordinarily go. I am neither, yet here I am.

As I move slowly around the tower's rim, warily clinging to the old and eroded guardrail, I have a view of our entire district. Ganfield is like a shallow basin in form, gently sloping upward from the central spike that is the tower to a rise on the district perimeter. They say that a broad lake once occupied the site where Ganfield now stands; it was drained and covered over centuries ago, when the need for new living space became extreme. Yesterday I heard that great pumps are used to keep the ancient lake from breaking through into our cellars, and that before very long the pumps will fail or shut themselves down for maintenance, and we will be flooded. Perhaps so. Ganfield once devoured the lake; will the lake now have Ganfield? Will we tumble into the dark waters and be swallowed, with no one to mourn us?

I look out over Ganfield. These tall brick boxes are our dwellings, twenty stories high but dwarfed from my vantage point far above. This sliver of land, black in the smoky moonlight, is our pitiful scrap of community park. These low flat-topped buildings are our shops, a helter-skelter cluster. This is our industrial zone, such that it is. That squat shadow-cloaked bulk just north of the tower is Ganfield Hold, where our crippled computers slip one by one into idleness. I have spent nearly my whole life within this one narrow swing of the compasses that is Ganfield. When I was a boy and affairs were not nearly so harsh between one district and its neighbor, my father took me on holiday to Morton Court, and another time to the Mill. When I was a young man I was sent on business across three districts to Parley Close. I remember those journeys as clearly and vividly as though I had dreamed them. But everything is quite different now and it is twenty years since I last left Ganfield. I am not one of your privileged commuters, gaily making transit from zone to zone. All the world is one great city, so it is said, with the deserts settled and the rivers bridged and all the open places filled, a universal city that has abolished the old boundaries, and yet it is twenty years since I passed from one district to the next. I wonder: are we one city, then, or merely thousands of contentious fragmented tiny states?

Look here, along the perimeter. There are no more boundaries, but what is this? This is our boundary, Ganfield Crescent, that wide curving boulevard surrounding the district. Are you a man of some other zone? Then cross the Crescent at risk of life. Do you see our police machines, blunt-snouted, glossy, formidably powerful, strewn like boulders in the broad avenue? They will interrogate you, and if your answers are uneasy, they may destroy you. Of course they can do no one any harm tonight.

Look outward now, at our horde of brawling neighbors. I see beyond the Crescent to the east the gaunt spires of Conning Town, and on the west, descending stepwise into the jumbled valley, the shabby dark-walled buildings of the Mill, with happy Morton Court on the far side, and somewhere in the smoky distance other places, Folkstone and Budleigh and Hawk Nest and Parley Close and Kingston and Old Grove and all the rest, the districts, the myriad districts, part of the chain that stretches from sea to sea, from shore to shore, spanning our continent paunch by paunch, the districts, the chips of gaudy glass making up the global mosaic, the infinitely numerous communities that are the segments of the all-encompassing world-city.

Tonight at the capital they are planning next month's rainfall patterns for districts that the planners have never seen. District food allocations—inadequate, always inadequate—are being devised by men to whom our appetites are purely abstract entities. Do they believe in our existence, at the capital? Do they really think there is such a place as Ganfield? What if we sent them a delegation of notable citizens to ask for help in replacing our lost program? Would they care? Would they even listen? For that matter, is there a capital at all? How can I who have never seen nearby Old Grove accept, on faith alone, the existence of a far-off governing centre, aloof, inaccessible, shrouded in myth? Maybe it is only a construct of some cunning subterranean machine that is our real ruler. That would not surprise me. Nothing surprises me. There is no capital. There are no central planners. Beyond the horizon everything is mist.

3.

In the office, at least, no one dares show hostility to me. There are no scowls, no glares, no snide references to the missing program. I am, after all, chief deputy to the District Commissioner of Nutrition, and since the commissioner is usually absent, I am in effect in charge of the department. If Silena's crime does not destroy my career, it might prove to have been unwise for my subordinates to treat me with disdain. In any case we are so busy that there is no time for such gambits. We are responsible for keeping the community properly fed; our tasks have been greatly complicated by the loss of the program, for there is no reliable way now of processing our allocation sheets, and we must requisition and distribute food by guesswork and memory. How many bales of plankton cubes do we consume each week? How many kilos of proteoid mix? How much bread for the shops of Lower Ganfield? What fads of diet are likely to sweep the district this month? If demand and supply fall into imbalance as a result of our miscalculations, there could be widespread acts of violence, forays into neighboring districts, even renewed outbreaks of cannibalism within Ganfield itself. So we must draw up our estimates with the greatest precision. What a terrible spiritual isolation we feel, deciding such things with no computers to guide us!

4.

On the fourteenth day of the crisis the district captain summons me. His message comes in late afternoon, when we all are dizzy with fatigue, choked by humidity. For several hours I have been tangled in complex dealings with a high official of the Marine Nutrients Board; this is an arm of the central city government, and I must therefore show the greatest tact, lest Ganfield's plankton quotas be arbitrarily lowered by a bureaucrat's sudden pique. Telephone contact is uncertain—the Marine Nutrients Board has its headquarters in Melrose New Port, half a continent away on the southeastern coast—and the line sputters and blurs with distortions that our computers, if the master program were in operation, would normally erase. As we reach a crisis in the negotiation my subdeputy gives me a note: DISTRICT CAPTAIN WANTS TO SEE YOU. "Not now," I say in silent lip-talk. The haggling proceeds. A few minutes later comes another note: IT'S URGENT. I shake my head, brush the note from my desk. The subdeputy retreats to the outer office, where I see him engaged in frantic discussion with a man in the gray and green uniform of the district captain's staff. The messenger points vehemently at me. Just then the phone line goes dead. I slam the instrument down and call to the messenger, "What is it?"

"The captain, sir. To his office at once, please."

"Impossible."

He displays a warrant bearing the captain's seal. "He requires your immediate presence."

"Tell him I have delicate business to complete," I reply. "Another fifteen minutes, maybe."

He shakes his head. "I am not empowered to allow a delay."

"Is this an arrest, then?"

"A summons."

"But with the force of an arrest?"

"With the force of an arrest, yes," he tells me.

I shrug and yield. All burdens drop from me. Let the subdeputy deal with the Marine Nutrients Board; let the clerk in the outer office do it, or no one at all; let the whole district starve. I no longer care. I am summoned. My responsibilities are discharged. I give over my desk to the subdeputy and summarize for him, in perhaps a hundred words, my intricate hours of negotiation. All that is someone else's problem now.

The messenger leads me from the building into the hot, dank street.

The sky is dark and heavy with rain, and evidently it has been raining some while, for the sewers are backing up and angry swirls of muddy water run shin-deep through the gutters. The drainage system, too, is controlled from Ganfield Hold, and must now be failing. We hurry across the narrow plaza fronting my office, skirt a gush of sewage-laden outflow, push into a close-packed crowd of irritable workers heading for home. The messenger's uniform creates an invisible sphere of untouchability for us; the throngs part readily and close again behind us. Wordlessly I am conducted to the stone-faced building of the district captain, and quickly to his office. It is no unfamiliar place to me, but coming here as a prisoner is quite different from attending a meeting of the district council. My shoulders are slumped, my eyes look toward the threadbare carpeting.

The district captain appears. He is a man of sixty, silver-haired, upright, his eyes frank and direct, his features reflecting little of the strain his position must impose. He has governed our district ten years. He greets me by name, but with warmth, and says, "You've heard nothing from your woman?"

"I would have reported it if I had."

"Perhaps. Perhaps. Have you any idea where she is?"

"I know only the common rumors," I say. "Conning Town, Morton Court, the Mill."

"She is in none of those places."

"Are you sure?"

"I have consulted the captains of those districts," he says. "They deny any knowledge of her. Of course, one has no reason to trust their word, but on the other hand, why would they bother to deceive me?" His eyes fasten on mine. "What part did you play in the stealing of the program?"

"None, sir."

"She never spoke to you of treasonable things?"

"Never."

"There is strong feeling in Ganfield that a conspiracy existed."

"If so, I knew nothing of it."

He judges me with a piercing look. After a long pause he says heavily, "She has destroyed us, you know. We can function at the present level of order for another six weeks, possibly, without the program—if there is no plague, if we are not flooded, if we are not overrun with bandits from outside. After that the accumulated effects of many minor breakdowns will paralyze us. We will fall into chaos. We will strangle on our own wastes, starve, suffocate, revert to savagery, live like beasts until the end—who knows? Without the master program we are lost. Why did she do this to us?"

"I have no theories," I say. "She kept her own counsel. Her independence of soul is what attracted me to her."

"Very well. Let her independence of soul be what attracts you to her now. Find her and bring back the program."

"Find her? Where?"

"That is for you to discover."

"I know nothing of the world outside Ganfield!"

"You will learn," the captain says coolly. "There are those here who would indict you for treason. I see no value in this. How does it help us to punish you? But we can *use* you. You are a clever and resourceful man; you can make your way through the hostile districts, and you can gather information, and you could well succeed in tracking her. If anyone has influence over her, you do—if you find her, you perhaps can induce her to surrender the program. No one else could hope to accomplish that. Go. We offer you immunity from prosecution in return for your cooperation."

The world spins wildly about me. My skin burns with shock. "Will I have safe conduct through the neighboring districts?" I ask.

"To whatever extent we can arrange. That will not be much, I fear."

"You'll give me an escort, then? Two or three men?"

"We feel you will travel more effectively alone. A party of several men takes on the character of an invading force. You would be met with suspicion and worse."

"Diplomatic credentials, at least?"

"A letter of identification, calling on all captains to honor your mission and treat you with courtesy."

I know how much value such a letter will have in Hawk Nest or Folkstone.

"This frightens me," I say.

He nods, not unkindly. "I understand that. Yet someone must seek her, and who else is there but you? We grant you a day to make your preparations. You will depart on the morning after next, and God hasten your return."

5.

Preparations. How can I prepare myself? What maps should I collect, when my destination is unknown? Returning to the office is unthinkable; I go straight home, and for hours I wander from one room to the other as if I face execution at dawn. At last I gather myself and fix a small meal, but most of it remains on my plate. No friends call; I call no one. Since Silena's disappearance my friends have fallen away from me. I sleep poorly. During the night there are hoarse shouts and shrill alarms in the street; I learn from the morning newscast that five men of Conning Town, here to loot, had been seized by one of the new vigilante groups that have replaced the police machines and were summarily put to death. I find no cheer in that, thinking that I might be in Conning Town in a day or so.

What clues to Silena's route? I ask to speak with the guard from whom she wangled entry into Ganfield Hold. He has been a prisoner ever since; the captain is too busy to decide his fate, and he languishes meanwhile. He is a small thick-bodied man with stubbly red hair and a sweaty forehead; his eyes are bright with anger and his nostrils quiver. "What is there to say?" he demands. "I was on duty at the Hold. She came in. I had never seen her before, though I knew she must be high-caste. Her cloak was open. She seemed naked beneath it. She was in a state of excitement."

"What did she tell you?"

"That she desired me. Those were her first words." Yes. I could see Silena doing that, though I had difficulty in imagining her long slender form enfolded in that squat little man's embrace. "She said she knew of me and was eager for me to have her."

"And then?"

"I sealed the gate. We went to an inner room where there is a cot. It was a quiet time of day, I thought no harm would come. She dropped her cloak. Her body—"

"Never mind her body." I could see it all too well in the eye of my mind, the sleek thighs, the taut belly, the small high breasts, the cascade of chocolate hair falling to her shoulders. "What did you talk about? Did she say anything of a political kind? Some slogan, some words against the government?"

"Nothing. We lay together naked awhile, only fondling one another. Then she said she had a drug with her, one which would enhance the sensations of love tenfold. It was a dark powder. I drank it in water; she drank it also, or seemed to. Instantly I was asleep. When I awoke, the Hold was in uproar and I was a prisoner." He glowers at me. "I should have suspected a trick from the start. Such women do not hunger for men like me. How did I ever injure you? Why did you choose me to be the victim of your scheme?"

"Her scheme," I say. "Not mine. I had no part in it. Her motive is a mystery to me. If I could discover where she has gone, I would seek her and wring answers from her. Any help you could give me might earn you a pardon and your freedom."

"I know nothing," he says sullenly. "She came in, she snared me, she drugged me, she stole the program."

"Think. Not a word? Possibly she mentioned the name of some other district."

"Nothing."

A pawn is all he is, innocent, useless. As I leave he cries out to me to intercede for him, but what can I do? "Your woman ruined me!" he roars.

"She may have ruined us all," I reply.

At my request a district prosecutor accompanies me to Silena's apartment, which has been under official seal since her disappearance. Its contents have been thoroughly examined, but maybe there is some clue I alone would notice. Entering, I feel a sharp pang of loss, for the sight of Silena's possessions reminds me of happier times. These things are painfully familiar to me: her neat array of books, her clothing, her furnishings, her bed. I knew her only eleven weeks, she was my monthwife only for two; I had not realized she had come to mean so much to me so quickly. We look around, the prosecutor and I. The books testify to the agility of her restless mind: little light fiction, mainly works of serious history, analyses of social problems, forecasts of conditions to come. Holman, *The Era of the World City.* Sawtelle, *Megalopolis Triumphant.* Doxiadis, *The New World of Urban Man.* Heggebend, *Fifty Billion Lives.* Marks, *Calcutta Is Everywhere.* Chasin, *The New Community.* I take a few of the books down, fondling them as though they were Silena. Many times when I had spent an evening here she reached for one of those books, Sawtelle or Heggebend or Marks or Chasin, to read me a passage that amplified some point she was making. Idly I turn pages. Dozens of paragraphs are underscored with fine, precise lines, and lengthy marginal comments are abundant. "We've analyzed all of that for possible significance," the prosecutor remarks. "The only thing we've concluded is that she thinks the world is too crowded for comfort." A racheting laugh. "As who doesn't?" He points to a stack of green-bound pamphlets at the end of a lower shelf. "These, on the other hand, may be useful in your search. Do you know anything about them?"

The stack consists of nine copies of something called *Walden Three:* a Utopian fantasy, apparently, set in an idyllic land of streams and forests. The booklets are unfamiliar to me; Silena must have obtained them recently. Why nine copies? Was she acting as a distributor? They bear the imprint of a publishing house in Kingston. Ganfield and Kingston severed trade relations long ago; material published there is uncommon here. "I've never seen them," I say. "Where do you think she got them?"

"There are three main routes for subversive literature originating in Kingston. One is—"

"Is this pamphlet subversive, then?"

"Oh, very much so. It argues for complete reversal of the social trends of the last hundred years. As I was saying, there are three main routes for subversive literature originating in Kingston. We have traced one chain of distribution running by way of Wisleigh and Cedar Mall, another through Old Grove, Hawk Nest, and Conning Town, and the third via Parley Close and the Mill. It is plausible that your woman is in Kingston now, having traveled along one of these underground distribution routes, sheltered by her fellow subversives all the way. But we have no way of confirming this." He smiles emptily. "She could be in any of the other communities along the three routes. Or in none of them."

"I should think of Kingston, though, as my ultimate goal, until I learn anything to the contrary. Is that right?"

"What else can you do?"

What else, indeed? I must search at random through an unknown number of hostile districts, having no clue other than the vague one implicit in the place of origin of these nine booklets, while time ticks on and Ganfield slips deeper day by day into confusion.

The prosecutor's office supplies me with useful things: maps, letters of introduction, a commuter's passport that should enable me to cross at least some district lines unmolested, and an assortment of local currencies as well as banknotes issued by the central bank and therefore valid in most districts. Against my wishes I am given also a weapon—a small heat-pistol—and in addition a capsule that I can swallow in the event that a quick and easy death becomes desirable. As the final stage in my preparation I spend an hour conferring with a secret agent, now retired, whose career of espionage took him safely into hundreds of communities as far away as Threadmuir and Reed Meadow. What advice does he give someone about to try to get across? "Maintain your poise," he says. "Be confident and self-assured, as though you belong in whatever place you find yourself. Never slink. Look all men in the eye. However, say no more than is necessary. Be watchful at all times. Don't relax your guard." Such precepts I could have evolved without his aid. He has nothing in the nature of specific hints for survival. Each district, he says, presents unique problems, constantly changing; nothing can be anticipated, everything must be met as it arises. How comforting!

At nightfall I go to the soulfather's house, in the shadow of Ganfield Tower. To leave without a blessing seems unwise. But there is something stagy and unspontaneous about my visit, and my faith flees as I enter. In the dim antechamber I light the nine candles, I pluck the five blades of grass from the ceremonial vase, I do the other proper ritual things, but my spirit remains chilled and hollow, and I am unable to pray. The soulfather himself, having been told of my mission, grants me audience—gaunt old man with impenetrable eyes set in deep bony rims—and favors me with a gentle feather-light embrace. "Go in safety," he murmurs. "God watches over you." I wish I felt sure of that. Going home, I take the most roundabout possible route, as if trying to drink in as much of Ganfield as I can on my last night. The diminishing past flows through me like a river running dry. My birthplace, my school, the streets where I played, the dormitory where I spent my adolescence, the home of my first month-wife. Farewell. Farewell. Tomorrow I go across. I return to my apartment alone; once more my sleep is fitful; an hour after dawn I find myself, astonished by it, waiting in line among the commuters at the mouth of the transit tube, bound for Conning Town. And so my crossing begins.

6.

Aboard the tube no one speaks. Faces are tense, bodies are held rigid in the plastic seats. Occasionally someone on the other side of the aisle glances at me as though wondering who this newcomer to the commuter group may be, but his eyes quickly slide away as I take notice. I know none of these commuters, though they must have dwelled in Ganfield as long as I; their lives have never intersected mine before. Engineers, merchants, diplomats, whatever—their careers are tied to districts other than their own. It is one of the anomalies of our ever more fragmented and stratified society that some regular contact still survives between community and community; a certain number of people must journey each day to outlying districts, where they work encapsulated, isolated, among unfriendly strangers.

We plunge eastward at unimaginable speed. Surely we are past the boundaries of Ganfield by now and under alien territory. A glowing sign on the wall of the car announces our route: CONNING TOWN-HAWK NEST-OLD GROVE-KINGSTON-FOLKSTONE-PARLEY CLOSE-BUDLEIGH-CEDAR MALL-THE MILL-MORTON COURT-GANFIELD, a wide loop through our most immediate neighbors. I try to visualize the separate links in this chain of districts, each a community of three or four hundred thousand loyal and patriotic citizens, each with its own special tone, its flavor, its distinctive quality, its apparatus of government, its customs and rituals. But I can imagine them merely as a cluster of Ganfields, every place very much like the one I have just left. I know this is not so. The world-city is no homogenous collection of uniformities, a global bundle of indistinguishable suburbs. No, there is incredible diversity, a host of unique urban cores bound by common need into a fragile unity. No master plan brought them into being; each evolved at a separate point in time, to serve the necessities of a particular purpose. This community sprawls gracefully along a curving river, that one boldly mounts the slopes of stark hills; here the prevailing architecture reflects an easy, gentle climate, there it wars with unfriendly nature; form follows topography and local function, creating individuality. The world is a richness: why then do I see only ten thousand Ganfields?

Of course it is not so simple. We are caught in the tension between forces which encourage distinctiveness and forces compelling all communities toward identicality. Centrifugal forces broke down the huge ancient cities, the Londons and Tokyos and New Yorks, into neighborhood communities that seized quasi-autonomous powers. Those giant cities were too unwieldy to survive; density of population, making long-distance transport unfeasible and communication difficult, shattered the urban fabric, destroyed the authority of the central government, and left the closely knit small-scale subcity as the only viable unit. Two dynamic and contradictory processes now asserted themselves. Pride and the quest for local advantage led each community toward specialization: this one a center primarily of industrial production, this one devoted to advanced education, this to finance, this to the processing of raw materials, this to wholesale marketing of commodities, this to retail distribution, and so on, the shape and texture of each district defined by its chosen function. And yet the new decentralization required a high degree of redundancy, duplication of governmental structures, of utilities, of community services; for its own safety each district felt the need to transform itself into a microcosm of the former full city. Ideally we should have hovered in perfect balance between specialization and redundancy, all communities striving to fulfil the needs of all other communities with the least possible overlap and waste of resources; in fact, our human frailty has brought into being these irreversible trends of rivalry and irrational fear, dividing district from district, so that against our own self-interest we sever year after year our bonds of interdependence and stubbornly seek self-sufficiency at the district level. Since this is impossible, our lives grow constantly more impoverished. In the end all districts will be the same and we will have created a world of pathetic limping Ganfields, devoid of grace, lacking in variety.

So. The tube-train halts. This is Conning Town. I am across the first district line. I make my exit in a file of solemn-faced commuters. Imitating them, I approach a colossal cyclopean scanning machine and present my passport. It is unmarked by visas; theirs are gaudy with scores of them. I tremble, but the machine accepts me and slams down a stamp that fluoresces a brilliant shimmering crimson against the pale lavender page:

DISTRICT OF CONNING TOWN
ENTRY VISA
24-HOUR VALIDITY

Dated to the hour, minute, second. Welcome, stranger, but get out of town before sunrise!

Up the purring ramp, into the street. Bright morning sunlight pries apart the slim sooty close-ranked towers of Conning Town. The air is cool and sweet, strange to me after so many sweltering days in programless demechanized Ganfield. Does our foul air drift across the border and offend them? Sullen eyes study me; those about me know me for an outsider. Their clothing is alien in style, pinched in at the shoulders, flaring at the waist. I find myself adopting an inane smile in response to their dour glares.

For an hour I walk aimlessly through the downtown section until my first fears melt and a comic cockiness takes possession of me: I pretend to myself that I am a native, and enjoy the flimsy imposture. This place is not much unlike Ganfield, yet nothing is quite the same. The sidewalks are wider; the street lamps have slender arching necks instead of angular ones; the fire hydrants are green and gold, not blue and orange. The police machines have flatter domes than ours; ringed with ten or twelve spy-eyes where ours have six or eight. Different, different, all different.

Three times I am halted by police machines. I produce my passport, display my visa, am allowed to continue. So far getting across has been easier than I imagined. No one molests me here. I suppose I look harmless. Why did I think my foreignness alone would lead these people to attack me? Ganfield is not at war with its neighbors, after all.

Drifting eastward in search of a bookstore, I pass through a shabby residential neighborhood and through a zone of dismal factories before I reach an area of small shops. Then in late afternoon I discover three bookstores on the same block, but they are antiseptic places, not the sort that might carry subversive propaganda like *Walden Three*. The first two are wholly automated, blank-walled charge-plate-and-scanner operations. The third has a human clerk, a man of about thirty with drooping yellow mustachios and alert blue eyes. He recognizes the style of my clothing and says, "Ganfield, eh? Lot of trouble over there."

"You've heard?"

"Just stories. Computer breakdown, isn't it?"

I nod. "Something like that."

"No police, no garbage removal, no weather control, hardly anything working—that's what they say." He seems neither surprised nor disturbed to have an outlander in his shop. His manner is amiable and relaxed. Is he fishing for data about our vulnerability, though? I must be careful not to tell him anything that might be used against us. But evidently they already know everything here. He says, "It's a little like dropping back into the Stone Age for you people, I guess. It must be a real traumatic thing."

"We're coping," I say, stiffly casual.

"How did it happen, anyway?"

I give him a wary shrug. "I'm not sure about that." Still revealing nothing. But then something in his tone of a moment before catches me belatedly and neutralizes some of the reflexive automatic suspicion with which I have met his questions. I glance around. No one else is in the shop. I let something conspiratorial creep into my voice and say, "It might not even be so traumatic, actually, once we get used to it. I mean, there once was a time when we didn't rely so heavily on machines to do our thinking for us, and we survived and even managed pretty well. I was reading a little book last week that seemed to be saying we might profit by trying to return to the old way of life. Book published in Kingston."

"*Walden Three.*" Not a question but a statement.

"That's it." My eyes query his. "You've read it?"

"Seen it."

"A lot of sense in that book, I think."

He smiles warmly. "I think so too. You get much Kingston stuff over in Ganfield?"

"Very little, actually."

"Not much here, either."

"But there's some."

"Some, yes," he says.

Have I stumbled upon a member of Silena's underground movement? I say eagerly, "You know, maybe you could help me meet some people who—"

"No."

"No?"

"No." His eyes are still friendly but his face is tense. "There's nothing like that around here," he says, his voice suddenly flat and remote. "You'd have to go over into Hawk Nest."

"I'm told that that's a nasty place."

"Nevertheless. Hawk Nest is where you want to go. Nate and Holly Borden's shop, just off Box Street." Abruptly his manner shifts to one of exaggerated bland clerkishness. "Anything else I can do for you, sir? If you're interested in supernovels we've got a couple of good new double-amplified cassettes, just in. Perhaps I can show you—"

"Thank you, no." I smile, shake my head, leave the store. A police machine waits outside. Its dome rotates; eye after eye scans me intently; finally its resonant voice says, "Your passport, please." This routine is familiar by now. I produce the document. Through the bookshop window I see the clerk bleakly watching. The police machine says, "What is your place of residence in Conning Town?"

"I have none. I'm here on a twenty-four-hour visa."

"Where will you spend the night?"

"In a hotel, I suppose."

"Please show your room confirmation."

"I haven't made arrangements yet," I tell it.

A long moment of silence: the machine is conferring with its central, no doubt, keying into the master program of Conning Town for instructions. At length it says, "You are advised to obtain a legitimate reservation and display it to a monitor at the earliest opportunity within the next four hours. Failure to do so will result in cancellation of your visa and immediate expulsion from Conning Town." Some ominous clicks come from the depths of the machine. "You are now under formal surveillance," it announces.

Brimming with questions, I return hastily to the bookshop. The clerk is displeased to see me. Anyone who attracts monitors to his shop—"monitors" is what they call police machines here, it seems—is unwelcome. "Can you tell me how to reach the nearest decent hotel?" I ask.

"You won't find one."

"No decent hotels?"

"No hotels. None where you could get a room, anyway. We have only two or three transient houses, and accommodations are allocated months in advance to regular commuters."

"Does the monitor know that?"

"Of course."

"Where are strangers supposed to stay, then?"

The clerk shrugs. "There's no structural program here for strangers as such. The regular commuters have regular arrangements. Unauthorized intruders don't belong here at all. You fall somewhere in between, I imagine. There's no legal way for you to spend the night in Conning Town."

"But my visa—"

"Even so."

"I'd better go on into Hawk Nest, I suppose."

"It's late. You've missed the last tube. You've got no choice but to stay, unless you want to try a border crossing on foot in the dark. I wouldn't recommend that."

"Stay? But where?"

"Sleep in the street. If you're lucky the monitors will leave you alone."

"Some quiet back alley, I suppose."

"No," he says. "You sleep in an out-of-the-way place and you'll surely get sliced up by night-bandits. Go to one of the designated sleeping streets. In the middle of a big crowd you might just go unnoticed, even though you're under surveillance." As he speaks he moves about the shop, closing it down for the night. He looks restless and uncomfortable. I take out my map of Conning Town and he shows me where to go. The map is some years out of date, apparently; he corrects it with irritable swipes of his pencil. We leave the shop together. I invite him to come with me to some restaurant as my guest, but he looks at me as if I carry plague. "Goodbye," he says. "Good luck."

7.

Alone, apart from the handful of other diners, I take my evening meal at a squalid, dimly lit automated cafeteria at the edge of downtown. Silent machines offer me thin acrid soup, pale spongy bread, and a leaden stew containing lumpy ingredients of undeterminable origin, for which I pay with yellow plastic counters of Conning Town currency. Emerging undelighted, I observe a reddish glow in the western sky: it may be a lovely sunset or, for all I know, may be a sign that Ganfield is burning. I look about for monitors. My four-hour grace period has nearly expired. I must disappear shortly into a throng. It seems too early for sleep, but I am only a few blocks from the place where the bookshop clerk suggested I should pass the night, and I go to it. Just as well: when I reach it—a wide plaza bordered by gray buildings of ornate facade—I find it already filling up with street-sleepers. There must be eight hundred of them, men, women, family groups, settling down in little squares of cobbled territory that are obviously claimed night after night under some system of squatters' rights. Others constantly arrive, flowing inward from the plaza's three entrances, finding their places, laying out foam cushions or mounds of clothing as their mattresses. It is a friendly crowd: these people are linked by bonds of neighborliness, a common poverty. They laugh, embrace, play games of chance, exchange whispered confidences, bicker, transact business, and join together in the rites of the local religion, performing a routine that involves six people clasping hands and chanting. Privacy seems obsolete here. They undress freely before one another, and there are instances of open coupling. The gaiety of the scene—a medieval carnival is what it suggests to me, a Breughelesque romp—is marred only by my awareness that this horde of revelers is homeless under the inhospitable skies, vulnerable to rain, sleet, damp fog, snow, and the other unkindnesses of winter and summer in these latitudes. In Ganfield we have just a scattering of street-sleepers, those who have lost their residential licenses and are temporarily forced into the open, but here it seems to be an established institution, as though Conning Town declared a moratorium some years ago on new residential construction without at the same time checking the increase of population.

Stepping over and around and between people, I reach the center of the plaza and select an unoccupied bit of pavement. But in a moment a little ruddy-faced woman arrives, excited and animated, and with a Conning Town accent so thick I can barely understand her she tells me she holds claim here. Her eyes are bright with menace; her hands are not far from becoming claws; several nearby squatters sit up and regard me threateningly. I apologize for my error and withdraw, stumbling over a child and narrowly missing overturning a bubbling cooking pot. Onward. Not here. Not here. A hand emerges from a pile of blankets and strokes my leg as I look around in perplexity. Not here. A man with a painted face rises out of a miniature green tent and speaks to me in a language I do not understand. Not here. I move on again and again, thinking that I will be jostled out of the plaza entirely, excluded, disqualified even to sleep in this district's streets, but finally I find a cramped corner where the occupants indicate I am welcome. "Yes?" I say. They grin and gesture. Gratefully I seize the spot.

Darkness has come. The plaza continues to fill; at least a thousand people have arrived after me, cramming into every vacancy, and the flow does not abate. I hear booming laughter, idle chatter, earnest romantic persuasion, the brittle sound of domestic quarreling. Someone passes a jug of wine around, even to me: bitter stuff, fermented clam juice its probable base, but I appreciate the gesture. The night is warm, almost sticky. The scent of unfamiliar food drifts on the air, something sharp, spicy, a heavy pungent smell. Curry? Is this then truly Calcutta? I close my eyes and huddle into myself. The hard cobblestones are cold beneath me. I have no mattress and I feel unable to remove my clothes before so many strangers. It will be hard for me to sleep in this madhouse, I think. But gradually the hubbub diminishes and—exhausted, drained—I slide into a deep troubled sleep.

Ugly dreams. The asphyxiating pressure of a surging mob. Rivers leaping their channels. Towers toppling. Fountains of mud bursting from a thousand lofty windows. Bands of steel encircling my thighs; my legs, useless, withering away. A torrent of lice sweeping over me. A frosty hand touching me. Touching me. Touching me. Pulling me up from sleep.

Harsh white light drenches me. I blink, cringe, cover my eyes. Shortly I perceive that a monitor stands over me. About me the sleepers awake, backing away, murmuring, pointing.

"Your street-sleeping permit, please."

Caught. I mumble excuses, plead ignorance of the law, beg forgiveness. But a police machine is neither malevolent nor merciful; it merely follows its program. It demands my passport and scans my visa. Then it reminds me I have been under surveillance. Having failed to obtain a hotel room as ordered, having neglected to report to a monitor within the prescribed interval, I am subject to expulsion.

"Very well," I say. "Conduct me to the border of Hawk Nest."

"You will return at once to Ganfield."

"I have business in Hawk Nest."

"Illegal entrants are returned to their district of origin."

"What does it matter to you where I go, so long as I get out of Conning Town?"

"Illegal entrants are returned to their district of origin," the machine tells me inexorably.

I dare not go back with so little accomplished. Still arguing with the monitor, I am led from the plaza through dark cavernous streets toward the mouth of a transit tube. On the station level a second monitor is given charge of me. "In three hours," the monitor that apprehended me informs me, "the Ganfield-bound train will arrive."

The first monitor rolls away.

Too late I realize that the machine has neglected to return my passport.

8.

Monitor number two shows little interest in me. Patrolling the tube station, it swings in a wide arc around me, keeping a scanner perfunctorily trained on me but making no attempt to interfere with what I do.

If I try to flee, of course, it will destroy me. Fretfully I study my maps. Hawk Nest lies to the northeast of Conning Town; if this is the tube station that I think it is, the border is not far. Five minutes' walk, perhaps. Passportless, there is no place I can go except Ganfield; my commuter status is revoked. But legalities count for little in Hawk Nest.

How to escape?

I concoct a plan. Its simplicity seems absurd, yet absurdity is often useful when dealing with machines. The monitor is instructed to put me aboard the train for Ganfield, yes? But not necessarily to keep me there.

I wait out the weary hours to dawn. I hear the crash of compressed air far up the tunnel. Snub-nosed, silken-smooth, the train slides into the station. The monitor orders me aboard. I walk into the car, cross it quickly, and exit by the open door on the far side of the platform. Even if the monitor has observed this maneuver, it can hardly fire across a crowded train. As I leave the car I break into a trot, darting past startled travelers, and sprint upstairs into the misty morning. At street level running is unwise. I drop back to a rapid walking pace and melt into the throngs of early workers. The street is Crystal Boulevard. Good, I have memorized a route: Crystal Boulevard to Flagstone Square, thence via Mechanic Street to the border.

Presumably all monitors, linked to whatever central nervous system the machines of the district of Conning Town utilize, have instantaneously been apprised of my disappearance. But that is not the same as knowing where to find me. I head northward on Crystal Boulevard—its name shows a dark sense of irony, or else the severe transformations time can work—and, borne by the flow of pedestrian traffic, enter Flagstone Square, a grimy, lopsided plaza out of which, on the left, snakes curving Mechanic Street. I go unintercepted on this thoroughfare of small shops. The place to anticipate trouble is at the border.

I am there in a few minutes. It is a wide dusty street, silent and empty, lined on the Conning Town side by a row of blocky brick warehouses, on the Hawk Nest side by a string of low ragged buildings, some in ruins, the best of them defiantly slatternly. There is no barrier. To fence a district border is unlawful except in time of war, and I have heard of no war between Conning Town and Hawk Nest.

Dare I cross? Police machines of two species patrol the street: flat-domed ones of Conning Town and black, hexagon-headed ones of Hawk Nest. Surely one or the other will gun me down in the no man's land between districts. But I have no choice. I must keep going forward.

I run out into the street at a moment when two police machines, passing one another on opposite orbits, have left an unpatrolled space perhaps a block long. Midway in my crossing the Conning Town monitor spies me and blares a command. The words are unintelligible to me, and I keep running, zigzagging in the hope of avoiding the bolt that very likely will follow. But the machine does not shoot; I must already be on the Hawk Nest side of the line, and Conning Town no longer cares what becomes of me.

The Hawk Nest machine has noticed me. It rolls toward me as I stumble, breathless and gasping, onto the curb. "Halt!" it cries. "Present your documents!" At that moment a red-bearded man, fierce-eyed, wide-shouldered, steps out of a decaying building close by me. A scheme assembles itself in my mind. Do the customs of sponsorship and sanctuary hold good in this harsh district.

"Brother!" I cry. "What luck!" I embrace him, and before he can fling me off I murmur, "I am from Ganfield. I seek sanctuary here. Help me!"

The machine has reached me. It goes into an interrogatory stance and I say, "This is my brother who offers me the privilege of sanctuary. Ask him! Ask him!"

"Is this true?" the machine inquire.

Redbeard, unsmiling, spits and mutters, "My brother, yes. A political refugee. I'll stand sponsor to him. I vouch for him. Let him be."

The machine clicks, hums, assimilates. To me it says, "You will register as a sponsored refugee within twelve hours or leave Hawk Nest." Without another word it rolls away.

I offer my sudden savior warm thanks. He scowls, shakes his head, spits once again. "We owe each other nothing," he says brusquely and goes striding down the street.

9.

In Hawk Nest nature has followed art. The name, I have heard, once had purely neutral connotations: some real-estate developer's high-flown metaphor, nothing more. Yet it determined the district's character, for gradually Hawk Nest became the home of predators that it is today, where all men are strangers, where every man is his brother's enemy.

Other districts have their slums. Hawk Nest *is* a slum. I am told they live here by looting, cheating, extorting, and manipulating. An odd economic base for an entire community, but maybe it works for them. The atmosphere is menacing. The only police machines seem to be those that patrol the border. I sense emanations of violence just beyond the corner of my eye: rapes and garrottings in shadowy byways, flashing knives and muffled groans, covert cannibal feasts. Perhaps my imagination works too hard. Certainly I have gone unthreatened so far; those I meet on the streets pay no heed to me, indeed will not even return my glance. Still, I keep my heat-pistol close by my hand as I walk through these shabby, deteriorating outskirts. Sinister faces peer at me through cracked, dirt-veiled windows. If I am attacked, will I have to fire in order to defend myself? God spare me from having to answer that.

10.

Why is there a bookshop in this town of murder and rubble and decay? Here is Box Street, and here, in an oily pocket of spare-parts depots and fly-specked quick-lunch counters, is Nate and Holly Borden's place. Five times as deep as it is broad, dusty, dimly lit, shelves overflowing with old books and pamphlets: an improbable outpost of the nineteenth century, somehow displaced in time. There is no one in it but a large, impassive woman seated at the counter, fleshy, puffy-faced, motionless. Her eyes, oddly intense, glitter like glass discs set in a mound of dough. She regards me without curiosity.

I say, "I'm looking for Holly Borden."

"You've found her," she replies, deep in the baritone range.

"I've come across from Ganfield by way of Conning Town."

No response from her to this.

I continue, "I'm traveling without a passport. They confiscated it in Conning Town and I ran the border."

She nods. And waits. No show of interest.

"I wonder if you could sell me a copy of *Walden Three,*" I say.

Now she stirs a little. "Why do you want one?"

"I'm curious about it. It's not available in Ganfield."

"How do you know I have one?"

"Is anything illegal in Hawk Nest?"

She seems annoyed that I have answered a question with a question. "How do you know *I* have a copy of that book?"

"A bookshop clerk in Conning Town said you might."

A pause. "All right. Suppose I do. Did you come all the way from Ganfield just to buy a book?" Suddenly she leans forward and smiles—a warm, keen, penetrating smile that wholly transforms her face: now she is keyed up, alert, responsive, shrewd, commanding. "What's your game?" she asks.

"My game?"

"What are you playing? What are you up to here?"

It is the moment for total honesty. "I'm looking for a woman named Silena Ruiz, from Ganfield. Have you heard of her?"

"Yes. She's not in Hawk Nest."

"I think she's in Kingston. I'd like to find her."

"Why? To arrest her?"

"Just to talk to her. I have plenty to discuss with her. She was my month-wife when she left Ganfield."

"The month must be nearly up," Holly Borden says.

"Even so," I reply. "Can you help me reach her?"

"Why should I trust you?"

"Why not?"

She ponders that briefly. She studies my face. I feel the heat of her scrutiny. At length she says, "I expect to be making a journey to Kingston soon. I suppose I could take you with me."

11.

She opens a trapdoor; I descend into a room beneath the bookshop. After a good many hours a thin, gray-haired man brings me a tray of food. "Call me Nate," he says. Overhead I hear indistinct conversations, laughter, the thumping of boots on the wooden floor. In Ganfield famine may be setting in by now. Rats will be dancing around Ganfield Hold. How long will they keep me here? Am I a prisoner? Two days. Three. Nate will answer no questions. I have books, a cot, a sink, a drinking glass. On the third day the trapdoor opens. Holly Borden peers down. "We're ready to leave," she says.

The expedition consists just of the two of us. She is going to Kingston to buy books and travels on a commercial passport that allows for one helper. Nate drives us to the tube-mouth in midafternoon. It no longer seems unusual to me to be passing from district to district; they are not such alien and hostile places, merely different from the place I know. I see myself bound on an odyssey that carries me across hundreds of districts, even thousands, the whole patchwork frenzy of our world. Why return to Ganfield? Why not go on, ever eastward, to the great ocean and beyond, to the unimaginable strangenesses on the far side?

Here we are in Kingston. An old district, one of the oldest. We are the only ones who journey hither today from Hawk Nest. There is only a perfunctory inspection of passports. The police machines of Kingston are tall, long-armed, with fluted bodies ornamented in stripes of red and green: quite a gay effect. I am becoming an expert in local variations of police-machine design. Kingston itself is a district of low pastel buildings arranged in spokelike boulevards radiating from the famed university that is its chief enterprise. No one from Ganfield has been admitted to the university in my memory.

Holly is expecting friends to meet her, but they have not come. We wait fifteen minutes. "Never mind," she says. "We'll walk." I carry the luggage. The air is soft and mild; the sun, sloping toward Folkstone and Budleigh, is still high. I feel oddly serene. It is as if I have perceived a divine purpose, an overriding plan, in the structure of our society, in our sprawling city of many cities, our network of steel and concrete clinging like an armor of scales to the skin of our planet. But what is that purpose? What is that plan? The essence of it eludes me; I am aware only that it must exist. A cheery delusion.

Fifty paces from the station we are abruptly surrounded by a dozen or more buoyant young men who emerge from an intersecting street. They are naked but for green loincloths; their hair and beards are untrimmed and unkempt; they have a fierce and barbaric look. Several carry long unsheathed knives strapped to their waists. They circle wildly about us, laughing, jabbing at us with their fingertips. "This is a holy district!" they cry. "We need no blasphemous strangers here! Why must you intrude on us?"

"What do they want?" I whisper. "Are we in danger?"

"They are a band of priests," Holly replies. "Do as they say and we will come to no harm."

They press close. Leaping, dancing, they shower us with sprays of perspiration. "Where are you from?" they demand. "Ganfield," I say. "Hawk Nest," says Holly. They seem playful yet dangerous. Surging about me, they empty my pockets in a series of quick jostling forays: I lose my heat-pistol, my maps, my useless letters of introduction, my various currencies, everything, even my suicide capsule. These things they pass among themselves, exclaiming over them; then the heat-pistol and some of the currency are returned to me. "Ganfield," they murmur. "Hawk Nest!" There is distaste in their voices. "Filthy places," they say. "Places scorned by God," they say. They seize our hands and haul us about, making us spin. Heavy-bodied Holly is surprisingly graceful, breaking into a serene lumbering dance that makes them applaud in wonder.

One, the tallest of the group, catches our wrists and says, "What is your business in Kingston?"

"I come to purchase books," Holly declares.

"I come to find my month-wife Silena," say I.

"Silena! Silena! Silena!" Her name becomes a jubilant incantation on their lips. "His month-wife! Silena! His month-wife! Silena! Silena! Silena!"

The tall one thrusts his face against mine and says, "We offer you a choice. Come and make prayer with us, or die on the spot."

"We choose to pray," I tell him.

They tug at our arms, urging us impatiently onward. Down street after street until at last we arrive at holy ground: a garden plot, insignificant in area, planted with unfamiliar bushes and flowers, tended with evident care. They push us inside.

"Kneel," they say.

"Kiss the sacred earth."

"Adore the things that grow in it, strangers."

"Give thanks to God for the breath you have just drawn."

"And for the breath you are about to draw."

"Sing!"

"Weep!"

"Laugh!"

"Touch the soil!"

"Worship!"

12.

Silena's room is cool and quiet, in the upper story of a residence overlooking the university grounds. She wears a soft green robe of coarse texture, no jewelery, no face paint. Her demeanor is calm and self-assured. I had forgotten the delicacy of her features, the cool malicious sparkle of her dark eyes.

"The master program?" she says, smiling. "I destroyed it!"

The depth of my love for her unmans me. Standing before her, I feel my knees turning to water. In my eyes she is bathed in a glittering aura of sensuality. I struggle to control myself. "You destroyed nothing," I say. "Your voice betrays the lie."

"You think I still have the program?"

"I know you do."

"Well, yes," she admits coolly. "I do."

My fingers tremble. My throat parches. An adolescent foolishness seeks to engulf me.

"Why did you steal it?" I ask.

"Out of love of mischief."

"I see the lie in your smile. What was the true reason?"

"Does it matter?"

"The district is paralyzed, Silena. Thousands of people suffer. We are at the mercy of raiders from adjoining districts. Many have already died of the heat, the stink of garbage, the failure of the hospital equipment. Why did you take the program?"

"Perhaps I had political reasons."

"Which were?"

"To demonstrate to the people of Ganfield how utterly dependent on these machines they have allowed themselves to become."

"We knew that already," I say. "If you meant only to dramatize our weaknesses, you were pressing the obvious. What was the point of crippling us? What could you gain from it?"

"Amusement?"

"Something more than that. You're not that shallow, Silena."

"Something more than that, then. By crippling Ganfield I help to change things. That's the purpose of any political act. To display the need for change, so that change may come about."

"Simply displaying the need is not enough."

"It's a place to begin."

"Do you think stealing our program was a rational way to bring change, Silena?"

"Are you happy?" she retorts. "Is this the kind of world you want?"

"It's the world we have to live in whether we like it or not. And we need that program in order to go on coping. Without it we are plunged into chaos."

"Fine. Let chaos come. Let everything fall apart, so we can rebuild it."

"Easy enough to say, Silena. What about the innocent victims of your revolutionary zeal, though?"

She shrugs. "There are always innocent victims in any revolution." In a sinuous movement she rises and approaches me. The closeness of her body is dazzling and maddening. With exaggerated voluptuousness she croons, "Stay here. Forget Ganfield. Life is good here. These people are building something worth having."

"Let me have the program," I say.

"They must have replaced it by now."

"Replacing it is impossible. The program is vital to Ganfield, Silena. Let me have it."

She emits an icy laugh.

"I beg you, Silena."

"How boring you are!"

"I love you."

"You love nothing but the status quo. The shape of things as they are gives you great joy. You have the soul of a bureaucrat."

"If you have always had such contempt for me, why did you become my month-wife?"

She laughs again. "For sport, perhaps."

Her words are like knives. Suddenly, to my own astonishment, I am brandishing the heat-pistol. "Give me the program or I'll kill you!" I cry.

She is amused. "Go. Shoot. Can you get the program from a dead Silena?"

"Give it to me."

"How silly you look holding that gun!"

"I don't have to kill you," I tell her. "I can merely wound you. This pistol is capable of inflicting light burns that scar the skin. Shall I give you blemishes, Silena?"

"Whatever you wish. I'm at your mercy."

I aim the pistol at her thigh. Silena's face remains expressionless. My arm stiffens and begins to quiver. I struggle with the rebellious muscles, but I succeed in steadying my aim only for a moment before the tremors return. An exultant gleam enters her eyes. A flush of excitement spreads over her face. "Shoot," she says defiantly. "Why don't you shoot me?"

She knows me too well. We stand in a frozen tableau for an endless moment outside time—a minute, an hour, a second?—and then my arm sags to my side. I put the pistol away. It never would have been possible for me to fire it. A powerful feeling assails me of having passed through some subtle climax: it will all be downhill from here for me, and we both know it. Sweat drenches me. I feel defeated, broken.

Silena's features reveal intense scorn. She has attained some exalted level of consciousness in these past few moments where all acts become gratuitous, where love and hate and revolution and betrayal and loyalty are indistinguishable from one another. She smiles the smile of someone who has scored the winning point in a game, the rules of which will never be explained to me.

"You little bureaucrat," she says calmly. "Here!"

From a closet she brings forth a small parcel which she tosses disdainfully to me. It contains a drum of computer film. "The program?" I ask. "This must be some joke. You wouldn't actually give it to me, Silena."

"You hold the master program of Ganfield in your hand."

"Really, now?"

"Really, really," she says. "The authentic item. Go on. Go. Get out. Save your stinking Ganfield."

"Silena—"

"Go."

13.

The rest is tedious but simple. I locate Holly Borden, who has purchased a load of books. I help her with them, and we return via tube to Hawk Nest. There I take refuge beneath the bookshop once more while a call is routed through Old Grove, Parley Close, the Mill, and possibly some other districts to the district captain of Ganfield. It takes two days to complete the circuit, since district rivalries make a roundabout relay necessary. Ultimately I am connected and convey my happy news: I have the program, though I have lost my passport and am forbidden to cross Conning Town. Through diplomatic channels a new passport is conveyed to me a few days later, and I take the tube home the long way, via Budleigh, Cedar Mall, and Morton Court. Ganfield is hideous, all filth and disarray, close to the point of irreversible collapse; its citizens have lapsed into a deadly stasis and await their doom placidly. But I have returned with the program.

The captain praises my heroism. I will be rewarded, he says. I will have promotion to the highest ranks of the civil service, with hope of ascent to the district council.

But I take pale pleasure from his words. Silena's contempt still governs my thoughts. *Bureaucrat. Bureaucrat.*

14.

Still, Ganfield is saved. The police machines have begun to move again.

MS. FOUND IN AN ABANDONED TIME MACHINE

There was a time, back in the dear old dead 1960s, when "pertinence" and "relevance" were the watchwords of radical young America. College curricula had to be revised to eliminate "irrelevant" subjects (history, Elizabethan drama, organic chemistry) so that greater prominence could be given to "relevant" ones (ethnic studies, feminism, environmental issues). Writers of fiction were supposed to deal only with socially relevant themes. People were supposed to dress in relevant ways—the uniform of nonconformism—and use relevant vocabulary. I enjoyed the late 1960s as much as anyone, and I regarded much of the political ferment of the time as vital to the survival of our society—the Vietnam war might have gone on for many decades more without it. But the era did have its silly side, and the search for the immediately relevant at the expense of the less immediately practical side was, to me, one of the sillier aspects of it. Throwing most of past human knowledge overboard for the sake of bringing about instant social reform did not strike me as an effective way of achieving anything but ignorance. Evidently it seemed that way to others, too: after a while the traditional sciences and historical subjects returned to the curriculum, Shakespeare and Sophocles were allowed back in also, and not a great deal was heard from the earnest, deadly young decreers of non-negotiable demands who had had such power over academic life for a time. (Although a lot of them grew up and became university professors, and they are behind the modern craze for political correctness that has spread so much terror through our academic institutions.)

I have to point out that much of what was "relevant" to the Movement folks of the 1960s was also relevant to non-Movement me. But though I agreed with them on many social issues of the times, I disagreed fiercely on the need to discuss those issues, and only *those issues, in fiction, and steadfastly went on writing stories that refused to double as political tracts. (The notion that I could singlehandedly end the war in Vietnam, or the oppression of the oppressed, by writing a science-fiction story always seemed transcendentally dim-witted to me.) Nevertheless on at least one occasion I let myself be inveigled into contributing to an anthology of "relevant" science fiction stories that would be packaged for sale to politically conscious students, a sure-fire commercial idea marred only by the fact that very few of the campus radicals were so doctrinaire as to want to read political sermons disguised as science fiction. The inveigler was Roger Elwood, for his book* Ten Tomorrows.

I wrote "Ms. Found in an Abandoned Time Machine" in June, 1972, at a time when the current feminist usage of "Ms." had not evolved and the abbreviation was merely short for "manuscript." I suppose it could have been considered a properly "relevant" story, in the parlance of the day, since it did embody some thoughts about the need for transformation of contemporary society and did indeed, pre-Watergate, poke some fun at President Nixon, the Pentagon, the polluters of the environment, and other widely acknowledged villains of the day. I still don't think that stories like this are apt to change the world. I do think this one is a pretty funny story which amiably deflates a lot of contemporary nonsense.

Incidentally, by the time Ten Tomorrows *was published in 1973, the Vietnam war was over, nobody was making non-negotiable demands any more, the error of mellowness and self-realization was getting under way, and the publishers shrewdly didn't announce anywhere on the cover of the book that its contents were meant to be "relevant."*

Just as well, I thought. A few years later Elwood reprinted the story in another anthology called Visions of Tomorrow, *which also included fiction by such irrelevant old-guard types as Isaac Asimov, Poul Anderson, Arthur C. Clarke, and H.G. Wells, and achieved not one whit toward the betterment of humanity, though it did provide 390 pages of lively and entertaining reading.*

If life is to be worth living at all, we have to have at least the illusion that we are capable of making sweeping changes in the world we live in. I say *at least the illusion.* Real ability to effect change would obviously be preferable, but not all of us can get to that level, and even the illusion of power offers hope, and hope sustains life. The point is not to be a puppet, not to be a passive plaything of karma. I think you'll agree that sweeping changes in society have to be made. Who will make them, if not you and me? If we tell ourselves that we're helpless, that meaningful reform is impossible, that the status quo is here for keeps, then we might as well not bother going on living, don't you think? I mean, if the bus is breaking down and the driver is freaking out on junk and all the doors are jammed, it's cooler to take the cyanide than to wait around for the inevitable messy smashup. But naturally we don't want to let ourselves believe that we're helpless. We want to think that we can grab the wheel and get the bus back on course and steer it safely to the repair shop. Right? Right. That's what we want to think. Even if it's only an illusion. Because sometimes—who knows?—you can firm up an illusion and make it real.

The cast of characters. Thomas C—, our chief protagonist, age twenty. As we first encounter him he lies asleep with strands of his own long brown hair casually wrapped across his mouth. Tie-dyed jeans and an ECOLOGY NOW! sweat shirt are crumpled at the foot of the bed. He was raised in Elephant Mound, Wisconsin, and this is his third year at the university. He appears to be sleeping peacefully, but through his dreaming mind flit disturbing phantoms: Lee Harvey Oswald, George Lincoln Rockwell, Neil Armstrong, Arthur Bremer, Sirhan Sirhan, Hubert Humphrey, Mao Tse-tung, Lieutenant William Calley, John Lennon. Each in turn announces himself, does a light-footed little dance expressive of his character, vanishes and reappears elsewhere in Thomas's cerebral cortex. On the wall of Thomas's room are various contemporary totems: a giant photograph of Spiro Agnew playing golf, a gaudy VOTE FOR MCGOVERN sticker, and banners that variously proclaim FREE ANGELA, SUPPORT YOUR LOCAL PIG FORCE, POWER TO THE PEOPLE, and CHE LIVES! Thomas has an extremely contemporary sensibility, circa 1970-72. By 1997 he will feel terribly nostalgic for the causes and artefacts of his youth, as his grandfather now is for raccoon coats, bathtub gin, and flagpole sitters. He will say things like "Try it, you'll like it" or "Sock it to me" and no one under forty will laugh.

Asleep next to him is Katherine F—, blonde, nineteen years old. Ordinarily she wears steel-rimmed glasses, green hip-hugger bells, a silken purple poncho, and a macramé shawl, but she wears none of these things now. Katherine is not dreaming, but her next REM cycle is due shortly. She comes from Moose Valley, Minnesota, and lost her virginity at the age of fourteen while watching a Mastroianni-Loren flick at the North Star Drive-In. During her seduction she never took her eyes from the screen for a period longer than thirty seconds. Nowadays she's much more heavily into the responsiveness thing, but back then she was trying hard to be cool. Four hours ago she and Thomas performed an act of mutual oral-genital stimulation that is illegal in seventeen states and the Republic of Vietnam (South), although there is hope of changing that before long.

On the floor by the side of the bed is Thomas's dog Fidel, part beagle, part terrier. He is asleep too. Attached to Fidel's collar is a day-glo streamer that reads THREE WOOFS FOR PET LIB.

Without God, said one of the Karamazov boys, everything is possible. I suppose that's true enough, if you conceive of God as the force that holds things together, that keeps water from flowing uphill and the sun from rising in the west. But what a limited concept of God that is! *Au contraire*, Fyodor: *with* God everything is possible. And I would like to be God for a little while.

Q. *What did you do?*

A. *I yelled at Sergeant Bacon and told him to go and start searching hooches and get your people moving right on—not the hooches but the bunkers—and I started over to Mitchell's location. I came back out. Meadlo was still standing there with a group of Vietnamese, and I yelled at Meadlo and asked him—I told him if he couldn't move all those people, to get rid of them.*

Q. *Did you fire into that group of people?*

A. *No, sir, I did not.*

Q. *After that incident, what did you do?*

A. *Well, I told my men to get on across the ditch and to get into position after I had fired into the ditch.*

Q. *Now, did you have a chance to look and observe what was in the ditch?*

A. *Yes, sir.*

Q. *And what did you see?*
A. *Dead people, sir.*
Q. *Did you see any appearance of anybody being alive in there?*
A. *No, sir.*

This is Thomas talking. Listen to me. Just listen. Suppose you had a machine that would enable you to fix everything that's wrong in the world. Let's say that it draws on all the resources of modern technology, not to mention the powers of a rich, well-stocked imagination and a highly developed ethical sense. The machine can do anything. It makes you invisible; it gives you a way of slipping backward and forward in time; it provides telepathic access to the minds of others; it lets you reach into those minds and c-h-a-n-g-e them. And so forth. Call this machine whatever you want. Call it Everybody's Fantasy Actualizer. Call it a Time Machine Mark Nine. Call it a God Box. Call it a magic wand, if you like. Okay. I give you a magic wand. And you give me a magic wand too, because reader and writer have to be allies, co-conspirators. You and me, with our magic wands. What will you do with yours? What will I do with mine? Let's go.

The Revenge of the Indians. On the plains ten miles west of Grand Otter Falls, Nebraska, the tribes assemble. By pickup truck, camper, Chevrolet, bicycle, and microbus they arrive from every corner of the nation, the delegations of angry redskins. Here are the Onondagas, the Oglallas, the Hunkpapas, the Jicarillas, the Punxsatawneys, the Kickapoos, the Gros Ventres, the Nez Percés, the Lenni Lenapes, the Wepawaugs, the Pamunkeys, the Penobscots, and all that crowd. They are clad in the regalia that the white man expects them to wear: feather bonnets, buckskin leggings, painted faces, tomahawks. See the great bonfire burn! See the leaping seat-shiny braves dance the scalping dance! Listen to their weird barbaric cries! What terror these savages must inspire in the plump suburbanites who watch them on Channel Four!

Now the council meeting begins. The pipe passes. Grunts of approval are heard. The mighty Navaho chieftain, Hosteen Dollars, is the main orator. He speaks for the strongest of the tribes, for the puissant Navahos own motels, gift shops, oil wells, banks, coal mines, and supermarkets. They hold the lucrative national distributorships for the superb pottery of their Hopi and Pueblo neighbours. Quietly they have accumulated vast wealth and power, which they have surreptitiously devoted to the welfare of their less fortunate kinsmen of other tribes. Now the arsenal is fully stocked: the tanks, the flamethrowers, the automatic rifles, the halftracks, the crop-dusters primed with napalm. Only the Big Bang is missing. But that lack, Hosteen Dollars declares, has now been remedied through miraculous intervention. "This is our moment!" he cries. "Hiawatha! Hiawatha!" Solemnly I descend from the skies, drifting in a slow downward spiral, landing lithely on my feet. I am naked but for a fringed breechclout. My coppery skin gleams glossily. Cradled in my arms is a hydrogen bomb, armed and ready. "The Big Bang!" I cry. "Here, brothers! Here!" By nightfall Washington is a heap of radioactive ash. At dawn the Acting President capitulates. Hosteen Dollars goes on national television to explain the new system of reservations, and the roundup of palefaces commences.

Marin County District Attorney Bruce Bales, who disqualified himself as Angela Davis's prosecutor, said yesterday he was "shocked beyond belief" at her acquittal.

In a bitter reaction, Bales said, "I think the jury fell for the very emotional pitch offered by the defense. She didn't even take the stand to deny her guilt. Despite what has happened, I still maintain she was as responsible for the death of Judge Haley and the crippling of my assistant, Gary Thomas, as Jonathan Jackson. Undoubtedly more so, because of her age, experience, and intelligence."

Governor Ronald Reagan, a spokesman at the capital said, was not available for comment on the verdict.

The day we trashed the Pentagon was simply beautiful, a landmark in the history of the Movement. It took years of planning and a tremendous cooperative effort, but the results were worth the heroic struggle and then some.

This is how we did it:

With the help of our IBM 2020 multiphasic we plotted a ring of access points around the whole District of Columbia. Three sites were in Maryland—Hyattsville, Suitland, and Wheaton—and two were on the Virginia side, at McLean and Merrifield. At each access point we dropped a vertical shaft six hundred feet deep, using our Hughes fluid-intake rotary reamer coupled with a GM twin-core extractor unit. Every night we transported the excavation tailings by truck to Kentucky and Tennessee, dumping them as fill in strip-mining scars. When we reached the six-hundred-foot level we began laying down a thirty-six-inch pipeline route straight to the Pentagon from each of our five loci, employing an LTV molecular compactor to convert the soil castings into semi-liquid form. This slurry we pumped into five huge adjacent underground retaining pockets that we carved with our Gardner-Denver hemispherical subsurface backhoe. When the pipelines were laid we started to pump the stored slurry toward the Pentagon at a constant rate calculated for us by our little XDS computer and monitored at five-hundred-meter intervals along the route by our Control Data 106a sensor system. The pumps, of course, were heavy-duty Briggs and Stratton 580's.

Over a period of eight months we succeeded in replacing the subsoil beneath the Pentagon's foundation with an immense pool of slurry, taking care, however, to avoid causing any seismological disturbances that the Pentagon's own equipment might detect. For this part of the operation we employed Bausch and Lomb spectrophotometers and Perkin-Elmer scanners, rigged in series with a Honeywell 990 vibration-damping integrator. Our timing was perfect. On the evening of July 3 we pierced the critical destruct threshold. The Pentagon was now floating on a lake of mud nearly a kilometre in diameter. A triple bank of Dow autonomic stabilizers maintained the building at its normal elevation; we used Ampex homeostasis equipment to regulate flotation pressures. At noon on the Fourth of July Katherine and I held a press conference on the steps of the Library of Congress, attended chiefly by representatives of the underground media although there were a few nonfreak reporters there too. I demanded an immediate end to all Amerikan overseas military adventures and gave the President one hour to reply. There was no response from the White House, of course, and at five minutes to one I activated the sluices by whistling three bars of "The Star-Spangled Banner" into a pay telephone outside FBI headquarters. By doing so I initiated a slurry-removal process and by five after one the Pentagon was sinking. It went down slowly enough so that there was no loss of life: the evacuation was complete within two hours and the uppermost floor of the building didn't go under the mud until five in the afternoon.

Two lions that killed a youth at the Portland Zoo Saturday night were dead today, victims of a night-time rifleman.

Roger Dean Adams, nineteen years old, of Portland, was the youth who was killed. The zoo was closed Saturday night when he and two companions entered the zoo by climbing a fence.

The companions said that the Adams youth first lowered himself over the side of the grizzly bear pit, clinging by his hands to the edge of the wall, then pulling himself up. He tried it again at the lions' pit after first sitting on the edge.

Kenneth Franklin Bowers of Portland, one of young Adams's companions, said the youth lowered himself over the edge and as he hung by his fingers he kicked at the lions. One slapped at him, hit his foot, and the youth fell to the floor of the pit, sixteen feet below the rim of the wall. The lions then mauled him and it appeared that he bled to death after an artery in his neck was slashed.

One of the lions, Caesar, a sixteen-year-old male, was killed last night by two bullets from a foreign-made rifle. Sis, an eleven-year-old female, was shot in the spine. She died this morning.

The police said they had few clues to the shootings.

Jack Marks, the zoo director, said the zoo would prosecute anyone charged with the shootings. "You'd have to be sick to shoot an animal that has done nothing wrong by its own standards," Mr. Marks said. "No right-thinking person would go into the zoo in the middle of the night and shoot an animal in captivity."

Do you want me to tell you who I really am? You may think I am a college student of the second half of the twentieth century but in fact I am a visitor from the far future, born in a year which by your system of reckoning would be called A.D. 2806. I can try to describe my native era to you, but there is little likelihood you would comprehend what I say. For instance, does it mean anything to you when I tell you that I have two womb-mothers, one ovarian and one uterine, and that my sperm-father in the somatic line was, strictly speaking, part dolphin and part ocelot? Or that I celebrated my fifth neurongate raising by taking part in an expedition to Proxy Nine, where I learned the eleven soul-diving drills and the seven contrary mantras? The trouble is that from your point of view we have moved beyond the technological into the incomprehensible. You could explain television to a man of the eleventh century in such a way that he would grasp the essential concept, if not the actual operative principles ("We have this box on which we are able to make pictures of faraway places appear, and we do this by taming the same power that makes lightning leap across the sky"), but how can I find even the basic words to help you visualize our simplest toys?

At any rate it was eye-festival time, and for my project I chose to live in the year 1972. This required a good deal of preparation. Certain physical alterations were necessary—synthesizing body hair, for example—but the really difficult part was creating the cultural camouflage. I had to pick up speech patterns, historical background, a whole sense of *context.* (I also had to create a convincing autobiography. The time-field effect provides travelers like myself with an instant retroactive existence in the past, an established background of schooling and parentage and whatnot stretching over any desired period prior to point of arrival, but only if the appropriate programming is done.) I drew on the services of our leading historians and archeologists, who supplied me with everything I needed, including an intensive training in late-twentieth-century youth culture. How glib I became! I can talk all your dialects: macrobiotics, ecology, hallucinogens, lib-sub-aleph, rock, astrology, yoga. Are you a *sanpaku* Capricorn? Are you plagued by sexism, bum trips, wobbly karma, malign planetary conjunctions? Ask me for advice. I know this stuff. I'm into everything that's current. I'm with the Revolution all the way. Do you want to know something else? I think I may not be the only time traveler who's here right now. I'm starting to form a theory that this entire generation may have come here from the future.

BELFAST, Northern Ireland, May 28—Six people were killed early today in a big bomb explosion in Short Strand, a Roman Catholic section of Belfast.

Three of the dead, all men, were identified later as members of the Irish Republican Army. Security forces said they believed the bomb blew up accidentally while it was being taken to another part of the city.

> One of the dead was identified as a well-known IRA explosives expert who had been high on the British Army's wanted list for some time. The three other victims, two men and a woman, could not be identified immediately.
>
> Seventeen persons, including several children, were injured by the explosion, and twenty houses in the narrow street were so badly damaged that they will have to be demolished.

One day I woke up and could not breathe. All that day and through the days after, in the green parks and in the rooms of friends and even beside the sea, I could not breathe. The air was used up. Each thing I saw that was ugly was ugly because of man—man-made or man-touched. And so I left my friends and lived alone.

> EUGENE, Ore. (UPI)—A retired chef and his dog were buried together recently as per the master's wish.
>
> Horace Lee Edwards, seventy-one years old, had lived alone with his dog for twenty-two years, since it was a pup. He expressed the wish that when he died the dog be buried with him.
>
> Members of Mr. Edwards's family put the dog to death after Mr. Edwards's illness. It was placed at its master's feet in his coffin.

I accept chaos. I am not sure whether it accepts me.

A memo to the Actualizer.

Dear Machine:

We need more assassins. The system itself is fundamentally violent and we have tried to transform it through love. That didn't work. We gave them flowers and they gave us bullets. All right. We've reached such a miserable point that the only way we can fight their violence is with violence of our own. The time has come to rip off the rippers-off. Therefore, old machine, your assignment for today is to turn out a corps of capable assassins, a cadre of convincing-looking artificial human beings who will serve the needs of the Movement. Killer androids, that's what we want.

These are the specs:

AGE—between nineteen and twenty-five years old.

HEIGHT—from five feet to five feet nine.

WEIGHT—on the low side, or else very heavy.

RACE—white, more or less.

REIGION—Former Christian, now agnostic or atheist. Ex-Fundamentalist will do nicely.

PSYCHOLOGICAL PROFILE—intense, weird, a loner, a loser. A bad sexual history: impotence, premature ejaculation, inability to find willing partners. A bad relationship with siblings (if any) and parents. Subject should be a hobbyist (stamp or coin collecting, trap-shooting, cross-country running, etc.) but not an "intellectual." A touch of paranoia is desirable. Also free-floating ambitions impossible to fulfil.

POLITICAL CONVICTIONS—any. Preferably highly flexible. Willing to call himself a libertarian anarchist on Tuesday and a dedicated Marxist on Thursday if he thinks it'll get him somewhere to make the switch. Willing to shoot with equal enthusiasm at presidential candidates, incumbent senators, baseball players, rock stars, traffic cops, or any other components of the mysterious "they" that hog the glory and keep him from attaining his true place in the universe.

Okay. You can supply the trimmings yourself, machine. Any color eyes so long as the eyes are a little bit on the glassy hyperthyroid side. Any color hair, although it will help if the hair is prematurely thinning and our man blames his lack of success with women in part on that. Any marital history (single, divorced, widowed, married) provided whatever liaison may have existed was unsatisfactory. The rest is up to you. Get with the job and use your creativity. Start stamping them out in quantity:

Oswald Sirhan Bremer Ray Czolgosz Guiteau
Oswald Sirhan Bremer Ray Czolgosz Guiteau
Oswald Sirhan Bremer Ray Czolgosz Guiteau
Oswald Sirhan Bremer Ray Czolgosz Guiteau
Oswald Sirhan Bremer Ray Czolgosz Guiteau
Oswald Sirhan Bremer Ray Czolgosz Guiteau
Oswald Sirhan Bremer Ray Czolgosz Guiteau
Oswald Sirhan Bremer Ray Czolgosz Guiteau

Give us the men. We'll find uses for them. And when they've done their filthy thing we'll throw them back into the karmic hopper to be recycled, and God help us all.

Every day thousands of ships routinely stain the sea with oily wastes. When an oil tanker has discharged its cargo, it might add weight of some other kind to remain stable; this is usually done by filling some of the ship's storage tanks with seawater. Before it can take on a new load of oil, the tanker must flush this watery ballast from its tanks; and as the water is pumped out, it takes with it the oily scum that had remained in the tanks when the last cargo was unloaded. Until 1964 each such flushing of an average 40,000-ton tanker sent eighty-three tons of oil into the sea. Improved flushing procedures have cut the usual oil discharge to about three tons. But there are so many tankers afloat—more than 4,000 of them—that they nevertheless release several million tons of oil a year in this fashion. The 44,000 passenger, cargo, military, and pleasure ships now in service add an equal amount of pollution by flushing oily wastes from their bilges. All told, according to one scientific estimate, man may be putting as much as ten million tons of oil a year into the sea. When the explorer Thor Heyerdahl made a 3,200-mile voyage from North Africa to the West Indies in a boat of papyrus reeds in the summer of 1970, he saw "a continuous stretch of at least 1,400 miles of open Atlantic polluted by floating lumps of solidified, asphalt-like oil." French oceanographer Jacques Yves Cousteau estimates that forty percent of the world's sea life has disappeared in the present century. The beaches near Boston Harbor have an average oil accumulation of 21.8 pounds of oil per mile, a figure that climbs to 1,750 pounds per mile on one stretch on Cape Cod. The Scientific

Centre of Monaco reports: "On the Mediterranean seaboard practically all the beaches are soiled by the petroleum refineries, and the sea bottom, which serves as a food reserve for marine fauna, is rendered barren by the same factors."

It's a coolish spring day and here I am in Washington, DC. That's the Capitol down there, and there's the White House. I can't see the Washington Monument, because they haven't finished it yet, and of course there isn't any Lincoln Memorial, because Honest Abe is alive and well on Pennsylvania Avenue. Today is Friday, April 14, 1865. And here I am. Far out!

—We hold the power to effect change. Very well, what shall we change? The whole ugly racial thing?

—That's cool. But how do we go about it?

—Well, what about uprooting the entire institution of slavery by going back to the sixteenth century and blocking it at the outset?

—No, too many ramifications. We'd have to alter the dynamics of the entire imperialist-colonial thrust, and that's just too big a job even for a bunch of gods. Omnipotent we may be, but not indefatigable. If we blocked that impulse there, it would only crop up somewhere else along the time-line; no force that powerful can be stifled altogether.

—What we need is a pinpoint way of reversing the racial mess. Let us find a single event that lies at a crucial nexus in the history of black-white relations in the United States and unhappen it. Any suggestions?

—Sure, Thomas. The Lincoln assassination.

—Far out! Run it through the machine; see what the consequences would be.

So we do the simulations and twenty times out of twenty they come out with a recommend that we de-assassinate Lincoln. Groovy. Any baboon with a rifle can do an assassination, but only we can do a de-assassination. *Alors*: Lincoln goes on to complete his second term. The weak, ineffectual Andrew Johnson remains Vice President, and the Radical Republican faction in Congress doesn't succeed in enacting its "humble the proud traitors" screw-the-South policies. Under Lincoln's even-handed guidance the South will be rebuilt sanely and welcomed back into the Union; there won't be any vindictive Reconstruction era, and there won't be the equally vindictive Jim Crow reaction against the carpetbaggers that led to all the lynchings and restrictive laws, and maybe we can blot out a century of racial bitterness. Maybe.

That's Ford's Theatre over there. *Our American Cousin* is playing tonight. Right now John Wilkes Booth is holed up in some downtown hotel, I suppose, oiling his gun, rehearsing his speech. "Sic semper tyrannis!" is what he'll shout, and he'll blow away poor old Abe.

—One ticket for tonight's performance, please.

Look at the elegant ladies and gentlemen descending from their carriages. They know the President will be at the theatre, and they're wearing their finest finery. And yes! That's the White House buggy! Is that imperious-looking lady Mary Todd Lincoln? It has to be. And there's the President, stepping right off the five-dollar bill. Graying beard, stooped shoulders, weary eyes, tired, wrinkled face. Poor old Abe. Am I doing you much of a favor by saving you tonight? Don't you want to lay your burden down? But history needs you, man. All dem li'l black boys and girls, dey needs you. The President waves. I wave back. Greetings from the twentieth century, Mr. Lincoln! I'm here to rob you of your martyrdom!

Curtain going up. Abe smiles in his box. I can't follow the play. Words, just words. Time crawls, tick-tock, tick-tock, tick-tock. Ten o'clock at last. The moment's coming close. There, do you see him? There: the wild-eyed man with the big gun. Wow, that gun's the size of a cannon! And he's creeping up on the President. Why doesn't anybody notice? Is the play so goddamned interesting that nobody notices—

"Hey! Hey you, John Wilkes Booth! Look over here, man! Look at me!"

Everybody turns as I shout. Booth turns too, and I rise and extend my arm and fire, not even needing to aim, just turning the weapon into an extension of my pointing hand as the Zen exercises have shown me how to do. The sound of the shot expands, filling the theatre with a terrible reverberating boom, and Booth topples, blood fountaining from his chest. Now, finally the President's bodyguards break from their freeze and come scrambling forward. I'm sorry, John. Nothing personal. History was in need of some changing, is all. Goodbye, 1865. Goodbye, President Abe. You've got an extension of your lease, thanks to me. The rest is up to you.

Our freedom…our liberation…can only come through a transformation of social structure and relationships…no one group can be free while another is still held in bonds. We want to build a world where people can choose their futures, where they can love without dependency games, where they do not starve. We want to create a world where men and women can relate to each other and to children as sharing, loving equals. We must eliminate the twin oppressors…hierarchical and exploitative capitalism and its myths that keep us so securely in bonds…sexism, racism, and other evils created by those who rule to keep the rest of us apart.

—Do you Alexander, take this man to be your lawful wedded mate?

—I do.

—Do you, George, take this man to be your lawful wedded mate?

—I do.

—Then, George and Alexander, by the power vested in me by the State of New York as ordained minister of the First Congregational Gay Communion of Upper Manhattan, I do hereby pronounce you man and man, wedded before God and in the eyes of mankind, and may you love happily ever after.

It's all done with the aid of a lot of science fiction gadgetry. I won't apologize for that part of it. Apologies just aren't necessary. If you need gadgetry to get yourself off, you use gadgetry; the superficials simply don't enter into any real consideration of how you get where you want to be from where you're at. The aim is to eradicate the well-known evils of our society, and if we have to get there by means of time machines, thought-amplification headbands, anti-uptightness rays, molecular interpenetrator beams, superheterodyning levitator rods, and all the rest of that gaudy comic-book paraphernalia, so be it. It's the results that count.

Like I mean, take the day I blew the President's mind. You think I could have done that without all this gadgetry? Listen, simply getting into the White House is a trip and a half. You can't get hold of a reliable map of the interior of the White House, the part that the tourists aren't allowed to see; the maps that exist are phonies, and actually they keep rearranging the rooms so that espionage agents and assassins won't be able to find their way around. What is a bedroom one month is an office the next and a switchboard room the month after that. Some rooms can be folded up and removed altogether. It's a whole wild cloak-and-dagger number. So we set up our ultrasonic intercavitation scanner in Lafayette Park and got ourselves a trustworthy holographic representation of the inside of the building. That data enabled me to get my bearings once I was in there. But I also needed to be able to find the President in a hurry. Our method was to slap a beep transponder on him, which we did by catching the White House's head salad chef, zonking him on narcoleptic strobes, and programming him to hide the gimmick inside a tomato. The President ate the tomato at dinnertime and from that moment on we could trace him easily. Also, the pattern of interference waves coming from the transponder told us whether anyone was with him.

So okay. I waited until he was alone one night, off in the Mauve Room rummaging through his file of autographed photos of football stars, and I levitated to a point ninety feet directly above that room, used our neutrinoflux desensitizer to knock out the White House security shield, and plummeted down via interpenetrator beam. I landed right in front of him. Give him credit: he didn't start to yell. He backed away and started to go for some kind of alarm button, but I said, "Cool it, Mr. President, you aren't going to get hurt. I just want to talk. Can you spare five minutes for a little rap?" And I beamed him with the conceptutron to relax him and make him receptive. "Okay, chief?"

"You may speak, son," he replied. "I'm always eager to hear the voice of the public, and I'm particularly concerned with being responsive to the needs and problems of our younger generation. Our gallant young people who—"

"Groovy, Dick. Okay—now dig this. The country's falling apart, right? The ecology is deteriorating, the cities are decaying, the blacks are up in arms, the right-wingers are stocking up on napalm, the kids are getting maimed in one crazy foreign war after another, the prisons are creating criminals instead of rehabilitating them, the Victorian sexual codes are turning millions of potentially beautiful human beings into sickniks, the drug laws don't make any sense, the women are still hung up on the mother-chauffeur-cook-chambermaid trip, the men are still into the booze-guns-broads trips, the population is still growing and filling up the clean open spaces, the economic structure is set up to be self-destructive since capital and labor are in cahoots to screw the consumer, and so on. I'm sure you know the problems, since you're the President and you read a lot of newspapers. Okay. How did we get into this bummer? By accident? No. Through bad karma? I don't really think so. Through inescapable deterministic forces? Uh-uh. We got into it through dumbness, greed, and inertia. We're so greedy we don't even realize that it's ourselves we're robbing. But it can be fixed, Dick, *it can all be fixed*! We just have to wake up! And you're the man who can do it. Don't you want to go down in history as the man who helped this great country get itself together? You and thirty influential congressmen and five members of the Supreme Court can do it. All you have to do is start reshaping the national consciousness through some executive directives backed up with congressional action. Get on the tube, man, and tell all your silent majoritarians to shape up. Proclaim the reign of love. No more war, hear? It's over tomorrow. No more economic growth: we just settle for what we have and we start cleaning up the rivers and lakes and forests. No more babies to be used as status symbols and pacifiers for idle housewives—from now on people will do babies only for the sake of bringing groovy new human beings into the world, two or three to a couple. As of tomorrow we abolish all laws against stuff that people do without hurting other people. And so on. We proclaim a new Bill of Rights granting every individual the right to a full and productive life according to his own style. Will you do that?"

"Well—"

"Let me make one thing perfectly clear," I said. "You're *going* to do it. You're going to decree an end to all the garbage that's been going down in this country. You know how I know you're going to do it? Because I've got this shiny little metal tube in my hand and it emits vibrations that are real strong stuff, vibrations that are going to get your head together when I press the button. Ready or not, here I go. One, two, three ...*zap*.

"Right on, baby," the President said.

The rest is history.

Oh. Oh. Oh. Oh, God. If it could only be that easy. One, two, three, zap. But it doesn't work like that. I don't have any magic wand. What makes you think I did? How was I able to trick you into a suspension of disbelief? You, reader, sitting there on your rear end, what do you think I really am? A miracle man? Some kind of superbeing from Galaxy Ten? I'll tell you what I really am, me, Thomas C—. I'm a bunch of symbols on a piece of paper. I'm just something abstract trapped within a mere fiction. A "hero" in a "story." Helpless, disembodied, unreal. UNREAL! Whereas you out there—you have eyes, lungs, feet, arms, a brain, a mouth, all that good stuff. You can function. You can move. You can act. Work for the Revolution! Strive for change! You're operating in the real world; you can do it if anybody can! Struggle toward...umph...glub.... Hey, get your filthy hands off me—power to the people! Down with the fascist pigs...hey—help—HELP!

THE SCIENCE FICTION HALL OF FAME

Here we have a slippery and involuted story, a symphony of mixed motives. The title is the giveaway, for it is the same as that of a well-known anthology that has gone through dozens of printings since I edited it on behalf of the Science Fiction Writers of America in 1968. And now you find me in June of 1972, just a few years later, writing a story of the same name, well aware of the confusion that is bound to ensue, slyly enjoying the bibliographic chaos.

What is worse, the story pretends to be a science-fiction story, but it really isn't. It's more of a parody, perhaps, or even an attack. Like most of my 1972 stories it shows the restlessness that was growing in me then as I struggled to redefine my attitude toward the genre to which I had devoted so much of my career. Terry Carr, for whom I had written a story for each of the first three issues of his anthology Universe, *had asked me for another one, and this is what I gave him. He read it right away—and returned it to me, looking crestfallen and dismayed, that evening. "You know how much I want to use something of yours in the next issue," he said. "But I can't publish* this, *Bob.* Universe *is supposed to be a book for people who* like *science fiction."*

I had to admit that Terry was right: this was a story written by a man who had developed a powerful love-hate relationship with his own field. I thought then, and think now, that it reflects more ambivalence than hostility—the work of a writer who had spent a quarter of a century deeply concerned with science fiction and who, for the moment, had grown a little cross with it. Terry was so upset by the whole episode that I promised to write another one for him, and did—"A Sea of Faces," which you'll encounter very shortly. I offered "The Science Fiction Hall of Fame" to another veteran editor, Bob Hoskins, who accepted it without any qualms and published it in the fifth issue of his anthology Infinity.

The look his remote grey eyes was haunted, terrified, beaten, as he came running in from the Projectorium. His shoulders were slumped; I had never before seen him betray the slightest surrender to despair, but now I was chilled by the completeness of his capitulation. With a shaking hand he thrust at me a slender yellow data slip, marked in red with the arcane symbols of cosmic computation. "No use," he muttered. "There's absolutely no use trying to fight any longer!"

"You mean—"

"Tonight," he said huskily, "the universe irrevocably enters the penumbra of the null point!"

The day Armstrong and Aldrin stepped out onto the surface of the moon—it was Sunday, July 20, 1969, remember?—I stayed home, planning to watch the whole thing on television. But it happened that I met an interesting woman at Leon and Helene's party the night before, and she came home with me. Her name is gone from my mind, if I ever knew it, but I remember how she looked: long soft golden hair, heart-shaped face with prominent ruddy cheeks, gentle gray-blue eyes, plump breasts, slender legs. I remember, too, how she wandered around my apartment, studying the crowded shelves of old paperbacks and magazines. "You're really into sci-fi, aren't you?" she said at last. And laughed and said, "I guess this must be your big weekend, then! Wow, the moon!" But it was all a big joke to her, that men should be cavorting around up there when there was still so much work left to do on earth. We had a shower and I made lunch and we settled down in front of the set to wait for the men to come out of their module, and—very easily, without a sense of transition—we found ourselves starting to screw, and it went on and on, one of those impossible impersonal mechanical screws in which body grinds against body for centuries, no feeling, no excitement, and as I rocked rhythmically on top of her, unable either to come or to quit, I heard Walter Cronkite telling the world that the module hatch was opening. I wanted to break free of her so I could watch, but she clawed at my back. With a distinct effort I pulled myself up on my elbows, pivoted the upper part of my body so I had a view of the screen, and waited for the ecstasy to hit me. Just as the first wavery image of an upside-down spaceman came into view on that ladder, she moaned and bucked her hips wildly and went into frenzied climax. I felt nothing. Nothing. Eventually she left, and I showered and had a snack and watched the replay of the moonwalk on the eleven o'clock news. And still I felt nothing.

"What is the answer?" said Gertrude Stein, about to die. Alice B. Toklas remained silent. "In that case," Miss Stein went on, "what is the question?"

Extract from *History of the Imperium*, Koeckert and Hallis, third edition (revised):

> The galactic empire was organized 190 standard universal centuries ago by the joint, simultaneous, and unanimous resolution of the governing bodies of eleven hundred worlds. By the present day the hegemony of the empire has spread to thirteen galactic sectors and embraces many thousands of planets, all of which entered the empire willingly and gladly. To remain outside the empire is to confess civic insanity, for the Imperium is unquestionably regarded throughout the cosmos as the most wholly sane construct ever created by the sentient mind. The decision-making processes of the Imperium are invariably determined by recourse to the Hermosillo Equations, which provide unambiguous and incontrovertibly rational guidance in any question of public policy. Thus the many worlds of the empire form a single coherent unit, as perfectly interrelated socially, politically, and economically as its component worlds are interrelated by the workings of the universal laws of gravitation.

Perhaps I spend too much time on other planets and in remote galaxies. It's an embarrassing addiction, this science fiction. (Horrible jingle! It jangles in my brain like an idiot's singsong chant.) Look at my bookshelves: hundreds of well-worn paperbacks, arranged alphabetically by authors, Aschenbach-Barger-Capwell-De Soto-Friedrich, all the greats of the genre out to Waldman and Zenger. The collection of magazines, every issue of everything back to the summer of 1953, a complete run of *Nova*, most issues of *Deep Space*, a thick file of *Tomorrow*. I suppose some of those magazines are quite rare now, though I've never looked closely into the feverish world of the s-f collector. I simply accumulate the publications I buy at the newsstand, never throwing any of them away. How could I part with them? Slices of my past, those magazines, those books. I can give dates to changes in my spirit, alterations in my consciousness, merely by picking up old magazines and reflecting on the associations they evoke. The issue showing the ropy-armed purple monster: it went on sale the month I discovered sex. This issue, cover painting of exploding spaceships: I read it my first month in college, by way of relief from Aquinas and Plato. Mileposts, landmarks, waterlines. An embarrassing addiction. My friends are good-humored about it. They think science fiction is a literature for children—God knows, they may be right—and they indulge my fancy for it in an affectionate way, giving me some fat anthology for Christmas, leaving a stack of current magazines on my desk while I'm out to lunch. But they wonder about me. Sometimes I wonder too. At the age of thirty-four should I still be able to react with such boyish enthusiasm to, say, Capwell's Solar League novels or Waldman's "Mindleech" series? What is there about the present that drives me so obsessively toward the future? The gray and vacant present, the tantalizing, inaccessible future.

His eyes were glittering with irrepressible excitement as he handed her the gleaming yellow dome that was the thought-transference helmet. "Put it on," he said tenderly.

"I'm afraid, Riik."

"Don't be. What's there to fear?"

"Myself. The real me. I'll be wide open, Riik. I fear what you may see in me, what it may do to you, to *us.*"

"Is it so ugly inside you?" he asked.

"Sometimes I think so."

"Sometimes everybody thinks that about himself, Juun. It's the old neurotic self-hatred welling up, the garbage that we can't escape until we're totally sane. You'll find that kind of stuff in me, too, once we have the helmets on. Ignore it. It isn't real. It isn't going to be a determining factor in our lives."

"Do you love me, Riik?"

"The helmet will answer that better than I can."

"All right. All right." She smiled nervously. Then with exaggerated care she lifted the helmet, put it in place, adjusted it, smoothed a vagrant golden curl back under the helmet's rim. He nodded and donned his own.

"Ready?" he asked.

"Ready."

"Now!"

He threw the switch. Their minds surged toward one another.

Then—

Oneness!

My mind is cluttered with other men's fantasies: robots, androids, starships, giant computers, predatory energy globes, false messiahs, real messiahs, visitors from distant worlds, time machines, gravity repellers. Punch my buttons and I offer you parables from the works of Hartzell or Marcus, appropriate philosophical gems borrowed from the collected editorial utterances of David Coughlin, or concepts dredged from my meditations on De Soto. I am a walking mass of secondhand imagination. I am the flesh-and-blood personification of the Science Fiction Hall of Fame.

"At last," cried Professor Kholgoltz triumphantly. "The machine is finished! The last solenoid is installed! Feed power, Hagley. Feed power! Now we will have the Answer we have sought for so many years!"

He gestured to his assistant, who gradually brought the great computer throbbingly to life. A subtle, barely perceptible flow of energy pervaded the air: the neutrino flux that the master equations had predicted. In the amphitheatre adjoining the laboratory, ten thousand people sat tensely frozen. All about the world, millions more, linked by satellite relay, waited with similar intensity. The professor nodded. Another gesture, and Hagley, with a grand flourish, fed the question tape—programmed under the supervision of a corps of multispan-trained philosophers—into the gaping jaws of the input slot.

"The meaning of life," murmured Kholgoltz. "The solution to the ultimate riddle. In just another moment it will be in our hands."

An ominous rumbling sound came from the depths of the mighty thinking machine. And then—

My recurring nightmare: A beam of dense emerald light penetrates my bedroom and lifts me with an irresistible force from my bed. I float through the window and hover high above the city. A zone of blackness engulfs me and I find myself transported to an endless onyx-walled tunnel-like hallway. I am alone. I wait, and nothing happens, and after an interminable length of time I begin to walk forward, keeping close to the left side of the hall. I am aware now that towering cone-shaped beings with saucer-size orange eyes and rubbery bodies are gliding past me on the right, paying no attention to me. I walk for days. Finally the hallway splits: nine identical tunnels confront me. Randomly I choose the leftmost one. It is just like the last, except that the beings moving toward me now are animated purple starfish, rough-skinned, many-tentacled, a globe of pale white fire glowing at their cores. Days again. I feel no hunger, no fatigue; I just go marching on. The tunnel forks once more. Seventeen options this time. I choose the rightmost branch. No change in the texture of the tunnel—smooth as always, glossy, bright with an inexplicable inner radiance—but now the beings flowing past me are spherical, translucent, paramecioid things filled with churning misty organs. On to the next forking place. And on. And on. Fork after fork, choice after choice, nothing the same, nothing ever different. I keep walking. On. On. On. I walk forever. I never leave the tunnel.

What's the purpose of life, anyway? Who if anybody put us here, and why? Is the whole cosmos merely a gigantic accident? Or was there a conscious and determined Prime Cause? What about free will? Do we have any, or are we only acting out the dictates of some unimaginable, unalterable program that was stencilled into the fabric of reality a billion years ago?

Big resonant questions. The kind an adolescent asks when he first begins to wrestle with the nature of the universe. What am I doing brooding over such stuff at my age? Who am I fooling?

This is the place. I have reached the center of the universe, where all vortices meet, where everything is tranquil, the zone of stormlessness. I drift becalmed, moving in a shallow orbit. This is ultimate peace. This is the edge of union with the All. In my tranquillity I experience a vision of the brawling, tempestuous universe that surrounds me. In every quadrant there are wars, quarrels, conspiracies, murders, air crashes, frictional losses, dimming suns, transfers of energy, colliding planets, a multitude of entropic interchanges. But here everything is perfectly still. Here is where I wish to be.

Yes! If only I could remain forever!

How, though? There's no way. Already I feel the tug of inexorable forces, and I have only just arrived. There is no everlasting peace. We constantly rocket past the miraculous center toward one zone of turbulence or another, driven always toward the periphery, driven, driven, helpless. I am drawn away from the place of peace. I spin wildly. The centrifuge of ego keeps me churning. Let me go back! Let me go! Let me lose myself in that place at the heart of the tumbling galaxies!

Never to die. That's part of the attraction. To live in a thousand civilizations yet to come, to see the future millennia unfold, to participate vicariously in the ultimate evolution of mankind—how to achieve all that, except through these books and magazines? That's what they give me: life eternal and a cosmic perspective. At any rate they give it to me from one page to the next.

The signal sped across the black bowl of night, picked up again and again by ultrawave repeater stations that kicked it to higher energy states. A thousand trembling laser nodes were converted to vapor in order to hasten the message to the galactic communications center on Manipool VI, where the emperor awaited news of the revolt. Through the data dome at last the story tumbled. Worlds aflame! Millions dead! The talismans of the Imperium trampled upon!

"We have no choice," said the emperor calmly. "Destroy the entire Rigel system at once."

The problem that arises when you try to regard science fiction as adult literature is that it's doubly removed from our "real" concerns. Ordinary mainstream fiction, your Faulkner and Dostoevsky and Hemingway, is by definition made-up stuff—the first remove. But at least it derives directly from experience, from contemplation of the empirical world of tangible daily phenomena. And so, while we are able to accept *The Possessed,* say, as an abstract thing, a verbal object, a construct of nouns and verbs and adjectives and adverbs, and while we can take it purely as a story, and aggregation of incidents and conversations and expository passages describing invented individuals and events, we can also *make use of it* as a guide to a certain aspect of Russian nineteenth-century sensibility and as a key to prerevolutionary radical thought. That is, it is of the nature of an historical artefact, a legacy of its own era, with real and identifiable extra literary values. Because it simulates actual people moving within a plausible and comprehensible real-world human situation, we can draw information from Dostoevsky's book that could conceivably aid us in understanding our own lives. What about science fiction, though, dealing with unreal situations set in places that do not exist and in eras that have not yet occurred? Can we take the adventures of Captain Zap in the eightieth century as a blueprint for self-discovery? Can we accept the collision of stellar federations in the Andromeda Nebula as an interpretation of the relationship of the United States and the Soviet Union circa 1950? I suppose we can, provided we can accept a science fiction story on a rarefied metaphorical level, as a set of symbolic structures generated in some way by the author's real-world experience. But it's much easier to hang in there with Captain Zap on his own level, for the sheer gaudy fun of it. And that's kiddie stuff.

Therefore we have two possible evaluations of science fiction:

—That it is simple-minded escape literature, lacking relevance to daily life and useful only as self-contained diversion.

—That its value is subtle and elusive, accessible only to those capable and willing to penetrate the experimental substructure concealed by those broad metaphors of galactic empires and supernormal powers.

I oscillate between the two attitudes. Sometimes I embrace both simultaneously. That's a trick I learned from science fiction, incidentally: "multispan logic," it was called in Zenger's famous novel *The Mind Plateau*. It took his hero twenty years of ascetic study in the cloisters of the Brothers of Aldebaran to master the trick. I've accomplished it in twenty years of reading *Nova* and *Deep Space* and *Solar Quarterly*. Yes: multispan logic. Yes. The art of embracing contradictory theses. Maybe "dynamic schizophrenia" would be a more expressive term, I don't know.

Is this the center? Am I there? I doubt it. Will I know it when I reach it, or will I deny it as I frequently do, will I say, *What else is there, where else should I look?*

The alien was a repellent thing, all lines and angles, its tendrils quivering menacingly, its slit-wide eyes revealing a somber bloodshot curiosity. Mortenson was unable to focus clearly on the creature; it kept slipping off at the edges into some other plane of being, an odd rippling effect that he found morbidly disquieting. It was no more than fifty meters from him now, and advancing steadily. When it gets to within ten meters, he thought, I'm going to blast it no matter what.

Five steps more; then an eerie metamorphosis. In place of this thing of harsh angular threat there stood a beaming, happy Golkon! The plump little creature waved its chubby tentacles and cooed a gleeful greeting!

"I am love," the Golkon declared. "I am the bringer of happiness! I welcome you to this world, dear friend!"

What do I fear? I fear the future. I fear the infinite possibilities that lie ahead. They fascinate and terrify me. I never thought I would admit that, even to myself. But what other interpretation can I place on my dream? That multitude of tunnels, that infinity of strange beings, all drifting toward me as I walk on and on? The embodiment of my basic fear. Hence my compulsive reading of science fiction: I crave road signs, I want a map of the territory that I must enter. That we all must enter. Yet the maps themselves are frightening. Perhaps I should look backward instead. It would be less terrifying to read historical novels. Yet I feed on these fantasies that obsess and frighten me. I derive energy from them. If I renounced them, what would nourish me?

The blood-collectors were out tonight, roving in thirsty packs across the blasted land. From the stone-walled safety of his cell he could hear them baying, could hear also the terrible cries of the victims, the old women, the straggling children. Four, five nights a week now, the fanged monsters broke loose and went marauding, and each night there were fewer humans left to hold back the tide. That was bad enough, but there was worse: his own craving. How much longer could he keep himself locked up in here? How long before he too was out there, prowling, questing for blood?

When I went to the newsstand at lunchtime to pick up the latest issue of *Tomorrow,* I found the first number of a new magazine: *Worlds of Wonder.* That startled me. It must be nine or ten years since anybody risked bringing out a new s-f title. We have our handful of long-established standbys, most of them founded in the thirties and even the twenties, which seem to be going to go on forever; but the failure of nearly all the younger magazines in the fifties was so emphatic that I suppose I came to assume there never again would be any new titles. Yet here is *Worlds of Wonder,* out today. There's nothing extraordinary about it. Except for the name it might very well be *Deep Space* or *Solar.* The format is the usual one, the size of *Reader's Digest.* The cover painting, unsurprisingly, is by Greenstone. The stories are by Aschenbach, Marcus, and some lesser names. The editor is Roy Schaefer, whom I remember as a competent but unspectacular writer in the fifties and sixties. I suppose I should be pleased that I'll have six more issues a year to keep me amused. In fact I feel vaguely threatened, as though the tunnel of my dreams has sprouted an unexpected new fork.

✹

The time machine hangs before me in the laboratory, a glittering golden ovoid suspended in ebony struts. Richards and Halleck smile nervously as I approach it. This, after all, is the climax of our years of research, and so much emotion rides on the success of the voyage I am about to take that every moment now seems freighted with heavy symbolic import. Our experiments with rats and rabbits seemed successful; but how can we know what it is to travel in time until a human being has made the journey?

All right. I enter the machine. Crisply we crackle instructions to one another across the intercom. Setting? Fifth of May, 2500 A.D.—a jump of nearly three and a half centuries. Power level? Energy feed? Go. Go. Dislocation circuit activated? Yes. All systems go. Bon voyage!

The control panel goes crazy. Dials spin. Lights flash. Everything's zapping at once. I plunge forward in time, going, going, going!

When everything is calm again I commence the emergence routines. The time capsule must be opened just so, unhurriedly. My hands tremble in anticipation of the strange new world that awaits me. A thousand hypotheses tumble through my brain. At last the hatch opens. "Hello," says Richards. "Hi there," Halleck says. We are still in the laboratory."

"I don't understand," I say. "My meters show definite temporal transfer."

"There was," says Richards. "You went forward to 2500 A.D., as planned. But you're still here."

"Where?"

"Here."

Halleck laughs. "You know what happened, Mike? You *did* travel in time. You jumped forward three hundred and whatever years. But you brought the whole present along with you. You pulled our own time into the future. It's like tugging a doughnut through its own hole. You see? Our work is kaput, Mike. We've got our answer. The present is always with us, no matter how far out we go."

⁂

Once about five years ago I took some acid, a little purple pill that a friend of mine mailed me from New Mexico. I had read a good deal about the psychedelics and I wasn't at all afraid; eager, in fact, hungry for the experience. I was going to float up into the cosmos and embrace it all. I was going to become a part of the nebulas and the supernovas, and they were going to become part of me; or rather, I would at last come to recognize that we had been part of each other all along. In other words, I imagined that LSD would be like an input of five hundred s-f novels all at once; a mind-blowing charge of imagery, emotion, strangeness, and transport to incredible unknowable places. The drug took about an hour to hit me. I saw the walls begin to flow and billow, and cascades of light streamed from the ceiling. Time became jumbled, and I thought three hours had gone by, but it was only about twenty minutes. Holly was with me. "What are you feeling?" she asked. "Is it mystical?" She asked a lot of questions like that. "I don't know," I said. "It's very pretty, but I just don't know." The drug wore off in about seven hours, but my nervous system was keyed up and lights kept exploding behind my eyes when I tried to go to sleep. So I sat up all night and read Marcus's *Starflame* novels, both of them, before dawn.

⁂

There is no galactic empire. There never will be any galactic empire. All is chaos. Everything is random. Galactic empires are puerile power-fantasies. Do I truly believe this? If not, why do I say it? Do I enjoy bringing myself down?

⁂

"Look over there!" the mutant whispered. Carter looked. An entire corner of the room had disappeared—melted away, as though it had been erased. Carter could see the street outside, the traffic, the building across the way. "Over there!" the mutant said. "Look!" The chair was gone. "Look!" The ceiling vanished. "Look! Look! Look!" Carter's head whirled. Everything was going, vanishing at the command of the inexorable golden-eyed mutant. "Do you see the stars?" the mutant asked. He snapped his fingers. "No!" Carter cried. "Don't!" Too late. The stars also were gone.

Sometimes I slip into what I consider the science fiction experience in everyday life. I mean, I can be sitting at my desk typing a report, or standing in the subway train waiting for the long grinding sweaty ride to end, when I feel a buzz, a rush, an upward movement of the soul similar to what I felt the time I took acid, and suddenly I see myself in an entirely new perspective—as a visitor from some other time, some other place, isolated in a world of alien beings known as Earth. Everything seems unfamiliar and baffling. I get that sense of doubleness, of *déjà vu,* as though I have read about this subway in some science fiction novel, as though I have seen this office described in a fantasy story, far away, long ago. The real world thus becomes something science fictional to me for twenty or thirty seconds at a stretch. The textures slide; the fabric strains. Sometimes, when that has happened to me, I think it's more exciting than having a fantasy world become "real" as I read. And sometimes I think I'm coming apart.

While we were sleeping there had been tragedy aboard our mighty starship. Our captain, our leader, our guide for two full generations, had been murdered in his bed! "Let me see it again!" I insisted, and Timothy held out the hologram. Yes! No doubt of it! I could see the blood stains in his thick white hair, I could see the frozen mask of anguish on his strong-featured face. Dead! The captain was dead! "What now?" I asked. "What will happen?"

"The civil war has already started on E Deck," Timothy said.

Perhaps what I really fear is not so much a dizzying multiplicity of futures but rather the absence of futures. When I end, will the universe end? Nothingness, emptiness, the void that awaits us all, the tunnel that leads not to everywhere but to nowhere—is that the only destination? If it is, is there any reason to feel fear? Why should I fear it? Nothingness is peace. Our nada who art in nada, nada be thy name, thy kingdom nada, thy will be nada, in nada as it is in nada. Hail nothing full of nothing, nothing is with thee. That's Hemingway. He felt the nada pressing in on all sides. Hemingway never wrote a word of science fiction. Eventually he delivered himself cheerfully to the great nada with a shotgun blast.

My friend Leon reminds me in some ways of Henry Darkdawn in De Soto's classic *Cosmos* trilogy. (If I said he reminded me of Stephen Dedalus or Raskolnikov or Julien Sorel, you would naturally need no further descriptions to know what I mean, but Henry Darkdawn is probably outside your range of literary experience. The De Soto trilogy deals with the formation, expansion, and decay of a quasi-religious movement spanning several galaxies in the years 30,000 to 35,000 A.D., and Darkdawn is a charismatic prophet, human but immortal or at any rate extraordinarily long-lived, who combines within himself the functions of Moses, Jesus and St. Paul: seer, intermediary with higher powers, organizer, leader, and ultimately martyr.) What makes the series so beautiful is the way De Soto gets inside Darkdawn's character, so that he's not merely a distant bas-relief—the Prophet—but a warm, breathing human being. That is, you see him warts and all—a sophisticated concept for science fiction, which tends to run heavily to marble statues in place of living protagonists.

Leon, of course, is unlikely ever to found a galaxy-spanning cult, but he has much of the intensity that I associate with Darkdawn. Oddly, he's quite tall—six feet two, I'd say—and has conventional good looks; people of his type don't generally run to high inner voltage, I've observed. But despite his natural physical advantages something must have compressed and redirected Leon's soul when he was young, because he's a brooder, a dreamer, a fire-breather, always coming up with visionary plans for reorganizing our office, stuff like that. He's the one who usually leaves s-f magazines on my desk as gifts, but he's also the one who pokes the most fun at me for reading what he considers to be trash. You see his contradictory nature right there. He's shy and aggressive, tough and vulnerable, confident and uncertain, the whole crazy human mix, everything right up front.

Last Tuesday I had dinner at his house. I often go there. His wife Helene is a superb cook. She and I had an affair five years ago that lasted about six months. Leon knew about it after the third meeting, but he never has said a word to me. Judging by Helene's desperate ardor, she and Leon must not have a very good sexual relationship; when she was in bed with me she seemed to want everything all at once, every position, every kind of sensation, as though she had been deprived much too long. Possibly Leon was pleased that I was taking some of the sexual pressure off him, and has silently regretted that I no longer sleep with his wife. (I ended the affair because she was drawing too much energy from me and because I was having difficulties meeting Leon's frank, open gaze.)

Last Tuesday just before dinner Helene went into the kitchen to check the oven. Leon excused himself and headed for the bathroom. Alone, I stood a moment by the bookshelf, checking in my automatic way to see if they had any s-f, and then I followed Helene into the kitchen to refill my glass from the martini pitcher in the refrigerator. Suddenly she was up against me, clinging tight, her lips seeking mine. She muttered my name; she dug her fingertips into my back. "Hey," I said softly. "Wait a second! We agreed that we weren't going to start that stuff again!"

"I want you!"

"Don't, Helene." Gently I pried her free of me. "Don't complicate things. Please."

I wriggled loose. She backed away from me, head down, and sullenly went to the stove. As I turned I saw Leon in the doorway. He must have witnessed the entire scene. His dark eyes were glossy with half-suppressed tears; his lips were quivering. Without saying anything he took the pitcher from me, filled his martini glass and drank the cocktail at a gulp. Then he went into the living room, and ten minutes later we were talking office politics as though nothing had happened. Yes, Leon, you're Henry Darkdawn to the last inch. Out of such stuff as you, Leon, are prophets created. Out of such stuff as you are cosmic martyrs made.

No one could tell the difference any longer. The sleek, slippery android had totally engulfed its maker's personality.

⁂

I stood at the edge of the cliff, staring in horror at the red, swollen thing that had been the life-giving sun of Earth.

⁂

The horde of robots—

⁂

The alien spaceship, plunging in a wild spiral—

⁂

Laughing, she opened her fist. The Q-bomb lay in the center of her palm. "Ten seconds," she cried.

⁂

How warm it is tonight! A dank glove of humidity enfolds me. Sleep will not come. I feel a terrible pressure all around me. Yes! The beam of green light! At last, at last, at last! Cradling me, lifting me, floating me through the open window. High over the dark city. On and on, through the void, out of space and time. To the tunnel. Setting me down. Here. Here. Yes, exactly as I imagined it would be: the onyx walls, the sourceless dull gleam, the curving vault far overhead, the silent alien figures drifting toward me. Here. The tunnel, at last. I take the first step forward. Another. Another. I am launched on my journey.

A SEA OF FACES

This is the story I wrote for Terry Carr in July, 1972, after he found himself unable to publish "The Science Fiction Hall of Fame" because of that story's anti-science-fiction subtext. He liked this one just fine; but at a somewhat later date he and I independently realized that the theme of the psychotherapist who disappears into his patient's consciousness had already been handled, and handled superbly, by Roger Zelazny in his novel The Dream Master.

The writer's mind plays odd tricks. There's always the danger of unconsciously plagiarizing some story that you admire, or accidentally reinventing some splendid line from somebody else's story that you now think is your own creation, because you've forgotten that you read it somewhere else. Anyone who has read as much as I have, and has written as much, is particularly prone to this syndrome, and more than once in my career I've belatedly discovered that I've unintentionally rewritten somebody else's story. (I've done it intentionally *a few times, too, as in "In Another Country," my version of C.L. Moore's "Vintage Season," but in such cases I always make it quite clear upon first publication that the work is a pastiche.) Zelazny's* The Dream Master *is one science-fiction story I very much wish I had written, but, since I was too late for that, I seem to have rewritten it instead in all blithe innocence, and Terry published it in the same way—leading to our "Oh, my God!" reactions afterward.*

Apart from theme, the stories don't really have much in common, and so I don't have any hesitation about reprinting my story here. A good theme can stand more than one handling; and in any case this sort of unconscious literary borrowing goes on all the time. (I've been on the other end of it, too.) I rather like my version of the idea, second-hand though it turned out to be, but I still wish I had written Zelazny's before he did.

Are not such floating fragments on the sea of the unconscious called Freudian ships?

JOSEPHINE SAXTON

Falling.

It's very much like dying, I suppose. That awareness of infinite descent, that knowledge of the total absence of support. It's all sky up here. Down below is neither land nor sea, only color without form, so distant that I can't even put a name to the color. The cosmos is torn open, and I plummet headlong, arms and legs pinwheeling wildly, the gray stuff in my skull centrifuging toward my ears. I'm dropping like Lucifer. *From morn to noon he fell, from noon to dewy eve, A summer's day; and with the setting sun Dropp'd from the zenith like a falling star.* That's Milton. Even now my old liberal-arts education stands me in good stead. *And when he falls, he falls like a Lucifer, Never to hope again.* That's Shakespeare. It's all part of the same thing. All of English literature was written by a single man, whose sly persuasive voice ticks in my dizzy head as I drop. God grant me a soft landing.

"She looks a little like you," I told Irene. "At least, it seemed that way for one quick moment, when she turned toward the window in my office and the sunlight caught the planes of her face. Of course, it's the most superficial resemblance only, a matter of bone structure, the placement of the eyes, the cut of the hair. But your expressions, your inner selves externally represented, are altogether dissimilar. You radiate unbounded good health and vitality, Irene, and she slips so easily into the classic schizoid fancies, the eyes alternately dreamy and darting, the forehead pale, flecked with sweat. She's very troubled."

"What's her name?"

"Lowry. April Lowry."

"A beautiful name. April. Young?"

"About twenty-three."

"How sad, Richard. Schizoid, you said?"

"She retreats into nowhere without provocation. Lord knows what triggers it. When it happens she can go six or eight months without saying a word. The last attack was a year ago. These days she's feeling much better, she's willing to talk about herself a bit. She says it's as though there's a zone of weakness in the walls of her mind, an opening, a trapdoor, a funnel, something like that, and from time to time her soul is irresistibly drawn toward it and goes pouring through and disappears into God knows what, and there's nothing left of her but a shell. And eventually she comes back through the same passage. She's convinced that one of these times she won't come back."

"Is there some way to help her?" Irene asked. "What will you try? Drugs? Hypnosis? Shock? Sensory deprivation?"

"They've all been tried."

"What then, Richard? What will you do?"

Suppose there is a way. Let's pretend there is a way. Is that an acceptable hypothesis? Let's pretend. Let's just pretend, and see what happens.

The vast ocean below me occupies the entirety of my field of vision. Its surface is convex, belly-up in the middle and curving vertiginously away from me at the periphery; the slope is so extreme that I wonder why the water doesn't all run off toward the edges and drown the horizon. Not far beneath that shimmering swollen surface a gigantic pattern of crosshatchings and countertextures is visible, like an immense mural floating lightly submerged in the water. For a moment, as I plunge, the pattern resolves itself and becomes coherent: I see the face of Irene, a calm pale mask, the steady blue eyes focused lovingly on me. She fills the ocean. Her semblance covers an area greater than any continental mass. Firm chin, strong full lips, delicate tapering nose. She emanates a serene aura of inner peace that buoys me like an invisible net: I am falling easily now, pleasantly, arms outspread, face down, my entire body relaxed. How beautiful she is! I continue to descend and the pattern shatters; the sea is abruptly full of metallic shards and splinters, flashing bright gold through the dark blue-green; then, when I am perhaps a thousand meters lower, the pattern suddenly reorganizes itself. A colossal face, again. I welcome Irene's return, but no, the face is the face of April, my silent sorrowful one. A haunted face, a face full of shadows: dark terrified eyes, flickering nostrils, sunken cheeks. A bit of one incisor is visible over the thin lower lip. O my poor sweet Taciturna. Needles of reflected sunlight glitter in her outspread waterborne hair. April's manifestation supplants serenity with turbulence; again I plummet out of control, again I am in the cosmic centrifuge, my breath is torn from me and a dread chill rushes past my tumbling body. Desperately I fight for poise and balance. I attain it, finally, and look down. The pattern has again broken; where April has been, I see only parallel bands of amber light, distorted by choppy refractions. Tiny white dots—islands, I suppose—now are evident in the glossy sea.

What a strange resemblance there is, at times, between April and Irene! How confusing for me to confuse them. How dangerous for me.

—It's the riskiest kind of therapy you could have chosen, Dr. Bjornstrand.

—Risky for me, or risky for her?

—Risky for you and for your patient, I'd say.

—So what else is new?

—You asked me for an impartial evaluation, Dr. Bjornstrand. If you don't care to accept my opinion—

—I value your opinion highly, Erik.

—But you're going to go through with the therapy as presently planned?

—Of course I am.

This is the moment of splashdown.

I hit the water perfectly and go slicing through the sea's shining surface with surgical precision, knifing fifty meters deep, eighty, a hundred, cutting smoothly through the oceanic epithelium and the sturdy musculature beneath. Very well done, Dr. Bjornstrand. High marks for form.

Perhaps this is deep enough.

I pivot, kick, turn upward, clutch at the brightness above me. I may have overextended myself, I realize. My lungs are on fire and the sky, so recently my home, seems terribly far away. But with vigorous strokes I pull myself up and come popping into the air like a stubborn cork.

I float idly a moment, catching my breath. Then I look around. The ferocious eye of the sun regards me from a late-morning height. The sea is warm and gentle, undulating seductively. There is an island only a few hundred meters away: an inviting beach of bright sand, a row of slender palms farther back. I swim toward it. As I near the shore, the bottomless dark depths give way to sandy outlying sunken shelf, and the hue of the sea changes from deep blue to light green. Yet it is taking longer to reach land than I had expected. Perhaps my estimate of the distance was overly optimistic; for all my efforts, the island seems to be getting no closer. At moments it actually appears to be retreating from me. My arms grow heavy. My kick becomes sluggish. I am panting, wheezing, sputtering; something throbs behind my forehead. Suddenly, though, I see sun-streaked sand just below me. My feet touch bottom. I wade wearily ashore and fall to my knees on the margin of the beach.

—Can I call you April, Miss Lowry?

—Whatever.

—I don't think that that's a very threatening level of therapist-patient intimacy, do you?

—Not really.

—Do you always shrug every time you answer a question?

—I didn't know I did.

—You shrug. You also studiously avoid any show of facial expression. You try to be very unreadable, April.

—Maybe I feel safer that way.

—But who's the enemy?

—You'd know more about that than I would, doctor.

—Do you actually think so? I'm all the way over here. You're right there inside your own head. You'll know more than I ever will about you.

—You could always come inside my head if you wanted to.

—Wouldn't that frighten you?

—It would kill me.

—I wonder, April. You're much stronger than you think you are. You're also very beautiful, April. I know, it's beside the point. But you are.

⁂

It's just a small island. I can tell that by the way the shoreline curves rapidly away from me. I lie sprawled near the water's edge, face down, exhausted, fingers digging tensely into the warm moist sand. The sun is strong; I feel waves of heat going *thratata thratata* on my bare back. I wear only a ragged pair of faded blue jeans, very tight, cut off choppily at the knee. My belt is waterlogged and salt-cracked, as though I was adrift for days before making landfall. Perhaps I was. It's hard to maintain a reliable sense of time in this place.

I should get up. I should explore.

Yes. Getting up, now. A little dizzy, eh? Yes. But I walk steadily up the gentle slope of the beach. Fifty meters inland, the sand shades into sandy soil, loose, shallow; rounded white coral boulders poke through from below. Thirsty soil. Nevertheless, how lush everything is here. A wall of tangled vines and creepers. Long glossy tropical green leaves, smooth-edged, big-veined. The corrugated trunks of the palms. The soft sound of the surf, *fwissh, fwissh,* underlying all other textures. How blue the sea. How green the sky. *Fwissh.*

Is that the image of a face in the sky?

A woman's face, yes. Irene? April? The features are indistinct. But I definitely see it, yes, hovering a few hundred meters above the water as if projected from the sun-streaked sheet that is the skin of the ocean: a glow, a radiance, having the form of a delicate face—nostrils, lips, brows, cheeks, certainly a face, and not just one, either, for in the intensity of my stare I cause it to split and then to split again, so that a row of them hangs in the air, ten faces, a hundred, a thousand faces, faces all about me, a sea of faces. They seem quite grave. Smile! On command, the faces smile. Much better. The air itself is brighter for that smile. The faces merge, blur, sharpen, blur again, overlap in part, dance, shimmer, melt, flow. Illusions born of the heat. Daughters of the sun. Sweet mirages. I look past them, higher, into the clear reaches of the cloudless heavens.

Hawks!

Hawks here? Shouldn't I be seeing gulls? The birds whirl and swoop, dark figures against the blinding sky, wings outspread, feathers like fingers. I see their fierce hooked beaks. They snap great beetles from the steaming air and soar away, digesting. Then there are no birds, only the faces, still smiling. I turn my back on them and slowly move off through the underbrush to see what sort of place the sea has given me.

So long as I stay near the shore, I have no difficulty in walking; cutting through the densely vegetated interior might be a different matter. I sidle off to the left, following the nibbled line of beach. Before I have walked a hundred paces I have made a new discovery: the island is adrift.

Glancing seaward, I notice that on the horizon there lies a dark shore rimmed by black triangular mountains, one or two days' sail distant. Minutes ago I saw only open sea in that direction. Maybe the mountains have just this moment sprouted, but more likely the island, spinning slowly in the currents, has only now turned to reveal them. That must be the answer. I stand quite still for a long while and it seems to me that I behold those mountains now from one angle, now from a slightly different one. How else to explain such effects of parallax? The island freely drifts. It moves, and I move with it, upon the breast of the changeless unbounded sea.

The celebrated young American therapist Richard Bjornstrand commenced his experimental treatment of Miss April Lowry on the third of August, 1987. Within fifteen days the locus of disturbance had been identified, and Dr. Bjornstrand had recommended consciousness-penetration treatment, a technique increasingly popular in the United States. Miss Lowry's physician was initially opposed to the suggestion, but further consultations demonstrated the potential value of such an approach, and on the nineteenth of September the entry procedures were initiated. We expect further reports from Dr. Bjornstrand as the project develops.

Leonie said, "But what if you fall in love with her?"

"What of it?" I asked. "Therapists are always falling in love with their patients. Reich married one of his patients, and so did Fenichel, and dozens of the early analysts had affairs with their patients, and even Freud, who didn't, was known to observe—"

"Freud lived a long time ago," Leonie said.

I have now walked entirely around the island. The circumambulation took me four hours, I estimate, since the sun was almost directly overhead when I began it and is now more than halfway toward the horizon. In these latitudes I suppose sunset comes quite early, perhaps by half past six, even in summer.

All during my walk this afternoon the island remained on a steady course, keeping one side constantly toward the sea, the other toward that dark mountain-girt shore. Yet it has continued to drift, for there are minor oscillations in the position of the mountains relative to the island, and the shore itself appears gradually to grow closer. (Although that may be an illusion.) Faces appear and vanish and reappear in the lower reaches of the sky according to no predictable schedule of event or identity: April, Irene, April, Irene, Irene, April, April, Irene. Sometimes they smile at me. Sometimes they do not. I thought I saw one of the Irenes wink; I looked again and the face was April's.

The island, though quite small, has several distinct geographical zones. On the side where I first came ashore there is a row of close-set palms, crown to crown, beyond which the beach slopes toward the sea. I have arbitrarily labeled that side of the island as *east.* The western side is low and parched, and the vegetation is a tangle of scrub. On the north side is a high coral ridge, flat-faced and involute, descending steeply into the water. White wavelets batter tirelessly against the rounded spires and domes of that pocked coral wall. The island's southern shore has dunes, quite Saharaesque, their yellowish-pink crests actually shifting ever so slightly as I watch. Inland, the island rises to a peak perhaps fifty meters above sea level, and evidently there are deep pockets of retained rainwater in the porous, decayed limestone of the undersurface, for the vegetation is profuse and vigorous. At several points I made brief forays to the interior, coming upon a swampy region of noisy sucking quicksand in one place, a cool dark glade interpenetrated with the tunnels and mounds of termites in another, a copse of wide-branching little fruit-bearing trees elsewhere.

Altogether the place is beautiful. I will have enough food and drink, and there are shelters. Nevertheless I long already for an end to the voyage. The bare sharp-tipped mountains of the mainland grow ever nearer; some day I will reach the shore, and my real work will begin.

The essence of this kind of therapy is risk. The therapist must be prepared to encounter forces well beyond his own strength, and to grapple with them in the knowledge that they might readily triumph over him. The patient, for her part, must accept the knowledge that the intrusion of the therapist into her consciousness may cause extensive alterations of the personality, not all of them for the better.

A bewildering day. The dawn was red-stained with purple veins—a swollen, grotesque, traumatic sky. Then came high winds; the palms rippled and swayed and great fronds were torn loose. A lull followed. I feared toppling trees and tidal waves, and pressed inland for half an hour, settling finally in a kind of natural amphitheatre of dead old coral, a weathered bowl thrust up from the sea millennia ago. Here I waited out the morning. Toward noon thick dark clouds obscured the heavens. I felt a sense of menace, of irresistible powers gathering their strength, such as I sometimes feel when I hear that tense little orchestral passage late in the Agnus Dei of the *Missa Solemnis*, and instants later there descended on me hail, rain, sleet, high wind, furious heat, even snow—all weathers at once. I thought the earth would crack open and pour forth magma upon me. It was all over in five minutes, and every trace of the storm vanished. The clouds parted; the sun emerged, looking gentle and innocent; birds of many plumages wheeled in the air, warbling sweetly. The faces of Irene and April, infinitely reduplicated, blinked on and off against the backdrop of the sky. The mountainous shore hung fixed on the horizon, growing no nearer, getting no farther away, as though the day's turmoils had caused the frightened island to put down roots.

Rain during the night, warm and steamy. Clouds of gnats. An evil humming sound, greasily resonant, pervading everything. I slept, finally, and was awakened by a sound like a mighty thunderclap, and saw an enormous distorted sun rising slowly in the west.

We sat by the redwood table on Donald's patio: Irene, Donald, Erik, Paul, Anna, Leonie, me. Paul and Erik drank bourbon, and the rest of us sipped Shine, the new drink, essence of cannabis mixed with (I think) ginger beer and strawberry syrup. We were very high. "There's no reason," I said, "why we shouldn't avail ourselves of the latest technological developments. Here's this unfortunate girl suffering from an undeterminable but crippling psychological malady, and the chance exists for me to enter her soul and—"

"Enter her *what?*" Donald asked.

"Her consciousness, her *anima*, her spirit, her mind, her whatever you want to call it."

"Don't interrupt him," Leonie said to Donald.

Irene said, "Will you bring her to Erik for an impartial opinion first, at least?"

"What makes you think Erik is impartial?" Anna asked.

"He tries to be," said Erik coolly. "Yes, bring her to me, Dr. Bjornstrand."

"I know what you'll tell me."

"Still. Even so."

"Isn't this terribly dangerous?" Leonie asked. "I mean, suppose your mind became stuck inside her, Richard."

"Stuck?"

"Isn't that possible? I don't actually know anything about the process but—"

"I'll be entering her only in the most metaphorical sense," I said. Irene laughed. Anna said, "Do you actually believe that?" and gave Irene a sly look. Irene merely shook her head. "I don't worry about Richard's fidelity," she said, drawling her words.

Her face fills the sky today.

April. Irene. Whoever she is. She eclipses the sun, and lights the day with her own supernal radiance.

The course of the island has been reversed, and now it drifts out to sea. For three days I have watched the mountains of the mainland growing smaller. Evidently the currents have changed; or perhaps there are zones of resistance close to the shore, designed to keep at bay such wandering islands as mine. I must find a way to deal with this. I am convinced that I can do nothing for April unless I reach the mainland.

I have entered a calm place where the sea is a mirror and the sweltering air reflects the images in an infinitely baffling regression. I see no face but my own, now, and I see it everywhere. A million versions of myself dance in the steamy haze. My jaws are stubbled and there is a bright red band of sunburn across my nose and upper cheeks. I grin and the multitudinous images grin at me. I reach toward them and they reach toward me. No land is in sight, no other islands—nothing, in fact, but this wall of reflections. I feel as though I am penned inside a box of polished metal. My shining image infests the burning atmosphere. I have a constant choking sensation; a terrible languor is coming over me; I pray for hurricanes, waterspouts, convulsions of the ocean bed, any sort of upheaval that will break the savage claustrophobic tension.

Is Irene my wife? My lover? My companion? My friend? My sister?

I am within April's consciousness and Irene is a figment.

It has begun to occur to me that this may be my therapy rather than April's.

I have set to work creating machinery to bring me back to the mainland. All this week I have painstakingly felled palm trees, using a series of blunt, soft hand axes chipped from slabs of dead coral. Hauling the trees to a promontory of the island's southern face, I lashed them loosely together with vines, setting them in the water so that they projected from both sides of the headland like the oars of a galley. By tugging at an unusually thick vine that runs down the spine of the whole construction, I am indeed able to make them operate like oars; and I have tied that master vine to an unusually massive palm that sprouts from the central ridge of the promontory. What I have built, in fact, is a kind of reciprocating engine; the currents, stirring the leafy crowns of my felled palms, impart a tension to the vines that link them, and the resistance of the huge central tree to the tug of the master vine causes the felled trees to sweep the water, driving the entire island shoreward. Through purposeful activity said Goethe, we justify our existence in the eyes of God.

The "oars" work well. I'm heading toward the mainland once again.

Heading toward the mainland very rapidly. Too rapidly, it seems. I think I may be caught in a powerful current.

The current definitely has seized my island and I'm being swept swiftly along, willy-nilly. I am approaching the isle where Scylla waits. That surely is Scylla: that creature just ahead. There is no avoiding her; the force of the water is inexorable and my helpless oars dangle limply. The many-necked monster sits in plain sight on a barren rock, coiled into herself, waiting. Where shall I hide? Shall I scramble into the underbrush and huddle there until I am past her? Look, there: six heads, each with three rows of pointed teeth, and twelve snaky limbs. I suppose I could hide, but how cowardly, how useless. I will show myself to her. I stand exposed on the shore. I listen to her dread barking. How may I guard myself against Scylla's fangs? Irene smiles out of the low fleecy clouds. There's a way, she seems to be saying. I gather a cloud and fashion it into a simulacrum of myself. See: another Bjornstrand stands here, sunburned, half naked. I make a second replica, a third, complete to the stubble, complete to the blemishes. A dozen of them. Passive, empty, soulless. Will they deceive her? We'll see. The barking is ferocious now. She is close. My island whips through the channel. Strike, Scylla! Strike! The long necks rise and fall, rise and fall. I hear the screams of my other selves; I see their arms and legs thrashing as she seizes them and lifts them. Them she devours. Me she spares. I float safely past the hideous beast. April's face, reduplicated infinitely in the blue vault above me, is smiling. I have gained power by this encounter. I need have no further fears: I have become invulnerable. Do your worst, ocean! Bring me the Charybdis. I'm ready. Yes. Bring me to Charybdis.

✹

The whole, D. H. Lawrence wrote, is a strange assembly of apparently incongruous parts, slipping past one another. I agree. But of course the incongruity is apparent rather than real, else there would be no whole.

✹

I believe I have complete control over the island now. I can redesign it to serve my needs, and I have streamlined it, making it shipshaped, pointed at the bow, blunt at the stern. My conglomeration of felled palms has been replaced; now flexible projections of island-stuff flail the sea, propelling me steadily toward the mainland. Broad-leafed shade trees make the heat of day more bearable. At my command fresh-water streams spring from the sand, cool, glistening.

Gradually I extend the sphere of my control beyond the perimeter of the island. I have established a shark-free zone just off shore within an encircling reef. There I swim in perfect safety, and when hunger comes, I draw friendly fishes forth with my hands.

I fashion images out of clouds: April, Irene. I simulate the features of Dr. Richard Bjornstrand in the heavens. I draw April and Irene together, and they blur, they become one woman.

✹

Getting close to the coast now. Another day or two and I'll be there.

✹

This is the mainland. I guide my island into a wide half-moon harbor, shadowed by the great naked mountains that rise like filed black teeth from the nearby interior. The island pushes out a sturdy woody cable that ties it to its berth; using the cable as a gangplank, I go ashore. The air is cooler here. The vegetation is sparse and cactusoidal: thick fleshy thorn-studded purplish barrels, mainly, taller than I. I strike one with a log and pale pink fluid gushes from it: I taste it and find it cool, sugary, vaguely intoxicating.

Cactus fluid sustains me during a five-day journey to the summit of the closest mountain. Bare feet slap against bare rock. Heat by day, lunar chill by night; the boulders twang at twilight as the warmth leaves them. At my back sprawls the sea, infinite, silent. The air is spangled with the frowning faces of women. I ascend by a slow spiral route, pausing frequently to rest, and push myself onward until at last I stand athwart the highest spine of the range. On the inland side the mountains drop away steeply into a tormented irregular valley, boulder-strewn and icy, slashed by glittering white lakes like so many narrow lesions. Beyond that is a zone of low breast-shaped hills, heavily forested, descending into a central lowlands out of which rises a pulsing fountain of light—jagged phosphorescent bursts of blue and gold and green and red that rocket into the air, attenuate, and are lost. I dare not approach that fountain; I will be consumed, I know, in its fierce intensity, for there the essence of April has its lair, the savage soul-core that must never be invaded by another.

I turn seaward and look to my left, down the coast. At first I see nothing extraordinary: a row of scalloped bays, some strips of sandy beach, a white line of surf, a wheeling flock of dark birds. But then I detect, far along the shore, a more remarkable feature. Two long slender promontories jut from the mainland like curved fingers, a thumb and a forefinger reaching toward one another, and in the wide gulf enclosed between them the sea churns in frenzy, as though it boils. At the vortex of the disturbance, though, all is calm. There! There is Charybdis! The maelstrom!

It would take me days to reach it overland. The sea route will be quicker. Hurrying down the slopes, I return to my island and sever the cable that binds it to shore. Perversely, it grows again. Some malign influence is negating my power. I sever; the cable reunites. I sever; it reunites. Again, again, again. Exasperated, I cause a fissure to pierce the island from edge to edge at the place where my cable is rooted; the entire segment surrounding that anchor breaks away and remains in the harbor, held fast, while the remainder of the island drifts toward the open sea.

Wait. The process of fission continues of its own momentum. The island is calving like a glacier, disintegrating, huge fragments breaking away. I leap desperately across yawning crevasses, holding always to the largest sector, struggling to rebuild my floating home, until I realize that nothing significant remains of the island, only an ever-diminishing raft of coral rock, halving and halving again. My island is no more than ten meters square now. Five. Less than five. Gone.

I always dreaded the ocean. That great inverted bowl of chilly water, resonating with booming salty sounds, infested with dark rubbery weeds, inhabited by toothy monsters—it preyed on my spirit, draining me, filling itself from me. Of course it was the northern sea I knew and hated, the dull dirty Atlantic, licking greasily at the Massachusetts coast. A black rocky shoreline, impenetrable mysteries of water, a line of morning debris cluttering the scanty sandy coves, a host of crabs and lesser scuttlers crawling everywhere. While swimming I imagined unfriendly sea beasts nosing around my dangling legs. I looked with distaste upon that invisible shimmering clutter of hairy-clawed planktonites, that fantasia of fibrous filaments and chittering antennae. And I dreaded most of all the slow lazy stirring of the Kraken, idly sliding its vast tentacles upward toward the boats of the surface. And here I am adrift on the sea's own breast. April's face in the sky wears a smile. The face of Irene flexes into a wink.

I am drawn toward the maelstrom. Swimming is unnecessary; the water carries me purposefully toward my goal. Yet I swim, all the same, stroke after stroke, yielding nothing to the force of the sea. The first promontory is coming into view. I swim all the more energetically. I will not allow the whirlpool to capture me; I must give myself willingly to it.

Now I swing round and round in the outer gyres of Charybdis. This is the place through which the spirit is drained: I can see April's pallid face like an empty plastic mask, hovering, drawn downward, disappearing chin-first through the whirlpool's vortex, reappearing, going down once more, an infinite cycle of drownings and disappearances and returns and resurrections. I must follow her.

No use pretending to swim here. One can only keep one's arms and legs pressed close together and yield, as one is sluiced down through level after level of the maelstrom until one reaches the heart of the eddy, and then—*swoosh!*—the ultimate descent. Now I plummet. The tumble takes forever. *From morn to noon he fell, from noon to dewy eve.* I rocket downward through the hollow heart of the whirlpool, gripped in a monstrous suction, until abruptly I am delivered to a dark region of cold quiet water: far below the surface of the sea. My lungs ache; my ribcage, distended over a bloated lump of hot depleted air, shoots angry protests into my armpits. I glide along the smooth vertical face of a submerged mountain. My feet find lodging on a ledge; I grope my way along it and come at length to the mouth of a cave, set at a sharp angle against the steep wall of stone. I topple into it.

Within, I find an air-filled pocket of a room, dank, slippery, lit by some inexplicable inner glow. April is there, huddled against the back of the cave. She is naked, shivering, sullen, her hair pasted in damp strands to the pale column of her neck. Seeing me, she rises but does not come forward. Her breasts are small, her hips narrow, her thighs slender: a child's body.

I reach a hand toward her. "Come. Let's swim out of here together, April."

"No. It's impossible. I'll drown."

"I'll be with you."

"Even so," she says. "I'll drown, I know it."

"What are you going to do, then? Just stay here?"

"For the time being."

"Until when?"

"Until it's safe to come out," she says.

"When will that be?"

"I'll know."

"I'll wait with you. All right?"

I don't hurry her. At last she says, "Let's go now."

This time I am the one who hesitates, to my own surprise. It is as if there has been an interchange of strength in this cave and I have been weakened. I draw back, but she takes my hand and leads me firmly to the mouth of the cave. I see the water swirling outside, held at bay because it has no way of expelling the bubble of air that fills our pocket in the mountain. April begins to glide down the slick passageway that takes us from the cave. She is excited, radiant, eyes bright, breasts heaving. "Come," she says. "Now! *Now!*"

We spill out of the cave together.

The water hammers me. I gasp, choke, tumble. The pressure is appalling. My eardrums scream shrill complaints. Columns of water force themselves into my nostrils. I feel the whirlpool dancing madly far above me. In terror I turn and try to scramble back into the cave, but it will not have me, and rebounding impotently against a shield of air, I let myself be engulfed by the water. I am beginning to drown, I think. My eyes deliver no images. Dimly I am aware of April tugging at me, grasping me, pulling me upward. What will she do, swim through the whirlpool from below? All is darkness. I perceive only the touch of her hand. I struggle to focus my eyes, and finally I see her through a purple chaos. How much like Irene she looks! Which is she, April or Irene? It scarcely matters. Drowning is my occupation now. It will all be over soon. Let me go, I tell her, let me go, let me do my drowning and be done with it. Save yourself. Save yourself. But she pays no heed and continues to tug.

We erupt into the sunlight.

Bobbing at the surface, we bask in glorious warmth. "Look," she cries. "There's an island! Swim, Richard, swim! We'll be there in ten minutes. We can rest there."

Irene's face fills the sky.

"Swim!" April urges.

I try. I am without strength. A few strokes and I lapse into stupor. April, apparently unaware, is far ahead of me. April, I call. April. April, help me. I think of the beach, the warm moist sand, the row of palms, the intricate texture of the white coral boulders. Yes. Time to go home. Irene is waiting for me. April! April!

She scrambles ashore. Her slim bare form glistens in the hot sunlight.

April?

The sea has me. I drift away, foolish flotsam, borne again toward the maelstrom.

Down. Down. No way to fight it. April is gone. I see only Irene, shimmering in the waves. Down.

This cool dark cave.

Where am I? I don't know.

Who am I? Dr. Richard Bjornstrand? April Lowry? Both of those? Neither of those? I think I'm Bjornstrand. Was. Here, Dickie Dickie Dickie.

How do I get out of here? I don't know.

I'll wait. Sooner or later I'll be strong enough to swim out. Sooner. Later. We'll see.

Irene?

April?

Here Dickie Dickie Dickie. Here.

Where?

Here.

THE DYBBUK OF MAZEL TOV IV

A certain ethnic quality had been creeping into my science fiction in the early 1970s—representing, I think, nothing more than boredom with the conventional Anglo-Saxonicity of most science fiction, to which I had generally adhered in my own writing. This rebellion against stereotype had surfaced fairly explicitly in the novels I wrote in 1971, Dying Inside *and* The Book of Skulls, *leading one perplexed admirer to tell me something like, "I sure do like your stuff, but why all the Jewishness?" (To which I replied, a little testily, "Why not?") But all my ethnic phase amounted to, really, was using characters with names like David Selig and Eli Steinfeld instead of Kimball Kinnison and Michael Valentine Smith. There was no real sense of Jewish cultural tradition about my characters: more of a New Yorkiness than a Jewishness, in fact, for they were, like their creator, assimilated, non-observing Jews, linked to the tribe only by inheritance and osmosis.*

Then my good friend Jack Dann asked me to do a story for a book called Wandering Stars, *an anthology of what he called "Jewish science fiction." I thought that was an odd idea for a book, even a wrong-headed one. The balkanization of s-f—Jewish s-f, black s-f, feminist s-f, WASP s-f—didn't seem right to me. Setting up such arbitrary divisions imposed limits on a field that ought to have infinite horizons. Then I came around to the other side of the issue: the very limitation Jack was imposing might just provide an interesting intellectual challenge. And so I signed on.*

"The Dybbuk of Mazel Tov IV" was written in July of 1972, at a time when most of my fiction was tending to be fragmentary and elliptical in manner, the work of a writer who had grown really weary of telling stories

in the conventional mode; and yet somehow this one came out pure storytelling, old-fashioned in construction and style, a refreshing relapse into a mode of fiction that I had nearly abandoned. It was a joy to write and I think it's fun to read. It's also the only story of mine that owes anything much to the cultural background in which I was ostensibly raised.

My grandson David will have his bar mitzvah next spring. No one in our family has undergone that rite in at least three hundred years—certainly not since we Levins settled in Old Israel, the Israel on Earth, soon after the European holocaust. My friend Eliahu asked me not long ago how I feel about David's bar mitzvah, whether the idea of it angers me, whether I see it as a disturbing element. No, I replied, the boy is a Jew, after all—let him have a bar mitzvah if he wants one. These are times of transition and upheaval, as all times are. David is not bound by the attitudes of his ancestors.

"Since when is a Jew not bound by the attitudes of his ancestors?" Eliahu asked.

"You know what I mean," I said.

Indeed he did. We are bound but yet free. If anything governs us out of the past it is the tribal bond itself, not the philosophies of our departed kinsmen. We accept what we choose to accept; nevertheless we remain Jews. I come from a family that has liked to say—especially to gentiles—that we are Jews but not Jewish; that is, we acknowledge and cherish our ancient heritage, but we do not care to entangle ourselves in outmoded rituals and folkways. This is what my forefathers declared, as far back as those secular-minded Levins who three centuries ago fought to win and guard the freedom of the land of Israel. (Old Israel, I mean.) I would say the same here, if there were any gentiles on this world to whom such things had to be explained. But of course in this New Israel in the stars we have only ourselves, no gentiles within a dozen light-years, unless you count our neighbors the Kunivaru as gentiles. (Can creatures that are not human rightly be called gentiles? I'm not sure the term applies. Besides, the Kunivaru now insist that they are Jews. My mind spins. It's an issue of Talmudic complexity, and God knows I'm no Talmudist. Hillel, Akiva, Rashi, help me!) Anyway, come the fifth day of Sivan my son's son will have his bar mitzvah, and I'll play the proud grandpa as pious old Jews have done for six thousand years.

All things are connected. That my grandson would have a bar mitzvah is merely the latest link in a chain of events that goes back to—when? To the day the Kunivaru decided to embrace Judaism? To the day the dybbuk entered Seul the Kunivar? To the day we refugees from Earth discovered the fertile planet that we sometimes call New Israel and sometimes call Mazel Tov IV? To the day of the Final Pogrom on Earth? Reb Yossele the Hasid might say that David's bar mitzvah was determined on the day the Lord God fashioned Adam out of dust. But I think that would be overdoing things.

The day the dybbuk took possession of the body of Seul the Kunivar was probably where it really started. Until then things were relatively uncomplicated here. The Hasidim had their settlement, we Israelis had ours, and the natives, the Kunivaru, had the rest of the planet; and generally we all kept out of one another's way. After the dybbuk everything changed. It happened more than forty years ago, in the first generation after the Landing, on the ninth day of Tishri in the year 6302. I was working in the fields, for Tishri is a harvest month. The day was hot, and I worked swiftly, singing and humming. As I moved down the long rows of cracklepods, tagging those that were ready to be gathered, a Kunivar appeared at the crest of the hill that overlooks our kibbutz. It seemed to be in some distress, for it came staggering and lurching down the hillside with extraordinary clumsiness, tripping over its own four legs as if it barely knew how to manage them. When it was about a hundred meters from me, it cried out, "Shimon! Help me, Shimon! In God's name help me!"

There were several strange things about this outcry, and I perceived them gradually, the most trivial first. It seemed odd that a Kunivar would address me by my given name, for they are a formal people. It seemed more odd that a Kunivar would speak to me in quite decent Hebrew, for at that time none of them had learned our language. It seemed most odd of all—but I was slow to discern it—that a Kunivar would have the very voice, dark and resonant, of my dear dead friend Joseph Avneri.

The Kunivar stumbled into the cultivated part of the field and halted, trembling terribly. Its fine green fur was pasted into hummocks by perspiration, and its great golden eyes rolled and crossed in a ghastly way. It stood flat-footed, splaying its legs out under the four corners of its chunky body like the legs of a table, and clasped its long powerful arms around its chest. I recognized the Kunivar as Seul, a subchief of the local village, with whom we of the kibbutz had had occasional dealings.

"What help can I give you?" I asked. "What has happened to you, Seul?"

"Shimon—Shimon—" A frightful moan came from the Kunivar. "Oh, God, Shimon, it goes beyond all belief! How can I bear this? How can I even comprehend it?"

No doubt of it. The Kunivar was speaking in the voice of Joseph Avneri.

"Seul?" I said hesitantly.

"My name is Joseph Avneri."

"Joseph Avneri died a year ago last Elul. I didn't realize you were such a clever mimic, Seul."

"Mimic? You speak to me of mimicry, Shimon? It's no mimicry. I am your Joseph, dead but still aware, thrown for my sins into this monstrous alien body. Are you Jew enough to know what a dybbuk is, Shimon?"

"A wandering ghost, yes, who takes possession of the body of a living being."

"I have become a dybbuk."

"There are no dybbuks. Dybbuks are phantoms out of medieval folklore," I said.

"You hear the voice of one."

"This is impossible," I said.

"I agree, Shimon, I agree." He sounded calmer now. "It's entirely impossible. I don't believe in dybbuks either, any more than I believe in Zeus, the Minotaur, werewolves, gorgons, or golems. But how else do you explain me?"

"You are Seul the Kunivar, playing a clever trick."

"Do you really think so? Listen to me, Shimon. I knew you when we were boys in Tiberias. I rescued you when we were fishing in the lake and our boat overturned. I was with you the day you met Leah whom you married. I was godfather to your son Yigal. I studied with you at the university in Jerusalem. I fled with you in the fiery days of the Final Pogrom. I stood watch with you aboard the Ark in the years of our flight from Earth. Do you remember, Shimon? Do you remember Jerusalem?

The Old City, the Mount of Olives, the Tomb of Absalom, the Western Wall? Am I a Kunivar, Shimon, to know of the Western Wall?"

"There is no survival of consciousness after death," I said stubbornly.

"A year ago I would have agreed with you. But who am I if I am not the spirit of Joseph Avneri? How can you account for me any other way? Dear God, do you think I want to believe this, Shimon? You know what a scoffer I was. But it's real."

"Perhaps I'm having a very vivid hallucination."

"Call the others, then. If ten people have the same hallucination, is it still a hallucination? Be reasonable, Shimon! Here I stand before you, telling you things that only I could know, and you deny that I am—"

"Be reasonable?" I said. "Where does reason enter into this? Do you expect me to believe in ghosts, Joseph, in wandering demons, in dybbuks? Am I some superstition-ridden peasant out of the Polish woods? Is this the Middle Ages?"

"You called me Joseph," he said quietly.

"I can hardly call you Seul when you speak in that voice."

"Then you believe in me!"

"No."

"Look, Shimon, did you ever know a bigger sceptic than Joseph Avneri? I had no use for the Torah, I said Moses was fictional, I plowed the fields on Yom Kippur, I laughed in God's nonexistent face. What is life, I said? And I answered: a mere accident, a transient biological phenomenon. Yet here I am. I remember the moment of my death. For a full year I've wandered this world, bodiless, perceiving things, unable to communicate. And today I find myself cast into this creature's body, and I know myself for a dybbuk. If *I* believe, Shimon, how can you dare disbelieve? In the name of our friendship, have faith in what I tell you!"

"You have actually become a dybbuk?"

"I have become a dybbuk," he said.

I shrugged. "Very well, Joseph. You're a dybbuk. It's madness but I believe." I stared in astonishment at the Kunivar. Did I believe? Did I believe that I believed? How could I not believe? There was no other way for the voice of Joseph Avneri to be coming from the throat of a Kunivar. Sweat streamed down my body. I was face to face with the impossible, and all my philosophy was shattered. Anything was possible now. God might appear as a burning bush. The sun might stand still. No, I told myself. Believe only one irrational thing at a time,

Shimon. Evidently there are dybbuks; well, then, there are dybbuks. But everything else pertaining to the Invisible World remains unreal until it manifests itself.

I said, "Why do you think this has happened to you?"

"It could only be as a punishment."

"For what, Joseph?"

"My experiments. You knew I was doing research into the Kunivaru metabolism, didn't you?"

"Yes, certainly. But—"

"Did you know I performed surgical experiments on live Kunivaru in our hospital? That I used patients, without informing them or anyone else, in studies of a forbidden kind? It was vivisection, Shimon."

"What?"

"There were things I needed to know, and there was only one way I could discover them. The hunger for knowledge led me into sin. I told myself that these creatures were ill, that they would shortly die anyway, and that it might benefit everyone if I opened them while they still lived, you see? Besides, they weren't human beings, Shimon, they were only animals—very intelligent animals, true, but still only—"

"No, Joseph. I can believe in dybbuks more readily than I can believe this. You, doing such a thing? My calm rational friend, my scientist, my wise one?" I shuddered and stepped a few paces back from him. "Auschwitz!" I cried. "Buchenwald! Dachau! Do those names mean anything to you? 'They weren't human beings,' the Nazi surgeon said. 'They were only Jews, and our need for scientific knowledge is such that—' That was only three hundred years ago, Joseph. And you, a Jew, a Jew of all people, to—"

"I know, Shimon, I know. Spare me the lecture. I sinned terribly, and for my sins I've been given this grotesque body, this gross, hideous, heavy body, these four legs which I can hardly coordinate, this crooked spine, this foul, hot furry pelt. I still don't believe in a God, Shimon, but I think I believe in some sort of compensating force that balances accounts in this universe, and the account has been balanced for me, oh, yes, Shimon! I've had six hours of terror and loathing today such as I never dreamed could be experienced. To enter this body, to fry in this heat, to wander these hills trapped in such a mass of flesh, to feel myself being bombarded with the sensory perceptions of a being so alien—it's been hell, I tell you that without exaggeration. I would have died of shock in the first ten minutes if I didn't already happen to be dead. Only now, seeing you, talking to you, do I begin to get control of myself. Help me, Shimon."

"What do you want me to do?"

"Get me out of here. This is torment. I'm a dead man—I'm entitled to rest the way the other dead ones rest. Free me, Shimon."

"How?"

"How? How? Do I know? Am I an expert on dybbuks? Must I direct my own exorcism? If you knew what an effort it is simply to hold this body upright, to make its tongue form Hebrew words, to say things in a way you'll understand—" Suddenly the Kunivar sagged to his knees, a slow, complex folding process that reminded me of the manner in which the camels of Old Earth lowered themselves to the ground. The alien creature began to sputter and moan and wave his arms about; foam appeared on his wide rubbery lips. "God in Heaven, Shimon," Joseph cried, "set me free!"

I called for my son Yigal and he came running swiftly from the far side of the fields, a lean healthy boy, only eleven years old but already long-legged, strong-bodied. Without going into details, I indicated the suffering Kunivar and told Yigal to get help from the kibbutz. A few minutes later he came back leading seven or eight men—Abrasha, Itzhak, Uri, Nahum, and some others. It took the full strength of all of us to lift the Kunivar into the hopper of a harvesting machine and transport him to our hospital. Two of the doctors—Moshe Shiloah and someone else—began to examine the stricken alien, and I sent Yigal to the Kunivaru village to tell the chief that Seul had collapsed in our fields.

The doctors quickly diagnosed the problem as a case of heat prostration. They were discussing the sort of injection the Kunivar should receive when Joseph Avneri, breaking a silence that had lasted since Seul had fallen, announced his presence within the Kunivar's body. Uri and Nahum had remained in the hospital room with me; not wanting this craziness to become general knowledge in the kibbutz, I took them outside and told them to forget whatever ravings they had heard. When I returned, the doctors were busy with their preparations and Joseph was patiently explaining to them that he was a dybbuk who had involuntarily taken possession of the Kunivar. "The heat has driven the poor creature insane," Moshe Shiloah murmured, and rammed a huge needle into one of Seul's thighs.

"Make them listen to me," Joseph said.

"You know that voice," I told the doctors. "Something very unusual has happened here."

But they were no more willing to believe in dybbuks than they were in rivers that flow uphill. Joseph continued to protest, and the doctors continued methodically to fill Seul's body with sedatives and restoratives and other potions. Even when Joseph began to speak of last year's kibbutz gossip—who had been sleeping with whom behind whose back, who had illicitly been peddling goods from the community storehouse to the Kunivaru—they paid no attention. It was as though they had so much difficulty believing that a Kunivar could speak Hebrew that they were unable to make sense out of what he was saying and took Joseph's words to be Seul's delirium. Suddenly Joseph raised his voice for the first time, calling out in a loud, angry tone, "You, Moshe Shiloah! Aboard the Ark I found you in bed with the wife of Teviah Kohn, remember? Would a Kunivar have known such a thing?"

Moshe Shiloah gasped, reddened, and dropped his hypodermic. The other doctor was nearly as astonished.

"What is this?" Moshe Shiloah asked. "How can this be?"

"Deny me now!" Joseph roared. "Can you deny me?"

The doctors faced the same problems of acceptance that I had had, that Joseph himself had grappled with. We were all of us rational men in this kibbutz, and the supernatural had no place in our lives. But there was no arguing the phenomenon away. There was the voice of Joseph Avneri emerging from the throat of Seul the Kunivar, and the voice was saying things that only Joseph would have said, and Joseph had been dead more than a year. Call it a dybbuk, call it hallucination, call it anything: Joseph's presence could not be ignored.

Locking the door, Moshe Shiloah said to me, "We must deal with this somehow."

Tensely we discussed the situation. It was, we agreed, a delicate and difficult matter. Joseph, raging and tortured, demanded to be exorcised and allowed to sleep the sleep of the dead; unless we placated him he would make us all suffer. In his pain, in his fury, he might say anything, he might reveal everything he knew about our private lives; a dead man is beyond all of society's rules of common decency. We could not expose ourselves to that. But what could we do about him? Chain him in an outbuilding and hide him in solitary confinement? Hardly. Unhappy Joseph deserved better of us than that; and there was Seul to consider, poor supplanted Seul, the dybbuk's unwilling host. We could not keep a Kunivar in the kibbutz, imprisoned or free, even if his body did house the spirit of one of our own people, nor could we let the shell of Seul go back to the Kunivaru village with Joseph as a furious passenger trapped inside. What to do? Separate soul from body, somehow: restore Seul to wholeness and send Joseph to the limbo of the dead. But how? There was nothing in the standard pharmacopoeia about dybbuks. What to do?

I sent for Shmarya Asch and Yakov Ben-Zion, who headed the kibbutz council that month, and for Shlomo Feig, our rabbi, a shrewd and sturdy man, very unorthodox in his orthodoxy, almost as secular as the rest of us. They questioned Joseph Avneri extensively, and he told them the whole tale—his scandalous secret experiments, his post-mortem year as a wandering spirit, his sudden painful incarnation within Seul. At length Shmarya Asch turned to Moshe Shiloah and snapped, "There must be some therapy for such a case."

"I know of none."

"This is schizophrenia," said Shmarya Asch in his firm, dogmatic way. "There are cures for schizophrenia. There are drugs, there are electric shock treatments, there are—you know these things better than I, Moshe."

"This is not schizophrenia," Moshe Shiloah retorted. "This is a case of demonic possession. I have no training in treating such maladies."

"Demonic possession?" Shmarya bellowed. "Have you lost your mind?"

"Peace, peace, all of you," Shlomo Feig said, as everyone began to shout at once. The rabbi's voice cut sharply through the tumult and silenced us all. He was a man of great strength, physical as well as moral, to whom the entire kibbutz inevitably turned for guidance although there was virtually no one among us who observed the major rites of Judaism. He said, "I find this as hard to comprehend as any of you. But the evidence triumphs over my scepticism. How can we deny that Joseph Avneri has returned as a dybbuk? Moshe, you know no way of causing this intruder to leave the Kunivar's body?"

"None," said Moshe Shiloah.

"Maybe the Kunivaru themselves know a way," Yakov Ben-Zion suggested.

"Exactly," said the rabbi. "My next point. These Kunivaru are a primitive folk. They live closer to the world of magic and witchcraft, of demons and spirits, than we do whose minds are schooled in the habits of reason. Perhaps such cases of possession occur often among them. Perhaps they have techniques for driving out unwanted spirits. Let us turn to them, and let them cure their own."

✹

Before long Yigal arrived, bringing with him six Kunivaru, including Gyaymar, the village chief. They wholly filled the little hospital room, bustling around in it like a delegation of huge furry centaurs; I was oppressed by the acrid smell of so many of them in one small space, and although they had always been friendly to us, never raising an objection when we appeared as refugees to settle on their planet, I felt fear of them now as I had never felt before. Clustering about Seul, they asked questions of him in their own supple language, and when Joseph Avneri replied in Hebrew they whispered things to each other unintelligible to us. Then, unexpectedly, the voice of Seul broke through, speaking in halting spastic monosyllables that revealed the terrible shock his nervous system must have received; then the alien faded and Joseph Avneri spoke once more with the Kunivar's lips, begging forgiveness, asking for release.

Turning to Gyaymar, Shlomo Feig said, "Have such things happened on this world before?"

"Oh, yes, yes," the chief replied. "Many times. When one of us dies having a guilty soul, repose is denied, and the spirit may undergo strange migrations before forgiveness comes. What was the nature of this man's sin?"

"It would be difficult to explain to one who is not Jewish," said the rabbi hastily, glancing away. "The important question is whether you have a means of undoing what has befallen the unfortunate Seul, whose sufferings we all lament."

"We have a means, yes," said Gyaymar, the chief.

The six Kunivaru hoisted Seul to their shoulders and carried him from the kibbutz; we were told that we might accompany them if we cared to do so. I went along, and Moshe Shiloah, and Shmarya Asch, and Yakov Ben-Zion, and the rabbi, and perhaps some others. The Kunivaru took their comrade not to their village but to a meadow several kilometers to the east, down in the direction of the place where the Hasidim lived. Not long after the Landing, the Kunivaru had let us know that the meadow was sacred to them, and none of us had ever entered it.

It was a lovely place, green and moist, a gently sloping basin crisscrossed by a dozen cool little streams. Depositing Seul beside one of the streams, the Kunivaru went off into the woods bordering the meadow to gather firewood and herbs. We remained close by Seul. "This will do no good," Joseph Avneri muttered more than once. "A waste of time, a foolish expense of energy." Three of the Kunivaru started to build a bonfire. Two sat nearby, shredding the herbs, making heaps of leaves, stems, roots. Gradually more of their kind appeared until the meadow was filled with them; it seemed that the whole village, some four hundred Kunivaru, was turning out to watch or to participate in the rite. Many of them carried musical instruments, trumpets and drums, rattles and clappers, lyres, lutes, small harps, percussive boards, wooden flutes, everything intricate and fanciful of design; we had not suspected such cultural complexity. The priests—I assume they were priests, Kunivaru of stature and dignity—wore ornate ceremonial helmets and heavy golden mantles of sea-beast fur. The ordinary townsfolk carried ribbons and streamers, bits of bright fabric, polished mirrors of stone, and other ornamental devices. When he saw how elaborate a function it was going to be, Moshe Shiloah, an amateur anthropologist at heart, ran back to the kibbutz to fetch camera and recorder. He returned, breathless, just as the rite commenced.

And a glorious rite it was: incense, a grandly blazing bonfire, the pungent fragrance of freshly picked herbs, some heavy-footed quasi-orgiastic dancing, and a choir punching out harsh, sharp-edged arrhythmic melodies. Gyaymar and the high priest of the village performed an elegant antiphonal chant, uttering long curling intertwining melismas and sprinkling Seul with a sweet-smelling pink fluid out of a baroquely carved wooden censer. Never have I beheld such stirring pageantry. But Joseph's gloomy prediction was correct; it was all entirely useless. Two hours of intensive exorcism had no effect. When the ceremony ended—the ultimate punctuation marks were five terrible shouts from the high priest—the dybbuk remained firmly in possession of Seul. "You have not conquered me," Joseph declared in a bleak tone.

Gyaymar said, "It seems we have no power to command an earthborn soul."

"What will we do now?" demanded Yakov Ben-Zion of no one in particular. "Our science and their witchcraft both fail."

Joseph Avneri pointed toward the east, toward the village of the Hasidim, and murmured something indistinct.

"No!" cried Rabbi Shlomo Feig, who stood closest to the dybbuk at that moment.

"What did he say?" I asked.

"It was nothing," the rabbi said. "It was foolishness. The long ceremony has left him fatigued, and his mind wanders. Pay no attention."

I moved nearer to my old friend. "Tell me, Joseph."

"I said," the dybbuk replied slowly, "that perhaps we should send for the Baal Shem."

"Foolishness!" said Shlomo Feig, and spat.

"Why this anger?" Shmarya Asch wanted to know. "You, Rabbi Shlomo, you were one of the first to advocate employing Kunivaru sorcerers in this business. You gladly bring in alien witch doctors, Rabbi, and grow angry when someone suggests that your fellow Jew be given a chance to drive out the demon? Be consistent, Shlomo!"

Rabbi Shlomo's strong face grew mottled with rage. It was strange to see this calm, even-tempered man becoming so excited. "I will have nothing to do with Hasidim!" he exclaimed.

"I think this is a matter of professional rivalries," Moshe Shiloah commented.

The rabbi said, "To give recognition to all that is most superstitious in Judaism, to all that is most irrational and grotesque and outmoded and medieval? No! No!"

"But dybbuks *are* irrational and grotesque and outmoded and medieval," said Joseph Avneri. "Who better to exorcise one than a rabbi whose soul is still rooted in ancient beliefs?"

"I forbid this!" Shlomo Feig sputtered. "If the Baal Shem is summoned I will—I will—"

"Rabbi," Joseph said, shouting now, "this is a matter of my tortured soul against your offended spiritual pride. Give way! Give way! Get me the Baal Shem!"

"I refuse!"

"Look!" called Yakov Ben-Zion. The dispute had suddenly become academic. Uninvited, our Hasidic cousins were arriving at the sacred meadow, a long procession of them, eerie prehistoric-looking figures clad in their traditional long black robes, wide-brimmed hats, heavy beards, dangling side-locks; and at the head of the group marched their tzaddik, their holy man, their prophet, their leader, Reb Shmuel the Baal Shem.

It was certainly never our idea to bring Hasidim with us when we fled out of the smoldering ruins of the Land of Israel. Our intention was to leave Earth and all its sorrows far behind, to start anew on another world where we could at last build an enduring Jewish homeland, free for once of our eternal gentile enemies and free, also, of the religious fanatics among our own kind whose presence had long been a drain on our vitality. We needed no mystics, no ecstatics, no weepers, no moaners, no leapers, no chanters; we needed only workers, farmers, machinists, engineers, builders. But how could we refuse them a place on the Ark? It was their good fortune to come upon us just as we were making the final preparations for our flight. The nightmare that had darkened our sleep for three centuries had been made real: the Homeland lay in flames, our armies had been shattered out of ambush, Philistines wielding long knives strode through our devastated cities. Our ship was ready to leap to the stars. We were not cowards but simply realists, for it was folly to think we could do battle any longer, and if some fragment of our ancient nation were to survive, it could only survive far from the bitter world Earth. So we were going to go; and here were suppliants asking us for succor, Reb Shmuel and his thirty followers. How could we turn them away, knowing they would certainly perish? They were human beings, they were Jews. For all our misgivings, we let them come on board.

And then we wandered across the heavens year after year, and then we came to a star that had no name, only a number, and then we found its fourth planet to be sweet and fertile, a happier world than Earth, and we thanked the God in whom we did not believe for the good luck that He had granted us, and we cried out to each other in congratulation, Mazel tov! Mazel tov! Good luck, good luck, good luck! And someone looked in an old book and saw that mazel once had had an astrological connotation, that in the days of the Bible it had meant not only "luck" but a lucky star, and so we named our lucky star Mazel Tov, and we made our landfall on Mazel Tov IV, which was to be the New Israel. Here we found no enemies, no Egyptians, no Assyrians, no Romans, no

Cossacks, no Nazis, no Arabs, only the Kunivaru, kindly people of a simple nature, who solemnly studied our pantomimed explanations and replied to us in gestures, saying, Be welcome, there is more land here than we will ever need. And we built our kibbutz.

But we had no desire to live close to those people of the past, the Hasidim, and they had scant love for us, for they saw us as pagans, godless Jews who were worse than gentiles, and they went off to build a muddy little village of their own. Sometimes on clear nights we heard their lusty singing, but otherwise there was scarcely any contact between us and them.

I could understand Rabbi Shlomo's hostility to the idea of intervention by the Baal Shem. These Hasidim represented the mystic side of Judaism, the dark uncontrollable Dionysiac side, the skeleton in the tribal closet; Shlomo Feig might be amused or charmed by a rite of exorcism performed by furry centaurs, but when Jews took part in the same sort of supernaturalism it was distressing to him. Then, too, there was the ugly fact that the sane, sensible Rabbi Shlomo had virtually no followers at all among the sane, sensible secularized Jews of our kibbutz, whereas Reb Shmuel's Hasidim looked upon him with awe, regarding him as a miracle worker, a seer, a saint. Still, Rabbi Shlomo's understandable jealousies and prejudices aside, Joseph Avneri was right: dybbuks were vapors out of the realm of the fantastic, and the fantastic was the Baal Shem's kingdom.

He was an improbably tall, angular figure, almost skeletal, with gaunt cheekbones, a soft, thickly curling beard, and gentle dreamy eyes. I suppose he was about fifty years old, though I would have believed it if they said he was thirty or seventy or ninety. His sense of the dramatic was unfailing; now—it was late afternoon—he took up a position with the setting sun at his back, so that his long shadow engulfed us all, and spread forth his arms and said, "We have heard reports of a dybbuk among you."

"There is no dybbuk!" Rabbi Shlomo retorted fiercely.

The Baal Shem smiled. "But there is a Kunivar who speaks with an Israeli voice?"

"There has been an odd transformation, yes," Rabbi Shlomo conceded. "But in this age, on this planet, no one can take dybbuks seriously."

"That is, *you* cannot take dybbuks seriously," said the Baal Shem.

"I do!" cried Joseph Avneri in exasperation. "I! I! I am the dybbuk! I, Joseph Avneri, dead a year ago last Elul, doomed for my sins to inhabit this Kunivar carcass. A Jew, Reb Shmuel, a dead Jew, a pitiful sinful miserable Yid. Who'll let me out? Who'll set me free?"

"There is no dybbuk?" the Baal Shem said amiably.

"This Kunivar has gone insane," said Shlomo Feig.

We coughed and shifted our feet. If anyone had gone insane it was our rabbi, denying in this fashion the phenomenon that he himself had acknowledged as genuine, however reluctantly, only a few hours before. Envy, wounded pride, and stubbornness had unbalanced his judgment. Joseph Avneri, enraged, began to bellow the Aleph Beth Gimel, the Shma Yisroel, anything that might prove his dybbukhood. The Baal Shem waited patiently, arms outspread, saying nothing. Rabbi Shlomo, confronting him, his powerful stocky figure dwarfed by the long-legged Hasid, maintained energetically that there had to be some rational explanation for the metamorphosis of Seul the Kunivar.

When Shlomo Feig at length fell silent, the Baal Shem said, "There is a dybbuk in this Kunivar. Do you think, Rabbi Shlomo, that dybbuks ceased their wanderings when the shtetls of Poland were destroyed? Nothing is lost in the sight of God, Rabbi. Jews go to the stars; the Torah and the Talmud and the Zohar have gone also to the stars; dybbuks too may be found in these strange worlds. Rabbi, may I bring peace to this troubled spirit and to this weary Kunivar?"

"Do whatever you want," Shlomo Feig muttered in disgust, and strode away, scowling.

Reb Shmuel at once commenced the exorcism. He called first for a minyan. Eight of his Hasidim stepped forward. I exchanged a glance with Shmarya Asch, and we shrugged and came forward too, but the Baal Shem, smiling, waved us away and beckoned two more of his followers into the circle. They began to sing; to my everlasting shame I have no idea what the singing was about, for the words were Yiddish of a Galitzianer sort, nearly as alien to me as the Kunivaru tongue. They sang for ten or fifteen minutes; the Hasidim grew more animated, clapping their hands, dancing about their Baal Shem; suddenly Reb Shmuel lowered his arms to his sides, silencing them, and quietly began to recite Hebrew phrases, which after a moment I recognized as those of the Ninety-first Psalm: The Lord is my refuge and my fortress, in him will I trust. The psalm rolled melodiously to its comforting conclusion, its promise of deliverance and salvation. For a long moment all was still. Then in a terrifying voice, not loud but immensely commanding, the Baal Shem ordered the spirit of Joseph Avneri to quit the body of

Seul the Kunivar. "Out! Out! God's name out, and off to your eternal rest!" One of the Hasidim handed Reb Shmuel a shofar. The Baal Shem put the ram's horn to his lips and blew a single titanic blast.

Joseph Avneri whimpered. The Kunivar that housed him took three awkward, toppling steps. "Oy, mama, mama," Joseph cried. The Kunivar's head snapped back; his arms shot straight out at his sides; he tumbled clumsily to his four knees. An eon went by. Then Seul rose—smoothly, this time, with natural Kunivaru grace—and went to the Baal Shem, and knelt, and touched the tzaddik's black robe. So we knew the thing was done.

Instants later the tension broke. Two of the Kunivaru priests rushed toward the Baal Shem, and then Gyaymar, and then some of the musicians, and then it seemed the whole tribe was pressing close upon him, trying to touch the holy man. The Hasidim, looking worried, murmured their concern, but the Baal Shem, towering over the surging mob, calmly blessed the Kunivaru, stroking the dense fur of their backs. After some minutes of this the Kunivaru set up a rhythmic chant, and it was a while before I realized what they were saying. Moshe Shiloah and Yakov Ben-Zion caught the sense of it about the same time I did, and we began to laugh, and then our laughter died away.

"What do their words mean?" the Baal Shem called out.

"They are saying," I told him, "that they are convinced of the power of your god. They wish to become Jews."

For the first time Reb Shmuel's poise and serenity shattered. His eyes flashed ferociously and he pushed at the crowding Kunivaru, opening an avenue between them. Coming up to me, he snapped, "Such a thing is an absurdity!"

"Nevertheless, look at them. They worship you, Reb Shmuel."

"I refuse their worship."

"You worked a miracle. Can you blame them for adoring you and hungering after your faith?"

"Let them adore," said the Baal Shem. "But how can they become Jews? It would be a mockery."

I shook my head. "What was it you told Rabbi Shlomo? Nothing is lost in the sight of God. There have always been converts to Judaism—we never invite them, but we never turn them away if they're sincere, eh, Reb Shmuel? Even here in the stars, there is continuity of tradition, and tradition says we harden not our hearts to those who seek the truth of God. These are a good people—let them be received into Israel."

"No," the Baal Shem said. "A Jew must first of all be human."

"Show me that in the Torah."

"The Torah! You joke with me. A Jew must first of all be human. Were cats allowed to become Jews? Were horses?"

"These people are neither cats nor horses, Reb Shmuel. They are as human as we are."

"No! No!"

"If there can be a dybbuk on Mazel Tov IV," I said, "then there can also be Jews with six limbs and green fur."

"No. No. No. *No!*"

The Baal Shem had had enough of this debate. Shoving aside the clutching hands of the Kunivaru in a most unsaintly way, he gathered his followers and stalked off, a tower of offended dignity, bidding us no farewells.

But how can true faith be denied? The Hasidim offered no encouragement, so the Kunivaru came to us; they learned Hebrew and we loaned them books, and Rabbi Shlomo gave them religious instruction, and in their own time and in their own way they entered into Judaism. All this was years ago, in the first generation after the Landing. Most of those who lived in those days are dead now—Rabbi Shlomo, Reb Shmuel the Baal Shem, Moshe Shiloah, Shmarya Asch. I was a young man then. I know a good deal more now, and if I am no closer to God than I ever was, perhaps He has grown closer to me. I eat meat and butter at the same meal, and I plow my land on the Sabbath, but those are old habits that have little to do with belief or the absence of belief.

We are much closer to the Kunivaru, too, than we were in those early days; they no longer seem like alien beings to us, but merely neighbors whose bodies have a different form. The younger ones of our kibbutz are especially drawn to them. The year before last Rabbi Lhaoyir the Kunivar suggested to some of our boys that they come for lessons to the Talmud Torah, the religious school, that he runs in the Kunivaru village; since the death of Shlomo Feig there has been no one in the kibbutz to give such instruction. When Reb Yossele, the son and successor of Reb Shmuel the Baal Shem heard this, he raised strong objections. If your boys will take instruction, he said, at least send them to us, and not to green monsters. My son Yigal threw him out of the kibbutz. We would rather let our boys learn the Torah from green monsters, Yigal told Reb Yossele, than have them raised to be Hasidim.

And so my son's son has had his lessons at the Talmud Torah of Rabbi Lhaoyir the Kunivar, and next spring he will have his bar mitzvah. Once I would have been appalled by such goings-on, but now I say only, How strange, how unexpected, how interesting! Truly the Lord, if He exists, must have a keen sense of humor. I like a god who can smile and wink, who doesn't take himself too seriously. The Kunivaru are Jews! Yes! They are preparing David for his bar mitzvah! Yes! Today is Yom Kippur, and I hear the sound of the shofar coming from their village! Yes! Yes. So be it. So be it, yes, and all praise be to Him.

BRECKENRIDGE AND THE CONTINUUM

September, 1972 found me still in an experimental mood as the first summer of my new California life goes on and on. Roger Elwood had asked me to contribute to yet another anthology of new stories, and as soon as I got back from the wild and woolly World Science Fiction Convention in Los Angeles, I complied. This book was called Showcase, *described as "In the tradition of Damon Knight's* Orbit *and Robert Silverberg's* New Dimensions,*" that is, an anthology without a theme, simply a collection of new stories, essentially a magazine in hardcover form. Perhaps the plan was to have it appear annually, as my anthology and Damon's did, but the volume that appeared in 1973 was the only one.*

The early 1970s were, as you may have heard, a pretty freaky time in Western culture, especially in California, and when I wasn't writing or swimming I was investigating a lot of odd corners of the intellectual life. Among them were the structuralist theories of the anthropologist Claude Levi-Strauss, who was analyzing the classical myths by breaking them down into their component parts through the use of diagrams. Since science fiction lends itself readily to the creation of new myths, I decided to invent a myth of my own and apply Levi-Strauss's structuralist principles to it, and the result was this wide-ranging tale—I suppose it would be called "edgy" today—complete with a Levi-Straussian structural chart a few pages from the end.

Then Breckenridge said, "I suppose I could tell you the story of Oedipus King of Thieves tonight."

The late afternoon sky was awful: gray, mottled, fierce. It resonated with a strange electricity. Breckenridge had never grown used to that sky. Day after day, as they crossed the desert, it transfixed him with the pain of incomprehensible loss.

"Oedipus King of Thieves," Scarp murmured. Arios nodded. Horn looked toward the sky. Militor frowned. "Oedipus," said Horn. "King of Thieves," Arios said.

Breckenridge and his four companions were camped in a ruined pavilion in the desert—a handsome place of granite pillars and black marble floors, constructed perhaps for some delicious paramour of some forgotten prince of the city-building folk. The pavilion lay only a short distance outside the walls of the great dead city that they would enter, at last, in the morning. Once, maybe, this place had been a summer resort, a place for sherbet and swimming, in that vanished time when this desert had bloomed and peacocks had strolled through fragrant gardens. A fantasy out of the Thousand and One Nights: long ago, long ago, thousands of years ago. How confusing it was for Breckenridge to remember that that mighty city, now withered by time, had been founded and had thrived and had perished all in an era far less ancient than his own. The bonds that bound the continuum had loosened. He flapped in the time-gales.

"Tell your story," Militor said.

They were restless, eager; they nodded their heads, they shifted positions. Scarp added fuel to the campfire. The sun was dropping behind the bare low hills that marked the desert's western edge; the day's smothering heat was suddenly rushing skyward, and a thin wind whistled through the colonnade of grooved gray pillars that surrounded the pavilion. Grains of pinkish sand danced in a steady stream across the floor of polished stone on which Breckenridge and those who traveled with him squatted. The lofty western wall of the nearby city was already sleeved in shadow.

Breckenridge drew his flimsy cloak closer around himself. He stared in turn at each of the four hooded figures facing him. He pressed his fingers against the cold smooth stone to anchor himself. In a low droning voice he said "This Oedipus was monarch of the land of Thieves, and a bold and turbulent man. He conceived an illicit desire for

Eurydice his mother. Forcing his passions upon her, he grew so violent that in their coupling she lost her life. Stricken with guilt and fearing that her kinsmen would exact reprisals, Oedipus escaped his kingdom through the air, having fashioned wings for himself under the guidance of the magician Prospero; but he flew too high and came within the ambit of the chariot of his father Apollo, god of the sun. Wrathful over this intrusion, Apollo engulfed Oedipus in heat, and the wax binding the feathers of his wings was melted. For a full day and a night Oedipus tumbled downward across the heavens, plummeting finally into the ocean, sinking through the sea's floor into the dark world below. There he dwells for all eternity, blind and lame, but each spring he reappears among men, and as he limps across the fields green grasses spring up in his tracks."

There was silence. Darkness was overtaking the sky. The four rounded fragments of the shattered old moon emerged and commenced their elegant, baffling saraband, spinning slowly, soaking one another in shifting patterns of cool white light. In the north the glittering violet and green bands of the aurora flickered with terrible abruptness, like the streaky glow of some monstrous searchlight. Breckenridge felt himself penetrated by gaudy ions, roasting him to the core. He waited, trembling.

"Is that all?" Militor said eventually. "Is that how it ends?"

"There's no more to the story," Breckenridge replied. "Are you disappointed?"

"The meaning is obscure. Why the incest? Why did he fly too high? Why was his father angry? Why does Oedipus reappear every spring? None of it makes sense. Am I too shallow to comprehend the relationships? I don't believe that I am."

"Oh, it's old stuff," said Scarp. "The tale of the eternal return. The dead king bringing the new year's fertility. Surely you recognize it, Militor." The aurora flashed with redoubled frenzy, a coded beacon, crying out, SPACE AND TIME, SPACE AND TIME, SPACE AND TIME. "You should have been able to follow the outline of the story," Scarp said. "We've heard it a thousand times in a thousand forms."

—SPACE AND TIME—

"Indeed we have," Militor said. "But the components of any satisfying tale have to have some logical necessity of sequence, some essential connection."—SPACE—"What we've just heard is a mass of random floating fragments. I see the semblance of myth but not the inner truth."

—TIME—

"A myth holds truth," Scarp insisted, "no matter how garbled its form, no matter how many irrelevant interpolations have entered it. The interpolations may even be one species of truth, and not the lowest species at that."

The Dow Jones Industrial Average, Breckenridge thought, closed today at 1100432.86—

"At any rate, he told it poorly," Arios observed. "No drama, no intensity, merely a bald outline of events. I've heard better from you on other nights, Breckenridge. Scheherazade and the Forty Giants—now, that was a story! Don Quixote and the Fountain of Youth, yes! But this—this—"

Scarp shook his head. "The strength of a myth lies in its content, not in the melody of its telling. I sense the inherent power of tonight's tale. I find it acceptable."

"Thank you," Breckenridge said quietly. He threw sour glares at Militor and Arios. It was hateful when they quibbled over the stories he told them. What gift did he have for these four strange beings, anyhow, except his stories? When they received that gift with poor grace they were denying him his sole claim to their fellowship.

A million years from nowhere—

SPACE—TIME—

Apollo—Jesus—Apollo—

The wind grew chillier. No one spoke. Beasts howled on the desert. Breckenridge lay back, feeling an ache in his shoulders, and wriggled against the cold stone floor.

Merry my wife, Cassandra my daughter, Noel my son—

SPACE—TIME—

SPACE—

His eyes hurt from the aurora's frosty glow. He felt himself stretched across the cosmos, torn between then and now, breaking, breaking, ripping into fragments like the moon—

The stars had come out. He contemplated the early constellations. They were unfamiliar; no matter how often Scarp or Horn pointed out the patterns to him, he saw only random sprinklings of light. In his other life he had been able to identify at least the more conspicuous constellations, but they did not seem to be here. How long does it take to effect a complete redistribution of the heavens? A million years? Ten million? Thank God Mars and Jupiter still were visible, the orange dot and the brilliant white one, to tell him that this place was his own world, his own solar system. Images danced in his aching skull. He saw everything double, suddenly. There was Pegasus, there was Orion, there was Sagittarius. An overlay, a mass of realities superimposed on realities.

"Listen to this music," Horn said after a long while, producing a fragile device of wheels and spindles from beneath his cloak.

He caressed it and delicate sounds came forth: crystalline, comforting, the music of dreams, sliding into the range of audibility with no perceptible instant of attack. Shortly Scarp began a wordless song, and one by one the others joined him—first Horn, then Militor, and lastly, in a dry, buzzing monotone, Arios.

"What are you singing?" Breckenridge asked.

"The hymn of Oedipus King of Thieves," Scarp told him

Had it been such a bad life? He had been healthy, prosperous, and beloved. His father was managing partner of Falkner, Breckenridge & Company, one of the most stable of the Wall Street houses, and Breckenridge, after coming up through the ranks in the family tradition, putting in his time as a customer's man and his time in the bond department and his time as a floor trader, was a partner too, only ten years out of Dartmouth. What was wrong with that? His draw in 1972 was $83,500—not as much as he had hoped for out of a partnership, but not bad, not bad at all, and next year might be much better. He had a wife and two children, an apartment on East 73rd Street, a country cabin on Candlewood Lake, a fair-size schooner that he kept in the Gulf Coast marina, and a handsome young mistress in an apartment of her own on the Upper West Side. What was wrong with that? When he burst through the fabric of the continuum and found himself in an unimaginably altered world at the end of time, he was astonished not that such a thing might happen but that it had happened to someone as settled and well established as himself.

While they slept, a corona of golden light sprang into being along the top of the city wall; the glow awakened Breckenridge, and he sat up quickly, thinking that the city was on fire. But the light seemed cool and supple, and appeared to be propagated in easy rippling waves, more like the aurora than like the raw blaze of flames. It sprang from the very rim of the wall and leaped high, casting blurred, rounded shadows at cross-angles to the sharp crisp shadows that the fragmented moon created. There seemed also to be a deep segment of blackness in the side of the wall; looking closely, Breckenridge saw that the huge gate on the wall's western face was standing open. Without telling the others he left the camp and crossed the flat sandy wasteland, coming to the gate after a brisk march of about an hour. Nothing prevented him from entering. Just within the wall was a wide cobbled plaza, and beyond that stretched broad avenues lined with buildings of a strange sort, rounded and rubbery, porous of texture, all humps and parapets. Black unfenced wells at the centre of each major intersection plunged to infinite depths. Breckenridge had been told that the city was empty, that it had been uninhabited for centuries since the spoiling of the climate in this part of the world, so he was surprised to find it occupied; pale figures flitted silently about, moving like wraiths, as though there were empty space between their feet and the pavement. He approached one and another and a third, but when he tried to speak no words would leave his lips. He seized one of the city dwellers by the wrist, a slender black-haired girl in a soft gray robe, and held her tightly, hoping that contact would lead to contact. Her dark somber eyes studied him without show of fear and she made no effort to break away. I am Noel Breckenridge, he said—Noel III—and I was born in the town of Greenwich, Connecticut in the year of our lord 1940, my wife's name is Merry and my daughter is Cassandra and my son is Noel Breckenridge IV, and I am not as coarse or stupid as you may think me to be. She made no reply and showed no change of expression. He asked, Can you understand anything I'm saying to you? Her face remained totally blank. He asked, Can you even hear the sound of my voice? There was no response. He went on: What is your name? What is this city called? When was it abandoned? What year is this on any calendar that I can comprehend? What do you know about me that I need to know? She continued to regard him in an altogether neutral way. He pulled her against his body and gripped her thin shoulders with his fingertips and kissed her urgently, forcing his tongue between her teeth. An instant later he found himself sprawled not far from the campsite with his face in the sand and sand in his mouth. Only a dream, he thought wearily, only a dream.

He was having lunch with Harry Munsey at the Merchants and Shippers Club: sleek chrome-and-redwood premises, sixty stories above William Street in the heart of the financial district. Subdued light fixtures glowed like pulsing red suns; waiters moved past the tables like silent moons. The club was over a century old, although the skyscraper in which it occupied a penthouse suite had been erected only in 1968—its fourth home, or maybe its fifth. Membership was limited to white male Christians, sober and responsible, who had important positions in the New York securities industry. There was nothing in the club's written constitution that explicitly limited its membership to white male Christians, but all the same there had never been any members who had not been white, male, and Christian. No one with a firm grasp of reality thought there ever would be.

Harry Munsey, like Noel Breckenridge, was white, male, and Christian. They had gone to Dartmouth together and they had entered Wall Street together, Breckenridge going into his family's firm and Munsey into his, and they had lunch together almost every day and saw each other almost every Saturday night, and each had slept with the other's wife, though each believed that the other knew nothing about that.

On the third martini Munsey said, "What's bugging you today, Noel?"

A dozen years ago Munsey had been an all-Ivy halfback; he was a big, powerful man, bigger even than Breckenridge, who was not a small man. Munsey's face was pink and unlined and his eyes were alive and youthful, but he had lost all his hair before he turned thirty.

"Is something bugging me?"

"Something's bugging you, yes. Why else would you look so uptight after you've had two and a half martinis?"

Breckenridge had found it difficult to grow used to the sight of the massive bright dome that was Munsey's skull.

He said, "All right. So I'm bugged."

"Want to talk about it?"

"No."

"Okay," Munsey said.

Breckenridge finished his drink. "As a matter of fact, I'm oppressed by a sophomoric sense of the meaninglessness of life, if you have to know."

"Really?"

"Really."

"The meaninglessness of life?"

"Life is empty, dumb, and mechanical," Breckenridge said.

"*Your* life?"

"Life."

"I know a lot of people who'd like to live your life. They'd trade with you, even up, asset for asset, liability for liability, life for life."

Breckenridge shook his head. "They're fools, then."

"It's that bad?"

"It all seems so pointless, Harry. Everything. We have a good time and con ourselves into thinking it means something. But what is there, actually? The pursuit of money? I have enough money. After a certain point it's just a game. French restaurants? Trips to Europe? Drinking? Sex? Swimming pools? Jesus! We're born, we grow up, we do a lot of stuff, we grow old, we die. Is that all? Jesus, Harry, is that *all?*"

Munsey looked embarrassed. "Well, there's family," he suggested. "Marriage, fatherhood, knowing that you're linking yourself into the great chain of life. Bringing forth a new generation. Transmitting your ideas, your standards, your traditions, everything that distinguishes us from the apes we used to be. Doesn't that count?"

Shrugging, Breckenridge said, "All right. Having kids, you say. We bring them into the world, we wipe their noses, we teach them to be little men and women, we send them to the right schools and get them into the right clubs, and they grow up to be carbon copies of their parents, lawyers or brokers or clubwomen or whatever—"

The lights fluttering. The aurora: red, green, violet, red, green. The straining fabric—the moon, the broken moon—the aurora—the lights—the fire atop the walls—

"—or else they grow up and deliberately fashion themselves into the opposites of their parents, and somewhere along the way the parents die off, and the kids have kids, and the cycle starts around again. Around and around, generation after generation, Noel Breckenridge III, Noel Breckenridge IV, Noel Breckenridge XVI—"

Arios—Scarp—Militor—Horn—

The city—the gate—

"—making money, spending money, living high, building nothing real, just occupying space on the planet for a little while, and what for? What for? What does it all mean?"

The granite pillars—the aurora—SPACE AND TIME—

"You're on a bummer today, Noel," Munsey said.

"I know. Aren't you sorry you asked what was bugging me?"

"Not particularly. Everybody goes through a phase like this."

"When he's seventeen, yes."

"And later, too."

"It's more than a phase," Breckenridge said. "It's a sickness. If I had any guts, Harry, I'd drop out. Drop right out and try to work out some meanings in the privacy of my own head."

"Why don't you? You can afford it. Go on. Why not?"

"I don't know," said Breckenridge.

Such strange constellations. Such a terrible sky.

Such a cold wind blowing out of tomorrow.

"I think it may be time for another martini," Munsey said.

They had been crossing the desert for a long time now—forty days and forty nights, Breckenridge liked to tell himself, but probably it had been more than that—and they moved at an unsparing pace, marching from dawn to sunset with as few rest periods as possible. The air was thin. His lungs felt leathery. Because he was the biggest man in the group, he carried the heaviest pack. That didn't bother him.

What did bother him was how little he knew about his expedition, its purposes, its origin, even how he had come to be a part of it. But asking such questions seemed somehow naive and awkward, and he never did. He went along, doing his share—making camp, cleaning up in the mornings—and tried to keep his companions amused with his stories. They demanded stories from him every night. "Tell us your myths," they urged. "Tell us the legends and fables you learned in your childhood."

After weeks of sharing this trek with them he knew little more about the other four than he had at the outset. His favorite among them was Scarp, who was sympathetic and flexible. He liked the hostile, contemptuous Militor the least. Horn—dreamy, poetic, unworldly, aloof—was beyond his reach; Arios, the most dry and objective and scientific of the group, did not seem worth trying to reach. So far as Breckenridge could determine they were human, although their skins were oddly glossy and of a peculiar olive hue, something on the far side of swarthy. They had strange noses, narrow, high-bridged noses of a kind he had never seen before, extremely fragile, like the noses of purebred society women carried to the ultimate possibilities of their design.

The desert was beautiful. A gaudy desolation, all dunes and sandy ripples, streaked blue and red and gold and green with brilliant oxides.

Sometimes when the aurora was going full blast—SPACE! TIME! SPACE! TIME!—the desert seemed merely to be a mirror for the sky. But in the morning, when the electronic furies of the aurora had died away, the sand still reverberated with its own inner pulses of bright color.

And the sun—pale, remorseless—Apollo's deathless fires—

I am Noel Breckenridge and I am nine years old and this is how I spent my summer vacation—

Oh Lord Jesus forgive me.

Scattered everywhere on the desert were outcroppings of ancient ruins—colonnades, halls of statuary, guardposts, summer pavilions, hunting lodges, the stumps of antique walls, and invariably the marchers made their camp beside one of these. They studied each ruin, measured its dimensions, recorded its salient details, poked at its sand-shrouded foundations. Around Scarp's neck hung a kind of mechanized map, a teardrop-shaped black instrument that could be made to emit—

PING!

—sounds which daily guided them toward the next ruin in the chain leading to the city. Scarp also carried a compact humming machine that generated sweet water from handfuls of sand. For solid food they subsisted on small yellow pellets, quite tasty.

PING!

At the beginning Breckenridge had felt constant fatigue, but under the grinding exertions of the march he had grown steadily in strength and endurance, and now he felt he could continue forever, never tiring, parading—

PING!

—endlessly back and forth across this desert which perhaps spanned the entire world. The dead city, though, was their destination, and finally it was in view. They were to remain there for an indefinite stay. He was not yet sure whether these four were archeologists or pilgrims. Perhaps both, he thought. Or maybe neither. Or maybe neither.

"How do you think you can make your life more meaningful, then?" Munsey asked.

"I don't know. I don't have any idea what would work for me. But I do know who the people are whose lives do have meaning."

"Who?"

"The creators, Harry. The shapers, the makers, the begetters. Beethoven, Rembrandt. Dr. Salk, Einstein, Shakespeare, that bunch. It isn't enough just to live. It isn't even enough just to have a good mind, to think clear thoughts. You have to add something to the sum of humanity's accomplishments, something real, something valuable. You have to *give.* Mozart. Newton. Columbus. Those who are able to reach into the well of creation, into that hot boiling chaos of raw energy down there, and pull something out, shape it, make something unique and new out of it. Making money isn't enough. Making more Breckenridges or Munseys isn't enough, either. You know what I'm saying, Harry? The well of creation. The reservoir of life, which is God. Do you ever think you believe in God? Do you wake up in the middle of the night sometimes saying, Yes, yes, there *is* Something after all, I believe, I believe! I'm not talking about churchgoing now, you understand. Churchgoing's nothing but a conditioned reflex these days, a twitch, a tic. I'm talking about faith. Belief. The state of enlightenment. I'm not talking about God as an old man with long white whiskers, either, Harry. I mean something abstract, a force, a power, a current, a reservoir of energy underlying everything and connecting everything. God is that reservoir. That reservoir is God. I think of that reservoir as being something like the sea of molten lava down beneath the earth's crust: it's there, it's full of heat and power, it's accessible for those who know the way. Plato was able to tap into the reservoir. Van Gogh. Joyce. Schubert. El Greco. A few lucky ones knew how to reach it. Most of us can't. Most of us can't. For those who can't, God is dead. Worse: for them, He never lived at all. Oh, Christ, how awful it is to be trapped in an era where everybody goes around like some sort of zombie, cut off from the energies of the spirit, ashamed even to admit there are such energies. I hate it. I hate the whole stinking twentieth century, do you know that? Am I making any sense? Do I seem terribly drunk? Am I embarrassing you, Harry? Harry? Harry?"

In the morning they struck camp and set out on the final leg of their journey toward the city. The sand here had a disturbing crusty quality: white saline outcroppings gave Breckenridge the feeling that they were crossing a tundra rather than a desert. The sky was clear and pale, and in its bleached cloudlessness it took on something of the quality of a shield, of a mirror, seizing the morning heat that rose from the ground and hurling it inexorably back, so that the five marchers felt themselves trapped in an infinite baffle of unendurable dry smothering warmth.

As they moved cityward Militor and Arios chattered compulsively, falling after a while into a quarrel over certain obscure and controversial points of historical theory. Breckenridge had heard them have their argument at least a dozen times in the last two weeks, and no doubt they had been battling it out for years. The main area of contention was the origin of the city. Who were its builders? Militor believed they were colonists from some other planet, strangers to earth, representatives of some alien species of immeasurable grandeur and nobility, who had crossed space thousands of years ago to build this gigantic monument on Asia's flank. Nonsense, retorted Arios: the city was plainly the work of human beings, unusually gifted and energetic but human nonetheless. Why multiply hypotheses needlessly? Here is the city; humans have built many cities nearly as great as this one in their long history; this city is only quantitatively superior to the others, merely a little bigger, merely a bit more daringly conceived; to invoke extraterrestrial architects is to dabble gratuitously in fantasy. But Militor maintained his position. Humans, he said, were plainly incapable of such immense constructions. Neither in this present decadent epoch, when any sort of effort is too great, nor at any time in the past could human resources have been equal to such a task as the building of this city must have been. Breckenridge had his doubts about that, having seen what the twentieth century had accomplished. He tended to side with Arios. But indeed the city was extraordinary, Breckenridge admitted: an ultimate urban glory, a supernal Babylon, a consummate Persepolis, the soul's own hymn in brick and stone. The wall that girdled it was at least two hundred feet high—why pour so much energy into a wall? were no better means of defense at hand, or was the wall mere exuberant decoration?—and, judging by the easy angle of its curve, it must be hundreds of miles in circumference. A city larger than New York, more sprawling even than Los Angeles, a giant antenna of turbulent consciousness set like a colossal gem into this vast plain, a throbbing antenna for all the radiance of the stars: yes, it was overwhelming, it was devastating to contemplate the planning and the building of it, it seemed almost to require the hypothesis of a superior alien race. And yet he refused to accept that hypothesis. Arios, he thought, I am with you.

The city was uninhabited, a hulk, a ruin. Why? What had happened here to turn this garden plain into a salt-crusted waste? The builders grew too proud, said Militor. They defied the gods, they overreached even their own powers, and stumbling, they fell headlong into decay. The life went out of the soil, the sky gave no rain, the spirit lost its energies; the city perished and was forgotten, and was whispered about by mythmakers, a city out of time, a city at the end of the world, a mighty mass of dead wonders, a habitation for jackals, a place where no one went. We are the first in centuries, said Scarp, to seek this city.

Halfway between dawn and noon they reached the wall and stood before the great gate. The gate alone was fifty feet high, a curving slab of burnished blue metal set smoothly into a recess in the tawny stucco of the wall. Breckenridge saw no way of opening it, no winch, no portcullis, no handles, no knobs. He feared that the impatient Militor would merely blow a hole in it. But, groping along the base of the gate, they found a small doorway, man-high and barely man-wide, near the left-hand edge. Ancient hinges yielded at a push. Scarp led the way inside.

The city was as Breckenridge remembered it from his dream: the cobbled plaza, the broad avenues, the humped and rubbery buildings. The fierce sunlight, deflected and refracted by the undulant roof lines, reverberated from every flat surface and rebounded in showers of brilliant energy. Breckenridge shaded his eyes. It was as though the sky were full of pulsars. His soul was frying on a cosmic griddle, cooking in a torrent of hard radiation.

The city was inhabited.

Faces were visible at windows. Elusive figures emerged at street corners, peered, withdrew. Scarp called to them; they shrank back into the hard-edged shadows.

"Well?" Arios demanded. "They're human, aren't they?"

"What of it?" said Militor. "Squatters, that's all. You saw how easy it was to push open that door. They've come in out of the desert to live in the ruins."

"Maybe not. Descendants of the builders, I'd say. Perhaps the city never really was abandoned." Arios looked at Scarp. "Don't you agree?"

"They might be anything," Scarp said. "Squatters, descendants, even synthetics, even servants without masters, living on, waiting, living on, waiting—"

"Or projections cast by ancient machines," Militor said. "No human hand built this city."

Arios snorted. They advanced quickly across the plaza and entered into the first of the grand avenues. The buildings flanking it were sealed. They proceeded to a major intersection, where they halted to inspect an open circular pit, fifteen feet in diameter, smooth-rimmed, descending into infinite darkness. Breckenridge had seen many such dark wells in his vision of the night before. He did not doubt now that he had left his sleeping body and had made an actual foray into the city last night.

Scarp flashed a light into the well. A copper-colored metal ladder was visible along one face.

"Shall we go down?" Breckenridge asked.

"Later," said Scarp.

The famous anthropologist had been drinking steadily all through the dinner party—wine, only wine, but plenty of it—and his eyes seemed glazed, his face flushed; nevertheless he continued to talk with superb clarity of perception and elegant precision of phrase, hardly pausing at all to construct his concepts. Perhaps he's merely quoting his own latest book from memory, Breckenridge thought, as he strained to follow the flow of ideas. "—A comparison between myth and what appears to have largely replaced it in modern societies, namely, politics. When the historian refers to the French Revolution it is always as a sequence of past happenings, a nonreversible series of events the remote consequences of which may still be felt at present. But to the French politician, as well as to his followers, the French Revolution is both a sequence belonging to the past—as to the historian—and an everlasting pattern which can be detected in the present French social structure and which provides a clue for its interpretation, a lead from which to infer the future developments. See, for instance, Michelet, who was a politically minded historian. He describes the French Revolution thus: 'This day…everything was possible…future became present…that is, no more time, a glimpse of eternity.'" The great man reached decisively for another glass of claret. His hand wavered; the glass toppled; a dark red torrent stained the table cloth. Breckenridge experienced a sudden terrifying moment of complete disorientation, as though the walls and floor were shifting places: he saw a parched desert plateau, four hooded figures, a blazing sky of strange constellations, a pulsating aurora sweeping the heavens with old fire. A mighty walled city dominated the plain, and its frosty shadow, knifeblade-sharp, cut across Breckenridge's path. He shivered. The woman on Breckenridge's right laughed lightly and began to recite:

> I saw Eternity the other night
> Like a great ring of pure and endless light.
> All calm, as it was bright;
> And round beneath it, Time in hours, days, years,
> Driv'n by the spheres
> Like a vast shadow mov'd; in which the world
> And all her train were hurl'd.

"Excuse me," Breckenridge said. "I think I'm unwell." He rushed from the dining room. In the hallway he turned toward the washroom and found himself staring into a steaming tropical marsh, all ferns and horsetails and giant insects. Dragonflies the size of pigeons whirred past him. The sleek rump of a brontosaurus rose like a bubbling aneurysm from the black surface of the swamp. Breckenridge recoiled and staggered away. On the other side of the hall lay the desert under the lash of a frightful noonday sun. He gripped the frame of a door and held himself upright, trembling, as his soul oscillated wildly across the hallucinatory eons. "I am Scarp," said a quiet voice within him. "You have come to the place where all times are one, where all errors can be unmade, where past and future are fluid and subject to redefinition." Breckenridge felt powerful arms encircling and supporting him. "Noel? Noel? Here, sit down." Harry Munsey. Shiny pink skull, searching blue eyes. "Jesus, Noel, you look like you're having some kind of bad trip. Merry sent me after you to find out—"

"It's okay," Breckenridge said hoarsely. "I'll be all right."

"You want me to get her?"

"I'll be *all right*. Just let me steady myself a second." He rose uncertainly. "Okay. Let's go back inside."

The anthropologist was still talking. A napkin covered the wine stain and he held a fresh glass aloft like a sacramental chalice. "The key to everything, I think, lies in an idea that Franz Boas offered in 1898: 'It would seem that mythological worlds have been built up only to be shattered again, and that new worlds were built from the fragments.'"

Breckenridge said, "The first men lived underground and there was no such thing as private property. One day there was an earthquake and the earth was rent apart. The light of day flooded the subterranean cavern where mankind dwelled. Clumsily, for the light dazzled their eyes, they came upward into the world of brightness and learned how to see. Seven days later they divided the fields among themselves and began to build the first walls as boundaries marking the limits of their land."

By midday the city dwellers were losing their fear of the five intruders. Gradually, in twos and threes, they left their hiding places and gathered around the visitors until a substantial group had collected. They were dressed simply, in light robes, and they said nothing to the strangers, though they whispered frequently to one another. Among the group was the slender, dark-haired girl of Breckenridge's dream. "Do you remember me?" he asked. She smiled and shrugged and answered softly in a liquid, incomprehensible language. Arios questioned her in six or seven tongues, but she shook her head to everything. Then she took Breckenridge by the hand and led him a few paces away, toward one of the street-wells. Pointing into it, she smiled. She pointed to Breckenridge, pointed to herself, to the surrounding buildings. She made a sweeping gesture taking in all the sky. She pointed again into the well. "What are you trying to tell me?" he asked her. She answered in her own language. Breckenridge shook his head apologetically. She did a simple pantomime: eyes closed, head lolling against pressed-together hands. An image of sleep, certainly. She pointed to him. To herself. To the well. "You want me to sleep with you?" he blurted. "Down there?" He had to laugh at his own foolishness. It was ridiculous to assume the persistence of a cowardly, euphemistic metaphor like that across so many millennia. He gaped stupidly at her. She laughed—a silvery, tinkling laugh—and danced away from him, back toward her own people.

Their first night in the city they made camp in one of the great plazas. It was an octagonal space surrounded by low green buildings, sharp-angled, each faced on its plaza side with mirror-bright stone. About a hundred of the city-dwellers crouched in the shadows of the plaza's periphery, watching them. Scarp sprinkled fuel pellets and kindled a fire; Militor distributed dinner; Horn played music as they ate; Arios, sitting apart, dictated a commentary into a recording device he carried, the size and texture of a large pearl. Afterward they asked Breckenridge to tell a story, as usual, and he told them the tale of how Death Came to the World.

"Once upon a time," he began, "there were only a few people in the world and they lived in a green and fertile valley where winter never came and gardens bloomed all the year round. They spent their days laughing and swimming and lying in the sun, and in the evenings they feasted and sang and made love, and this went on without change, year in, year out, and no one ever fell ill or suffered from hunger, and no one ever died. Despite the serenity of this existence, one man in the village was unhappy. His name was Faust, and he was a restless, intelligent man with intense, burning eyes and a lean, unsmiling face. Faust felt that life must consist of something more than swimming and making love and plucking ripe fruit off vines. 'There is something else to life,' Faust insisted, 'something unknown to us, something that eludes our grasp, something the lack of which keeps us from being truly happy. We are incomplete.' The others listened to him and at first they were puzzled, for they had not known they were unhappy or incomplete, they had mistaken the ease and placidity of their existence for happiness. But after a while they started to believe that Faust might be right. They had not known how vacant their lives were until Faust had pointed it out. What can we do, they asked? How can we learn what the thing is that we lack? A wise old man suggested that they might ask the gods. So they elected Faust to visit the god Prometheus, who was said to be a friend to mankind, and ask him. Faust crossed hill and dale, mountain and river, and came at last to Prometheus on the storm-swept summit where he dwelled. He explained the situation and said, 'Tell me, O Prometheus, why we feel so incomplete.' The god replied, 'It is because you do not have the use of fire. Without fire there can be no civilization; you are uncivilized, and your barbarism makes you unhappy. With fire you can cook your food and enjoy many interesting new flavors. With fire you can work metals, and create effective weapons and other tools.' Faust considered this and said, 'But where can we obtain fire? What is it? How is it used?'

"'I will bring fire to you,' Prometheus answered.

"Prometheus then went to Zeus, the greatest of the gods, and said, 'Zeus, the humans desire fire, and I seek your permission to bestow it upon them.' But Zeus was hard of hearing and Prometheus lisped badly and in the language of the gods the words for fire and for death were very similar, and Zeus misunderstood and said, 'How odd of them to desire such a thing, but I am a benevolent god, and deny my creatures nothing that they crave.' So Zeus created a woman named Pandora and put death inside her and gave her to Prometheus, who took her back to the valley where mankind lived. 'Here is Pandora,' said Prometheus. 'She will give you fire.'

"As soon as Prometheus took his leave Faust came forward and embraced Pandora and lay with her. Her body was hot as flame, and as he held her in his arms death came forth from her and entered him, and he shivered and grew feverish, and cried out in ecstasy, 'This is fire! I have mastered fire!' Within the hour death began to consume him so that he grew weak and thin, and his skin became parched and yellowish, and he trembled like a leaf in a breeze. 'Go!' he cried to the others. 'Embrace her—she is the bringer of fire!' And he staggered off into the wilderness beyond the valley's edge, murmuring, 'Thanks be to Prometheus for this gift.' He lay down beneath a huge tree, and there he died, and it was the first time that death had visited a human being. And the tree died also.

"Then the other men of the village embraced Pandora, one after another, and death entered into them too, and they went from her to their own women and embraced them, so that soon all the men and women of the village were ablaze with death, and one by one their lives reached an end. Death remained in the village, passing into all who lived and into all who were born from their loins, and this is how death came to the world. Afterward, during a storm, lightning struck the tree that had died when Faust had died, and set it ablaze, and a man whose name is forgotten thrust a dry branch into the blaze and lit it, and learned how to build a fire and how to keep the fire alive, and after that time men cooked their food and used fire to work metal into weapons, and so it was that civilization began."

It was time to investigate one of the wells. Scarp, Arios, and Breckenridge would make the descent, with Militor and Horn remaining on the surface to cope with contingencies. They chose a well half a day's march from their campsite, deep into the city, a big one, broader and deeper than most they had seen. At its rim Scarp mounted a spherical fist-size light that cast a dazzling blue-white beam into the opening. Then, lightly swinging himself out onto the metal ladder, he began to climb down, shrouded in a nimbus of molten brightness. Breckenridge peered after him. Scarp's head and shoulders remained visible for a long while, dwindling until he was only a point of darkness in motion deep within the cone of light, and then he could no longer be seen. "Scarp?" Breckenridge called. After a moment came a muffled reply out of the depths. Scarp had reached bottom, somewhere beyond the range of the beam, and wanted them to join him.

Breckenridge followed. The descent seemed infinite. There was a stiffness in his left knee. He became a mere automaton, mechanically seizing the rungs; they were warm in his hands. His eyes, fixed on the pocked gray skin of the well's wall inches from his nose, grew glassy and unfocused. He passed through the zone of light as though sliding through the face of a mirror and moved downward in darkness without a change of pace until his boot slammed unexpectedly into a solid floor where he had thought to encounter the next rung. The left boot; his knee, jamming, protested. Scarp lightly touched his shoulder. "Step back here next to me," he said. "Take sliding steps and make sure you have a footing. For all we know, we're on some sort of ledge with a steep drop on all sides."

They waited while Arios came down. His footfalls were like thunder in the well: boom, boom, boom, transmitted and amplified by the rungs. Then the men at the surface lowered the light, fixed to the end of a long cord, and at last they could look around.

They were in a kind of catacomb. The floor of the well was a platform of neatly dressed stone slabs which gave access to horizontal tunnels several times a man's height, stretching away to right and left, to fore and aft. The mouth of the well was a dim dot of light far above. Scarp, after inspecting the perimeter of the platform, flashed the beam into one of the tunnels, stared a moment, and cautiously entered. Breckenridge heard him cough. "Dusty in here," Scarp muttered. Then he said, "You told us a story once about the King of the Dead Lands, Breckenridge. What was his name?"

"Thanatos."

"Thanatos, yes. This must be his kingdom. Come and look."

Arios and Breckenridge exchanged shrugs. Breckenridge stepped into the tunnel. The walls on both sides were lined from floor to ceiling with tiers of coffins, stacked eight or ten high and extending as far as the beam of light reached. The coffins were glass-faced and covered over with dense films of dust. Scarp drew his fingers through the dust over one coffin and left deep tracks; clouds rose up, sending Breckenridge back, coughing and choking, to stumble into Arios. When the dust cleared they could see a figure within, seemingly asleep, the nude figure of a young man lying on his back. His expression was one of great serenity. Breckenridge shivered. Death's kingdom, yes, the place of Thanatos, the house of Pluto. He walked down the row, wiping coffin after coffin. An old man. A child. A young woman. An older woman. A whole population lay embalmed here. I died long ago, he thought, and I don't even sleep. I walk about beneath the earth. The silence was frightening here. "The people of the city?" Scarp asked. "The ancient inhabitants?"

"Very likely," said Arios. His voice was as crisp as ever. He alone was not trembling. "Slain in some inconceivable massacre? But what? But how?"

"They appear to have died natural deaths," Breckenridge pointed out. "Their bodies look whole and healthy. As though they were lying here asleep. Not dead, only sleeping."

"A plague?" Scarp wondered. "A sudden cloud of deadly gas? A taint of poison in their water supply?"

"If it had been sudden," said Breckenridge, "how would they have had time to build all these coffins? This whole tunnel—catacomb upon catacomb—" A network of passageways spanning the city's entire subterrane. Thousands of coffins. Millions. Breckenridge felt dazed by the presence of death on such a scale. The skeleton with the scythe, moving briskly about its work. Severed heads and hands and feet scattered like dandelions in the springtime meadow. The reign of Thanatos, King of Swords, Knight of Wands.

Thunder sounded behind them. Footfalls in the well.

Scarp scowled. "I told them to wait up there. That fool Militor—"

Arios said, "Militor should see this. Undoubtedly it's the resting place of the city dwellers. Undoubtedly these are human beings. Do you know what I imagine? A mass suicide. A unanimous decision to abandon the world of life. Years of preparation. The construction of tunnels, of machines for killing, a whole vast apparatus of immolation. And then the day appointed—long lines waiting to be processed—millions of men and women and children passing through the machines, gladly giving up their lives, going willingly to the coffins that await them—"

"And then," Scarp said, "there must have been only a few left and no one to process them. Living on, caretakers for the dead, perhaps, maintaining the machinery that preserves these millions of bodies—"

"Preserves them for what?" Arios asked.

"The day of resurrection," said Breckenridge.

The footfalls in the well grew louder. Scarp glanced toward the tunnel's mouth. "Militor?" he called. "Horn?" He sounded angry. He walked toward the well. "You were supposed to wait for us up—"

Breckenridge heard a grinding sound and whirled to see Arios tugging at the lid of a coffin—the one that held the serene young man. Instinctively he moved to halt the desecration, but he was too slow; the glass plate rose as Arios broke the seals, and, with a quick whooshing sound, a burst of greenish vapor rushed from the coffin. It hovered a moment in midair, speared by Arios's beam of light; then it congealed into a yellow precipitant and broke in a miniature rainstorm that stained the tunnel's stone floor. To Breckenridge's horror the young man's body jerked convulsively: muscles tightened into knots and almost instantly relaxed. "He's alive!" Breckenridge cried.

"Was," said Scarp.

Yes. The figure in the glass case was motionless. It changed color and texture, turning black and withered. Scarp shoved Arios aside and slammed the lid closed, but that could do no good now. A dreadful new motion commenced within the coffin. In moments something shriveled and twisted lay before them.

"Suspended animation," said Arios. "The city builders—they lie here, as human as we are, sleeping, not dead, sleeping. Sleeping! Militor! Militor, come quickly!"

Feingold said, "Let me see if I have it straight. After the public offering our group will continue to hold eighty-three percent of the Class B stock and thirty-four percent of the voting common, which constitutes a controlling block. We'll let you have 100,000 five-year warrants and we'll agree to a conversion privilege on the 1992 6½ percent debentures, plus we allow you the stipulated underwriting fee, providing your Argentinian friend takes up the agreed-upon allotment of debentures and follows through on his deal with us in Colorado. Okay? Now, then, assuming the SEC has no objections, I'd like to outline the proposed interlocking directorates with Heitmark A.G. in Liechtenstein and Hellaphon S.A. in Athens, after which—"

The high, clear, rapid voice went on and on. Breckenridge toyed with his lunch, smiled frequently, nodded whenever he felt it was appropriate, and otherwise remained disconnected, listening only with the automatic-recorder part of his mind. They were sitting on the terrace of an open-air restaurant in Tiberias, at the edge of the Sea of Galilee, looking across to the bleak, brown Syrian hills on the far side. The December air was mild, the sun bright. Last week Breckenridge had visited Monaco, Zurich, and Milan. Yesterday Tel Aviv, tomorrow Haifa, next Tuesday Istanbul. Then on to Nairobi, Johannesburg, Peking, Singapore. Finally San Francisco and then home. Zap! Zap! A crazy round-the-world scramble in twenty days, cleaning up a lot of international business for the firm. It could all have been handled by telephone, or else some of these foreign tycoons could have come to New York, but Breckenridge had volunteered to do the junket. Why? Why? Sitting here ten thousand miles from home having lunch with a man whose office was down the street from his own. Crazy. Why all this running, Noel? Where do you think you'll get?

"Some more wine?" Feingold asked. "What do you think of this Israeli stuff, anyway?"

"It goes well with the fish." Breckenridge reached for Feingold's copy of the agreement. "Here, let me initial all that."

"Don't you want to check it over first?"

"Not necessary. I have faith in you, Sid."

"Well, I wouldn't cheat you, that's true. But I could have made a mistake. I'm capable of making mistakes."

"I don't think so," Breckenridge said. He grinned. Feingold grinned. Behind the grin there was something chilly. Breckenridge looked away. You think I'm bending over backward to treat you like a gentleman, he thought, because you know what people like me are really supposed to think about Jews, and I know you know, and you know I know you know, and—and—well, screw it, Sid. Do I trust you? Maybe I do. Maybe I don't. But the basic fact is I just don't care. Stack the deck any way you like, Feingold. I just don't care. I wish I was on Mars. Or Pluto. Or the year Two Billion. Zap! Right across the whole continuum! Noel Breckenridge, freaking out! He heard himself say, "Do you want to know my secret fantasy, Sid? I dream of waking up Jewish one day. It's so damned boring being a gentile, do you know that? I feel so bland, so straight, so sunny. I envy you all that feverish kinky complexity of soul. All that history. Ghettos, persecutions, escapes, schemes for survival and revenge, a sense of tribal unity born out of shared pain. It's so hard for a goy to develop some honest paranoia, you know? Let alone a little schiziness." Feingold was still grinning. He filled Breckenridge's wineglass again. He showed no sign of having heard anything that might offend him. Maybe I didn't say anything, Breckenridge thought.

Feingold said, "When you get back to New York, Noel, I'd like you out to our place for dinner. You and your wife. A weekend, maybe. Logs on the fire, thick steaks, plenty of good wine. You'll love our place." Three Israeli jets roared low over Tiberias and vanished in the direction of Lebanon. "Will you come? Can you fit it into your schedule?"

Some possible structural hypotheses:

LIFE AS MEANINGLESS CONDITION		
Breckenridge on Wall Street.	The four seekers moving randomly.	The dead city.
LIFE RENDERED MEANINGFUL THROUGH ART		
Breckenridge recollects ancient myths.	The four seekers elicit his presence and request the myths.	The dead city inhabited after all. The inhabitants listen to Breckenridge.
THE IMPACT OF ENTROPY		
His tales are garbled dreams.	The seekers quarrel over theory.	The city dwellers speak an unknown language.
ASPECTS OF CONSCIOUSNESS		
He is a double self.	The four seekers are unsure of the historical background.	Most of the city dwellers are asleep.

His audience was getting larger every night. They came from all parts of the city, silently arriving, drawn at sundown to the place where the visitors camped. Hundreds, now, squatting beyond the glow of he campfire. They listened intently, nodded, seemed to comprehend, murmured occasional comments to one another. How strange: they seemed to comprehend.

"The story of Samson and Odysseus," Breckenridge announced.

"Samson is blind but mighty. His woman is known as Delilah. To them comes the wily chieftain Odysseus, making his way homeward from the land of Ithaca. He penetrates the maze in which Samson and Delilah live and hires himself to them as bondservant, giving his name as No Man. Delilah entices him to carry her off, and he abducts her. Samson is aware of the abduction but is unable to find them in the maze; he cries out in pain and rage, 'No Man steals my wife! No Man steals my wife!' His servants are baffled by this and take no action. In fury Samson brings the maze crashing down on himself and dies, while Odysseus carries Delilah off to Sparta, where she is seduced by Paris, Prince of Troy. Odysseus thus loses her and by way of gaining revenge he seduces Helen, the Queen of Troy, and the Trojan War begins."

And then he told the story of how mankind was created:

"In the beginning there was only a field of white sand. Lightning struck it, and where the lightning hit the sand it coagulated into a vessel of glass, and rainwater ran into the vessel and brought it to life, and from the vessel a she-wolf was born. Thunder entered her womb and fertilized her and she gave birth to twins, and they were not wolves but a human boy and a human girl. The wolf suckled the twins until they reached adulthood. Then they copulated and engendered children of their own. Because they were ashamed of their nakedness they killed the old wolf and made garments from her hide."

And then he told them the myth of the Wandering Jew, who scoffed at God and was condemned to drift through time until he himself was able to become God.

And he told them of the Golden Age and the Iron Age and the Age of Uranium.

And he told them how the waters and winds came into being, and the seasons, the months, day and night.

And he told them how art was born:

"Out of a hole in space pours a stream of life force. Many men and women attempted to seize the flow, but they were burned to ashes by its intensity. At last, however, a man devised a way. He hollowed himself out until there was nothing at all inside his body, and had himself dragged by a faithful dog to the place where the stream of energy descended from the heavens. Then the life force entered him and filled him, and instead of destroying him it took possession of him and restored him to life. But the force overflowed within him, brimming over, and the only way he could deal with that was to fashion stories and sculptures and songs, for otherwise the force would engulf him and drown him. His name was Gilgamesh and he was the first of the artists of mankind."

The city dwellers came by the thousands now. They listened and wept at Breckenridge's words.

Hypothesis of structural resolution:

He finds creative fulfilment.	The four seekers have bridged space and time to bring life out of death.	The sleeping city dwellers will be awakened.

Gradually the outlines of a master myth took place: the creation, the creation of man, the origin of private property, the origin of death, the loss of faith, the end of the world, the coming of a redeemer to start the cycle anew. Soon the structure would be complete. When it was,

Breckenridge thought, perhaps rains would fall on the desert, perhaps the world would be reborn.

Breckenridge slept. Sleeping, he experienced an inward glow of golden light. The girl he had encountered before came to him and took his hand and led him through the city. They walked for hours, it seemed, until they came to a well different from all the others, rectangular rather than circular and surrounded at street level by a low railing of bright metal mesh. "Go down into this one," she told him. "When you reach the bottom, keep walking until you reach the room where the mechanisms of awakening are located." He looked at her in amazement, realizing that her words had been comprehensible. "Are you speaking my language," he asked, "or am I speaking yours?" She answered by smiling and pointing toward the well.

He stepped over the railing and began his descent. The well was deeper than the other one; the air in its depths was stale and dry. The golden glow lit his way for him to the bottom and thence along a low passageway with a rounded vault of a ceiling. After a long time he came to a large, brightly lit room filled with sleek gray machinery. It was much like the computer room at any large bank. Mounted on the walls were control panels, labeled in an unknown language but also clearly marked with sequential symbols:

I II III IIII IIIII IIIIII

While he studied these he became aware of a sliding, hissing sound from the corridor beyond. He thought of sturdy metal cables passing one against the other; but then into the control room slowly came a creature something like a scorpion in form, considerably greater than a man in size. Its curved tubular thorax was dark and of a waxen texture; a dense mat of brown bristles, thick as straws, sprouted on its abdomen; its many eyes were bright, alert, and malevolent. Breckenridge snatched up a steel bar that lay near his feet and tried to wield it like a lance as the monster approached. From its jaws, though, there looped a sudden lasso of newly spun silken thread that caught the end of the bar and jerked it from Breckenridge's grasp. Then a second loop, entangling his arms and shoulders. Struggle was useless. He was caught. The creature pulled him closer. Breckenridge saw fangs, powerful palpi, a scythe of a tail in which a dripping stinger had become erect. Breckenridge writhed in the monster's grip. He felt neither surprise nor fear; this seemed a necessary working out of some ancient foreordained pattern.

A cool, silent voice within his skull said, "Who are you?"

"Noel Breckenridge of New York City, born A.D. 1940."

"Why do you intrude here?"

"I was summoned. If you want to know why, ask someone else."

"Is it your purpose to awaken the sleepers?"

"Very possibly," Breckenridge said.

"So the time has come?"

"Maybe it has," said Breckenridge. All was still for a long moment. The monster made no hostile move. Breckenridge grew impatient. "Well, what's the arrangement?" he said finally.

"The arrangement?"

"The terms under which I get my freedom. Am I supposed to tell you a lot of diverting stories? Will I have to serve you six months out of the year, forevermore? Is there some precious object I'm obliged to bring you from the bottom of the sea? Maybe you have a riddle that I'm supposed to answer."

The monster made no reply.

"Is that it?" Breckenridge demanded. "A riddle?"

"Do you want it to be a riddle?"

"A riddle, yes."

There was another endless pause. Breckenridge met the beady gaze steadily. At last the voice said, "A riddle. A riddle. Very well. Tell me the answer to this. What goes on four legs in the morning, on two legs in the afternoon, on three legs in the evening."

Breckenridge repeated it. He pondered. He frowned. He coughed. Then he laughed. "A baby," he said, "crawls on all fours. A grown man walks upright. An old man requires the assistance of a cane. Therefore the answer to your riddle is—"

He left the sentence unfinished. The gleam went out of the monster's eyes; the silken loop binding Breckenridge dissolved; the creature began slowly and sadly to back away, withdrawing into the corridor from which it came. Its hissing, rustling sound persisted for a time, growing ever more faint.

Breckenridge turned and without hesitation pulled the switch marked I.

The aurora no longer appears in the night sky. A light rain has been falling frequently for some days, and the desert is turning green. The sleepers are awakening, millions of them, called forth from their coffins by the workings of automatic mechanisms. Breckenridge stands in the central plaza of the city, arms outspread, and the city dwellers, as they emerge from the subterranean sleeping places, make their way toward him. I am the resurrection and the life, he thinks. I am Orpheus the sweet singer. I am Homer the blind. I am Noel Breckenridge. He looks across the eons to Harry Munsey. "I was wrong," he says. "There's meaning everywhere, Harry. For Sam Smith as well as for Beethoven. For Noel Breckenridge as well as for Michelangelo. Dawn after dawn, simply being alive, being part of it all, part of the cosmic dance of life—that's the meaning, Harry. Look! Look!" The sun is high now—not a cruel sun but a mild, gentle one, its heat softened by a humid haze. This is the dream-time, when all mistakes are unmade, when all things become one. The city folk surround him. They come closer. Closer yet. They reach toward him. He experiences a delicious flash of white light. The world disappears.

"JKF Airport," he told the taxi driver. The cab zoomed away. From the front seat came the voice of the radio with today's closing Dow Jones Industrials: 948.72, down 6.11. He reached the airport by half past five, and at seven he boarded a Pan Am flight for London. The next morning at nine, London time, he cabled his wife to say that he was well and planned to head south for the winter. Then he reported to the Air France counter for the nonstop flight to Morocco. Over the next week he cabled home from Rabat, Marrakech, and Timbuktu in Mali. The third cable said:

> GUESS WHAT STOP I'M REALLY IN TIMBUKTU STOP HAVE RENTED JEEP STOP I SET OUT INTO SAHARA TOMORROW STOP AM VERY HAPPY STOP YES STOP VERY HAPPY STOP VERY VERY HAPPY STOP STOP STOP.

It was the last message he sent. The night it arrived in New York there was a spectacular celestial display, an aurora that brought thousands of people out into Central Park. There was rain in the southeastern Sahara four days later, the first recorded precipitation there in eight years and seven months. An earthquake was reported in southern Sicily, but it did little damage. Things were much quieter after that for everybody.

CAPRICORN GAMES

Jesus was a Capricorn, so was Richard M. Nixon, and so am I. I am not much of a believer in the astrological sciences—in fact, I put no credence in them at all—but I do maintain a notion of the sort of people that Capricorns, in astrological parlance, are supposed to be. (Stubborn, dedicated, talented, self-centered, always working things out in advance. I think of Capricorns as the sort of people who would be superb chess players, although I confess that I'm a lousy one myself.) I look upon Capricorns as somewhat manipulative, which is not necessarily a negative attribute: "manipulative" can apply to jugglers, novelists, surgeons, musicians, and others who are quick with their hands in a literal or metaphorical sense. But some of the Capricorn energy does flow into the work of organizing other human beings into patterns that serve the needs of the Capricorn who's doing the organizing, I feel. Certainly that's the sort of Capricorn that Nikki is in this story, which dates from October, 1972.

This is another of the many stories that I wrote at the behest of the prodigious anthologist Roger Elwood (it appeared in his book The Far Side of Time *in 1974), and has always been a particular favorite of mine, not just because its January-born author often sees himself as sitting at the keyboard playing games with his characters and playing games with his readers' minds. Nikki's birthdate happens—by sheer one-out-of-365 coincidence—to be the same as that of a young woman who was living in Houston, Texas in 1981 when I—also by sheer coincidence—was in town to speak at a local university. She came upon the story somehow, was startled and amused to find that she shared a birthdate with its protagonist and that the author of the story was making a public appearance locally that day, and went to meet him. It turned out that we had a lot to say to each other. Her name was Karen Haber and—to make a long story short—we play our Capricorn games under the same roof these days.*

Nikki stepped into the conical field of the ultrasonic cleanser, wriggling so that the unheard droning out of the machine's stubby snout could more effectively shear her skin of dead epidermal tissue, globules of dried sweat, dabs of yesterday's scents, and other debris; after three minutes she emerged clean, bouncy, ready for the party. She programmed her party outfit: green buskins, lemon-yellow tunic of gauzy film, pale orange cape soft as a clam's mantle, and nothing underneath but Nikki—smooth, glistening, satiny Nikki. Her body was tuned and fit. The party was in her honor, though she was the only one who knew that. Today was her birthday, the seventh of January, 1999: twenty-four years old, no sign yet of bodily decay. Old Steiner had gathered an extraordinary assortment of guests: he promised to display a reader of minds, a billionaire, an authentic Byzantine duke, an Arab rabbi, a man who had married his own daughter, and other marvels. All of these, of course, subordinate to the true guest of honor, the evening's prize, the real birthday boy, the lion of the season—the celebrated Nicholson, who had lived a thousand years and who said he could help others to do the same. Nikki...Nicholson. Happy assonance, portending close harmony. You will show me, dear Nicholson, how I can live forever and never grow old. A cozy soothing idea.

The sky beyond the sleek curve of her window was black, snow-dappled; she imagined she could hear the rusty howl of the wind and feel the sway of the frost-gripped building, ninety stories high. This was the worst winter she had ever known. Snow fell almost every day, a planetary snow, a global shiver, not even sparing the tropics. Ice hard as iron bands bound the streets of New York. Walls were slippery, the air had a cutting edge. Tonight Jupiter gleamed fiercely in the blackness like a diamond in a raven's forehead. Thank God she didn't have to go outside. She could wait out the winter within this tower. The mail came by pneumatic tube. The penthouse restaurant fed her. She had friends on a dozen floors. The building was a world, warm, snug. Let it snow.

Let the sour gales come. Nikki checked herself in the all-around mirror: very nice, very very nice. Sweet filmy yellow folds. Hint of thigh, hint of breasts. More than a hint when there's a light-source behind her. She glowed. Fluffed her short glossy black hair. Dab of scent. Everyone loved her. Beauty is a magnet: repels some, attracts many, leaves no one unmoved. It was nine o'clock.

"Upstairs," she said to the elevator. "Steiner's place."

"Eighty-eighth floor," the elevator said.

"I know that. You're so sweet."

Music in the hallway: Mozart, crystalline and sinuous. The door to Steiner's apartment was a half-barrel of chromed steel, like the entrance to a bank vault. Nikki smiled into the scanner. The barrel revolved. Steiner held his hands like cups, centimeters from her chest, by way of greeting. "Beautiful," he murmured.

"So glad you asked me to come."

"Practically everybody's here already. It's a wonderful party, love."

She kissed his shaggy cheek. In October they had met in the elevator. He was past sixty and looked less than forty. When she touched his body she perceived it as an object encased in milky ice, like a mammoth fresh out of the Siberian permafrost. They had been lovers for two weeks. Autumn had given way to winter and Nikki had passed out of his life, but he had kept his word about the parties: here she was, invited.

"Alexius Ducas," said a short, wide man with a dense black beard, parted in the middle. He bowed. A good flourish. Steiner evaporated and she was in the keeping of the Byzantine duke. He maneuvered her at once across the thick white carpet to a place where clusters of spotlights, sprouting like angry fungi from the wall, revealed the contours of her body. Others turned to look. Duke Alexius favored her with a heavy stare. But she felt no excitement. Byzantium had been over for a long time. He brought her a goblet of chilled green wine and said, "Are you ever in the Aegean Sea? My family has its ancestral castle on an island eighteen kilometers east of—"

"Excuse me, but which is the man named Nicholson?"

"Nicholson is merely the name he currently uses. He claims to have had a shop in Constantinople during the reign of my ancestor the Basileus Manuel Comnenus." A patronizing click, tongue on teeth. "Only a shopkeeper." The Byzantine eyes sparkled ferociously. "How beautiful you are!"

"Which one is he?"

"There. By the couch."

Nikki saw only a wall of backs. She tilted to the left and peered. No use. She would get to him later. Alexius Ducas continued to offer her his body with his eyes. She whispered languidly, "Tell me all about Byzantium."

He got as far as Constantine the Great before he bored her. She finished her wine, and, coyly extending the glass, persuaded a smooth young man passing by to refill it for her. The Byzantine looked sad. "The empire then was divided," he said, "among—"

"This is my birthday," she announced.

"Yours also? My congratulations. Are you as old as—"

"Not nearly. Not by half. I won't even be five hundred for some time," she said, and turned to take her glass. The smooth young man did not wait to be captured. The party engulfed him like an avalanche. Sixty, eighty guests, all in motion. The draperies were pulled back, revealing the full fury of the snowstorm. No one was watching it. Steiner's apartment was like a movie set: great porcelain garden stools, Ming or even Sung; walls painted with flat sheets of bronze and scarlet; pre-Columbian artefacts in spotlit niches; sculptures like aluminum spiderwebs; Dürer etchings—the loot of the ages. Squat shaven-headed servants, Mayans or Khmers or perhaps Olmecs, circulated impassively offering trays of delicacies: caviar, sea urchins, bits of roasted meat, tiny sausages, burritos in startling chili sauce. Hands darted unceasingly from trays to lips. This was a gathering of life-eaters, world-swallowers. Duke Alexius was stroking her arm. "I will leave at midnight," he said gently. "It would be a delight if you left with me."

"I have other plans," she told him.

"Even so." He bowed courteously, outwardly undisappointed. "Possibly another time. My card?" It appeared as if by magic in his hand: a sliver of tawny cardboard, elaborately engraved. She put it in her purse and the room swallowed him. Instantly a big, wild-eyed man took his place before her. "You've never heard of me," he began.

"Is that a boast or an apology?"

"I'm quite ordinary. I work for Steiner. He thought it would be amusing to invite me to one of his parties."

"What do you do?"

"Invoices and debarkations. Isn't this an amazing place?"

"What's your sign?" Nikki asked him.

"Libra."

"I'm Capricorn. Tonight's my birthday as well as *his*. If you're really Libra, you're wasting your time with me. Do you have a name?"

"Martin Bliss."

"Nikki."

"There isn't any Mrs. Bliss, hah-hah."

Nikki licked her lips. "I'm hungry. Would you get me some canapés?"

She was gone as soon as he moved toward the food. Circumnavigating the long room—past the string quintet, past the bartender's throne, past the window—until she had a good view of the man called Nicholson. He didn't disappoint her. He was slender, supple, not tall, strong in the shoulders. A man of presence and authority. She wanted to put her lips to him and suck immortality out. His head was a flat triangle, brutal cheekbones, thin lips, dark mat of curly hair, no beard, no moustache. His eyes were keen, electric, intolerably wise. He must have seen everything twice, at the very least. Nikki had read his book. Everyone had. He had been a king, a lama, a slave trader, a slave. Always taking pains to conceal his implausible longevity, now offering his terrible secret freely to the members of the Book-of-the-Month Club. Why had he chosen to surface and reveal himself? Because this is the necessary moment of revelation, he had said. When he must stand forth as what he is, so that he might impart his gift to others, lest he lose it. Lest he lose it. At the stroke of the new century he must share his prize of life. A dozen people surrounded him, catching his glow. He glanced through a palisade of shoulders and locked his eyes on hers; Nikki felt impaled, exalted, chosen. Warmth spread through her loins like a river of molten tungsten, like a stream of hot honey. She started to go to him. A corpse got in her way. Death's-head parchment skin, nightmare eyes. A scaly hand brushed her bare biceps. A frightful eroded voice croaked, "How old do you think I am?"

"Oh, God!"

"How old?"

"Two thousand?"

"I'm fifty-eight. I won't live to see fifty-nine. Here, smoke one of these."

With trembling hands he offered her a tiny ivory tube. There was a Gothic monogram near one end—FXB—and a translucent green capsule at the other. She pressed the capsule, and a flickering blue flame sprouted. She inhaled. "What is it?" she asked.

"My own mixture. Soma Number Five. You like it?"

"I'm smeared," she said. "Absolutely smeared. Oh, God!" The walls were flowing. The snow had turned to tinfoil. An instant hit. The corpse had a golden halo. Dollar signs rose into view like stigmata on his furrowed forehead. She heard the crash of the surf, the roar of the waves. The deck was heaving. The masts were cracking. *Woman overboard!* she cried, and heard her inaudible voice disappearing down a tunnel of echoes, boingg boingg boingg. She clutched at his frail wrists. "You bastard, what did you *do* to me?"

"I'm Francis Xavier Byrne."

Oh. The billionaire. Byrne Industries, the great conglomerate. Steiner had promised her a billionaire tonight.

"Are you going to die soon?" she asked.

"No later than Easter. Money can't help me now. I'm a walking metastasis." He opened his ruffled shirt. Something bright and metallic, like chain mail, covered his chest. "Life-support system," he confided. "It operates me. Take it off for half an hour and I'd be finished. Are you a Capricorn?"

"How did you know?"

"I may be dying, but I'm not stupid. You have the Capricorn gleam in your eyes. What am I?"

She hesitated. His eyes were gleaming too. Self-made man, fantastic business sense, energy, arrogance. Capricorn, of course. No, too easy. "Leo," she said.

"No. Try again." He pressed another monogrammed tube into her hand and strode away. She hadn't yet come down from the last one, although the most flamboyant effects had ebbed. Party guests swirled and flowed around her. She no longer could see Nicholson. The snow seemed to be turning to hail, little hard particles spattering the vast windows and leaving white abraded tracks: or were her perceptions merely sharper? The roar of conversation seemed to rise and fall as if someone were adjusting a volume control. The lights fluctuated in a counterpointed rhythm. She felt dizzy. A tray of golden cocktails went past her and she hissed, "Where's the bathroom?"

Down the hall. Five strangers clustered outside it, talking in scaly whispers. She floated through them, grabbed the sink's cold edge, thrust her face to the oval concave mirror. A death's-head. Parchment skin, nightmare eyes. No! No! She blinked and her own features reappeared. Shivering, she made an effort to pull herself together. The medicine cabinet held a tempting collection of drugs, Steiner's all-purpose remedies. Without looking at labels Nikki seized a handful of vials and gobbled pills at random. A flat red one, a tapering green one, a succulent yellow gelatin capsule. Maybe headache remedies, maybe hallucinogens. Who knows, who cares? We Capricorns are not always as cautious as you think.

Someone knocked at the bathroom door. She answered and found the bland, hopeful face of Martin Bliss hovering near the ceiling. Eyes protruding faintly, cheeks florid. "They said you were sick. Can I do anything for you?" So kind, so sweet. She touched his arm, grazed his cheek with her lips. Beyond him in the hall stood a broad-bodied man with close-cropped blond hair, glacial blue eyes, a plump perfect face. His smile was intense and brilliant. "That's easy," he said. "Capricorn."

"You can guess my—" She stopped, stunned. "Sign?" she finished, voice very small. "How did you do that? Oh."

"Yes. I'm that one."

She felt more than naked, stripped down to the ganglia, to the synapses. "What's the trick?"

"No trick. I listen. I hear."

"You hear people thinking?"

"More or less. Do you think it's a party game?" He was beautiful but terrifying, like a Samurai sword in motion. She wanted him but she didn't dare. He's got my number, she thought. I would never have any secrets from him. He said sadly, "I don't mind that. I know I frighten a lot of people. Some don't care."

"What's your name?"

"Tom," he said. "Hello, Nikki."

"I feel very sorry for you."

"Not really. You can kid yourself if you need to. But you can't kid me. Anyway, you don't sleep with men you feel sorry for."

"I don't sleep with you."

"You will," he said.

"I thought you were just a mind-reader. They didn't tell me you did prophecies too."

He leaned close and smiled. The smile demolished her. She had to fight to keep from falling. "I"ve got your number, all right," he said in a low, harsh voice. "I'll call you next Tuesday." As he walked away he said, "You're wrong. I'm a Virgo. Believe it or not."

Nikki returned, numb, to the living room. "...the figure of the mandala," Nicholson was saying. His voice was dark, focused, a pure basso cantante. "The essential thing that every mandala has is a center—the place where everything is born, the eye of God's mind, the heart of darkness and of light, the core of the storm. All right. You must move toward the center, find the vortex at the boundary of Yang and Yin, place yourself right at the mandala's midpoint. *Center yourself.* Do you follow the metaphor? Center yourself at *now,* the eternal *now.* To move off center is to move forward toward death, backward toward birth, always the fatal polar swings. But if you're capable of positioning yourself constantly at the focus of the mandala, right on center, you have access to the fountain of renewal, you become an organism capable of constant self-healing, constant self-replenishment, constant expansion into regions beyond self. Do you follow? The power of..."

Steiner, at her elbow, said tenderly, "How beautiful you are in the first moments of erotic fixation."

"It's a marvelous party."

"Are you meeting interesting people?"

"Is there any other kind?" she asked.

Nicholson abruptly detached himself from the circle of his audience and strode across the room, alone, in a quick decisive knight's move toward the bar. Nikki, hurrying to intercept him, collided with a shaven-headed tray-bearing servant. The tray slid smoothly from the man's thick fingertips and launched itself into the air like a spinning shield; a rainfall of skewered meat in an oily green curry sauce spattered the white carpet. The servant was utterly motionless. He stood frozen like some sort of Mexican stone idol, thick-necked, flat-nosed, for a long painful moment; then he turned his head slowly to the left and regretfully contemplated his rigid outspread hand, shorn of its tray; finally he swung his head toward Nikki, and his normally expressionless granite face took on for a quick flickering instant a look of total hatred, a coruscating emanation of contempt and disgust that faded immediately. He laughed: hu-hu-hu, a neighing snicker. His superiority was overwhelming. Nikki floundered in quicksands of humiliation. Hastily she escaped, a zig and a zag, around the tumbled goodies and across to the bar. Nicholson, still by himself. Her face went crimson. She felt short of breath. Hunting for words, tongue all thumbs. Finally, in a catapulting blurt: "Happy birthday!"

"Thank you," he said solemnly.

"Are you enjoying your birthday?"

"Very much."

"I'm amazed that they don't bore you. I mean, having had so many of them."

"I don't bore easily." He was awesomely calm, drawing on some bottomless reservoir of patience. He gave her a look that was at the same time warm and impersonal. "I find everything interesting," he said.

"That's curious. I said more or less the same thing to Steiner just a few minutes ago. You know, it's my birthday too."

"Really?"

"The seventh of January, 1975 for me."

"Hello, 1975. I'm—" He laughed. "It sounds absolutely absurd, doesn't it?"

"The seventh of January, 982."

"You've been doing your homework."

"I've read your book," she said. "Can I make a silly remark? My God, you don't *look* like you're a thousand and seventeen years old."

"How should I look?"

"More like him," she said, indicating Francis Xavier Byrne.

Nicholson chuckled. She wondered if he liked her. Maybe. Maybe. Nikki risked some eye contact. He was hardly a centimeter taller than she was, which made it a terrifyingly intimate experience. He regarded her steadily, centerdly; she imagined a throbbing mandala surrounding him, luminous turquoise spokes emanating from his heart, radiant red and green spiderweb rings connecting them. Reaching from her loins, she threw a loop of desire around him. Her eyes were explicit. His were veiled. She felt him calmly retreating. Take me inside, she pleaded, take me to one of the back rooms. Pour life into me. She said, "How will you choose the people you're going to instruct in the secret?"

"Intuitively."

"Refusing anybody who asks directly, of course."

"Refusing anybody who asks."

"Did *you* ask?"

"You said you read my book."

"Oh. Yes. I remember—you didn't know what was happening, you didn't understand anything until it was over."

"I was a simple lad," he said. "That was a long time ago." His eyes were alive again. He's drawn to me. He sees that I'm his kind, that I deserve him. Capricorn, Capricorn, Capricorn you and me, he-goat and she-goat. Play my game, Cap. "How are you named?" he asked.

"Nikki."

"A beautiful name. A beautiful woman."

The emptiness of the compliments devastated her. She realized she had arrived with mysterious suddenness at a necessary point of tactical withdrawal; retreat was obligatory, lest she push too hard and destroy the tenuous contact so tensely established. She thanked him with a glance and gracefully slipped away, pivoting toward Martin Bliss, slipping her arm through his. Bliss quivered at the gesture, glowed, leaped into a higher energy state. She resonated to his vibrations, going up and up. She was at the heart of the party, the center of the mandala: standing flat-footed, legs slightly apart, making her body a polar axis, with lines of force zooming up out of the earth, up through the basement levels of this building, up the eighty-eight stories of it, up through her sex, her heart, her head. This is how it must feel, she thought, when undyingness is conferred on you. A moment of spontaneous grace, the kindling of an inner light. She looked love at poor sappy Bliss. You dear heart, you dumb walking pun. The string quintet made molten sounds. "What is that?" she asked. "Brahms?" Bliss offered to find out. Alone, she was vulnerable to Francis Xavier Byrne, who brought her down with a single cadaverous glance.

"Have you guessed it yet?" he asked. "The sign."

She stared through his ragged cancerous body, blazing with decomposition. "Scorpio," she told him hoarsely.

"Right! Right!" He pulled a pendant from his breast and draped its golden chain over her head. "For you," he rasped, and fled. She fondled it. A smooth green stone. Jade? Emerald? Lightly engraved on its domed face was the looped cross, the crux ansata. Beautiful. The gift of life, from the dying man. She waved fondly to him across a forest of heads and winked. Bliss returned.

"They're playing something by Schönberg," he reported. "*Verklärte Nacht.*"

"How lovely." She flipped the pendant and let it fall back against her breasts. "Do you like it?"

"I'm sure you didn't have it a moment ago."

"It sprouted," she told him. She felt high, but not as high as she had been just after leaving Nicholson. That sense of herself as focal point had departed. The party seemed chaotic. Couples were forming, dissolving, reforming; shadowy figures were stealing away in twos and threes toward the bedrooms; the servants were more obsessively thrusting their trays of drinks and snacks at the remaining guests; the hail had reverted to snow, and feathery masses silently struck the windows, sticking there, revealing their glistening mandalic structures for painfully brief moments before they deliquesced. Nikki struggled to regain her centered position. She indulged in a cheering fantasy: Nicholson coming to her, formally touching her cheek, telling her, "You will be one of the elect." In less than twelve months the time would come for him to gather with his seven still unnamed disciples to see in the new century, and he would take their hands into his hands, he would pump the vitality of the undying into their bodies, sharing with them the secret that had been shared with him a thousand years ago. Who? Who? Who? Me. Me. Me. But where had Nicholson gone? His aura, his glow, that cone of imaginary light that had appeared to surround him—nowhere.

A man in a lacquered orange wig began furiously to quarrel, almost under Nikki's nose, with a much younger woman wearing festoons of bioluminescent pearls. Man and wife, evidently. They were both sharp-featured, with glossy, protuberant eyes, rigid faces, cheek muscles working intensely. Live together long enough, come to look alike. Their dispute had a stale, ritualistic flavor, as though they had staged it all too many times before. They were explaining to each other the events that had caused the quarrel, interpreting them, recapitulating them, shading them, justifying, attacking, defending—you said this because and that led me to respond that way because...no, on the contrary, I said this because you said that—all of it in a quiet screechy tone, sickening, agonizing, pure death.

"He's her biological father," a man next to Nikki said. "She was one of the first of the in vitro babies, and he was the donor, and five years ago he tracked her down and married her. A loophole in the law." Five years? They sounded as if they had been married for fifty. Walls of pain and boredom encased them. Only their eyes were alive. Nikki found it impossible to imagine those two in bed, bodies entwined in the act of love. Act of love, she thought, and laughed. Where was Nicholson? Duke Alexius, flushed and sweat-beaded, bowed to her. "I will leave soon," he announced, and she received the announcement gravely but without reacting, as though he had merely commented on the fluctuations of the storm, or had spoken in Greek. He bowed again and went away. Nicholson? Nicholson? She grew calm again, finding her center. He will come to me when he is ready. There was contact between us, and it was real and good.

Bliss, beside her, gestured and said, "A rabbi of Syrian birth, formerly Muslim, highly regarded among Jewish theologians."

She nodded but didn't look.

"An astronaut just back from Mars. I"ve never seen anyone's skin tanned quite that color."

The astronaut held no interest for her. She worked at kicking herself back into high. The party was approaching a climactic moment, she felt, a time when commitments were being made and decisions taken. The clink of ice in glasses, the foggy vapors of psychedelic inhalants, the press of warm flesh all about her—she was wired into everything, she was alive and receptive, she was entering into the twitching hour, the hour of galvanic jerks. She grew wild and reckless. Impulsively she kissed Bliss, straining on tiptoes, jabbing her tongue deep into his startled mouth. Then she broke free. Someone was playing with the lights: they grew redder, then gained force and zoomed to blue-white ferocity. Far across the room a crowd was surging and billowing around the fallen figure of Francis Xavier Byrne, slumped loose-jointedly against the base of the bar. His eyes were open but glassy. Nicholson crouched over him, reaching into his shirt, making delicate adjustments of the controls of the chain mail beneath. "It's all right," Steiner was saying. "Give him some air. It's all right!" Confusion. Hubbub. A torrent of tangled input.

"—they say there's been a permanent change in the weather patterns. Colder winters from now on, because of accumulations of dust in the atmosphere that screen the sun's rays. Until we freeze altogether by around the year 2200—"

"—but the carbon dioxide is supposed to start a greenhouse effect that's causing *warmer* weather, I thought, and—"

"—the proposal to generate electric power from—"

"—the San Andreas fault—"

"—financed by debentures convertible into—"

"—capsules of botulism toxin—"

"—to be distributed at a ratio of one per thousand families, throughout Greenland and the Kamchatka Metropolitan Area—"

"—in the sixteenth century, when you could actually hope to found your own empire in some unknown part of the—"

"—unresolved conflicts of Capricorn personality—"

"—intense concentration and meditation upon the completed mandala so that the contents of the work are transferred to and identified with the mind and body of the beholder. I mean, technically what occurs is the reabsorption of cosmic forces. In the process of construction these forces—"

"—butterflies, which are no longer to be found anywhere in—"

"—were projected out from the chaos of the unconscious; in the process of absorption, the powers are drawn back in again—"

"—reflecting transformations of the DNA in the light-collecting organ, which—"

"—the snow—"

"—a thousand years, can you imagine that? And—"

"—her body—"

"—formerly a toad—"

"—just back from Mars, and there's that *look* in his eye—"

"Hold me," Nikki said. "Just hold me. I'm very dizzy."

"Would you like a drink?"

"Just hold me." She pressed against cool sweet-smelling fabric. His chest unyielding beneath it. Steiner. Very male. He steadied her, but only for a moment. Other responsibilities summoned him. When he released her, she swayed. He beckoned to someone else, blond, soft-faced. The mind-reader, Tom. Passing her along the chain from man to man.

"You feel better now," the telepath told her.

"Are you positive of that?"

"Very."

"Can you read any mind in the room?" she asked.

He nodded.

"Even *his*?"

Again a nod. "He's the clearest of all. He's been using it so long, all the channels are worn deep."

"Then he really is a thousand years old?"

"You didn't believe it?"

Nikki shrugged. "Sometimes I don't know what I believe."

"He's *old.*"

"You'd be the one to know."

"He's a phenomenon. He's absolutely extraordinary." A pause—quick, stabbing. "Would you like to see into his mind?"

"How can I?"

"I'll patch you right in, if you'd like me to." The glacial eyes flashed sudden mischievous warmth. "Yes?"

"I'm not sure I want to."

"You're very sure. You're curious as hell. Don't kid me. Don't play games, Nikki. You want to see into him."

"Maybe." Grudgingly.

"You do. Believe me, you do. Here. Relax, let your shoulders slump a little, loosen up, make yourself receptive, and I'll establish the link."

"Wait," she said.

But it was too late. The mind-reader serenely parted her consciousness like Moses doing the Red Sea and rammed something into her forehead, something thick but insubstantial, a truncheon of fog. She quivered and recoiled. She felt violated. It was like her first time in bed, in that moment when all the fooling around at last was over, the kissing and the nibbling and the stroking, and suddenly there was this object deep inside her body. She had never forgotten that sense of being impaled. But of course it had been not only an intrusion but also a source of ecstasy. As was this. The object within her was the consciousness of Nicholson. In wonder she explored its surface, rigid and weathered, pitted with the myriad ablations of reentry. Ran her trembling hands over its bronzy roughness. Remained outside it. Tom, the mind-reader, gave her a nudge. Go on, go on. Deeper. Don't hold back. She folded herself around Nicholson and drifted into him like ectoplasm seeping into sand. Suddenly she lost her bearings. The discrete and impermeable boundary marking the end of her self and the beginning of his became indistinct. It was impossible to distinguish between her experiences and his, nor could she separate the pulsations of her nervous system from the impulses traveling along his. Phantom memories assailed and engulfed her. She was transformed into a node of pure perception: a steady, cool, isolated eye, surveying and recording. Images flashed. She was toiling upward along a dazzling snowy crest, with jagged Himalayan fangs hanging above her in the white sky and a warm-muzzled yak snuffling wearily at her side.

A platoon of swarthy little men accompanied her, slanty eyes, heavy coats, thick boots. The stink of rancid butter, the cutting edge of an impossible wind: and there, gleaming in the sudden sunlight, a pile of fire-bright yellow plaster with a thousand winking windows, a building, a lamasery strung along a mountain ridge. The nasal sound of distant horns and trumpets. The hoarse chanting of lotus-legged monks. What were they chanting? Om? Om? Om! *Om,* and flies buzzed around her nose, and she lay hunkered in a flimsy canoe, coursing silently down a midnight river in the heart of Africa; drowning in humidity. Brawny naked men with purple-black skins crouching close. Sweaty fronds dangling from flamboyantly excessive shrubbery; the snouts of crocodiles rising out of the dark water like toothy flowers; great nauseating orchids blossoming high in the smooth-shanked trees. And on shore, five white men in Elizabethan costume, wide-brimmed hats, drooping sweaty collars, lace, fancy buckles, curling red beards. Errol Flynn as Sir Francis Drake, blunderbuss dangling in crook of arm. The white men laughing, beckoning, shouting to the men in the canoe. Am I slave or slavemaster? No answer. Only a blurring and a new vision: autumn leaves blowing across the open doorways of straw-thatched huts, shivering oxen crouched in bare stubble-strewn fields, grim long-mustachioed men with close-cropped hair riding diagonal courses toward the horizon. Crusaders, are they? Or warriors of Hungary on their way to meet the dread Mongols? Defenders of the imperiled Anglo-Saxon realm against the Norman invaders? They could be any of these: But always that steady cool eye, always that unmoving consciousness at the center of every scene. *Him,* eternal, all-enduring. And then: the train rolling westward, belching white smoke, the plains unrolling infinityward, the big brown fierce-eyed bison standing in shaggy clumps along the right of way, the man with turbulent shoulder-length hair laughing, slapping a twenty-dollar gold piece on the table. Picking up his rifle—a .50-calibre breech-loading Springfield—he aims casually through the door of the moving train, he squeezes off a shot, another, another. Three shaggy brown corpses beside the tracks, and the train rolls onward, honking raucously.

Her arm and shoulder tingled with the impact of those shots. Then: a fetid waterfront, bales of cloves and peppers and cinnamon, small brown-skinned men in turbans and loincloths arguing under a terrible sun. Tiny irregular silver coins glittering in the palm of her hand. The jabber of some Malabar dialect counterpointed with fluid mocking Portuguese. Do we sail now with Vasco da Gama? Perhaps. And then a gray Teutonic street, windswept, medieval, bleak Lutheran faces scowling from leaded windows. And then the Gobi steppe, with horsemen and campfires and dark tents. And then New York City, unmistakably New York City, with square black automobiles scurrying between the stubby skyscrapers like glossy beetles, a scene out of some silent movie. And then. And then. Everywhere, everything, all times, all places, a discontinuous flow of events but always that clarity of vision, that rock-steady perception, that solid mind at the center, that unshakeable identity, that unchanging self—with whom I am inextricably enmeshed—

There was no "I," there was no "he," there was only the one ever-perceiving point of view. But abruptly she felt a change of focus; a distancing effect, a separation of self and self, so that she was looking at him as he lived his many lives, seeing him from the outside, seeing him plainly changing identities as others might change clothing, growing beards and moustaches, shaving them, cropping his hair, letting his hair grow, adopting new fashions, learning languages, forging documents. She saw him in all his thousand years of guises and subterfuges, saw him real and unified and centered beneath his obligatory camouflages—and saw him seeing her.

Instantly contact broke. She staggered. Arms caught her. She pulled away from the smiling plump-faced blond man, muttering, "What have you done? You didn't tell me you'd show *me* to *him.*"

"How else can there be a linkage?" the telepath asked.

"You didn't tell me. You should have told me." Everything was lost. She couldn't bear to be in the same room as Nicholson now. Tom reached for her, but she stumbled past him, stepping on people. They winked up at her. Someone stroked her leg. She forced her way through improbable laocoons, three women and two servants, five men and a tablecloth. A glass door, a gleaming silvery handle: she pushed. Out onto the terrace. The purity of the gale might cleanse her. Behind her, faint gasps, a few shrill screams, annoyed expostulations: "Close that thing!" She slammed it. Alone in the night, eighty-eight stories above street level, she offered herself to the storm. Her filmy tunic shielded her not at all. Snowflakes burned against her breasts. Her nipples hardened and rose like fiery beacons, jutting against the soft fabric. The snow stung her throat, her shoulders, her arms. Far below, the wind churned newly fallen crystals into spiral galaxies. The street was invisible. Thermal confusions brought updrafts that seized the edge of her tunic and whipped it outward from her body. Fierce, cold particles of hail were driven into her bare pale thighs. She stood with her back to the party. Did anyone in there notice her? Would someone think she was contemplating suicide and come rushing gallantly out to save her? Capricorns didn't commit suicide. They might threaten it, yes, they might even tell themselves quite earnestly that they were really going to do it, but it was only a game, only a game. No one came to her. She didn't turn. Gripping the railing, she fought to calm herself.

No use. Not even the bitter air could help. Frost in her eyelashes, snow on her lips. The pendant Byrne had given her blazed between her breasts. The air was white with a throbbing green underglow. It seared her eyes. She was off-center and floundering. She felt herself still reverberating through the centuries, going back and forth across the orbit of Nicholson's interminable life. What year is this? Is it 1386, 1912, 1532, 1779, 1043, 1977, 1235, 1129, 1836? So many centuries. So many lives. And yet always the one true self, changeless, unchangeable.

Gradually the resonances died away. Nicholson's unending epochs no longer filled her mind with terrible noise. She began to shiver, not from fear but merely from cold, and tugged at her moist tunic, trying to shield her nakedness. Melting snow left hot clammy tracks across her breasts and belly. A halo of steam surrounded her. Her heart pounded.

She wondered if what she had experienced had been genuine contact with Nicholson's soul, or rather only some trick of Tom's, a simulation of contact. Was it possible, after all, even for Tom to create a linkage between two non-telepathic minds such as hers and Nicholson's? Maybe Tom had fabricated it all himself, using images borrowed from Nicholson's book.

In that case there might still be hope for her.

A delusion, she knew. A fantasy born of the desperate optimism of the hopeless. But nevertheless—

She found the handle, let herself back into the party. A gust accompanied her, sweeping snow inward. People stared. She was like death arriving at the feast. Doglike, she shook off the searing snowflakes. Her clothes were wet and stuck to her skin; she might as well have been naked. "You poor shivering thing," a woman said. She pulled Nikki into a tight embrace. It was the sharp-faced woman, the bulgy-eyed bottle-born one, bride of her own father. Her hands traveled swiftly over Nikki's body, caressing her breasts, touching her cheek, her forearm, her haunch. "Come inside with me," she crooned. "I"ll make you warm." Her lips grazed Nikki's. A playful tongue sought hers.

For a moment, needing the warmth, Nikki gave herself to the embrace. Then she pulled away. "No," she said. "Some other time. Please." Wriggling free, she started across the room. An endless journey. Like crossing the Sahara by pogo stick. Voices, faces, laughter. A dryness in her throat. Then she was in front of Nicholson.

Well. Now or never.

"I have to talk to you," she said.

"Of course." His eyes were merciless. No wrath in them, not even disdain, only an incredible patience more terrifying than anger or scorn. She would not let herself bend before that cool level gaze.

She said, "A few minutes ago, did you have an odd experience, a sense that someone was—well, looking into your mind? I know it sounds foolish, but—?"

"Yes. It happened." So calm. How did he stay that close to his center? That unwavering eye, that uniquely self-contained self, perceiving all: the lamasery, the slave depot, the railroad train, everything, all time gone by, all time to come—how did he manage to be so tranquil? She knew she never could learn such calmness. She knew he knew it. *He has my number, all right.* She found that she was looking at his cheekbones, at his forehead, at his lips. Not into his eyes.

"You have the wrong image of me," she told him.

"It isn't an image," he said. "What I have is you."

"No."

"Face yourself, Nikki. If you can figure out where to look." He laughed. Gently, but she was demolished.

An odd thing, then. She forced herself to stare into his eyes and felt a snapping of awareness from one mode into some other, and he turned into an old man. That mask of changeless early maturity dissolved and she saw the frightening yellowed eyes, the maze of furrows and gullies, the toothless gums, the drooling lips, the hollow throat, the self beneath the face. A thousand years, a thousand years! And every moment of those thousand years was visible. "You're old," she whispered. "You disgust me. I wouldn't want to be like you, not for anything!" She backed away, shaking. "An old, old, old man. All a masquerade!"

He smiled. "Isn't that pathetic?"

"Me or you? *Me or you?*"

He didn't answer. She was bewildered. When she was five paces away from him there came another snapping of awareness, a second changing of phase, and suddenly he was himself again, taut-skinned, erect, appearing to be perhaps thirty-five years old. A globe of silence hung between them. The force of his rejection was withering. She summoned her last strength for a parting glare. *I didn't want you either, friend, not any single part of you.* He saluted cordially. Dismissal.

Martin Bliss, grinning vacantly, stood near the bar. "Let's go," she said savagely. "Take me home!"

"But—"

"It's just a few floors below." She thrust her arm through his. He blinked, shrugged, fell into step.

"I"ll call you Tuesday, Nikki," Tom said as they swept past him.

Downstairs, on her home turf, she felt better. In the bedroom they quickly dropped their clothes. His body was pink, hairy, serviceable. She turned the bed on, and it began to murmur and throb. "How old do you think I am?" she asked.

"Twenty-six?" Bliss said vaguely.

"Bastard!" She pulled him down on top of her. Her hands raked his skin. Her thighs parted. Go on. Like an animal, she thought. Like an animal! She was getting older moment by moment, she was dying in his arms.

"You're much better than I expected," she said eventually.

He looked down, baffled, amazed. "You could have chosen anyone at that party. Anyone."

"Almost anyone," she said.

When he was asleep she slipped out of bed. Snow was still falling. She heard the thunk of bullets and the whine of wounded bison. She heard the clangor of swords on shields. She heard lamas chanting: Om, Om, Om. No sleep for her this night, none. The clock was ticking like a bomb. The century was flowing remorselessly toward its finish. She checked her face for wrinkles in the bathroom mirror. Smooth, smooth, all smooth under the blue fluorescent glow. Her eyes looked bloody. Her nipples were still hard. She took a little alabaster jar from one of the bathroom cabinets and three slender red capsules fell out of it, into her palm. Happy birthday, dear Nikki, happy birthday to you. She swallowed all three. Went back to bed. Waited, listening to the slap of snow on glass, for the visions to come and carry her away.

SHIP-SISTER, STAR-SISTER

At the time I wrote this story—November, 1972—I was going through a prolonged period of skepticism about the value and merit of science fiction, as you will see if you go back to my introduction to "The Science Fiction Hall of Fame," a story written a few months earlier in that troubled year. I was having difficulties making myself believe in the classic furnishings of s-f. All those starships, telepaths, galactic empires and time machines, all the stuff I had been dealing with as reader and writer for twenty-plus years, had become monstrously unreal, implausible, impossible to me.

That seemed like an unhealthy attitude for a science-fiction writer to hold; and so, when that hyperactive anthology editor Roger Elwood asked me for a longish story for a book called Tomorrow's Alternatives, *I took a deep breath and reached for one of the most far-out Stapledonian concepts in my science-fiction idea file, figuring that if I could write that with some conviction, I'd be able to handle less audacious themes without any problem afterward. Somehow it worked. While I was writing "Ship-Sister" I made myself believe in half a dozen different astonishments at once, long enough (five weeks) for me to bring off this story in, I hope, fairly convincing manner.*

When I wrote an introduction to "Ship-Sister" in 1992 for an earlier collection of my stories, I concluded by saying, "The material of this story still fascinates me and I have a feeling that I may return to it some day and deal with it at book length." Indeed so. I did just that very thing a couple of years later, expanding the orignal novelette into the novel Starborne, *which was published in 1996.*

Sixteen light-years from Earth today, in the fifth month of the voyage, and the silent throb of acceleration continues to drive the velocity higher. Three games of Go are in progress in the ship's lounge. The year-captain stands at the entrance to the lounge, casually watching the players: Roy and Sylvia, Leon and Chiang, Heinz and Elliot. Go has been a craze aboard ship for weeks. The players—some eighteen or twenty members of the expedition have caught the addiction by now—sit hour after hour, contemplating strategies, devising variations, grasping the smooth black or white stones between forefinger and second finger, putting the stones down against the wooden board with the proper smart sharp clacking sound. The year-captain himself does not play, though the game once interested him to the point of obsession, long ago; he finds his responsibilities so draining that an exercise in simulated territorial conquest does not attract him now. He comes here often to watch, however, remaining five or ten minutes, then going on about his duties.

The best of the players is Roy, the mathematician, a large, heavy man with a soft sleepy face. He sits with his eyes closed, awaiting in tranquillity his turn to play. "I am purging myself of the need to win," he told the year-captain yesterday when asked what occupies his mind while he waits. Purged or not, Roy wins more than half of his games, even though he gives most of his opponents a handicap of four or five stones.

He gives Sylvia a handicap of only two. She is a delicate woman, fine-boned and shy, a geneticist, and she plays well although slowly. She makes her move. At the sound of it Roy opens his eyes. He studies the board, points, and says, "*Atari,*" the conventional way of calling to his opponent's attention the fact that her move will enable him to capture several of her stones. Sylvia laughs lightly and retracts her move. After a moment she moves again. Roy nods and picks up a white stone, which he holds for nearly a minute before he places it.

The year-captain would like to speak with Sylvia about one of her experiments, but he sees she will be occupied with the game for another hour or more. The conversation can wait. No one hurries aboard this ship. They have plenty of time for everything: a lifetime, maybe, if no habitable planet can be found. The universe is theirs. He scans the board and tries to anticipate Sylvia's next move. Soft footsteps sound behind him. The year-captain turns. Noelle, the ship's communicator, is approaching the lounge. She is a slim sightless girl with long dark hair, and she customarily walks the corridors unaided: no sensors for her, not even a cane. Occasionally she stumbles, but usually her balance is excellent and her sense of the location of obstacles is superb. It is a kind of arrogance for the blind to shun assistance, perhaps. But also it is a kind of desperate poetry.

As she comes up to him she says, "Good morning, year-captain."

Noelle is infallible in making such identifications. She claims to be able to distinguish members of the expedition by the tiny characteristic sounds they make: their patterns of breathing, their coughs, the rustling of their clothing. Among the others there is some scepticism about this. Many aboard the ship believe that Noelle is reading their minds. She does not deny that she possesses the power of telepathy; but she insists that the only mind to which she has direct access is that of her twin sister Yvonne, far away on Earth.

He turns to her. His eyes meet hers: an automatic act, a habit. Hers, dark and clear, stare disconcertingly through his forehead. He says, "I'll have a report for you to transmit in about two hours."

"I'm ready whenever." She smiles faintly. She listens a moment to the clacking of the Go stones. "Three games being played?" she asks.

"Yes."

"How strange that the game hasn't begun to lose its hold on them by this time."

"Its grip is powerful," the year-captain says.

"It must be. How good it is to be able to give yourself so completely to a game."

"I wonder. Playing Go consumes a great deal of valuable time."

"Time?" Noelle laughs. "What is there to do with time, except to consume it?" After a moment she says, "Is it a difficult game?"

"The rules are simple enough. The application of the rules is another matter entirely. It's a deeper and more subtle game than chess, I think."

Her blank eyes wander across his face and suddenly lock into his. "How long would it take for me to learn how to play?"

"You?"

"Why not? I also need amusement, year-captain."

"The board has hundreds of intersections. Moves may be made at any of them. The patterns formed are complex and constantly changing. Someone who is unable to see—"

"My memory is excellent," Noelle says. "I can visualize the board and make the necessary corrections as play proceeds. You need only tell me where you put down your stones. And guide my hand, I suppose, when I make my moves."

"I doubt that it'll work, Noelle."

"Will you teach me anyway?"

•

The ship is sleek, tapered, graceful: a silver bullet streaking across the universe at a velocity that has at this point come to exceed a million kilometers per second. No. In fact the ship is no bullet at all, but rather something squat and awkward, as clumsy as any ordinary spacegoing vessel, with an elaborate spidery superstructure of extensor arms and antennas and observation booms and other externals. Yet because of its incredible speed the year-captain persists in thinking of it as sleek and tapered and graceful. It carries him without friction through the vast empty gray cloak of nospace at a velocity greater than that of light. He knows better, but he is unable to shake that streamlined image from his mind.

Already the expedition is sixteen light-years from Earth. That isn't an easy thing for him to grasp. He feels the force of it, but not the true meaning. He can tell himself, *Already we are sixteen kilometers from home,* and understand that readily enough. *Already we are sixteen hundred kilometers from home*—yes, he can understand that too. What about *Already we are sixteen million kilometers from home?* That much strains comprehension—a gulf, a gulf, a terrible empty dark gulf—but he thinks he is able to understand even so great a distance, after a fashion. Sixteen light-years, though? How can he explain that to himself? Brilliant stars flank the tube of nospace through which the ship now travels, and he knows that his gray-flecked beard will have turned entirely white before the light of those stars glitters in the night sky of Earth. Yet only a few months have elapsed since the departure of the expedition. How miraculous it is, he thinks, to have come so far so swiftly.

Even so, there is a greater miracle. He will ask Noelle to relay a message to Earth an hour after lunch, and he knows that he will have an acknowledgment from Control Central in Brazil before dinner. That seems an even greater miracle to him.

•

Her cabin is neat, austere, underfurnished: no paintings, no light-sculptures, nothing to please the visual sense, only a few small sleek bronze statuettes, a smooth oval slab of green stone, and some objects evidently chosen for their rich textures—a strip of nubby fabric stretched across a frame, a sea-urchin's stony test, a collection of rough sandstone chunks. Everything is meticulously arranged. Does someone help her keep the place tidy? She moves serenely from point to point in the little room, never in danger of a collision; her confidence of motion is unnerving to the year-captain, who sits patiently waiting for her to settle down. She is pale, precisely groomed, her dark hair drawn tightly back from her forehead and held by an intricate ivory clasp. Her lips are full, her nose is rounded. She wears a soft flowing robe. Her body is attractive: he has seen her in the baths and knows of her high full breasts, her ample curving hips, her creamy perfect skin. Yet so far as he has heard she has had no shipboard liaisons. Is it because she is blind? Perhaps one tends not to think of a blind person as a potential sexual partner. Why should that be? Maybe because one hesitates to take advantage of a blind person in a sexual encounter, he suggests, and immediately catches himself up, startled, wondering why he should think of any sort of sexual relationship as "taking advantage." Well, then, possibly compassion for her handicap gets in the way of erotic feeling; pity too easily becomes patronizing and kills desire. He rejects that theory: glib, implausible. Could it be that people fear to approach her, suspecting that she is able to read their inmost thoughts? She has repeatedly denied any ability to enter minds other than her sister's. Besides, if you have nothing to hide, why be put off by her telepathy? No, it must be something else, and now he thinks he has isolated it: that Noelle is so self-contained, so serene, so much wrapped up in her blindness and her mind-power and her unfathomable communion with her distant sister, that no one dares to breach the crystalline barricades that guard her inner self. She is unapproached because she seems unapproachable; her strange perfection of soul sequesters her, keeping others at a distance the way extraordinary physical beauty can sometimes keep people at a distance. She does not arouse desire because she does not seem at all human. She gleams. She is a flawless machine, an integral part of the ship.

He unfolds the text of today's report to Earth. "Not that there's anything new to tell them," he says, "but I suppose we have to file the daily communiqué all the same."

"It would be cruel if we didn't. We mean so much to them."

"I wonder."

"Oh, yes. Yvonne says they take our messages from her as fast as they come in, and send them out on every channel. Word from us is terribly important to them."

"As a diversion, nothing more. As the latest curiosity. Intrepid explorers venturing into the uncharted wilds of interstellar nospace." His voice sounds harsh to him, his rhythms of speech coarse and blurting. His words surprise him. He had not known he felt this way about Earth. Still, he goes on. "That's all we represent: a novelty, vicarious adventure, a moment of amusement."

"Do you mean that? It sounds so awfully cynical."

He shrugs. "Another six months and they'll be completely bored with us and our communiqués. Perhaps sooner than that. A year and they'll have forgotten us."

She says, "I don't see you as a cynical man. Yet you often say such"—she falters—"such—"

"Such blunt things? I'm a realist, I guess. Is that the same as a cynic?"

"Don't try to label yourself, year-captain."

"I only try to look at things realistically."

"You don't know what real is. You don't know what you are, year-captain."

The conversation is suddenly out of control: much too charged, much too intimate. She has never spoken like this before. It is as if there is a malign electricity in the air, a prickly field that distorts their normal selves, making them unnaturally tense and aggressive. He feels panic. If he disturbs the delicate balance of Noelle's consciousness, will she still be able to make contact with far-off Yvonne?

He is unable to prevent himself from parrying: "Do *you* know what I am, then?"

She tells him, "You're a man in search of himself. That's why you volunteered to come all the way out here."

"And why did you volunteer to come all the way out here, Noelle?" he asks helplessly.

She lets the lids slide slowly down over her unseeing eyes and offers no reply. He tries to salvage things a bit by saying more calmly into her tense silence, "Never mind. I didn't intend to upset you. Shall we transmit the report?"

"Wait."

"All right."

She appears to be collecting herself. After a moment she says less edgily, "How do you think they see us at home? As ordinary human beings doing an unusual job or as superhuman creatures engaged in an epic voyage?"

"Right now, as superhuman creatures, epic voyage."

"And later we'll become more ordinary in their eyes?"

"Later we'll become nothing to them. They'll forget us."

"How sad." Her tone tingles with a grace note of irony. She may be laughing at him. "And you, year-captain? Do you picture yourself as ordinary or as superhuman?"

"Something in between. Rather more than ordinary, but no demigod."

"I regard myself as quite ordinary except in two respects," she says sweetly.

"One is your telepathic communication with your sister and the other—" He hesitates, mysteriously uncomfortable at naming it. "The other is your blindness."

"Of course," she says. Smiles. Radiantly. "Shall we do the report now?"

"Have you made contact with Yvonne?"

"Yes. She's waiting."

"Very well, then." Glancing at his notes, he begins slowly to read: "Ship-day 117. Velocity…Apparent location…"

She naps after every transmission. They exhaust her. She was beginning to fade even before he reached the end of today's message; now, as he steps into the corridor, he knows she will be asleep before he closes the door. He leaves, frowning, troubled by the odd outburst of tension between them and by his mysterious attack of "realism." By what right does he say Earth will grow jaded with the voyagers? All during the years of preparation for his first interstellar journey the public excitement never flagged, indeed spurred the voyagers themselves on at times when their interminable training routines threatened *them* with boredom. Earth's messages, relayed by Yvonne to Noelle, vibrate with eager queries; the curiosity of the home-world has been overwhelming since the start. Tell us, tell us, tell us!

But there is so little to tell, really, except in that one transcendental area where there is so much. And how, really, can any of that be told?

How can *this*—

He pauses by the viewplate in the main transit corridor, a rectangular window a dozen meters long that gives direct access to the external environment. The pearl-gray emptiness of nospace, dense and pervasive, presses tight against the skin of the ship. During the training period the members of the expedition had been warned to anticipate nothing in the way of outside inputs as they crossed the galaxy; they would be shuttling through a void of infinite length, a matter-free tube, and there would be no sights to entertain them, no backdrop of remote nebulae, no glittering stars, no stray meteors, not so much as a pair of colliding atoms yielding the tiniest momentary spark, only an external sameness, like a blank wall. They had been taught methods of coping with that: turn inward, demand no delights from the universe beyond the ship, make the ship itself your universe. And yet, and yet, how misguided those warnings had been! Nospace was not a wall but rather a window. It was impossible for those on Earth to understand what revelations lay in that seeming emptiness. The year-captain, head throbbing from his encounter with Noelle, now revels in his keenest pleasure. A glance at the viewplate reveals that place where the immanent becomes the transcendent: the year-captain sees once again the infinite reverberating waves of energy that sweep through the grayness. What lies beyond the ship is neither a blank wall nor an empty tube; it is a stunning profusion of interlocking energy fields, linking everything to everything; it is music that also is light, it is light that also is music, and those aboard the ship are sentient particles wholly enmeshed in that vast all-engulfing reverberation, that radiant song of gladness that is the universe. The voyagers journey joyously toward the center of all things, giving themselves gladly into the care of cosmic forces far surpassing human control and understanding. He presses his hands against the cool glass. He puts his face close to it. *What do I see, what do I feel, what am I experiencing?* It is instant revelation, every time. It is almost, *almost!*—the sought after oneness. Barriers remain, but yet he is aware of an altered sense of space and time, a knowledge of the awesome something that lurks in the vacancies between the spokes of the cosmos, something majestic and powerful; he knows that that something is part of himself, and he is part of it. When he stands at the viewplate he yearns to open the ship's great hatch and tumble into the eternal. But not yet, not yet. Barriers remain. The voyage has only begun. They grow closer every day to that which they seek, but the voyage has only begun.

How could we convey any of this to those who remain behind? How could we make them understand?

Not with words. Never with words.

Let them come out here and see for themselves—

He smiles. He trembles and does a little shivering wriggle of delight. He turns away from the viewplate, drained, ecstatic.

Noelle lies in uneasy dreams. She is aboard a ship, an archaic three-master struggling in an icy sea. The rigging sparkles with fierce icicles, which now and again snap free in the cruel gales and smash with little tinkling sounds against the deck. The deck wears a slippery shiny coating of thin hard ice, and footing is treacherous. Great eroded bergs heave wildly in the gray water, rising, slapping the waves, subsiding. If one of those bergs hits the hull, the ship will sink. So far they have been lucky about that, but now a more subtle menace is upon them. The sea is freezing over. It congeals, coagulates, becomes a viscous fluid, surging sluggishly. Broad glossy plaques toss on the waves: new ice floes, colliding, grinding, churning; the floes are at war, destroying one another's edges, but some are making treaties, uniting to form a single implacable shield. When the sea freezes altogether the ship will be crushed. And now it is freezing. The ship can barely make headway. The sails belly out uselessly, straining at their lines. The wind makes a lyre out of the rigging as the ice-coated ropes twang and sing. The hull creaks like an old man; the grip of the ice is heavy. The timbers are yielding. The end is near. They will all perish. They will all perish. Noelle emerges from her cabin, goes above, seizes the railing, sways, prays, wonders when the wind's fist will punch through the stiff frozen canvas of the sails. Nothing can save them. But now! yes, yes! A glow overhead! Yvonne! Yvonne! She comes. She hovers like a goddess in the black star-pocked sky. Soft golden light streams from her. She is smiling, and her smile thaws the sea. The ice relents. The air grows gentle. The ship is freed. It sails on, unhindered, toward the perfumed tropics.

In late afternoon Noelle drifts silently, wraithlike, into the control room where the year-captain is at work; she looks so weary and drawn that she is almost translucent; she seems unusually vulnerable, as though a harsh sound would shatter her. She has brought the year-captain Earth's answer to this morning's transmission. He takes from her the small, clear data-cube on which she has recorded her latest conversation with her sister. As Yvonne speaks in her mind, Noelle repeats the message aloud into a sensor disc, and it is captured on the cube. He wonders why she looks so wan. "Is anything wrong?" he asks. She tells him that she has had some difficulty receiving the message; the signal from Earth was strangely fuzzy. She is perturbed by that.

"It was like static," she says.

"Mental static?"

She is puzzled. Yvonne's tone is always pure, crystalline, wholly undistorted. Noelle has never had an experience like this before.

"Perhaps you were tired," he suggests. "Or maybe she was."

He fits the cube into the playback slot, and Noelle's voice comes from the speakers. She sounds unfamiliar, strained and ill at ease; she fumbles words frequently and often asks Yvonne to repeat. The message, what he can make out of it, is the usual cheery stuff, predigested news from the home-world—politics, sports, the planetary weather, word of the arts and sciences, special greetings for three or four members of the expedition, expressions of general good wishes—everything light, shallow, amiable. The static disturbs him. What if the telepathic link should fail? What if they were to lose contact with Earth altogether? He asks himself why that should trouble him so. The ship is self-sufficient; it needs no guidance from Earth in order to function properly, nor do the voyagers really have to have daily information about events on the mother planet. Then why care if silence descends? Why not accept the fact that they are no longer earthbound in any way, that they have become virtually a new species as they leap, faster than light, outward into the stars? No. He cares. The link matters. He decides that it has to do with what they were experiencing in relation to the intense throbbing grayness outside, that interchange of energies, that growing sense of universal connection. They are making discoveries every day, not astronomical but—well, spiritual—and, the year-captain thinks, what a pity if none of this can ever be communicated to those who have remained behind. We must keep the link open.

"Maybe," he says, "we ought to let you and Yvonne rest for a few days."

They look upon me as some sort of nun because I'm blind and special. I hate that, but there's nothing I can do to change it. I am what they think I am. I lie awake imagining men touching my body. The year-captain stands over me. I see his face clearly, the skin flushed and sweaty, the eyes gleaming. He strokes my breasts. He puts his lips to my lips. Suddenly, terribly, he embraces me and I scream. Why do I scream?

"You promised to teach me how to play," she says, pouting a little. They are in the ship's lounge. Four games are under way: Elliot with Sylvia, Roy and Paco, David and Heinz, Mike and Bruce. Her pout fascinates him: such a little-girl gesture, so charming, so human. She seems to be in much better shape today, even though there was trouble again in the transmission, Yvonne complaining that the morning report was coming through indistinctly and noisily. Noelle has decided that the noise is some sort of local phenomenon, something like a sunspot effect, and will vanish once they are far enough from this sector of nospace. He is not as sure of this as she is, but she probably has a better understanding of such things than he. "Teach me, year-captain," she prods. "I really do want to know how to play. Have faith in me."

"All right," he says. The game may prove valuable to her, a relaxing pastime, a timely distraction. "This is the board. It has nineteen horizontal lines, nineteen vertical lines. The stones are played on the intersections of these lines, not on the squares that they form." He takes her hand and traces, with the tip of her fingers, the pattern of intersecting lines. They have been printed with a thick ink, easily discernible against the flatness of the board. "These nine dots are called stars," he tells her. "They serve as orientation points." He touches her fingertips to the nine stars. "We give the lines in this direction numbers, from one to nineteen, and we give the lines in the other direction letters, from A to T, leaving out I. Thus we can identify positions on the board. This is B10, this is D18, this is J4, do you follow?" He feels despair. How can she ever commit the board to memory? But she looks untroubled as she runs her hand along the edges of the board, murmuring, "A, B, C, D..."

The other games have halted. Everyone in the lounge is watching them. He guides her hand toward the two trays of stones, the white and the black, and shows her the traditional way of picking up a stone between two fingers and clapping it down against the board. "The stronger player uses the white stones," he says. "Black always moves first. The players take turns placing stones, one at a time, on any unoccupied intersection. Once a stone is placed it is never moved unless it is captured, when it is removed at once from the board."

"And the purpose of the game?" she asks.

"To control the largest possible area with the smallest possible number of stones. You build walls. The score is reckoned by counting the number of vacant intersections within your walls, plus the number of prisoners you have taken." Methodically he explains the technique of play to her: the placing of stones, the seizure of territory, the capture of opposing stones. He illustrates by setting up simulated situations on the board, calling out the location of each stone as he places it: "Black holds P12, Q12, R12, S12, T12, and also P11, P10, P9, Q8, R8, S8, T8. White holds—" somehow she visualizes the positions; she repeats the patterns after him, and asks questions that show she sees the board clearly in her mind. Within twenty minutes she understands the basic ploys. Several times, in describing maneuvers to her, he gives her an incorrect coordinate—the board, after all, is not marked with numbers and letters, and he misgauges the point occasionally—but each time she corrects him, gently, saying, "N13? Don't you mean N12?"

At length she says, "I think I follow everything now. Would you like to play a game?"

Consider your situation carefully. You are twenty years old, female, sightless. You have never married or even entered into a basic pairing. Your only real human contact is your twin sister, who is like yourself blind and single. Her mind is fully open to yours. Yours is to hers. You and she are two halves of one soul, inexplicably embedded in separate bodies. With her, only with her, do you feel complete. Now you are asked to take part in a voyage to the stars, without her, a voyage that is sure to cut you off from her forever. You are told that if you leave Earth aboard the starship there is no chance that you will ever see your sister again. You are also told that your presence is important to the success of the voyage, for without your help it would take decades or even centuries for news of the starship to reach Earth, but if you are aboard it will be possible to maintain instantaneous communication across any distance. What should you do? Consider. Consider.

You consider. And you volunteer to go, of course. You are needed: how can you refuse? As for your sister, you will naturally lose the opportunity to touch her, to hold her close, to derive direct comfort from her presence. Otherwise you will lose nothing. Never "see" her again? No. You can "see" her just as well, certainly, from a distance of a million light-years as you can from the next room. There can be no doubt of that.

The morning transmission. Noelle, sitting with her back to the year-captain, listens to what he reads her and sends it coursing over a gap of more than sixteen light-years. "Wait," she says. "Yvonne is calling for a repeat. From *'metabolic.'*" He pauses, goes back, reads again: *"Metabolic balances remain normal, although, as earlier reported, some of the older members of the expedition have begun to show trace deficiencies of manganese and potassium. We are taking appropriate corrective steps, and—"* Noelle halts him with a brusque gesture. He waits, and she bends forward, forehead against the table, hands pressed tightly to her temples. "Static again," she says. "It's worse today."

"Are you getting through at all?"

"I'm getting through, yes. But I have to push, to push, to push. And still Yvonne asks for repeats. I don't know what's happening, year-captain."

"The distance—"

"No."

"Better than sixteen light-years."

"No," she says. "We've already demonstrated that distance effects aren't a factor. If there's no falling off of signal after a million kilometres, after one light-year, after ten light-years—no perceptible drop in clarity and accuracy whatever—then there shouldn't be any qualitative diminution suddenly at sixteen light-years. Don't you think I've thought about this?"

"Noelle—"

"Attenuation of signal is one thing, and interference is another. An attenuation curve is a gradual slope. Yvonne and I have had perfect contact from the day we left Earth until just a few days ago. And now—no, year-captain, it can't be attenuation. It has to be some sort of interference. A local effect."

"Yes, like sunspots, I know. But—"

"Let's start again. Yvonne's calling for signal. Go on from '*manganese and potassium.*' "

"—*manganese and potassium. We are taking appropriate corrective steps*—"

Playing Go seems to ease her tension. He has not played in years, and he is rusty at first, but within minutes the old associations return and he finds himself setting up chains of stones with skill. Although he expects her to play poorly, unable to remember the patterns on the board after the first few moves, she proves to have no difficulty keeping the entire array in her mind. Only in one respect has she overestimated herself: for all her precision of coordination, she is unable to place the stones exactly, tending rather to disturb the stones already on the board as she makes her moves. After a little while she admits failure and thenceforth she calls out the plays she desires—M17, Q6, P6, R4, C11—and he places the stones for her. In the beginning he plays unaggressively, assuming that as a novice she will be haphazard and weak, but soon he discovers that she is adroitly expanding and protecting her territory while pressing a sharp attack against his, and he begins to devise more cunning strategies. They play for two hours and he wins by sixteen points, a comfortable margin but nothing to boast about, considering that he is an experienced and adept player and that this is her first game.

The others are sceptical of her instant ability. "Sure she plays well," Heinz mutters. "She's reading your mind, isn't she? She can see the board through your eyes and she knows what you're planning."

"The only mind open to her is her sister's," the year-captain says vehemently.

"How can you be sure she's telling the truth?"

The year-captain scowls. "Play a game with her yourself. You'll see whether it's skill or mind-reading that's at work."

Heinz, looking sullen, agrees. That evening he challenges Noelle; later he comes to the year-captain, abashed. "She plays well. She almost beat me, and she did it fairly."

The year-captain plays a second game with her. She sits almost motionless, eyes closed, lips compressed, offering the coordinates of her moves in a quiet bland monotone, like some sort of game-playing mechanism. She rarely takes long to decide on a move and she makes no blunders that must be retracted. Her capacity to devise game patterns has grown astonishingly; she nearly shuts him off from the center, but he recovers the initiative and manages a narrow victory. Afterward she loses once more to Heinz, but again she displays an increase of ability, and in the evening she defeats Chiang, a respected player. Now she becomes invincible. Undertaking two or three matches every day, she triumphs over Heinz, Sylvia, the year-captain, and Leon; Go has become something immense to her, something much more than a mere game, a simple test of strength; she focuses her energy on the board so intensely that her playing approaches the level of a religious discipline, a kind of meditation. On the fourth day she defeats Roy, the ship's champion, with such economy that everyone is dazzled. Roy can speak of nothing else. He demands a rematch and is defeated again.

Noelle wondered, as the ship was lifting from Earth, whether she really would be able to maintain contact with Yvonne across the vast span of interstellar space. She had nothing but faith to support her belief that the power that joined their minds was wholly unaffected by distance. They had often spoken to each other without difficulty from opposite sides of the planet, yes, but would it be so simple when they were half a galaxy apart? During the early hours of the voyage she and Yvonne kept up a virtually continuous linking, and the signal remained clear and sharp, with no perceptible falling off of reception, as the ship headed outward. Past the orbit of the moon, past the million-kilometer mark, past the orbit of Mars: clear and sharp, clear and sharp. They had passed the first test: clarity of signal was not a quantitative function of distance. But Noelle remained unsure of what would happen once the ship abandoned conventional power and shunted into nospace in order to attain faster-than-light velocity. She would then be in a space apart from Yvonne; in effect she would be in another universe; would she still be able to reach her sister's mind? Tension rose in her as the moment of the shunt approached, for she had no idea what life would be like for her in the absence of Yvonne. To face that dreadful silence, to find herself thrust into such terrible isolation—but it did not happen. They entered nospace and her awareness of Yvonne never flickered. *Here we are, wherever we are,* she said, and moments later came Yvonne's response, a cheery greeting from the old continuum. Clear and sharp, clear and sharp. Nor did the signal grow more tenuous in the weeks that followed. Clear and sharp, clear and sharp, until the static began.

The year-captain visualizes the contact between the two sisters as an arrow whistling from star to star, as fire speeding through a shining tube, as a river or pure force coursing down a celestial wave guide. He sees the joining of those two minds as a stream of pure light binding the moving ship to the far-off mother world. Sometimes he dreams of Yvonne and Noelle, Noelle and Yvonne, and the glowing bond that stretches between the sisters gives off so brilliant a radiance that he stirs and moans and presses his forehead into the pillow.

The interference grows worse. Neither Noelle nor Yvonne can explain what is happening; Noelle clings without conviction to her sunspot analogy. They still manage to make contact twice daily, but it is increasingly a strain on the sisters' resources, for every sentence must be repeated two or three times, and whole blocks of words now do not get through at all. Noelle has become thin and haggard. Go refreshes her, or at least diverts her from this failing of her powers. She has become a master of the game, awarding even Roy a two-stone handicap; although she occasionally loses, her play is always distinguished, extraordinarily original in its sweep and design. When she is not playing she tends to be remote and aloof. She is in all respects a more elusive person than she was before the onset of this communications crisis.

Noelle dreams that her blindness has been taken from her. Sudden light surrounds her, and she opens her eyes, sits up, looks about in awe and wonder, saying to herself, This is a table, this is a chair, this is how my statuettes look, this is what my sea urchin is like. She is amazed by the beauty of everything in her room. She rises, goes forward, stumbling at first, groping, then magically gaining poise and balance, learning how to walk in this new way, judging the positions of things not by echoes and air currents but rather by using her eyes. Information floods her. She moves about the ship, discovering the faces of her ship-mates. You are Roy, you are Sylvia, you are Heinz, you are the year-captain. They look, surprisingly, very much as she had imagined them: Roy fleshy and red-faced, Sylvia fragile, the year-captain lean and fierce, Heinz like this, Elliot like that, everyone matching expectations. Everyone beautiful. She goes to the window of which the others all talk, and looks out into the famous grayness. Yes, yes, it is as they say it is: a cosmos of wonders, a miracle of complex pulsating tones, level after level of incandescent reverberation sweeping outward toward the rim of the boundless universe. For an hour she stands before that dense burst of rippling energies, giving herself to it and taking it into herself, and then, and then, just as the ultimate moment of illumination is coming over her, she realizes that something is wrong. Yvonne is not with her. She reaches out and does not reach Yvonne. She has somehow traded her power for the gift of sight. Yvonne? Yvonne? All is still. Where is Yvonne? Yvonne is not with her. This is only a dream, Noelle tells herself, and I will soon awaken. But she cannot awaken. In terror she cries out. "It's all right," Yvonne whispers. "I'm here, love, I'm here, I'm here, just as always." Yes. Noelle feels the closeness. Trembling, she embraces her sister. Looks at her. I can see, Yvonne! I can see! Noelle realizes that in her first rapture she quite forgot to look at herself, though she rushed about looking at everything else. Mirrors have never been part of her world. She looks at Yvonne, which is like looking at herself, and Yvonne is beautiful, her hair dark and silken and lustrous, her face smooth and pale, her features fine of outline, her eyes—her blind eyes—alive and sparkling. Noelle tells Yvonne how beautiful she is, and Yvonne nods, and they laugh and hold one another close, and they begin to weep with pleasure and love, and Noelle awakens, and the world is dark around her.

"I have the new communiqué to send," the year-captain says wearily. "Do you feel like trying again?"

"Of course I do." She gives him a ferocious smile. "Don't even hint at giving up, year-captain. There absolutely has to be some way around this interference."

"Absolutely," he says. He rustles his papers restlessly. "Okay, Noelle. Let's go. Shipday 128. Velocity…"

"Give me another moment to get ready," Noelle says.

He pauses. She closes her eyes and begins to enter the transmitting state. She is conscious, as ever, of Yvonne's presence. Even when no specific information is flowing between them, there is perpetual low-level contact, there is the sense that the other is near, that warm proprioceptive awareness such as one has of one's own arm or leg or lip. But between that impalpable subliminal contact and the actual transmission of specific content lie several key steps. Yvonne and Noelle are human biopsychic resonators constituting a long-range communications network; there is a tuning procedure for them as for any transmitters and receivers. Noelle opens herself to the radiant energy spectrum, vibratory, pulsating, that will carry her message to her earthbound sister. As the transmitting circuit in this interchange she must be the one to attain maximum energy flow. Quickly, intuitively, she activates her own energy centers, the one in the spine, the one in the solar plexus, the one at the top of the skull; energy pours from her and instantaneously spans the galaxy. But today there is an odd and troublesome splashback effect: monitoring the circuit, she is immediately aware that the signal has failed to reach Yvonne. Yvonne is there, Yvonne is tuned and expectant, yet something is jamming the channel and nothing gets through, not a single syllable. "The interference is worse than ever," she tells the year-captain. "I feel as if I could put my hand out and touch Yvonne. But she's not reading me and nothing's coming back from her." With a little shake of her shoulders Noelle alters the sending frequency; she feels a corresponding adjustment at Yvonne's end of the connection; but again they are thwarted, again there is total blockage. Her signal is going forth and is being soaked up by—what? How can such a thing happen?

Now she makes a determined effort to boost the output of the system. She addresses herself to the neural center in her spine, exciting its energies, using them to drive the next center to a more intense vibrational tone, harnessing that to push the highest center of all to its greatest harmonic capacity. Up and down the energy bands she roves. Nothing. Nothing. She shivers; she huddles; she is physically emptied by the strain. "I can't get through," she murmurs. "She's there, I can feel her there, I know she's working to read me. But I can't transmit any sort of intelligible coherent message."

*

Almost seventeen light-years from Earth and the only communication channel is blocked. The year-captain is overwhelmed by frosty terrors. The ship, the self-sufficient autonomous ship, has become a mere gnat blowing in a hurricane. The voyagers hurtle blindly into the depths of an unknown universe, alone, alone, alone. He was so smug about not needing any link to Earth, but now that the link is gone he shivers and cowers. Everything has been made new. There are no rules. Human beings have never been this far from home. He presses himself against the viewplate and the famous grayness just beyond, swirling and eddying, mocks him with its immensity. Leap into me, it calls, leap, leap, leap, lose yourself in me, drown in me.

Behind him: the sound of soft footsteps. Noelle. She touches his hunched, knotted shoulders. "It's all right," she whispers. "You're overreacting. Don't make such a tragedy out of it." But it is. Her tragedy, more than anyone's, hers and Yvonne's. But also his, theirs, everybody's. Cut off. Lost in a foggy silence.

Down in the lounge people are singing. Boisterous voices, Elliot, Chiang, Leon.

Travelin' Dan was a spacefarin' man
He jumped in the nospace tube.

The year-captain whirls, seizes Noelle, pulls her against him. Feels her trembling. Comforts her, where a moment before she had been comforting him. "Yes, yes, yes, yes," he murmurs. With his arm around her shoulders he turns, so that both of them are facing the viewplate. As if she could see. Nospace dances and churns an inch from his nose. He feels a hot wind blowing through the ship, the khamsin, the sirocco, the simoom, the leveche, a sultry wind, a killing wind coming out of the grey strangeness, and he forces himself not to fear that wind. It is a wind of life, he tells himself, a wind of joy, a cool sweet wind, the mistral, the tramontana. Why should he think there is anything to fear in the realm beyond the viewplate? How beautiful it is out there how ecstatically beautiful! How sad that we can never tell anyone about it, now, except one another. A strange peace unexpectedly descends on him. Everything is going to be all right, he insists. No harm will come of what has happened. And perhaps some good. And perhaps some good. Benefits lurk in the darkest places.

She plays Go obsessively, beating everyone. She seems to live in the lounge twenty hours a day. Sometimes she takes on two opponents at once—an incredible feat, considering that she must hold the constantly changing intricacies of both boards in her memory—and defeats them both: two days after losing verbal-level contact with Yvonne, she simultaneously triumphs over Roy and Heinz before an audience of thirty. She looks animated and buoyant; the sorrow she must feel over the snapping of the link she takes care to conceal. She expresses it, the others suspect, only by her manic Go-playing. The year-captain is one of her most frequent adversaries, taking his turn at the board in the time he would have devoted to composing and dictating the communiqués for Earth. He had thought Go was over for him years ago, but he too is playing obsessively now, building walls and the unassailable fortresses known as eyes. There is reassurance in the rhythmic clacking march of the black and white stones. Noelle wins every game against him. She covers the board with eyes.

Who can explain the interference? No one believes that the problem is a function of anything so obvious as distance. Noelle has been quite convincing on that score: a signal that propagates perfectly for the first sixteen light-years of a journey ought not suddenly to deteriorate. There should at least have been prior sign of attenuation, and there was no attenuation, only noise interfering with and ultimately destroying the signal. Some force is intervening between the sisters. But what can it be? The idea that it is some physical effect analogous to sunspot static, that it is the product of radiation emitted by some giant star in whose vicinity they have lately been traveling, must in the end be rejected. There is no energy interface between realspace and nospace, no opportunity for any kind of electromagnetic intrusion. That much had been amply demonstrated long before any manned voyages were undertaken. The nospace tube is an impermeable wall. Nothing that has mass or charge can leap the barrier between the universe of accepted phenomena and the cocoon of nothingness that the ship's drive mechanism has woven about them, nor can a photon get across, nor even a slippery neutrino.

Many speculations excite the voyagers. The one force that can cross the barrier, Roy points out, is thought: intangible, unmeasurable, limitless. What if the sector of realspace corresponding to this region of the nospace tube is inhabited by beings of powerful telepathic capacity whose transmissions, flooding out over a sphere with a radius of many light-years, are able to cross the barrier just as readily as those of Yvonne? The alien mental emanations, Roy supposes, are smothering the signal from Earth.

Heinz extends this theory into a different possibility: that the interference is caused by denizens of nospace. There is a seeming paradox in this, since it has been shown mathematically that the nospace tube must be wholly matter-free except for the ship that travels through it; otherwise a body moving at speeds faster than light would generate destructive resonances as its mass exceeds infinity. But perhaps the equations are imperfectly understood. Heinz imagines giant incorporeal beings as big as asteroids, as big as planets, masses of pure energy or even pure mental force that drift freely through the tube. These beings may be sources of biopsychic transmissions that disrupt the Yvonne-Noelle circuit, or maybe they are actually feeding on the sisters' mental output, Heinz postulates. "Angels," he calls them. It is an implausible but striking concept that fascinates everyone for several days. Whether the "angels" live within the tube as proposed by Heinz, or on some world just outside it as pictured by Roy, is unimportant at the moment; the consensus aboard the ship is that the interference is the work of an alien intelligence, and that arouses wonder in all.

What to do? Leon, inclining toward Roy's hypothesis, moves that they leave nospace immediately and seek the world or worlds where the "angels" dwell. The year-captain objects, noting that the plan of the voyage obliges them to reach a distance of one hundred light-years from Earth before they begin their quest for habitable planets. Roy and Leon argue that the plan is merely a guide, arbitrarily conceived, and not received scriptural writ; they are free to depart from it if some pressing reason presents itself. Heinz, supporting the year-captain, remarks that there is no need actually to leave nospace regardless of the source of the alien transmissions; if the thoughts of these creatures can come in from beyond the tube, then Noelle's thoughts can surely go outward through the tube to them, and contact can be established without the need of deviating from the plan. After all, if the interference is the work of beings sharing the tube with them, and the voyagers seek them in vain outside the tube, it may be impossible to find them again once the ship returns to nospace. This approach seems reasonable, and the question is put to Noelle: Can you attempt to open a dialogue with these beings?

She laughs. "I make no guarantees. I've never tried to talk to angels before. But I'll try, my friends, I'll try."

<table>
<tr><th>Black
(Year-Captain)</th><th>White
(Noelle)</th><td rowspan="16">Black remains on offensive through Move 89. White then breaks through weak north stones and encloses a major center territory. Black is unable to reply adequately and White runs a chain of stones along the 19th line. At Move 141 Black launches a hopeless attack, easily crushed by White, inside White's territory. Game ends at Move 196 after Black is faced with the cat-in-the-basket trap, by which it will lose a large group in the process of capturing one stone. Score: White 81, Black 62.</td></tr>
<tr><td>R16</td><td>Q4</td></tr>
<tr><td>C4</td><td>E3</td></tr>
<tr><td>D17</td><td>D15</td></tr>
<tr><td>E16</td><td>K17</td></tr>
<tr><td>O17</td><td>E15</td></tr>
<tr><td>H17</td><td>M17</td></tr>
<tr><td>R6</td><td>Q6</td></tr>
<tr><td>Q7</td><td>P6</td></tr>
<tr><td>R5</td><td>R4</td></tr>
<tr><td>D6</td><td>C11</td></tr>
<tr><td>K3</td><td>H3</td></tr>
<tr><td>N4</td><td>O4</td></tr>
<tr><td>N3</td><td>O3</td></tr>
<tr><td>R10</td><td>O8</td></tr>
<tr><td>O15...</td><td>M15...</td></tr>
</table>

She has never done anything like this before. It seems almost an act of infidelity, this opening of her mind to something or someone who is not Yvonne. But it must be done. She extends a tenuous tendril of thought that probes like a rivulet of quicksilver. Through the wall of the ship, into the surrounding grayness, upward, outward, toward, toward—

—angels?—

Angels. Oh. Brightness. Strength. Magnetism. Yes. Awareness now of a fierce roiling mass of concentrated energy close by. A mass in motion, laying a terrible stress on the fabric of the cosmos: the angel has angular momentum. It tumbles ponderously on its colossal axis. Who would have thought an angel could be so huge? Noelle is oppressed by the shifting weight of it as it makes its slow heavy axial swing. She moves closer. Oh. She is dazzled. *Too much light! Too much power!* She draws back, overwhelmed by the intensity of the other being's output. Such a mighty mind: she feels dwarfed. If she touches it with her mind she will be destroyed. She must step down the aperture, establish some kind of transformer to shield herself against the full blast of power that comes from it. It requires time and discipline. She works steadily, making adjustments, mastering new techniques, discovering capacities she had not known she possessed. And now. Yes. Try again. Slowly, slowly, slowly, with utmost care. Outward goes the tendril.

Yes.

Approaching the angel.

See? Here am I. Noelle. Noelle. Noelle. I come to you in love and fear. Touch me lightly. Just touch me—

Just a touch—

Touch—

Oh. Oh.

I see you. The light—eye of crystal—fountains of lava—oh, the light—your light—I see—I see—

Oh, like a god—

—and Semele wished to behold Zeus in all his brightness, and Zeus would have discouraged her, but Semele insisted and Zeus who loved her could not refuse her; so Zeus came upon her in full majesty and Semele was consumed by his glory, so that only the ashes of her remained, but the son she had conceived by Zeus, the boy Dionysus, was not destroyed, and Zeus saved Dionysus and took him away sealed in his thigh, bringing him forth afterward and bestowing godhood upon him—

—Oh God I am Semele—

She withdraws again. Rests, regroups her powers. The force of this being is frightening. But there are ways of insulating herself against destruction, of letting the overflow of energy dissipate itself. She will try once more. She knows she stands at the brink of wonders. Now. Now. The questing mind reaches forth.

I am Noelle. I come to you in love, angel.

Contact.

The universe is burning. Bursts of wild silver light streak across the metal dome of the sky. Words turn to ash. Walls smolder and burst into flames. There is contact. A dancing solar flare—a stream of liquid fire—a flood tide of brilliant radiance, irresistible, unendurable, running into her, sweeping over her, penetrating her. Light everywhere.

—*Semele.*

The angel smiles and she quakes. *Open to me,* cries the vast tolling voice, and she opens and the force enters fully, sweeping through her.

optic chiasma

thalamus

Sylvian fissure

hypothalamus

medulla
oblongata

limbic system

reticular
system

pons varolii

corpus
callosum

cingulate
sulcus

cuneas

orbital gyri

cingulate
gyrus

caudate
nucleus

—
cerebrum!
—

claustrum

operculum

putamen

fornix

chloroid
glomus

medial
lemniscus

—MESEN-
CEPHALON!
—

dura mater

dural sinus

arachnoid
granulation

subarachnoid
space

pia mater

cerebellum

cerebellum

cerebellum

She has been in a coma for days, wandering in delirium. Troubled, fearful, the year-captain keeps a somber vigil at her bedside. Sometimes she seems to rise toward consciousness; intelligible words, even whole sentences, bubble dreamily from her lips. She talks of light, of a brilliant unbearable white glow, of arcs of energy, of intense solar eruptions. A star holds me, she mutters. She tells him that she has been conversing with a star. How poetic, the year-captain thinks: what a lovely metaphor. Conversing with a star. But where is she, what is happening to her? Her face is flushed; her eyes move about rapidly, darting like trapped fish beneath her closed lids, Mind to mind, she whispers, the star and I, mind to mind. She begins to hum—an edgy whining sound, climbing almost toward inaudibility, a high-frequency keening. It pains him to hear it: hard aural radiation. Then she is silent.

Her body goes rigid. A convulsion of some sort? No. She is awakening. He sees lightning bolts of perception flashing through her quivering musculature; the galvanized frog, twitching at the end of its leads. Her eyelids tremble. She makes a little moaning noise.

She looks up at him.

The year-captain says gently, "Your eyes are open. I think you can see me now, Noelle. Your eyes are tracking me, aren't they?"

"I can see you, yes." Her voice is hesitant, faltering, strange for a moment, a foreign voice, but then it becomes more like its usual self as she asks, "How long was I away?"

"Eight ship-days. We were worried."

"You look exactly as I thought you would," she says. "Your face is hard. But not a dark face. Not a hostile face."

"Do you want to talk about where you went, Noelle?"

She smiles. "I talked with the…angel."

"Angel?"

"Not really an angel, year-captain. Not a physical being, either, not any kind of alien species. More like the energy creatures Heinz was discussing. But bigger. Bigger. I don't know what it was, year-captain."

"You told me you were talking with a star."

"—a star!"

"In your delirium. That's what you said."

Her eyes blaze with excitement. "A star! Yes! Yes, year-captain! I think I was, yes!"

"But what does that mean: talking to a star?"

She laughs. "It means talking to a star, year-captain. A great ball of fiery gas, year-captain, and it has a mind, it has a consciousness. I think that's what it was. I'm sure now. I'm sure!"

"But how can a—"

The light goes abruptly from her eyes. She is traveling again; she is no longer with him. He waits beside her bed. An hour, two hours, half a day. What bizarre realm has she penetrated? Her breathing is a distant, impersonal drone. So far away from him now, so remote from any place he comprehends. At last her eyelids flicker. She looks up. Her face seems transfigured. To the year-captain she still appears to be partly in that other world beyond the ship. "Yes," she says. "Not an angel, year-captain. A sun. A living intelligent sun." Her eyes are radiant. "A sun, a star, a sun," she murmurs. "I touched the consciousness of a sun. Do you believe that, year-captain? I found a network of stars that live, that think, that have minds, that have souls. That communicate. The whole universe is alive."

"A star," he says dully. "The stars have minds."

"Yes."

"All of them? Our own sun too?"

"All of them. We came to the place in the galaxy where this star lives, and it was broadcasting on my wavelength, and its output began overriding my link with Yvonne. That was the interference, year-captain. The big star broadcasting."

This conversation has taken on for him the texture of a dream. He says quietly, "Why didn't Earth's sun override you and Yvonne when you were on Earth?"

She shrugs. "It isn't old enough. It takes—I don't know, billions of years—until they're mature, until they can transmit. Our sun isn't old enough, year-captain. None of the stars close to Earth is old enough. But out here—"

"Are you in contact with it now?"

"Yes. With it and with many others. And with Yvonne."

"Yvonne too?"

"She's back in the link with me. She's in the circuit." Noelle pauses. "I can bring others into the circuit. I could bring you in, year-captain."

"Me?"

"You. Would you like to touch a star with your mind?"

"What will happen to me? Will it harm me?"

"Did it harm me, year-captain?"

"Will I still be me afterward?"

"Am I still me, year-captain?"

"I'm afraid."

"Open to me. Try. See what happens."

"I'm afraid."

"Touch a star, year-captain."

He puts his hand on hers. "Go ahead," he says, and his soul becomes a solarium.

Afterward, with the solar pulsations still reverberating in the mirrors of his mind, with blue-white sparks leaping in his synapses, he says, "What about the others?"

"I'll bring them in too."

He feels a flicker of momentary resentment. He does not want to share the illumination. But in the instant that he conceives his resentment, he abolishes it. *Let them in.*

"Take my hand," Noelle says.

They reach out together. One by one they touch the others. Roy. Sylvia. Heinz. Elliot. He feels Noelle surging in tandem with him, feels Yvonne, feels greater presences, luminous, eternal. All are joined. Ship-sister, star-sister: all become one. The year-captain realizes that the days of playing Go have ended. They are one person; they are beyond games.

"And now," Noelle whispers, "now we reach toward Earth. We put our strength into Yvonne, and Yvonne—"

Yvonne draws Earth's seven billion into the network.

The ship hurtles through the nospace tube. Soon the year-captain will initiate the search for a habitable planet. If they discover one, they will settle there. It not, they will go on, and it will not matter at all, and the ship and its seven billion passengers will course onward forever, warmed by the light of the friendly stars.

THIS IS THE ROAD

As this volume demonstrates, many were the anthologies of original science fiction that were spawned in the early 1970s, and not a few of them were edited by me. One format that I particularly liked was the novella trio, in which some writer would propound a theme for stories and three other writers independently worked to that theme at short-novel length. Usually I chose myself as one of the three writers for each trio volume, a process that produced novellas such as "How It Was When the Past Went Away," "Thomas the Proclaimer," and "The Feast of St. Dionysus," all of them reprinted in earlier volumes of this series.

Of all these trio books of mine, I have particular affection for the one called No Mind of Man, *which got put together around a living-room table in Berkeley, California, one day in the spring or summer of 1972. All three authors were present—Terry Carr, Richard A. Lupoff, and me—three old-time science-fiction fans who had gone on to become professional writers, who had known each other well when we all lived in New York City, and now, in the 1970s, had all turned up living in the San Francisco Bay Area. One of us—I don't remember who it was—suggested that the three of us ought to do a novella book together. Someone else—I don't remember which one of us that was, either—proposed that we write stories of transformation. Lupoff—that I do remember—provided the title,* No Mind of Man. *And off we went to write our novellas.*

Dick Lupoff, who had worked for IBM before becoming a freelance writer, did a splendid high-tech story, "The Partridge Project." Terry Carr, whose stories often had soaring, joyous spiritual themes, produced the exhilarating "The Winds at Starmont". And my contribution was the novella reprinted here, which I wrote in January of 1973, and of which I always have been fond, particularly for the elegiac final page or so, beginning with the lines, "These are the times we were meant to live in, and no asking why...."

Close students of my work may find a few familiar passages in the text. Half a dozen years later, when I was writing the novel Lord Valentine's Castle, *I coolly plagiarized myself to the tune of a few hundred words, transforming the wagon journey of Crown and Leaf and Sting and Shadow into an incident involving my band of iterinant jugglers on the giant planet Majipoor. There is otherwise no connection between the two stories: I needed a tense wagon journey through a forest, and I knew where a good one was available, and without any hesitation I lifted a few choice bits from it and put them in place in my new book. But I did get the permission of the original author first, at least. Most plagiarists are not that courteous.*

Leaf, lolling cozily with Shadow on a thick heap of furs in the air wagon's snug passenger castle, heard rain beginning to fall and made a sour face: very likely he would soon have to get up and take charge of driving the wagon, if the rain was the sort of rain he thought it was.

This was the ninth day since the Teeth had begun to lay waste to the eastern provinces. The airwagon, carrying four who were fleeing the invaders' fierce appetites, was floating along Spider Highway somewhere between Theptis and Northman's Rib, heading west, heading west as fast as could be managed. Jumpy little Sting was at the power reins, beaming dream commands to the team of six nightmares that pulled the wagon along; burly Crown was amidwagon, probably plotting vengeance against the Teeth, for that was what Crown did most of the time; that left Leaf and Shadow at their ease, but not for much longer. Listening to the furious drumming of the downpour against the wagon's taut-stretched canopy of big-veined stickskin, Leaf knew that this was no ordinary rain, but rather the dread purple rain that runs the air foul and brings the no-leg spiders out to hunt. Sting would never be able to handle the wagon in a purple rain. What a nuisance, Leaf thought, cuddling close against Shadow's sleek, furry blue form. Before long he heard the worried snorting of the nightmares and felt the wagon jolt and buck: yes, beyond any doubt, purple rain, no-leg spiders. His time of relaxing was just about over.

Not that he objected to doing his fair share of the work. But he had finished his last shift of driving only half an hour ago. He had earned his rest. If Sting was incapable of handling the wagon in this weather—and Shadow too, Shadow could never manage in a purple rain—then Crown ought to take the reins himself. But of course Crown would do no such thing. It was Crown's wagon and he never drove it himself. "I have always had underbreeds to do the driving for me," Crown had said ten days ago, as they stood in the grand plaza of Holy Town with the fires of the Teeth blazing in the outskirts.

"Your underbreeds have all fled without waiting for their master," Leaf had reminded him.

"So? There are others to drive."

"Am I to be your underbreed?" Leaf asked calmly. "Remember, Crown, I'm of the Pure Stream stock."

"I can see that by your face, friend. But why get into philosophical disputes? This is my wagon. The invaders will be here before nightfall. If you would ride west with me, these are the terms. If they're too bitter for you to swallow, well, stay here and test your luck against the mercies of the Teeth."

"I accept your terms," Leaf said.

So he had come aboard—and Sting, and Shadow—under the condition that the three of them would do all the driving. Leaf felt degraded by that—hiring on, in effect, as an indentured underbreed—but what choice was there for him? He was alone and far from his people; he had lost all his wealth and property; he faced sure death as the swarming hordes of Teeth devoured the eastland. He accepted Crown's terms. An aristocrat knows the art of yielding better than most. Resist humiliation until you can resist no longer, certainly, but then accept, accept, accept. Refusal to bow to the inevitable is vulgar and melodramatic. Leaf was of the highest caste, Pure Stream, schooled from childhood to be pliable, a willow in the wind, bending freely to the will of the Soul. Pride is a dangerous sin; so is stubbornness; so too, more than the others, is foolishness. Therefore, he labored while Crown lolled. Still, there were limits even to Leaf's capacity for acceptance, and he suspected those limits would be reached shortly.

⁂

On the first night, with only two small rivers between them and the Teeth and the terrible fires of Holy Town staining the sky, the fugitives halted briefly to forage for jellymelons in an abandoned field, and as they squatted there, gorging on ripe succulent fruit, Leaf said to Crown, "Where will you go, once you're safe from the Teeth on the far side of the Middle River?"

"I have distant kinsmen who live in the Flatlands," Crown replied. "I'll go to them and tell them what has happened to the Dark Lake folk in the east, and I'll persuade them to take up arms and drive the Teeth back into the icy wilderness where they belong. An army of liberation, Leaf, and I'll lead it." Crown's dark face glistened with juice. He wiped at it. "What are your plans?"

"Not nearly so grand. I'll seek kinsmen too, but not to organize an army. I wish simply to go to the Inland Sea, to my own people, and live quietly among them once again. I've been away from home too many years. What better time to return?" Leaf glanced at Shadow. "And you?" he asked her. "What do you want out of this journey?"

"I want only to go wherever you go," she said.

Leaf smiled. "You, Sting?"

"To survive," Sting said. "Just to survive."

Mankind had changed the world, and the changed world had worked changes in mankind. Each day the wagon brought the travelers to some new and strange folk who claimed descent from the old ancestral stock, though they might be water-breathers or have skins like tanned leather or grow several pairs of arms. Human, all of them, human, human, human. Or so they insisted. If you call yourself human, Leaf thought, then I will call you human too. Still, there were gradations of humanity. Leaf, as a Pure Stream, thought of himself as more nearly human than any of the peoples along their route, more nearly human even than his three companions; indeed, he sometimes tended to look upon Crown, Sting, and Shadow as very much other than human, though he did not consider that a fault in them. Whatever dwelled in the world was without fault, so long as it did no harm to others. Leaf had been taught to respect every breed of mankind, even the underbreeds. His companions were certainly no underbreeds: they were solidly midcaste, all of them, and ranked not far below Leaf himself. Crown, the biggest and strongest and most violent of them, was of the Dark Lake line. Shadow's race was Dancing Stars, and she was the most elegant, the most supple of the group. She was the only female aboard the wagon. Sting, who sprang from the White Crystal stock, was the quickest of body and spirit, mercurial, volatile. An odd assortment, Leaf thought. But in extreme times one takes one's traveling companions as they come. He had no complaints. He found it possible to get along with all of them, even Crown. Even Crown.

The wagon came to a jouncing halt. There was the clamor of hooves stamping the sodden soil; then shrill high-pitched cries from Sting and angry booming bellowings from Crown; and finally a series of muffled hissing explosions. Leaf shook his head sadly. "To waste our ammunition on no-leg spiders—"

"Perhaps they're harming the horses," Shadow said. "Crown is rough, but he isn't stupid."

Tenderly Leaf stroked her smooth haunches. Shadow tried always to be kind. He had never loved a Dancing Star before, though the sight of them had long given him pleasure: they were slender beings, bird-boned and shallow-breasted, and covered from their ankles to their crested skulls by fine dense fur the color of the twilight sky in winter. Shadow's voice was musical and her motions were graceful; she was the antithesis of Crown.

Crown now appeared, a hulking figure thrusting bluntly through the glistening beaded curtains that enclosed the passenger castle. He glared malevolently at Leaf. Even in his pleasant moments Crown seemed angry, an effect perhaps caused by his eyes, which were bright red where those of Leaf and most other kinds of humans were white. Crown's body was a block of meat, twice as broad as Leaf and half again as tall, though Leaf did not come from a small-statured race. Crown's skin was glossy, greenish-purple in colour, much like burnished bronze; he was entirely without hair and seemed more like a massive statue of an oiled gladiator than a living being. His arms hung well below his knees; equipped with extra joints and terminating in hands the size of great baskets, they were superb instruments of slaughter. Leaf offered him the most agreeable smile he could find. Crown said, without smiling in return, "You better get back on the reins, Leaf. The road's turning into one big swamp. The horses are uneasy. It's a purple rain."

Leaf had grown accustomed, in these nine days, to obeying Crown's brusque orders. He started to obey now, letting go of Shadow and starting to rise. But then, abruptly, he arrived at the limits of his acceptance.

"My shift just ended," he said.

Crown stared. "I know that. But Sting can't handle the wagon in this mess. And I just killed a bunch of mean-looking spiders. There'll be more if we stay around here much longer."

"So?"

"What are you trying to do, Leaf?"

"I guess I don't feel like going up front again so soon."

"You think Shadow here can hold the reins in this storm?" Crown asked coldly.

Leaf stiffened. He saw the wrath gathering in Crown's face. The big man was holding his natural violence in check with an effort, there would be trouble soon if Leaf remained defiant. This rebelliousness went against all of Leaf's principles, yet he found himself persisting in it and even taking a wicked pleasure in it. He chose to risk the confrontation and discover how firm Crown intended to be. Boldly he said, "You might try holding the reins yourself, friend."

"Leaf!" Shadow whispered, appalled.

Crown's face became murderous. His dark, shining cheeks puffed and went taut; his eyes blazed like molten nuggets; his hands closed and opened, closed and opened, furiously grasping air. "What kind of crazy stuff are you trying to give? We have a contract, Leaf. Unless you've suddenly decided that a Pure Stream doesn't need to abide by—"

"Spare me the class prejudice, Crown. I'm not pleading Pure Stream as an excuse to get out of working. I'm tired and I've earned my rest."

Shadow said softly, "Nobody's denying you your rest, Leaf. But Crown's right that I can't drive in a purple rain. I would if I could. And Sting can't do it either. That leaves only you."

"And Crown," Leaf said obstinately.

"There's only you," Shadow murmured. It was like her to take no sides, to serve ever as a mediator. "Go on, Leaf. Before there's real trouble. Making trouble like this isn't your usual way."

Leaf felt bound to pursue his present course, however perilous. He shook his head. "You, Crown. You drive."

In a throttled voice Crown said, "You're pushing me too far. We have a contract."

All Leaf's Pure Stream temperance was gone now. "Contract? I agreed to do my fair share of the driving, not to let myself be yanked up from my rest at a time when—"

Crown kicked at a low wickerwork stool, splitting it. His rage was boiling close to the surface. Swollen veins throbbed in his throat. He said, still controlling himself, "Get out there right now, Leaf, or by the Soul I'll send you into the All-Is-One!"

"Beautiful, Crown. Kill me, if you feel you have to. Who'll drive your damned wagon for you then?"

"I'll worry about that then."

Crown started forward, swallowing air, clenching fists.

Shadow sharply nudged Leaf's ribs. "This is going beyond the point of reason," she told him. He agreed. He had tested Crown and he had his answer, which was that Crown was unlikely to back down; now enough was enough, for Crown was capable of killing. The huge Dark Laker loomed over him, lifting his tremendous arms as though to bring them crashing against Leaf's head. Leaf held up his hands, more a gesture of submission than of self-defence.

"Wait," he said. "Stop it, Crown. I'll drive."

Crown's arms descended anyway. Crown managed to halt the killing blow midway, losing his balance and lurching heavily against the side of the wagon. Clumsily he straightened. Slowly he shook his head. In a low, menacing voice he said, "Don't ever try something like this again, Leaf."

"It's the rain," Shadow said. "The purple rain. Everybody does strange things in a purple rain."

"Even so," Crown said, dropping onto the pile of furs as Leaf got up. "The next time, Leaf, there'll be bad trouble. Now go ahead. Get up front."

Nodding to him, Leaf said, "Come up front with me, Shadow."

She did not answer. A look of fear flickered across her face.

Crown said, "The driver drives alone. You know that, Leaf. Are you still testing me? If you're testing me, say so and I'll know how to deal with you."

"I just want some company, as long as I have to do an extra shift."

"Shadow stays here."

There was a moment of silence. Shadow was trembling. "All right," Leaf said finally. "Shadow stays here."

"I'll walk a little way toward the front with you," Shadow said, glancing timidly at Crown. Crown scowled but said nothing. Leaf stepped out of the passenger castle; Shadow followed. Outside, in the narrow passageway leading to the midcabin, Leaf halted, shaken, shaking, and seized her. She pressed her slight body against him and they embraced, roughly, intensely. When he released her she said, "Why did you try to cross him like that? It was such a strange thing for you to do, Leaf."

"I just didn't feel like taking the reins again so soon."

"I know that."

"I want to be with you."

"You'll be with me a little later," she said. "It didn't make sense for you to talk back to Crown. There wasn't any choice. You had to drive."

"Why?"

"You know. Sting couldn't do it. I couldn't do it."

"And Crown?"

She looked at him oddly. "Crown? How would Crown have taken the reins?"

From the passenger castle came Crown's angry growl: "You going to stand there all day, Leaf? Go on! Get in here, Shadow!"

"I'm coming," she called.

Leaf held her a moment. "Why not? Why couldn't he have driven? He may be proud, but not so proud that—"

"Ask me another time," Shadow said, pushing him away. "Go. Go. You have to drive. If we don't move along we'll have the spiders upon us."

On the third day westward they had arrived at a village of Shapechangers. Much of the countryside through which they had been passing was deserted, although the Teeth had not yet visited it, but these Shapechangers went about their usual routines as if nothing had happened in the neighboring provinces. These were angular, long-legged people, sallow of skin, nearly green in hue, who were classed generally somewhere below the midcastes, but above the underbreeds. Their gift was metamorphosis, a slow softening of the bones under voluntary control that could, in the course of a week, drastically alter the form of their bodies, but Leaf saw them doing none of that, except for a few children who seemed midway through strange transformations, one with ropy, seemingly boneless arms, one with grotesquely distended shoulders, one with stiltlike legs. The adults came close to the wagon, admiring its beauty with soft cooing sounds, and Crown went out to talk with them. "I'm on my way to raise an army," he said. "I'll be back in a month or two, leading my kinsmen out of the Flatlands. Will you fight in our ranks? Together we'll drive out the Teeth and make the eastern provinces safe again."

The Shapechangers laughed heartily. "How can anyone drive out the Teeth?" asked an old one with a greasy mop of blue-white hair. "It was the will of the Soul that they burst forth as conquerors, and no one can quarrel with the Soul. The Teeth will stay in these lands for a thousand thousand years."

"They can be defeated!" Crown cried.

"They will destroy all that lies in their path, and no one can stop them."

"If you feel that way, why don't you flee?" Leaf asked.

"Oh, we have time. But we'll be gone long before your return with your army." There were giggles. "We'll keep ourselves clear of the Teeth. We have our ways. We make our changes and we slip away."

Crown persisted. "We can use you in our war against them. You have valuable gifts. If you won't serve as soldiers, at least serve us as spies. We'll send you into the camps of the Teeth, disguised as—"

"We will not be here," the old Shapechanger said, "and no one will be able to find us," and that was the end of it.

As the airwagon departed from the Shapechanger village, Shadow at the reins, Leaf said to Crown, "Do you really think you can defeat the Teeth?"

"I have to."

"You heard the old Shapechanger. The coming of the Teeth was the will of the Soul. Can you hope to thwart that will?"

"A rainstorm is the will of the Soul also," Crown said quietly. "All the same, I do what I can to keep myself dry. I've never known the Soul to be displeased by that."

"It's not the same. A rainstorm is a transaction between the sky and the land. We aren't involved in it; if we want to cover our heads, it doesn't alter what's really taking place. But the invasion of the Teeth is a transaction between tribe and tribe, a reordering of social patterns. In the great scheme of things, Crown, it may be a necessary process, preordained to achieve certain ends beyond our understanding. All events are part of some larger whole, and everything balances out, everything compensates for something else. Now we have peace, and now it's the time for invaders, do you see? If that's so, it's futile to resist."

"The Teeth broke into the eastlands," said Crown, "and they massacred thousands of Dark Lake people. My concern with necessary processes begins and ends with that fact. My tribe has nearly been wiped out. Yours is still safe, up by its ferny shores. I will seek help and gain revenge."

"The Shapechangers laughed at you. Others will also. No one will want to fight the Teeth."

"I have cousins in the Flatlands. If no one else will, they'll mobilize themselves. They'll want to repay the Teeth for their crime against the Dark Lakers."

"Your western cousins may tell you, Crown, that they prefer to remain where they are safe. Why should they go east to die in the name of vengeance? Will vengeance, no matter how bloody, bring any of your kinsmen back to life?"

"They will fight," Crown said.

"Prepare yourself for the possibility that they won't."

"If they refuse," said Crown, "then I'll go back east myself, and wage my war alone until I'm overwhelmed. But don't fear for me, Leaf. I'm sure I'll find plenty of willing recruits."

"How stubborn you are, Crown. You have good reason to hate the Teeth, as do we all. But why let that hatred cost you your only life? Why not accept the disaster that has befallen us, and make a new life for yourself beyond the Middle River, and forget this dream of reversing the irreversible?"

"I have my task," said Crown.

Forward through the wagon Leaf moved, going slowly, head down, shoulders hunched, feet atickle with the urge to kick things. He felt sour of spirit, curdled with dull resentment. He had let himself become angry at Crown, which was bad enough; but worse, he had let that anger possess and poison him. Not even the beauty of the wagon could lift him: ordinarily its superb construction and elegant furnishings gave him joy, the swirl-patterned fur hangings, the banners of gossamer textiles, the intricate carved inlays, the graceful strings of dried seeds and tassels that dangled from the vaulted ceilings, but these wonders meant nothing to him now. That was no way to be, he knew.

The airwagon was longer than ten men of the Pure Stream lying head to toe, and so wide that it spanned nearly the whole roadway. The finest workmanship had gone into its making: Flower Giver artisans, no doubt of it, only Flower Givers could build so well. Leaf imagined dozens of the fragile little folk toiling earnestly for months, all smiles and silence, long, slender fingers and quick, gleaming eyes, shaping the great wagon as one might shape a poem. The main frame was of lengthy pale spears of light, resilient wingwood, elegantly laminated into broad curving strips with a colorless fragrant mucilage and bound with springy withes brought from the southern marshes. Over this elaborate armature tanned sheets of stickskin had been stretched and stitched into place with thick yellow fibers drawn from the stick-creatures' own gristly bodies. The floor was of dark shining nightflower-wood planks, buffed to a high finish and pegged together with great skill. No metal had been employed in the construction of the wagon, nor any artificial substances: nature had supplied everything. Huge and majestic though the wagon was, it was airy and light, light enough to float on a vertical column of warm air generated by magnetic rotors whirling in its belly; so long as the earth turned, so would the rotors, and when the rotors were spinning the wagon drifted cat-high above the ground, and could be tugged easily along by the team of nightmares.

It was more a mobile palace than a wagon, and wherever it went it stirred excitement: Crown's love, Crown's joy, Crown's estate, a wondrous toy. To pay for the making of it Crown must have sent many souls into the All-Is-One, for that was how Crown had earned his livelihood in the old days, as a hired warrior, a surrogate killer, fighting one-on-one duels for rich eastern princelings too weak or too lazy to defend their own honor. He had never been scratched, and his fees had been high; but all that was ended now that the Teeth were loose in the eastlands.

Leaf could not bear to endure being so irritable any longer. He paused to adjust himself, closing his eyes and listening for the clear tone that sounded always at the center of his being. After a few minutes he found it, tuned himself to it, let it purify him. Crown's unfairness ceased to matter. Leaf became once more his usual self, alert and outgoing, aware and responsive.

Smiling, whistling, he made his way swiftly through the wide, comfortable, brightly lit midcabin, decorated with Crown's weapons and other grim souvenirs of battle, and went on into the front corridor that led to the driver's cabin.

Sting sat slumped at the reins. White Crystal folk such as Sting generally seemed to throb and tick with energy; but Sting looked exhausted, emptied, half dead of fatigue. He was a small, sinewy being, narrow of shoulder and hip, with colorless skin of a waxy, horny texture, pocked everywhere with little hairy nodes and whorls. His muscles were long and flat; his face was cavernous, beaked nose and tiny chin, dark mischievous eyes hidden in bony recesses. Leaf touched his shoulder. "It's all right," he said. "Crown sent me to relieve you." Sting nodded feebly but did not move. The little man was quivering like a frog. Leaf had always thought of him as indestructible, but in the grip of this despondency Sting seemed more fragile even than Shadow.

"Come," Leaf murmured. "You have a few hours for resting. Shadow will look after you."

Sting shrugged. He was hunched forward, staring dully through the clear curving window, stained now with splashes of muddy tinted water.

"The dirty spiders," he said. His voice was hoarse and frayed. "The filthy rain. The mud. Look at the horses, Leaf. They're dying of fright, and so am I. We'll all perish on this road, Leaf, if not of spiders then of poisoned rain, if not of rain then of the Teeth, if not of the Teeth then of something else. There's no road for us but this one, do you realize that? This is the road, and we're bound to it like helpless underbreeds, and we'll die on it."

"We'll die when our turn comes, like everything else, Sting, and not a moment before."

"Our turn is coming. Too soon. Too soon. I feel death-ghosts close at hand."

"Sting!"

Sting made a weird ratcheting sound low in his throat, a sort of rusty sob. Leaf lifted him and swung him out of the driver's seat, settling him gently down in the corridor. It was as though he weighed nothing at all. Perhaps just then that was true. Sting had many strange gifts. "Go on," Leaf said. "Get some rest while you can."

"How kind you are, Leaf."

"And no more talk of ghosts."

"Yes," Sting said. Leaf saw him struggling against fear and despair and weariness. Sting appeared to brighten a moment, flickering on the edge of his old vitality; then the brief glow subsided, and, smiling a pale smile, offering a whisper of thanks, he went aft.

Leaf took his place in the driver's seat.

Through the window of the wagon—thin, tough sheets of stickskin, the best quality, carefully matched, perfectly transparent—he confronted a dismal scene. Rain dark as blood was falling at a steep angle, scourging the spongy soil, kicking up tiny fountains of earth. A bluish miasma rose from the ground, billows of dark, steamy fog, the acrid odour of which had begun to seep into the wagon. Leaf sighed and reached for the reins. Death-ghosts, he thought. Haunted. Poor Sting, driven to the end of his wits.

And yet, and yet, as he considered the things Sting had said, Leaf realized that he had been feeling somewhat the same way, these past few days: tense, driven, haunted. *Haunted.* As though unseen presences, mocking, hostile, were hovering near. Ghosts? The strain, more likely, of all that he had gone through since the first onslaught of the Teeth. He had lived through the collapse of a rich and intricate civilization. He moved now through a strange world, all ashes and seaweed. He was haunted, perhaps, by the weight of the unburied past, by the memory of all that he had lost.

A rite of exorcism seemed in order.

Lightly he said, aloud, "If there are any ghosts in here, I want you to listen to me. *Get out of this cabin.* That's an order. I have work to do."

He laughed. He picked up the reins and made ready to take control of the team of nightmares.

The sense of an invisible presence was overwhelming.

Something at once palpable and intangible pressed clammily against him. He felt surrounded and engulfed. It's the fog, he told himself. Dark blue fog, pushing at the window, sealing the wagon into a pocket of vapor. Or was it? Leaf sat quite still for a moment, listening. Silence. He relinquished the reins, swung about in his seat, carefully inspected the cabin. No one there. An absurdity to be fidgeting like this. Yet the discomfort remained. This was no joke now. Sting's anxieties had infected him, and the malady was feeding on itself, growing more intense from moment to moment, making him vulnerable to any stray terror that whispered to him. Only with a tranquil mind could he attain the state of trance a nightmare-driver must enter; and trance seemed unattainable so long as he felt the prickle of some invisible watcher's gaze on the back of his neck. This rain, he thought, this damnable rain. It drives everybody crazy. In a clear, firm voice Leaf said, "I'm altogether serious. Show yourself and get yourself out of this cabin."

Silence.

He took up the reins again. No use. Concentration was impossible. He knew many techniques for centering himself, for leading his consciousness to a point of unassailable serenity. But could he achieve that now, jangled and distracted as he was? He would try. He had to succeed. The wagon had tarried in this place much too long already. Leaf summoned all his inner resources; he purged himself, one by one, of every discord; he compelled himself to slide into trance.

It seemed to be working. Darkness beckoned to him. He stood at the threshold. He started to step across.

"Such a fool, such a foolish fool," said a sudden dry voice out of nowhere that nibbled at his ears like the needle-toothed mice of the White Desert.

The trance broke. Leaf shivered as if stabbed and sat up, eyes bright, face flushed with excitement.

"Who spoke?"

"Put down those reins, friend. Going forward on this road is a heavy waste of spirit."

"Then I wasn't crazy and neither was Sting. There is something in here!"

"A ghost, yes a ghost, a ghost, a ghost!" The ghost showered him with laughter.

Leaf's tension eased. Better to be troubled by a real ghost than to be vexed by a fantasy of one's own disturbed mind. He feared madness far more than he did the invisible. Besides, he thought he knew what this creature must be.

"Where are you, ghost?"

"Not far from you. Here I am. Here. Here." From three different parts of the cabin, one after another. The invisible being began to sing. Its song was high-pitched, whining, a grinding tone that stretched Leaf's patience intolerably. Leaf still saw no one, though he narrowed his eyes and stared as hard as he could. He imagined he could detect a faint veil of pink light floating along the wall of the cabin, a smoky haze moving from place to place, a shimmering film like thin oil on water, but whenever he focused his eyes on it the misty presence appeared to evaporate.

Leaf said, "How long have you been aboard this wagon?"

"Long enough."

"Did you come aboard at Theptis?"

"Was that the name of the place?" asked the ghost disingenuously. "I forget. It's so hard to remember things."

"Theptis," said Leaf. "Four days ago."

"Perhaps it was Theptis," the ghost said. "Fool! Dreamer!"

"Why do you call me names?"

"You travel a dead road, fool, and yet nothing will turn you from it." The invisible one snickered. "Do you think I'm a ghost, Pure Stream?"

"I know what you are."

"How wise you've become!"

"Such a pitiful phantom. Such a miserable drifting wraith. Show yourself to me, ghost."

Laughter reverberated from the corners of the cabin. The voice said, speaking from a point close to Leaf's left ear, "The road you choose to travel has been killed ahead. We told you that when you came to us, and yet you went onward, and still you go onward. Why are you so rash?"

"Why won't you show yourself? A gentleman finds it discomforting to speak to the air."

Obligingly the ghost yielded, after a brief pause, some fraction of its invisibility. A vaporous crimson stain appeared in the air before Leaf, and he saw within it dim, insubstantial features, like projections on a screen of thick fog. He believed he could make out a wispy white beard, harsh glittering eyes, lean curving lips; a whole forbidding face, a fleshless torso. The stain deepened momentarily to scarlet and for a moment Leaf saw the entire figure of the stranger revealed, a long narrow-bodied man, dried and withered, grinning ferociously at him. The edges of the figure softened and became mist. Then Leaf saw only vapor again, and then nothing.

"I remember you from Theptis," Leaf said. "In the tent of Invisibles."

"What will you do when you come to the dead place on the highway?" the invisible one demanded. "Will you fly over it? Will you tunnel under it?"

"You were asking the same things at Theptis," Leaf replied. "I will make the same answer that the Dark Laker gave you then. We will go forward, dead place or no. This is the only road for us."

They had come to Theptis on the fifth day of their flight—a grand city, a splendid mercantile emporium, the gateway to the west, sprawling athwart a place where two great rivers met and many highways converged. In happy times any and all peoples might be found in Theptis, Pure Streams and White Crystals and Flower Givers and Sand Shapers and a dozen others jostling one another in the busy streets, buying and selling, selling and buying, but mainly Theptis was a city of Fingers—the merchant caste, plump and industrious, thousands upon thousands of them concentrated in this one city.

The day Crown's airwagon reached Theptis much of the city was ablaze, and they halted on a broad stream-split plain just outside the metropolitan area. An improvised camp for refugees had sprouted there, and tents of black and gold and green cloth littered the meadow like new nightshoots. Leaf and Crown went out to inquire after the news. Had the Teeth sacked Theptis as well? No, an old and sagging Sand Shaper told them. The Teeth, so far as anyone had heard, were still well to the east, rampaging through the coastal cities. Why the fires, then? The old man shook his head. His energy was exhausted, or his patience, or his courtesy. If you want to know anything else, he said, ask *them*. They know everything. And he pointed toward a tent opposite his.

Leaf looked into the tent and found it empty; then he looked again and saw upright shadows moving about in it, tenuous figures that existed at the very bounds of visibility and could be perceived only by tricks of the light as they changed place in the tent. They asked him within, and Crown came also. By the smoky light of their tentfire they were more readily seen: seven or eight men of the Invisible stock, nomads, ever mysterious, gifted with ways of causing beams of light to travel around or through their bodies so that they might escape the scrutiny of ordinary eyes. Leaf, like everyone else not of their kind, was uncomfortable among Invisibles. No one trusted them; no one was capable of predicting their actions, for they were creatures of whim and caprice, or else followed some code the logic of which was incomprehensible to outsiders. They made Leaf and Crown welcome, adjusting their bodies until they were in clear sight, and offering the visitors a flagon of wine, a bowl of fruit. Crown gestured toward Theptis. Who had set the city afire? A red-bearded Invisible with a raucous rumbling voice answered that on the second night of the invasion the richest of the Fingers had panicked and had begun to flee the city with their most precious belongings, and as their wagons rolled through the gates the lesser breeds had begun to loot the Finger mansions, and brawling had started once the wine cellars were pierced, and fires broke out, and there was no one to make the fire wardens do their work, for they were all underbreeds and the masters had fled. So the city burned and was still burning, and the survivors were huddled here on the plain, waiting for the rubble to cool so that they might salvage valuables from it, and hoping that the Teeth would not fall upon them before they could do their sifting. As for the Fingers, said the Invisible, they were all gone from Theptis now.

Which way had they gone? Mainly to the northwest, by way of Sunset Highway, at first; but then the approach to that road had become choked by stalled wagons butted one up against another, so that the only way to reach the Sunset now was by making a difficult detour through the sand country north of the city, and once that news became general the Fingers had turned their wagons southward. Crown wondered why no one seemed to be taking Spider Highway westward. At this a second Invisible, white-bearded, joined the conversation. Spider Highway, he said, is blocked just a few days' journey west of here: a dead road, a useless road. Everyone knows that, said the white-bearded Invisible.

"That is our route," said Crown.

"I wish you well," said the Invisible. "You will not get far."

"I have to get to the Flatlands."

"Take your chances with the sand country," the red-bearded one advised, "and go by way of the Sunset."

"It would waste two weeks or more," Crown replied. "Spider Highway is the only road we can consider." Leaf and Crown exchanged wary glances. Leaf asked the nature of the trouble on the highway, but the Invisibles said only that the road had been "killed," and would offer no amplification. "We will go forward," Crown said, "dead place or no."

"As you choose," said the older Invisible, pouring more wine. Already both Invisibles were fading; the flagon seemed suspended in mist. So, too, did the discussion become unreal, dreamlike, as answers no longer followed closely upon the sense of questions, and the words of the Invisibles came to Leaf and Crown as though swaddled in thick wool. There was a long interval of silence, at last, and when Leaf extended his empty glass the flagon was not offered to him, and he realized finally that he and Crown were alone in the tent. They left it and asked at other tents about the blockage on Spider Highway, but no one knew anything of it, neither some young Dancing Stars nor three flat-faced Water Breather women nor a family of Flower Givers.

How reliable was the word of Invisibles? What did they mean by a "dead" road? Suppose they merely thought the road was ritually impure, for some reason understood only by Invisibles. What value, then, would their warning have to those who did not subscribe to their superstitions? Who knew at any time what the words of an Invisible meant? That night in the wagon the four of them puzzled over the concept of a road that has been "killed," but neither Shadow's intuitive perceptions nor Sting's broad knowledge of tribal dialects and customs could provide illumination. In the end Crown reaffirmed his decision to proceed on the road he had originally chosen, and it was Spider Highway that they took out of Theptis. As they proceeded westward they met no one traveling the opposite way, though one might expect the eastbound lanes to be thronged with a flux of travelers turning back from whatever obstruction might be closing the road ahead. Crown took cheer in that; but Leaf observed privately that their wagon appeared to be the only vehicle on the road in either direction, as if everyone else knew better than to make the attempt. In such stark solitude they journeyed four days west of Theptis before the purple rain hit them.

Now the Invisible said, "Go into your trance and drive your horses. I'll dream beside you until the awakening comes."

"I prefer privacy."

"You won't be disturbed."

"I ask you to leave."

"You treat your guests coldly."

"Are you my guest?" Leaf asked. "I don't remember extending an invitation."

"You drank wine in our tent. That creates in you an obligation to offer reciprocal hospitality." The Invisible sharpened his bodily intensity until he seemed as solid as Crown; but even as Leaf observed the effect he grew thin again, fading in patches. The far wall of the cabin showed through his chest, as if he were hollow. His arms had disappeared, but not his gnarled long-fingered hands. He was grinning, showing crooked close-set teeth. There was a strange scent in the cabin, sharp and musky, like vinegar mixed with honey. The Invisible said, "I'll ride with you a little longer," and vanished altogether.

Leaf searched the corners of the cabin, knowing that an Invisible could always be felt even if he eluded the eyes. His probing hands encountered nothing. Gone, gone, gone, whisking off to the place where snuffed flames go, eh? Even that odor of vinegar and honey was diminishing. "Where are you?" Leaf asked. "Still hiding somewhere else?" Silence. Leaf shrugged. The stink of the purple rain was the dominant scent again. Time to move on, stowaway or no. Rain was hitting the window in huge murky windblown blobs. Once more Leaf picked up the reins. He banished the Invisible from his mind.

These purple rains condensed out of drifting gaseous clots in the upper atmosphere—dank clouds of chemical residues that arose from the world's most stained, most injured places and circled the planet like malign tempests. Upon colliding with a mass of cool air such a poisonous cloud often discharged its burden of reeking oils and acids in the form of a driving rainstorm; and the foulness that descended could be fatal to plants and shrubs, to small animals, sometimes even to man.

A purple rain was the cue for certain somber creatures to come forth from dark places: scuttering scavengers that picked eagerly through the dead and dying, and larger, more dangerous things that preyed on the dazed and choking living. The no-leg spiders were among the more unpleasant of these.

They were sinister spherical beasts the size of large dogs, voracious in the appetite and ruthless in the hunt. Their bodies were plump, covered with coarse, rank brown hair; they bore eight glittering eyes above sharp-fanged mouths. No-legged they were indeed, but not immobile, for a single huge fleshy foot, something like that of a snail, sprouted from the underbellies of these spiders and carried them along at a slow, inexorable pace. They were poor pursuers, easily avoided by healthy animals; but to the numbed victims of a purple rain they were deadly, moving in to strike with hinged, poison-barbed claws that leaped out of niches along their backs. Were they truly spiders? Leaf had no idea. Like almost everything else, they were a recent species, mutated out of the-Soul-only-knew-what during the period of stormy biological upheavals that had attended the end of the old industrial civilization, and no one yet had studied them closely, or cared to.

Crown had killed four of them. Their bodies lay upside down at the edge of the road, upturned feet wilting and drooping like plucked toadstools. About a dozen more spiders had emerged from the low hills flanking the highway and were gliding slowly toward the stalled wagon; already several had reached their dead comrades and were making ready to feed on them, and some of the others were eyeing the horses.

The six nightmares, prisoners of their harnesses, prowled about uneasily in their constricted ambits, anxiously scraping at the muddy ground with their hooves. They were big, sturdy beasts, black as death, with long feathery ears and high-domed skulls that housed minds as keen as many human's, sharper than some. The rain annoyed the horses but could not seriously harm them, and the spiders could be kept at bay with kicks, but plainly the entire situation disturbed them.

Leaf meant to get them out of here as rapidly as he could.

A slimy coating covered everything the rain had touched, and the road was a miserable quagmire, slippery as ice. There was peril for all of them in that. If a horse stumbled and fell it might splinter a leg, causing such confusion that the whole team might be pulled down; and as the injured nightmares thrashed about in the mud the hungry spiders would surely move in on them, venomous claws rising, striking, delivering stings that stunned, and leaving the horses paralyzed, helpless, vulnerable to eager teeth and strong jaws. As the wagon traveled onward through this swampy rainsoaked district Leaf would constantly have to steady and reassure the nightmares, pouring his energy into them to comfort them, a strenuous task, a task that had wrecked poor Sting.

Leaf slipped the reins over his forehead. He became aware of the consciousness of the six fretful horses.

Because he was still awake, contact was misty and uncertain. A waking mind was unable to communicate with the animals in any useful way. To guide the team he had to enter a trance state, a dream state; they would not respond to anything so gross as conscious intelligence. He looked about for manifestations of the Invisible. No, no sign of him. Good. Leaf brought his mind to dead center.

He closed his eyes. The technique of trance was easy enough for him, when there were no distractions.

He visualized a tunnel, narrow-mouthed and dark, slanting into the ground. He drifted toward its entrance.

Hovered there a moment.

Went down into it.

Floating, floating, borne downward by warm, gentle currents: he sinks in a slow spiral descent, autumn leaf on a springtime breeze. The tunnel's walls are circular, crystalline, lit from within, the light growing in brightness as he drops toward the heart of the world. Gleaming scarlet and blue flowers, brittle as glass, sprout from crevices at meticulously regular intervals.

He goes deep, touching nothing. Down.

Entering a place where the tunnel widens into a round smooth-walled chamber, sealed at the end. He stretches full-length on the floor. The floor is black stone, slick and slippery; he dreams it soft and yielding, womb-warm. Colors are muted here, sounds are blurred. He hears far-off music, percussive and muffled, *rat-a-rat, rat-a-rat, bllllooom, bllllooom.*

Now at least he is able to make full contact with the minds of the horses.

His spirit expands in their direction; he envelops them, he takes them into himself. He senses the separate identity of each, picks up the shifting play of their emotions, their prancing fantasies, their fears. Each mare has her own distinct response to the rain, to the spiders, to the sodden highway. One is restless, one is timid, one is furious, one is sullen, one is tense, one is torpid. He feeds energy to them. He pulls them together. Come, gather your strength, take us onward: this is the road, we must be on our way.

The nightmares stir.

They react well to his touch. He believes that they prefer him over Shadow and Sting as a driver: Sting is too manic, Shadow too permissive. Leaf keeps them together, directs them easily, gives them the guidance they need. They are intelligent, yes, they have personalities and goals and ideals, but also they are beasts of burden, and Leaf never forgets that, for the nightmares themselves do not.

Come, now. Onward.

The road is ghastly. They pick at it and their hooves make sucking sounds coming up from the mud. They complain to him. *We are cold, we are wet, we are bored.* He dreams wings for them to make their way easier. To soothe them he dreams sunlight for them, bountiful warmth, dry highway, an easy trot. He dreams green hillsides, cascades of yellow blossoms, the flutter of hummingbirds' wings, the droning of bees. He gives the horses sweet summer, and they grow calm; they lift their heads; they fan their dream-wings and preen; they are ready now to resume the journey. They pull as one. The rotors hum happily. The wagon slides forward with a smooth coasting motion.

Leaf, deep in trance, is unable to see the road, but no matter; the horses see it for him and send him images, fluid, shifting dream-images, polarized and refracted and diffracted by the strangenesses of their vision and the distortions of dream communication, six simultaneous and individual views. Here is the road, bordered by white birches whipped by an angry wind. Here is the road, an earthen swath slicing through a forest of mighty pines bowed down by white new snow. Here is the road, a ribbon of fertility, from which dazzling red poppies spring wherever a hoof strikes. Fleshy-finned blue fishes do headstands beside the road. Paunchy burghers of the Finger tribe spread brilliantly laundered tablecloths along the grassy margin and make lunch out of big-eyed reproachful oysters. Masked figures dart between the horses' legs. The road curves, curves again; doubles back on itself, crosses itself in a complacent loop. Leaf integrates this dizzying many-hued inrush of data, sorting the real from the unreal, blending and focusing the input and using it to guide himself in guiding the horses. Serenely he coordinates their movements with quick confident impulses of thought, so that each animal will pull with the same force. The wagon is precariously balanced on its column of air, and an unequal tug could well send it slewing into the treacherous thicket to the left of the road. He sends quicksilver messages down the thick conduit from his mind to theirs. Steady there, steady, watch that boggy patch coming up! Ah! Ah, that's my girl! Spiders on the left, careful! Good! Yes, yes, ah, yes! He pats their heaving flanks with a strand of his mind. He rewards their agility with dreams of the stable, of newly mown hay, of stallions waiting at journey's end.

From them—for they love him, he knows they love him—he gets warm dreams of the highway, all beauty and joy, all images converging into a single idealized view, majestic groves of wingwood trees and broad meadows through which clear brooks flow. They dream his own past life for him, too, feeding back to him nuggets of random autobiography mined in the seams of his being. What they transmit is filtered and transformed by their alien sensibilities, colored with hallucinatory glows and tugged and twisted into other-dimensional forms, but yet he is able to perceive the essential meaning of each tableau: his childhood among the parks and gardens of the Pure Stream enclave near the Inland Sea, his wanderyears among the innumerable, unfamiliar, not-quite-human breeds of the hinterlands, his brief, happy sojourn in the fog-swept western country, his eastward journey in early manhood, always following the will of the Soul, always bending to the breezes, accepting whatever destiny seizes him, eastward now, his band of friends closer than brothers in his adopted eastern province, his sprawling lakeshore home there, all polished wood and billowing tented pavilions, his collection of relics of mankind's former times—pieces of machinery, elegant coils of metal, rusted coins, grotesque statuettes, wedges of imperishable plastic—housed in its own wing with its own curator. Lost in these reveries he ceases to remember that the home by the lake has been reduced to ashes by the Teeth, that his friends of kinder days are dead, his estates overrun, his pretty things scattered in the kitchen-middens.

Imperceptibly, the dream turns sour.

Spiders and rain and mud creep back into it. He is reminded, through some darkening of tone of the imagery pervading his dreaming mind, that he has been stripped of everything and has become, now that he has taken flight, merely a driver hired out to a bestial Dark Lake mercenary who is himself a fugitive.

Leaf is working harder to control the team now. The horses seem less sure of their footing, and the pace slows; they are bothered about something, and a sour, querulous anxiety tinges their messages to him. He catches their mood. He sees himself harnessed to the wagon alongside the nightmares, and it is Crown at the reins, Crown wielding a terrible whip, driving the wagon frenziedly forward, seeking allies who will help him fulfil his fantasy of liberating the lands the Teeth have taken. There is no escape from Crown. He rises above the landscape like a monster of congealed smoke, growing more huge until he obscures the sky. Leaf wonders how he will disengage himself from Crown. Shadow runs beside him, stroking his cheeks, whispering to him, and he asks her to undo the harness, but she says she cannot, that it is their duty to serve Crown, and Leaf turns to Sting, who is harnessed on his other side, and he asks Sting for help, but Sting coughs and slips in the mud as Crown's whip flicks his backbone. There is no escape. The wagon heels and shakes. The right-hand horse skids, nearly falls, recovers. Leaf decides he must be getting tired. He has driven a great deal today, and the effort is telling. But the rain is still falling—he breaks through the veil of illusions, briefly, past the scenes of spring and summer and autumn, and sees the blue-black water dropping in wild handfuls from the sky—and there is no one else to drive, so he must continue.

He tries to submerge himself in deeper trance, where he will be less readily deflected from control.

But no, something is wrong, something plucks at his consciousness, drawing him toward the waking state. The horses summon him to wakefulness with frightful scenes. One beast shows him the wagon about to plunge through a wall of fire. Another pictures them at the brink of a vast impassable crater. Another gives him the image of giant boulders strewn across the road; another, a mountain of ice blocking the way; another, a pack of snarling wolves; another, a row of armored warriors standing shoulder to shoulder, lances at the ready. No doubt of it. Trouble. Trouble. Trouble. Perhaps they have come to the dead place in the road. No wonder that Invisible was skulking around. Leaf forces himself to awaken.

There was no wall of fire. No warriors, no wolves, none of those things. Only a palisade of newly felled timbers facing him some hundred paces ahead on the highway, timbers twice as tall as Crown, sharpened to points at both ends and thrust deep into the earth one up against the next and bound securely with freshly cut vines. The barricade spanned the highway completely from edge to edge; on its right it was bordered by a tangle of impenetrable thorny scrub; on its left it extended to the brink of a steep ravine.

They were stopped.

Such a blockade across a public highway was inconceivable. Leaf blinked, coughed, rubbed his aching forehead. Those last few minutes of discordant dreams had left a murky, gritty coating on his brain. This wall of wood seemed like some sort of dream too, a very bad one. Leaf imagined he could hear the Invisible's cool laughter somewhere close at hand. At least the rain appeared to be slackening, and there were no spiders about. Small consolations, but the best that were available.

Baffled, Leaf freed himself of the reins and awaited the next event. After a moment or two he sensed the joggling rhythms that told of Crown's heavy forward progress through the cabin. The big man peered into the driver's cabin.

"What's going on? Why aren't we moving?"

"Dead road."

"What are you talking about?"

"See for yourself," Leaf said wearily, gesturing toward the window.

Crown leaned across Leaf to look. He studied the scene an endless moment, reacting slowly. "What's that? A *wall*?"

"A wall, yes."

"A wall across a highway? I never heard of anything like that."

"The Invisibles at Theptis may have been trying to warn us about this."

"A wall. A wall." Crown shook with perplexed anger. "It violates all the maintenance customs! Soul take it, Leaf, a public highway is—"

"—sacred and inviolable. Yes. What the Teeth have been doing in the east violates a good many maintenance customs too," Leaf said. "And territorial customs as well. These are unusual times everywhere." He wondered if he should tell Crown about the Invisible who was on board. One problem at a time, he decided. "Maybe this is how these people propose to keep the Teeth out of their country, Crown."

"But to block a public road—"

"We were warned."

"Who could trust the word of an Invisible?"

"There's the wall," Leaf said. "Now we know why we didn't meet anyone else on the highway. They probably put this thing up as soon as they heard about the Teeth, and the whole province knows enough to avoid Spider Highway. Everyone but us."

"What folk dwell here?"

"No idea. Sting's the one who would know."

"Yes, Sting would know," said the high, clear, sharp-edged voice of Sting from the corridor. He poked his head into the cabin. Leaf saw Shadow just behind him. "This is the land of the Tree Companions," Sting said. "Do you know of them?"

Crown shook his head. "Not I," said Leaf.

"Forest-dwellers," Sting said. "Tree-worshippers. Small heads, slow brains. Dangerous in battle—they use poisoned darts. There are nine tribes of them in this region, I think, under a single chief. Once they paid tribute to my people, but I suppose in these times all that has ended."

"They worship trees?" Shadow said lightly. "And how many of their gods, then, did they cut down to make this barrier?"

Sting laughed. "If you must have gods, why not put them to some good use?"

Crown glared at the wall across the highway as he once might have glared at an opponent in the duelling ring. Seething, he paced a narrow path in the crowded cabin. "We can't waste any more time. The Teeth will be coming through this region in a few days, for sure. We've got to reach the river before something happens to the bridges ahead."

"The wall," Leaf said.

"There's plenty of brush lying around out there," said Sting. "We could build a bonfire and burn it down."

"Green wood," Leaf said. "It's impossible."

"We have hatchets," Shadow pointed out. "How long would it take for us to cut through timbers as thick as those?"

Sting said, "We'd need a week for the job. The Tree Companions would fill us full of darts before we'd been chopping an hour."

"Do you have any ideas?" Shadow said to Leaf.

"Well, we could turn back toward Theptis and try to find our way to Sunset Highway by way of the sand country. There are only two roads from here to the river, this and the Sunset. We lose five days, though, if we decide to go back, and we might get snarled up in whatever chaos is going on in Theptis, or we could very well get stranded in the desert trying to reach the highway. The only other choice I see is to abandon the wagon and look for some path around the wall on foot, but I doubt very much that Crown would—"

"Crown wouldn't," said Crown, who had been chewing his lip in tense silence. "But I see some different possibilities."

"Go on."

"One is to find these Tree Companions and compel them to clear this trash from the highway. Darts or no darts, one Dark Lake and one Pure Stream side by side ought to be able to terrify twenty tribes of pin-head forest folk."

"And if we can't?" Leaf asked.

"That brings us to the other possibility, which is that this wall isn't particularly intended to protect the neighborhood against the Teeth at all, but that these Tree Companions have taken advantage of the general confusion to set up some sort of toll-raising scheme. In that case, if we can't force them to open the road, we can find out what they want, what sort of toll they're asking, and pay it if we can and be on our way."

"Is that Crown who's talking?" Sting asked. "Talking about paying a toll to underbreeds of the forest? Incredible!"

Crown said, "I don't like the thought of paying toll to anybody. But it may be the simplest and quickest way to get out of here. Do you think I'm entirely a creature of pride, Sting?"

Leaf stood up. "If you're right that this is a toll station, there'd be some kind of gate in the wall. I'll go out there and have a look at it."

"No," said Crown, pushing him lightly back into his seat. "There's danger here, Leaf. This part of the work falls to me." He strode toward the midcabin and was busy there a few minutes. When he returned he was in his full armor: breastplates, helmet, face mask, greaves, everything burnished to a high gloss. In those few places where his bare skin showed through, it seemed but a part of the armor. Crown looked like a machine. His mace hung at his hip, and the short shaft of his extensor sword rested easily along the inside of his right wrist, ready to spring to full length at a squeeze. Crown glanced toward Sting and said, "I'll need your nimble legs. Will you come?"

"As you say."

"Open the midcabin hatch for us, Leaf."

Leaf touched a control on the board below the front window. With a soft, whining sound a hinged door near the middle of the wagon swung upward and out, and a stepladder sprouted to provide access to the ground. Crown made a ponderous exit. Sting, scorning the ladder, stepped down: it was the special gift of the White Crystal people to be able to transport themselves short distances in extraordinary ways.

Sting and Crown began to walk warily toward the wall. Leaf, watching from the driver's seat, slipped his arm lightly about the waist of Shadow, who stood beside him, and caressed her smooth fur. The rain had ended; a gray cloud still hung low, and the gleam of Crown's armor was already softened by fine droplets of moisture. He and Sting were nearly to the palisade, now, Crown constantly scanning the underbrush as if expecting a horde of Tree Companions to spring forth. Sting, loping along next to him, looked like some agile little two-legged beast, the top of his head barely reaching to Crown's hip.

They reached the palisade. Thin, late-afternoon sunlight streamed over its top. Kneeling, Sting inspected the base of the wall, probing at the soil with his fingers, and said something to Crown, who nodded and pointed upward. Sting backed off, made a short running start, and lofted himself, rising almost as though he were taking wing. His leap carried him soaring to the wall's jagged crest in a swift blurred flight. He appeared to hover for a long moment while choosing a place to land. At last he alighted in a precarious, uncomfortable-looking position, sprawled along the top of the wall with his body arched to avoid the timber's sharpened tips, his hands grasping two of the stakes and his feet wedged between two others. Sting remained in this desperate contortion for a remarkably long time, studying whatever lay beyond the barricade; then he let go his hold, sprang lightly outward, and floated to the ground, a distance some three times his own height. He landed upright, without stumbling. There was a brief conference between Crown and Sting. Then they came back to the wagon.

"It's a toll-raising scheme, all right," Crown muttered. "The middle timbers aren't embedded in the earth. They end just at ground level and form a hinged gate, fastened by two heavy bolts on the far side."

"I saw at least a hundred Tree Companions back of the wall," Sting said. "Armed with blowdarts. They'll be coming around to visit us in a moment."

"We should arm ourselves," Leaf said.

Crown shrugged. "We can't fight that many of them. Not twenty-five to one, we can't. The best hand-to-hand man in the world is helpless against little forest folk with poisoned blowdarts. If we aren't able to awe them into letting us go through, we'll have to buy them off somehow. But I don't know. That gate isn't nearly wide enough for the wagon."

He was right about that. There was the dry scraping squeal of wood against wood—the bolts were being unfastened—and then the gate swung slowly open. When it had been fully pushed back it provided an opening through which any good-size cart of ordinary dimensions might pass, but not Crown's magnificent vehicle. Five or six stakes on each side of the gate would have to be pulled down in order for the wagon to go by.

Tree Companions came swarming toward the wagon, scores of them—small, naked folk with lean limbs and smooth blue-green skin. They looked like animated clay statuettes, casually pinched into shape: their hairless heads were narrow and elongated, with flat sloping foreheads, and their long necks looked flimsy and fragile. They had shallow chests and bony, meatless frames. All of them, men and women both, wore reed dart-blowers strapped to their hips. As they danced and frolicked about the wagon they set up a ragged, irregular chanting, tuneless and atonal, like the improvised songs of children caught up in frantic play.

"We'll go out to them," Crown said. "Stay calm, make no sudden moves. Remember that these are underbreeds. So long as we think of ourselves as men and them as nothing more than monkeys, and make them realize we think that way, we'll be able to keep them under control."

"They're men," said Shadow quietly. "Same as we. Not monkeys."

"Think of them as like monkeys," Crown told her. "Otherwise we're lost. Come, now."

They left the wagon, Crown first, then Leaf, Sting, Shadow. The cavorting Tree Companions paused momentarily in their sport as the four travelers emerged; they looked up, grinned, chattered, pointed, did handsprings and headstands. They did not seem awed. Did Pure Stream mean nothing to them? Had they no fear of Dark Lake? Crown, glowering, said to Sting, "Can you speak their language?"

"A few words."

"Speak to them. Ask them to send their chief here to me."

Sting took up a position just in front of Crown, cupped his hands to his mouth, and shouted something high and piercing in a singsong language. He spoke with exaggerated, painful clarity, as one does in addressing a blind person or a foreigner. The Tree Companions snickered and exchanged little yipping cries. Then one of them came dancing forward, planted his face a handsbreadth from Sting's, and mimicked Sting's words, catching the intonation with comic accuracy. Sting looked frightened, and backed away half a pace, butting accidentally into Crown's chest. The Tree Companion loosed a stream of words, and when he fell silent Sting repeated his original phrase in a more subdued tone.

"What's happening?" Crown asked. "Can you understand anything?"

"A little. Very little."

"Will they get the chief?"

"I'm not sure. I don't know if he and I are talking about the same things."

"You said these people pay tribute to White Crystal."

"Paid," Sting said. "I don't know if there's any allegiance any longer. I think they may be having some fun at our expense. I think what he said was insulting, but I'm not sure. I'm just not sure."

"Stinking monkeys!"

"Careful, Crown," Shadow murmured. "We can't speak their language, but they may understand ours."

Crown said, "Try again. Speak more slowly. Get the monkey to speak more slowly. The chief, Sting, we want to see the chief! Isn't there any way you can make contact?"

"I could go into trance," Sting said. "And Shadow could help me with the meanings. But I'd need time to get myself together. I feel too quick now, too tense." As if to illustrate his point he executed a tiny jumping movement, blur-snap-hop, that carried him laterally a few paces to the left. Blur-snap-hop and he was back in place again. The Tree Companion laughed shrilly, clapped his hands, and tried to imitate Sting's little shuttling jump. Others of the tribe came over; there were ten or twelve of them now, clustered near the entrance to the wagon. Sting hopped again: it was like a twitch, a tic. He started to tremble. Shadow reached toward him and folded her slender arms about his chest, as though to anchor him. The Tree Companions grew more agitated; there was a hard, intense quality about their playfulness now. Trouble seemed imminent. Leaf, standing on the far side of Crown, felt a sudden knotting of the muscles at the base of his stomach. Something nagged at his attention, off to his right out in the crowd of Tree Companions; he glanced that way and saw an azure brightness, elongated and upright, a man-size strip of fog and haze, drifting and weaving among the forest folk. Was it the Invisible? Or only some trick of the dying daylight, slipping through the residual vapor of the rainstorm? He struggled for a sharp focus, but the figure eluded his gaze, slipping ticklingly beyond sight as Leaf followed it with his eyes. Abruptly he heard a howl from Crown and turned just in time to see a Tree Companion duck beneath the huge man's elbow and go sprinting into the wagon. "Stop!" Crown roared. "Come back!" And, as if a signal had been given, seven or eight others of the lithe little tribesmen scrambled aboard.

There was death in Crown's eyes. He beckoned savagely to Leaf and rushed through the entrance. Leaf followed. Sting, sobbing, huddled in the entranceway, making no attempt to halt the Tree Companions who were streaming into the wagon. Leaf saw them climbing over everything, examining, inspecting, commenting. Monkeys, yes. Down in the front corridor Crown was struggling with four of them, holding one in each vast hand, trying to shake free two others who were climbing his armored legs. Leaf confronted a miniature Tree Companion woman, a gnomish bright-eyed creature whose bare lean body glistened with sour sweat, and as he reached for her she drew not a dart-blower but a long narrow blade from the tube at her hip, and slashed Leaf fiercely along the inside of his left forearm. There was a quick, frightening gush of blood, and only some moments afterward did he feel the fiery lick of the pain. A poisoned knife? Well, then, into the All-Is-One with you, Leaf. But if there had been poison, he felt no effects of it; he wrenched the knife from her grasp, jammed it into the wall, scooped her up, and pitched her lightly through the open hatch of the wagon. No more Tree Companions were coming in, now. Leaf found two more, threw them out, dragged another out of the roofbeams, tossed him after the others, went looking for more. Shadow stood in the hatchway, blocking it with her frail arms outstretched. Where was Crown? Ah. There. In the trophy room. "Grab them and carry them to the hatch!" Leaf yelled. "We're rid of most of them!"

"The stinking monkeys," Crown cried. He gestured angrily. The Tree Companions had seized some treasure of Crown's, some ancient suit of mail, and in their childish buoyancy had ripped the fragile links apart with their tug-of-war. Crown, enraged, bore down on them, clamped one hand on each tapering skull—*"Don't!"* Leaf shouted, fearing darts in vengeance—and squeezed, cracking them like nuts. He tossed the corpses aside and, picking up his torn trophy, stood sadly pressing the sundered edges together in a clumsy attempt at repair.

"You've done it now," Leaf said. "They were just being inquisitive. Now we'll have war, and we'll be dead before nightfall."

"Never," Crown grunted.

He dropped the chainmail, scooped up the dead Tree Companions, carried them dangling through the wagon, and threw them like offal into the clearing. Then he stood defiantly in the hatchway, inviting their darts. None came. Those Tree Companions still aboard the wagon, five or six of them, appeared empty-handed, silent, and slipped hastily around the hulking Dark Laker. Leaf went forward and joined Crown. Blood was still dripping from Leaf's wound; he dared not induce clotting nor permit the wound to close until he had been purged of whatever poison might have been on the blade. A thin, straight cut, deep and painful, ran down his arm from elbow to wrist. Shadow gave a soft little cry and seized his hand. Her breath was warm against the edges of the gash. "Are you badly injured?" she whispered.

"I don't think so. It's just a question of whether the knife was poisoned."

"They poison only their darts," said Sting. "But there'll be infection to cope with. Better let Shadow look after you."

"Yes," Leaf said. He glanced into the clearing. The Tree Companions, as though thrown into shock by the violence that had come from their brief invasion of the wagon, stood frozen along the road in silent groups of nine or ten, keeping their distance. The two dead ones lay crumpled where Crown had hurled them. The unmistakable figure of the Invisible, transparent but clearly outlined by a dark perimeter, could be seen to the right, near the border of the thicket: his eyes glittered fiercely, his lips were twisted in a strange smile. Crown was staring at him in slack-jawed astonishment. Everything seemed suspended, held floating motionless in the bowl of time. To Leaf the scene was an eerie tableau in which the only sense of ongoing process was supplied by the throbbing in his slashed arm. He hung moored at the center, waiting, waiting, incapable of action, trapped like others in timelessness. In that long pause he realized that another figure had appeared during the melee, and stood now calmly ten paces or so to the left of the grinning Invisible: a Tree Companion, taller than the others of his kind, clad in beads and gimcracks but undeniably a being of presence and majesty.

"The chief has arrived," Sting said hoarsely.

The stasis broke. Leaf released his breath and let his rigid body slump. Shadow tugged at him, saying, "Let me clean that cut for you." The chief of the Tree Companions stabbed the air with three outstretched fingers, pointing at the wagon, and called out five crisp, sharp, jubilant syllables; slowly and grandly he began to stalk toward the wagon. At the same moment the Invisible flickered brightly, like a sun about to die, and disappeared entirely from view. Crown, turning to Leaf, said in a thick voice, "It's all going crazy here. I was just imagining I saw one of the Invisibles from Theptis skulking around by the underbrush."

"You weren't imagining anything," Leaf told him. "He's been riding secretly with us since Theptis. Waiting to see what would happen to us when we came to the Tree Companions' wall."

Crown looked jarred by that. "When did you find that out?" he demanded.

Shadow said, "Let him be, Crown. Go and parley with the chief. If I don't clean Leaf's wound soon—"

"Just a minute. I need to know the truth. Leaf, when did you find out about this Invisible?"

"When I went up front to relieve Sting. He was in the driver's cabin. Laughing at me, jeering. The way they do."

"And you didn't tell me? Why?"

"There was no chance. He bothered me for a while, and then he vanished, and I was busy driving after that, and then we came to the wall, and then the Tree Companions—"

"What does he want from us?" Crown asked harshly, face pushed close to Leaf's.

Leaf was starting to feel fever rising. He swayed and leaned on Shadow. Her taut, resilient little form bore him with surprising strength. He said tiredly, "I don't know. Does anyone ever know what one of them wants!" The Tree Companion chief, meanwhile, had come up beside them and in a lusty, self-assured way slapped his open palm several times against the side of the wagon, as though taking possession of it. Crown whirled. The chief coolly spoke, voice level, inflections controlled. Crown shook his head. "What's he saying?" he barked. "Sting? *Sting*?"

"Come," Shadow said to Leaf. "Now. Please."

She led him toward the passenger castle. He sprawled on the furs while she searched busily through her case of unguents and ointments; then she came to him with a long green vial in her hand and said, "There'll be pain for you now."

"Wait."

He centered himself and disconnected, as well as he was able, the network of sensory apparatus that conveyed messages of discomfort from his arm to his brain. At once he felt his skin growing cooler, and he realized for the first time since the battle how much pain he had been in: so much that he had not had the wisdom to do anything about it. Dispassionately he watched as Shadow, all efficiency, probed his wound, parting the lips of the cut without squeamishness and swabbing its red interior. A faint tickling, unpleasant but not painful, was all he sensed. She looked up, finally, and said, "There'll be no infection. You can allow the wound to close now." In order to do that Leaf had to reestablish the neural connections to a certain degree, and as he unblocked the flow of impulses he felt sudden startling pain, both from the cut itself and from Shadow's medicines; but quickly he induced clotting, and a moment afterward he was deep in the disciplines that would encourage the sundered flesh to heal. The wound began to close. Lightly Shadow blotted the fresh blood from his arm and prepared a poultice; by the time she had it in place, the gaping slash had reduced itself to a thin raw line. "You'll live," she said. "You were lucky they don't poison their knives." He kissed the tip of her nose and they returned to the hatch area.

Sting and the Tree Companion chief were conducting some sort of discussion in pantomime, Sting's motions sweeping and broad, the chief's the merest flicks of fingers, while Crown stood by, an impassive column of darkness, arms folded sombrely. As Leaf and Shadow reappeared Crown said, "Sting isn't getting anywhere. It has to be a trance parley or we won't make contact. Help him, Shadow."

She nodded. To Leaf, Crown said, "How's the arm?"

"It'll be all right."

"How soon?"

"A day. Two, maybe. Sore for a week."

"We may be fighting again by sunrise."

"You told me yourself that we can't possibly survive a battle with these people."

"Even so," Crown said. "We may be fighting again by sunrise. If there's no other choice, we'll fight."

"And die?"

"And die," Crown said.

Leaf walked slowly away. Twilight had come. All vestiges of the rain had vanished, and the air was clear, crisp, growing chill, with a light wind out of the north that was gaining steadily in force. Beyond the thicket the tops of tall ropy-limbed trees were whipping about. The shards of the moon had moved into view, rough daggers of whiteness doing their slow dance about one another in the darkening sky. The poor old shattered moon, souvenir of an era long gone: it seemed a scratchy mirror for the tormented planet that owned it, for the fragmented race of races that was mankind. Leaf went to the nightmares, who stood patiently in harness, and passed among them, gently stroking their shaggy ears, caressing their blunt noses. Their eyes, liquid, intelligent, watchful, peered into his almost reproachfully. You promised us a stable, they seemed to be saying. Stallions, warmth, newly mown hay. Leaf shrugged. In this world, he told them wordlessly, it isn't always possible to keep one's promises. One does one's best, and one hopes that that is enough.

✹

Near the wagon Sting has assumed a cross-legged position on the damp ground. Shadow squats beside him; the chief, mantled in dignity, stands stiffly before them, but Shadow coaxes him with gentle gestures to come down to them. Sting's eyes are closed and his head lolls forward. He is already in trance. His left hand grasps Shadow's muscular furry thigh; he extends his right, palm upward, and after a moment the chief puts his own palm to it. Contact: the circuit is closed.

Leaf has no idea what messages are passing among the three of them, but yet, oddly, he does not feel excluded from the transaction. Such a sense of love and warmth radiates from Sting and Shadow and even from the Tree Companion that he is drawn in, he is enfolded by their communion. And Crown, too, is engulfed and absorbed by the group aura; his rigid martial posture eases, his grim face looks strangely peaceful. Of course it is Sting and Shadow who are most closely linked; Shadow is closer now to Sting than she has ever been to Leaf, but Leaf is untroubled by this. Jealousy and competitiveness are inconceivable now. He is Sting, Sting is Leaf, they all are Shadow and Crown, there are no boundaries separating one from another, just as there will be no boundaries in the All-Is-One that awaits every living creature, Sting and Crown and Shadow and Leaf, the Tree Companions, the Invisibles, the nightmares, the no-leg spiders.

They are getting down to cases now. Leaf is aware of strands of opposition and conflict manifesting themselves in the intricate negotiation that is taking, place. Although he is still without a clue to the content of the exchange, Leaf understands that the Tree Companion chief is stating a position of demand—calmly, bluntly, immovable—and Sting and Shadow are explaining to him that Crown is not at all likely to yield. More than that Leaf is unable to perceive, even when he is most deeply enmeshed in the larger consciousness of the trance-wrapped three. Nor does he know how much time is elapsing. The symphonic interchange—demand, response, development, climax—continues repetitively, indefinitely, reaching no resolution.

He feels, at last, a running-down, an attenuation of the experience. He begins to move outside the field of contact, or to have it move outside him. Spiderwebs of sensibility still connect him to the others even as Sting and Shadow and the chief rise and separate, but they are rapidly thinning and fraying, and in a moment they snap.

The contact ends.

The meeting was over. During the trance-time night had fallen, an extraordinarily black night against which the stars seemed unnaturally bright. The fragments of the moon had traveled far across the sky. So it had been a lengthy exchange; yet in the immediate vicinity of the wagon nothing seemed altered. Crown stood like a statue beside the wagon's entrance; the Tree Companions still occupied the cleared ground between the wagon and the gate. Once more a tableau, then: how easy it is to slide into motionlessness, Leaf thought, in these impoverished times. Stand and wait, stand and wait; but now motion returned. The Tree Companion pivoted and strode off without a word, signaling to his people, who gathered up their dead and followed him through the gate. From within they tugged the gate shut; there was the screeching sound of the bolts being forced home. Sting, looking dazed, whispered something to Shadow, who nodded and lightly touched his arm. They walked haltingly back to the wagon.

"Well?" Crown asked finally.

"They will allow us to pass," Sting said.

"How courteous of them."

"But they claim the wagon and everything that is in it."

Crown gasped. "By what right?"

"Right of prophecy," said Shadow. "There is a seer among them, an old woman of mixed stock, part White Crystal, part Tree Companion, part Invisible. She has told them that everything that has happened lately in the world was caused by the Soul for the sake of enriching the Tree Companions."

"Everything? They see the onslaught of the Teeth as a sign of divine favor?"

"Everything," said Sting. "The entire upheaval. All for their benefit. All done so that migrations would begin and refugees would come to this place, carrying with them valuable possessions, which they would surrender to those whom the Soul meant should own them, meaning the Tree Companions."

Crown laughed roughly. "If they want to be brigands, why not practice brigandage outright, with the right name on it, and not blame their greed on the Soul?"

"They don't see themselves as brigands," Shadow said. "There can be no denying the chief's sincerity. He and his people genuinely believe that the Soul has decreed all this for their own special good, that the time has come—"

"*Sincerity!*"

"—for the Tree Companions to become people of substance and property. Therefore they've built this wall across the highway, and as refugees come west, the Tree Companions relieve them of their possessions with the blessing of the Soul."

"I'd like to meet their prophet," Crown muttered.

Leaf said, "It was my understanding that Invisibles were unable to breed with other stocks."

Sting told him, with a shrug, "We report only what we learned as we sat there dreaming with the chief. The witch-woman is part Invisible, he said. Perhaps he was wrong, but he was doing no lying. Of that I'm certain."

"And I," Shadow put in.

"What happens to those who refuse to pay tribute?" Crown asked.

"The Tree Companions regard them as thwarters of the Soul's design," said Sting, "and fall upon them and put them to death. And then seize their goods."

Crown moved restlessly in a shallow circle in front of the wagon, kicking up gouts of soil out of the hard-packed roadbed. After a moment he said, "They dangle on vines. They chatter like foolish monkeys. What do they want with the merchandise of civilized folk? Our furs, our statuettes, our carvings, our flutes, our robes?"

"Having such things will make them equal in their own sight to the higher stocks," Sting said. "Not the things themselves, but the possession of them, do you see, Crown?"

"They'll have nothing of mine!"

"What will we do, then?" Leaf asked. "Sit here and wait for their darts?"

Crown caught Sting heavily by the shoulder. "Did they give us any sort of time limit? How long do we have before they attack?"

"There was nothing like an ultimatum. The chief seems unwilling to enter into warfare with us."

"Because he's afraid of his betters!"

"Because he thinks violence cheapens the decree of the Soul," Sting replied evenly. "Therefore he intends to wait for us to surrender our belongings voluntarily."

"He'll wait a hundred years!"

"He'll wait a few days," Shadow said. "If we haven't yielded, the attack will come. But what will you do, Crown? Suppose they were willing to wait your hundred years. Are you? We can't camp here forever."

"Are you suggesting we give them what they ask?"

"I merely want to know what strategy you have in mind," she said. "You admit yourself we can't defeat them in battle. We haven't done a very good job of aweing them into submission. You recognize that any attempt to destroy their wall will bring them upon us with their darts. You refuse to turn back and look for some other westward route. You rule out the alternative of yielding to them. Very well, Crown. What do you have in mind?"

"We'll wait a few days," Crown said thickly.

"The Teeth are heading this way!" Sting cried. "Shall we sit here and let them catch us?"

Crown shook his head. "Long before the Teeth get here, Sting, this place will be full of other refugees, many of them, as unwilling to give up their goods to these folk as we are. I can feel them already on the road, coming this way, two days' march from us, perhaps less. We'll make alliance with them. Four of us may be helpless against a swarm of poisonous apes, but fifty or a hundred strong fighters would send them scrambling up their own trees."

"No one will come this way," said Leaf. "No one but fools. Everyone passing through Theptis knows what's been done to the highway here. What good is the aid of fools?"

"We came this way," Crown snapped. "Are we such fools?"

"Perhaps we are. We were warned not to take Spider Highway, and we took it anyway."

"Because we refused to trust the word of Invisibles."

"Well, the Invisibles happened to be telling the truth, this time," Leaf said. "And the news must be all over Theptis. No one in his right mind will come this way now."

"I feel marchers already on the way, hundreds of them," Crown said. "I can sense these things, sometimes. What about you, Sting? You feel things ahead of time, don't you? They're coming, aren't they? Have no fear, Leaf. We'll have allies here in a day or so, and then let these thieving Tree Companions beware." Crown gestured broadly. "Leaf, set the nightmares loose to graze. And then everybody inside the wagon. We'll seal it and take turns standing watch through the night. This is a time for vigilance and courage."

"This is a time for digging graves," Sting murmured sourly, as they clambered into the wagon.

Crown and Shadow stood the first round of watches while Leaf and Sting napped in the back. Leaf fell asleep at once and dreamed he was living in some immense brutal eastern city—the buildings and street plan were unfamiliar to him, but the architecture was definitely eastern in style, gray and heavy, all parapets and cornices—that was coming under attack by the Teeth.

He observed everything from a many-windowed gallery atop an enormous square-sided brick tower that seemed like a survival from some remote prehistoric epoch. First, from the north, came the sound of the war song of the invaders, a nasty unendurable buzzing drone, piercing and intense, like the humming of highspeed polishing wheels at work on metal plates. That dread music brought the inhabitants of the city spilling into the streets—all stocks, Flower Givers and Sand Shapers and White Crystals and Dancing Stars and even Tree Companions, absurdly garbed in mercantile robes as though they were so many fat citified Fingers—but no one was able to escape, for there were so many people, colliding and jostling and stumbling and falling in helpless heaps, that they blocked every avenue and alleyway.

Into this chaos now entered the vanguard of the Teeth; shuffling forward in their peculiar bent-kneed crouch, trampling those who had fallen. They looked half-beast, half-demon: squat thick-thewed flat-headed long-muzzled creatures, naked, hairy, their skins the color of sand, their eyes glinting with insatiable hungers. Leaf's dreaming mind subtly magnified and distorted them so that they came hopping into the city like a band of giant toothy frogs, thump-thump, bare fleshy feet slapping pavement in sinister reverberations, short powerful arms swinging almost comically at each leaping stride. The kinship of mankind meant nothing to these carnivorous beings. They had been penned up too long in the cold, mountainous, barren country of the far northeast, living on such scraps and strings as the animals of the forest yielded, and they saw their fellow humans as mere meat stockpiled by the Soul against this day of vengeance. Efficiently, now, they began their round-up in the newly conquered city, seizing everyone in sight, cloistering the dazed prisoners in hastily rigged pens: these we eat tonight at our victory feast; these we save for tomorrow's dinner; these become dried meat to carry with us on the march; these we kill for sport; these we keep as slaves. Leaf watched the Teeth erecting their huge spits.

Kindling their fierce roasting-fires. Diligent search teams fanned out through the suburbs. No one would escape. Leaf stirred and groaned, reached the threshold of wakefulness, fell back into dream. Would they find him in his tower? Smoke, gray and greasy, boiled up out of a hundred parts of town. Leaping flames. Rivulets of blood ran in the streets. He was choking. A terrible dream. But was it only a dream? This was how it had actually been in Holy Town hours after he and Crown and Sting and Shadow had managed to get away, this was no doubt as it had happened in city after city along the tormented coastal strip, very likely something of this sort was going on now in—where?—Bone Harbor? Ved-uru? Alsandar? He could smell the penetrating odor of roasting meat. He could hear the heavy lalloping sound of a Teeth patrol running up the stairs of his tower. They had him. Yes, here, now, now, a dozen Teeth bursting suddenly into his hiding place, grinning broadly—Pure Stream, they had captured a Pure Stream! What a coup! Beasts. Beasts. Prodding him, testing his flesh. Not plump enough for them, eh? This one's pretty lean. We'll cook him anyway. Pure Stream meat, it enlarges the soul, it makes you into something more than you were. Take him downstairs! To the spit, to the spit, to the—

"Leaf?"

"I warn you—you won't like—the flavor—"

"Leaf, wake up!"

"The fires—oh, the stink!"

"Leaf!"

It was Shadow. She shook him gently, plucked at his shoulder. He blinked and slowly sat up. His wounded arm was throbbing again; he felt feverish. Effects of the dream. A dream, only a dream. He shivered and tried to center himself, working at it, banishing the fever, banishing the shreds of dark fantasy that were still shrouding his mind.

"Are you all right?" she asked.

"I was dreaming about the Teeth," he told her. He shook his head, trying to clear it. "Am I to stand watch now?"

She nodded. "Up front. Driver's cabin."

"Has anything been happening?"

"Nothing. Not a thing." She reached up and drew her fingertips lightly along the sides of his jaws. Her eyes were warm and bright, her smile was loving. "The Teeth are far away, Leaf."

"From us, maybe. Not from others."

"They were sent by the will of the Soul."

"I know, I know." How often had he preached acceptance! This is the will, and we bow to it. This is the road, and we travel it uncomplainingly. But yet, but yet—he shuddered. The dream mode persisted. He was altogether disoriented. Dream-Teeth nibbled at his flesh. The inner chambers of his spirit resonated to the screams of those on the spits, the sounds of rending and tearing, the unbearable reek of burning cities. In ten days, half a world torn apart. So much pain, so much death, so much that had been beautiful destroyed by relentless savages who would not halt until, the Soul only knew when, they had had their full measure of revenge. The will of the Soul sends them upon us. Accept. Accept. He could not find his center. Shadow held him, straining to encompass his body with her arms. After a moment he began to feel less troubled, but he remained scattered, diffused, present only in part, some portion of his mind nailed as if by spikes into that monstrous ash-strewn wasteland that the Teeth had created out of the fair and fertile eastern provinces.

She released him. "Go," she whispered. "It's quiet up front. You'll be able to find yourself again."

He took her place in the driver's cabin, going silently past Sting, who had replaced Crown on watch amidwagon. Half the night was gone. All was still in the roadside clearing; the great wooden gate was shut tight and nobody was about. By cold starlight Leaf saw the nightmares browsing patiently at the edge of the thicket. Gentle horses, almost human. If I must be visited by nightmares, he thought, let it be by their kind.

Shadow had been right. In the stillness he grew calm, and perspective returned. Lamentation would not restore the shattered eastland, expressions of horror and shock would not turn the Teeth into pious tillers of the soil. The Soul had decreed chaos: so be it. This is the road we must travel, and who dares ask why? Once the world had been whole and now it is fragmented, and that is the way things are because that is the way things were meant to be. He became less tense. Anguish dropped from him. He was Leaf again.

Toward dawn the visible world lost its sharp starlit edge; a soft fog settled over the wagon, and rain fell for a time, a light, pure rain, barely audible, altogether different in character from yesterday's vicious storm. In the strange light just preceding sunrise the world took on a delicate pearly mistiness; and out of that mist an apparition materialized. Leaf saw a figure come drifting through the closed gate—through it—a ghostly, incorporeal figure. He thought it might be the Invisible who had been lurking close by the wagon since Theptis, but no, this was a woman, old and frail, an attenuated woman, smaller even than Shadow, more slender. Leaf knew who she must be: the mixed-blood woman. The prophetess, the seer, she who had stirred up these Tree Companions to block the highway. Her skin had the White Crystal waxiness of texture and the White Crystal nodes of dark, coarse hair; the form of her body was essentially that of a Tree Companion, thin and long-armed; and from her Invisible forebears, it seemed, she had inherited that perplexing intangibility, that look of existing always on the borderland between hallucination and reality, between mist and flesh. Mixed-bloods were uncommon; Leaf had rarely seen one, and never had encountered one who combined in herself so many different stocks. It was said that people of mixed blood had strange gifts. Surely this one did. How had she bypassed the wall? Not even Invisibles could travel through solid wood. Perhaps this was just a dream, then, or possibly she had some way of projecting an image of herself into his mind from a point within the Tree Companion village. He did not understand.

He watched her a long while. She appeared real enough. She halted twenty paces from the nose of the wagon and scanned the entire horizon slowly, her eyes coming to rest at last on the window of the driver's cabin. She was aware, certainly, that he was looking at her, and she looked back, eye to eye, staring unflinchingly. They remained locked that way for some minutes. Her expression was glum and opaque, a withered scowl, but suddenly she brightened and smiled intensely at him and it was such a *knowing* smile that Leaf was thrown into terror by the old witch, and glanced away, shamed and defeated.

When he lifted his head she was out of view; he pressed himself against the window, craned his neck, and found her down near the middle of the wagon. She was inspecting its exterior workmanship at close range, picking and prying at the hull. Then she wandered away, out to the place where Sting and Shadow and the chief had had their conference, and sat down cross-legged where they had been sitting. She became extraordinarily still, as if she were asleep, or in trance. Just when Leaf began to think she would never move again, she took a pipe of carved bone from a pouch at her waist, filled it with a gray-blue powder, and lit it. He searched her face for tokens of revelation, but nothing showed on it; she grew ever more impassive and unreadable. When the pipe went out, she filled it again, and smoked a second time, and still Leaf watched her, his face pushed awkwardly against the window, his body growing stiff. The first rays of sunlight now arrived, pink shading rapidly into gold. As the brightness deepened the witch-woman imperceptibly became less solid; she was fading away, moment by moment, and shortly he saw nothing of her but her pipe and her kerchief, and then the clearing was empty. The long shadows of the six nightmares splashed against the wooden palisade. Leaf's head lolled. I've been dozing, he thought. It's morning, and all's well. He went to awaken Crown.

✹

They breakfasted lightly. Leaf and Shadow led the horses to water at a small clear brook five minutes' walk toward Theptis. Sting foraged awhile in the thicket for nuts and berries, and having filled two pails, went aft to doze in the furs. Crown brooded in his trophy room and said nothing to anyone. A few Tree Companions could be seen watching the wagon from perches in the crowns of towering red-leaved trees on the hillside just behind the wall. Nothing happened until midmorning. Then, at a time when all four travelers were within the wagon, a dozen newcomers appeared, forerunners of the refugee tribe that Crown's intuitions had correctly predicted. They came slowly up the road, on foot, dusty and tired-looking, staggering beneath huge untidy bundles of belongings and supplies. They were square-headed muscular people, as tall as Leaf or taller, with the look of warriors about them; they carried short swords at their waists, and both men and women were conspicuously scarred. Their skins were gray, tinged with pale green, and they had more fingers and toes than was usual among mankind.

Leaf had never seen their sort before. "Do you know them?" he asked Sting.

"Snow Hunters," Sting said. "Close kin to the Sand Shapers, I think. Midcaste and said to be unfriendly to strangers. They live southwest of Theptis, in the hill country."

"One would think they'd be safe there," said Shadow.

Sting shrugged. "No one's safe from the Teeth, eh? Not even on the highest hills. Not even in the thickest jungles."

The Snow Hunters dropped their packs and looked around. The wagon drew them first; they seemed stunned by the opulence of it.

They examined it in wonder, touching it as the witch-woman had, scrutinizing it from every side. When they saw faces looking out at them, they nudged one another and pointed and whispered, but they did not smile, nor did they wave greetings. After a time they went on to the wall and studied it with the same childlike curiosity. It appeared to baffle them. They measured it with their outstretched hands, pressed their bodies against it, pushed at it with their shoulders, tapped the timbers, plucked at the sturdy bindings of vine. By this time perhaps a dozen more of them had come up the road; they too clustered about the wagon, doing as the first had done, and then continued toward the wall. More and more Snow Hunters were arriving, in groups of three or four. One trio, standing apart from the others, gave the impression of being tribal leaders; they consulted, nodded, summoned and dismissed other members of the tribe with forceful gestures of their hands.

"Let's go out and parley," Crown said. He donned his best armor and selected an array of elegant dress weapons. To Sting he gave a slender dagger. Shadow would not bear arms, and Leaf preferred to arm himself in nothing but Pure Stream prestige. His status as a member of the ancestral stock, he found, served him as well as a sword in most encounters with strangers.

The Snow Hunters—about a hundred of them now had gathered, with still more down the way—looked apprehensive as Crown and his companions descended from the wagon. Crown's bulk and gladiatorial swagger seemed far more threatening to these strong-bodied warlike folk than they had been to the chattering Tree Companions, and Leaf's presence too appeared disturbing to them. Warily they moved to form a loose semicircle about their three leaders; they stood close by one another, murmuring tensely, and their hands hovered near the hilts of their swords.

Crown stepped forward. "Careful," Leaf said softly. "They're on edge. Don't push them."

But Crown, with a display of slick diplomacy unusual for him, quickly put the Snow Hunters at their ease with a warm gesture of greeting—hands pressed to shoulders, palms outward, fingers spread wide—and a few hearty words of welcome. Introductions were exchanged. The spokesman for the tribe, an iron-faced man with frosty eyes and hard cheekbones, was called Sky; the names of his co-captains were Blade and Shield. Sky spoke in a flat, quiet voice, everything on the same note. He seemed empty, burned out, a man who had entered some realm of exhaustion far beyond mere fatigue. They had been on the road for three days and three nights almost without a halt, said Sky. Last week a major force of Teeth had started westward through the mid-coastal lowlands bound for Theptis, and one band of these, just a few hundred warriors, had lost its way, going south into the hill country. Their aimless wanderings brought these straying Teeth without warning into the secluded village of the Snow Hunters, and there had been a terrible battle in which more than half of Sky's people had perished. The survivors, having slipped away into the trackless forest, had made their way by back roads to Spider Highway, and, numbed by shock and grief, had been marching like machines toward the Middle River, hoping to find some new hillside in the sparsely populated territories of the far northwest. They could never return to their old home, Shield declared, for it had been desecrated by the feasting of the Teeth.

"But what is this wall?" Sky asked.

Crown explained, telling the Snow Hunters about the Tree Companions and their prophetess, and of her promise that the booty of all refugees was to be surrendered to them. "They lie in wait for us with their darts," Crown said. "Four of us were helpless against them. But they would never dare challenge a force the size of yours. We'll have their wall smashed down by nightfall!"

"The Tree Companions are said to be fierce foes," Sky remarked quietly.

"Nothing but monkeys," said Crown. "They'll scramble to their treetops if we just draw our swords."

"And shower us with their poisoned arrows," Shield muttered. "Friend, we have little stomach for further warfare. Too many of us have fallen this week."

"What will you do?" Crown cried. "Give them your swords, and your tunics and your wives' rings and the sandals off your feet?"

Sky closed his eyes and stood motionless, remaining silent for a long moment. At length, without opening his eyes, he said in a voice that came from the center of an immense void, "We will talk with the Tree Companions and learn what they actually demand of us, and then we will make our decisions and form our plans."

"The wall—if you fight beside us, we can destroy this wall, and open the road to all who flee the Teeth!"

With cold patience Sky said, "We will speak with you again afterward," and turned away. "Now we will rest, and wait for the Tree Companions to come forth."

The Snow Hunters withdrew, sprawling out along the margin of the thicket just under the wall. There they huddled in rows, staring at the ground, waiting. Crown scowled, spat, shook his head. Turning to Leaf he said, "They have the true look of fighters. There's something that marks a fighter apart from other men, Leaf, and I can tell when it's there, and these Snow Hunters have it. They have the strength, they have the power; they have the spirit of battle in them. And yet, see them now! Squatting there like fat frightened Fingers!"

"They've been beaten badly," Leaf said. "They've been driven from their homeland. They know what it is to look back across a hilltop and see the fires in which your kinsmen are being cooked. That takes the fighting spirit out of a person, Crown."

"No. Losing makes the flame burn brighter. It makes you feverish with the desire for revenge."

"Does it? What do you know about losing? You were never so much as touched by any of your opponents."

Crown glared at him. "I'm not speaking of dueling. Do you think my life has gone untouched by the Teeth? What am I doing here on this dirt road with all that I still own packed into a single wagon? But I'm no walking dead man like these Snow Hunters. I'm not running away, I'm going to find an army. And then I'll go back east and take my vengeance. While they—afraid of monkeys—"

"They've been marching day and night," Shadow said. "They must have been on the road when the purple rain was falling. They've spent all their strength while we've been riding in your wagon, Crown. Once they've had a little rest, perhaps they—"

"Afraid of *monkeys*!"

Crown shook with wrath. He strode up and down before the wagon, pounding his fists into his thighs. Leaf feared that he would go across to the Snow Hunters and attempt by bluster to force them into an alliance. Leaf understood the mood of these people: shattered and drained though they were, they might lash out in sudden savage irritation if Crown goaded them too severely. Possibly some hours of rest, as Shadow had suggested, and they might feel more like helping Crown drive his way through the Tree Companions' wall. But not now. Not now.

The gate in the wall opened. Some twenty of the forest folk emerged, among them the tribal chief and—Leaf caught his breath in awe—the ancient seeress, who looked across the way and bestowed on Leaf another of her penetrating comfortless smiles.

"What kind of creature is that?" Crown asked.

"The mixed-blood witch," said Leaf. "I saw her at dawn, while I was standing watch."

"Look!" Shadow cried. "She flickers and fades like an Invisible! But her pelt is like yours, Sting, and her shape is that of—"

"She frightens me," Sting said hoarsely. He was shaking. "She foretells death for us. We have little time left to us, friends. She is the goddess of death, that one." He plucked at Crown's elbow, unprotected by the armour. "Come! Let's start back along Spider Highway! Better to take our chances in the desert than to stay here and die!"

"Quiet," Crown snapped. "There's no going back. The Teeth are already in Theptis. They'll be moving out along this road in a day or two. There's only one direction for us."

"But the wall," Sting said.

"The wall will be in ruins by nightfall," Crown told him.

The chief of the Tree Companions was conferring with Sky and Blade and Shield. Evidently the Snow Hunters knew something of the language of the Tree Companions, for Leaf could hear vocal interchanges, supplemented by pantomime and sign language. The chief pointed to himself often, to the wall, to the prophetess; he indicated the packs the Snow Hunters had been carrying; he jerked his thumb angrily toward Crown's wagon. The conversation lasted nearly half an hour and seemed to reach an amicable outcome. The Tree Companions departed, this time leaving the gate open. Sky, Shield, and Blade moved among their people, issuing instructions. The Snow Hunters drew food from their packs—dried roots, seeds, smoked meat—and lunched in silence. Afterward, boys who carried huge waterbags made of sewn hides slung between them on poles went off to the creek to replenish their supply, and the rest of the Snow Hunters rose, stretched, wandered in narrow circles about the clearing, as if getting ready to resume the march. Crown was seized by furious impatience. "What are they going to do?" he demanded. "What deal have they made?"

"I imagine they've submitted to the terms," Leaf said.

"No! No! I need their help!" Crown, in anguish, hammered at himself with his fists. "I have to talk to them," he muttered.

"Wait. Don't push them, Crown."

"What's the use? What's the use?" Now the Snow Hunters were hoisting their packs to their shoulders. No doubt of it; they were going to leave. Crown hurried across the clearing. Sky, busily directing the order of march, grudgingly gave him attention. "Where are you going?" Crown asked.

"Westward," said Sky.

"What about us?"

"March with us, if you wish."

"My wagon!"

"You can't get it through the gate, can you?"

Crown reared up as though he would strike the Snow Hunter in rage. "If you would aid us, the wall would fall! Look, how can I abandon my wagon? I need to reach my kinsmen in the Flatlands. I'll assemble an army; I'll return to the east and push the Teeth back into the mountains where they belong. I've lost too much time already. I must get through. Don't you want to see the Teeth destroyed?"

"It's nothing to us," Sky said evenly. "Our lands are lost to us forever. Vengeance is meaningless. Your pardon. My people need my guidance."

More than half the Snow Hunters had passed through the gate already. Leaf joined the procession. On the far side of the wall he discovered that the dense thicket along the highway's northern rim had been cleared for a considerable distance, and a few small wooden buildings, hostelries or depots, stood at the edge of the road. Another twenty or thirty paces farther along, a secondary path led northward into the forest; this was evidently the route to the Tree Companions' village. Traffic on that path was heavy just now. Hundreds of forest folk were streaming from the village to the highway, where a strange, repellent scene was being enacted. Each Snow Hunter in turn halted, unburdened himself of his pack, and laid it open. Three or four Tree Companions then picked through it, each seizing one item of value—a knife, a comb, a piece of jewelry, a fine cloak—and running triumphantly off with it. Once he had submitted to this harrying of his possessions, the Snow Hunter gathered up his pack, shouldered it, and marched on, head bowed, body slumping. Tribute. Leaf felt chilled. These proud warriors, homeless now, yielding up their remaining treasures to—he tried to choke off the word, and could not—to a tribe of monkeys. And moving onward, soiled, unmanned. Of all that he had seen since the Teeth had split the world apart, this was the most sad.

Leaf started back toward the wagon. He saw Sky, Shield, and Blade at the rear of the column of Snow Hunters. Their faces were ashen; they could not meet his eyes. Sky managed a half-hearted salute as he passed by.

"I wish you good fortune on your journey," Leaf said.

"I wish you better fortune than we have had," said Sky hollowly, and went on.

Leaf found Crown standing rigid in the middle of the highway, hands on hips. "Cowards!" he called in a bitter voice. "Weaklings!"

"And now it's our turn," Leaf said.

"What do you mean?"

"The time's come for us to face hard truths. We have to give up the wagon, Crown."

"Never."

"We agree that we can't turn back. And we can't go forward so long as the wall's there. If we stay here, the Tree Companions will eventually kill us, if the Teeth don't overtake us first. Listen to me, Crown. We don't have to give the Tree Companions everything we have. The wagon itself, some of our spare clothing, some trinkets, the furnishings of the wagon—they'll be satisfied with that. We can load the rest of our goods on the horses and go safely through the gate as foot-pilgrims."

"I ignore this, Leaf."

"I know you do. I also know what the wagon means to you. I wish you could keep it. I wish I could stay with the wagon myself. Don't you think I'd rather ride west in comfort than slog through the rain and the cold? But we can't keep it. *We can't keep it,* Crown, that's the heart of the situation. We can go back east in the wagon and get lost in the desert, we can sit here and wait for the Tree Companions to lose patience and kill us, or we can give up the wagon and get out of this place with our skins still whole. What sort of choices are those? We have no choice. I've been telling you that for two days. Be reasonable, Crown!"

Crown glanced coldly at Sting and Shadow. "Find the chief and go into trance with him again. Tell him that I'll give him swords, armor, his pick of the finest things in the wagon. So long as he'll dismantle part of the wall and let the wagon itself pass through."

"We made that offer yesterday," Sting said glumly.

"And?"

"He insists on the wagon. The old witch has promised it to him for a palace."

"No," Crown said. *"NO!"* His wild roaring cry echoed from the hills. After a moment, more calmly, he said, "I have another idea. Leaf, Sting, come with me. The gate's open. We'll go to the village and seize the witch-woman. We'll grab her quickly, before anyone realizes what we're doing. They won't dare molest us while she's in our hands. Then, Sting, you tell the chief that unless they open the wall for us, we'll kill her." Crown chuckled. "Once she realizes we're serious, she'll tell them to hop it. Anybody that old wants to live forever. And they'll obey her. You can bet on that. They'll obey her! Come, now." Crown started toward the gate at a vigorous pace. He took a dozen strides, halted, looked back. Neither Leaf nor Sting had moved.

"Well? Why aren't you coming?"

"I won't do it," said Leaf tiredly. "It's crazy, Crown. She's a witch, she's part Invisible—she already knows your scheme. She probably knew of it before you knew of it yourself. How can we hope to catch her?"

"Let me worry about that."

"Even if we did, Crown—no. No. I won't have any part of it. It's an impossible idea. Even if we did seize her. We'd be standing there holding a sword to her throat, and the chief would give a signal, and they'd put a hundred darts in us before we could move a muscle. It's insane, Crown."

"I ask you to come with me."

"You've had your answer."

"Then I'll go without you."

"As you choose," Leaf said quietly. "But you won't be seeing me again."

"Eh?"

"I'm going to collect what I own and let the Tree Companions take their pick of it, and then I'll hurry forward and catch up with the Snow Hunters. In a week or so I'll be at the Middle River. Shadow, will you come with me, or are you determined to stay here and die with Crown?"

The Dancing Star looked toward the muddy ground. "I don't know," she said. "Let me think a moment."

"Sting?"

"I'm going with you."

Leaf beckoned to Crown. "Please. Come to your senses, Crown. For the last time—give up the wagon and let's get going, all four of us."

"You disgust me."

"Then this is where we part," Leaf said. "I wish you good fortune. Sting, let's assemble our belongings. Shadow? Will you be coming with us?"

"We have an obligation toward Crown," she said.

"To help him drive his wagon, yes. But not to die a foolish death for him. Crown has lost his wagon, Shadow, though he won't admit that yet. If the wagon's no longer his, our contract is voided. I hope you'll join us."

He entered the wagon and went to the midcabin cupboard where he stored the few possessions he had managed to bring with him out of the east. A pair of glistening boots made of the leathery skins of stick-creatures, two ancient copper coins, three ornamental ivory medallions, a shirt of dark red silk, a thick, heavily worked belt—not much, not much at all, the salvage of a lifetime. He packed rapidly. He took with him a slab of dried meat and some bread; that would last him a day or two, and when it was gone he would learn from Sting or the Snow Hunters the arts of gathering food in the wilderness.

"Are you ready?"

"Ready as I'll ever be," Sting said. His pack was almost empty—a change of clothing, a hatchet, a knife, some smoked fish, nothing else.

"Let's go, then."

As Sting and Leaf moved toward the exit hatch, Shadow scrambled up into the wagon. She looked tight-strung and grave; her nostrils were flared, her eyes downcast. Without a word she went past Leaf and began loading her pack. Leaf waited for her. After a few minutes she reappeared and nodded to him.

"Poor Crown," she whispered. "Is there no way—"

"You heard him," Leaf said.

They emerged from the wagon. Crown had not moved. He stood as if rooted, midway between wagon and wall. Leaf gave him a quizzical look, as if to ask whether he had changed his mind, but Crown took no notice. Shrugging, Leaf walked around him, toward the edge of the thicket, where the nightmares were nibbling leaves. Affectionately he reached up to stroke the long neck of the nearest horse, and Crown suddenly came to life, shouting, "Those are my animals! Keep your hands off them!"

"I'm only saying goodbye to them."

"You think I'm going to let you have some? You think I'm that crazy, Leaf?"

Leaf looked sadly at him. "We plan to do our traveling on foot, Crown. I'm only saying goodbye. The nightmares were my friends. You can't understand that, can you?"

"Keep away from those animals! *Keep away*!"

Leaf sighed. "Whatever you say." Shadow, as usual, was right: poor Crown. Leaf adjusted his pack and moved off toward the gate, Shadow beside him, Sting a few paces to the rear. As he and Shadow reached the gate, Leaf looked back and saw Crown still motionless, saw Sting pausing, putting down his pack, dropping to his knees. "Anything wrong?" Leaf called.

"Tore a bootlace," Sting said. "You two go on ahead. It'll take me a minute to fix it."

"We can wait."

Leaf and Shadow stood within the frame of the gate while Sting knotted his lace. After a few moments he rose and reached for his pack, saying, "That ought to hold me until tonight, and then I'll see if I can't—"

"Watch out!" Leaf yelled.

Crown erupted abruptly from his freeze, and, letting forth a lunatic cry, rushed with terrible swiftness toward Sting. There was no chance for Sting to make one of his little leaps: Crown seized him, held him high overhead like a child, and, grunting in frantic rage, hurled the little man toward the ravine. Arms and legs flailing, Sting traveled on a high arc over the edge; he seemed to dance in midair for an instant, and then he dropped from view. There was a long diminishing shriek, and silence. Silence.

Leaf stood stunned. "Hurry," Shadow said. "Crown's coming!"

Crown, swinging around, now rumbled like a machine of death toward Leaf and Shadow. His wild red eyes glittered ferociously. Leaf did not move; Shadow shook him urgently, and finally he pushed himself into action. Together they caught hold of the massive gate and, straining, swung it shut, slamming it just as Crown crashed into it. Leaf forced the reluctant bolts into place. Crown roared and pounded at the gate, but he was unable to force it.

Shadow shivered and wept. Leaf drew her to him and held her for a moment. At length he said, "We'd better be on our way. The Snow Hunters are far ahead of us already."

"Sting—"

"I know. I know. Come, now."

Half a dozen Tree Companions were waiting for them by the wooden houses. They grinned, chattered, pointed to the packs. "All right," Leaf said. "Go ahead. Take whatever you want. Take everything, if you like."

Busy fingers picked through his pack and Shadow's. From Shadow the Tree Companions took a brocaded ribbon and a flat, smooth green stone. From Leaf they took one of the ivory medallions, both copper coins, and one of his stickskin boots. Tribute. Day by day, pieces of the past slipped from his grasp. He pulled the other boot from the pack and offered it to them, but they merely giggled and shook their heads. "One is of no use to me," he said. They would not take it. He tossed the boot into the grass beside the road.

The road curved gently toward the north and began a slow rise, following the flank of the forested hills in which the Tree Companions made their homes. Leaf and Shadow marched, mechanically, saying little. The bootprints of the Snow Hunters were everywhere along the road, but the Snow Hunters themselves were far ahead, out of sight. It was early afternoon, and the day had become bright, unexpectedly warm. After an hour Shadow said, "I must rest."

Her teeth were clacking. She crouched by the roadside and wrapped her arms about her chest. Dancing Stars, covered with thick fur, usually wore no clothing except in the bleakest winters; but her pelt did her no good now.

"Are you ill?" he asked.

"It'll pass. I'm reacting. Sting—"

"Yes."

"And Crown. I feel so unhappy about Crown."

"A madman," Leaf said. "A murderer."

"Don't judge him so casually, Leaf. He's a man under sentence of death, and he knows it, and he's suffering from it, and when the fear and pain became unbearable to him he reached out for Sting. He didn't know what he was doing. He needed to smash something, that was all, to relieve his own torment."

"We're all going to die sooner or later," Leaf said. "That doesn't generally drive us to kill our friends."

"I don't mean sooner or later. I mean that Crown will die tonight or tomorrow."

"Why should he?"

"What can he do now to save himself, Leaf?"

"He could yield to the Tree Companions and pass the gate on foot, as we've done."

"You know he'd never abandon the wagon."

"Well, then, he can harness the nightmares and turn around toward Theptis. At least he'd have a chance to make it through to the Sunset Highway that way."

"He can't do that either," Shadow said.

"Why not?"

"He can't drive the wagon."

"There's no one left to do it for him. His life's at stake. For once he could eat his pride and—"

"I didn't say *won't* drive the wagon, Leaf. I said *can't*. Crown's incapable. He isn't able to make dream contact with the nightmares. Why do you think he always used hired drivers? Why was he so insistent on making you drive in the purple rain? He doesn't have the mind-power. Did you ever see a Dark Laker driving nightmares? Ever?"

Leaf stared at her. "You knew this all along?"

"From the beginning, yes."

"Is that why you hesitated to leave him at the gate? When you were talking about our contract with him?"

She nodded. "If all three of us left him, we were condemning him to death. He has no way of escaping the Tree Companions now unless he forces himself to leave the wagon, and he won't do that. They'll fall on him and kill him, today, tomorrow, whenever."

Leaf closed his eyes, shook his head. "I feel a kind of shame. Now that I know we were leaving him helpless. He could have spoken."

"Too proud."

"Yes. Yes. It's just as well he didn't say anything. We all have responsibilities to one another, but there are limits. You and I and Sting were under no obligation to die simply because Crown couldn't bring himself to give up his pretty wagon. But still—still—" He locked his hands tightly together. "Why did you finally decide to leave, then?"

"For the reason you just gave. I didn't want Crown to die, but I didn't believe I owed him my life. Besides, you had said you were going to go, no matter what."

"Poor, crazy Crown."

"And when he killed Sting—a life for a life, Leaf. All vows are canceled now. I feel no guilt."

"Nor I."

"I think the fever is leaving me."

"Let's rest a few minutes more," Leaf said.

It was more than an hour before Leaf judged Shadow strong enough to go on. The highway now described a steady upgrade, not steep but making constant demands on their stamina, and they moved slowly. As the day's warmth began to dwindle, they reached the crest of the grade, and rested again at a place from which they could see the road ahead winding in switchbacks into a green, pleasant valley. Far below were the Snow Hunters, resting also by the side of a fair-size stream.

"Smoke," Shadow said. "Do you smell it?"

"Campfires down there, I suppose."

"I don't think they have any fires going. I don't see any."

"The Tree Companions, then."

"It must be a big fire."

"No matter," Leaf said. "Are you ready to continue?"

"I hear a sound—"

A voice from behind and uphill of them said, "And so it ends the usual way, in foolishness and death, and the All-Is-One grows greater."

Leaf whirled, springing to his feet. He heard laughter on the hillside and saw movements in the underbrush; after a moment he made out a dim, faintly outlined figure, and realized that an Invisible was coming toward them, the same one, no doubt, who had traveled with them from Theptis.

"What do you want?" Leaf called.

"Want? Want? I want nothing. I'm merely passing through." The Invisible pointed over his shoulder. "You can see the whole thing from the top of this hill. Your big friend put up a mighty struggle, he killed many of them, but the darts, the darts—" The Invisible laughed. "He was dying, but even so he wasn't going to let them have his wagon. Such a stubborn man. Such a foolish man. Well, a happy journey to you both."

"Don't leave yet!" Leaf cried. But even the outlines of the Invisible were fading. Only the laughter remained, and then that too was gone.

Leaf threw desperate questions into the air and, receiving no replies, turned and rushed up the hillside, clawing at the thick shrubbery. In ten minutes he was at the summit, and stood gasping and panting, looking back across a precipitous valley to the stretch of road they had just traversed. He could see everything clearly from here: the Tree Companion village nestling in the forest, the highway, the shacks by the side of the road, the wall, the clearing beyond the wall. And the wagon. The roof was gone and the sides had tumbled outward. Bright spears of flame shot high, and a black, billowing cloud of smoke stained the air. Leaf stood watching Crown's pyre a long while before returning to Shadow.

They descended toward the place where the Snow Hunters had made their camp. Breaking a long silence, Shadow said, "There must once have been a time when the world was different, when all people were of the same kind, and everyone lived in peace. A golden age, long gone. How did things change, Leaf? How did we bring this upon ourselves?"

"Nothing has changed," Leaf said, "except the look of our bodies. Inside we're the same. There never was any golden age."

"There were no Teeth, once."

"There were always Teeth, under one name or another. True peace never lasted long. Greed and hatred always existed."

"Do you believe that, truly?"

"I do. I believe that mankind is mankind, all of us the same whatever our shape, and such changes as come upon us are trifles, and the best we can ever do is find such happiness for ourselves as we can, however dark the times."

"These are darker times than most, Leaf."

"Perhaps."

"These are evil times. The end of all things approaches."

Leaf smiled. "Let it come. These are the times we were meant to live in, and no asking why, and no use longing for easier times. Pain ends when acceptance begins. This is what we have now. We make the best of it. This is the road we travel. Day by day we lose what was never ours, day by day we slip closer to the All-Is-One, and nothing matters, Shadow, nothing except learning to accept what comes. Yes?"

"Yes," she said. "How far is it to the Middle River?"

"Another few days."

"And from there to your kinsmen by the Inland Sea?"

"I don't know," he said. "However long it takes us is however long it will take. Are you very tired?"

"Not as tired as I thought I'd be."

"It isn't far to the Snow Hunters' camp. We'll sleep well tonight."

"Crown," she said. "Sting."

"What about them?"

"They also sleep."

"In the All-Is-One," Leaf said. "Beyond all trouble. Beyond all pain."

"And that beautiful wagon is a charred ruin!"

"If only Crown had had the grace to surrender it freely, once he knew he was dying. But then he wouldn't have been Crown, would he? Poor Crown. Poor crazy Crown." There was a stirring ahead, suddenly. "Look. The Snow Hunters see us. There's Sky. Blade." Leaf waved at them and shouted. Sky waved back, and Blade, and a few of the others. "May we camp with you tonight?" Leaf called. Sky answered something, but his words were blown away by the wind. He sounded friendly, Leaf thought. He sounded friendly. "Come," Leaf said, and he and Shadow hurried down the slope.

TRIPS

During the most active phase of my career in the 1960s and 1970s I wrote novels with almost obsessive regularity, but after 1972 or so I often needed to be prodded into writing short stories. Every one of the fourteen stories in this volume was written at some editor's direct request. It was all too easy, in that troubled era, for me not to write at all; but I had *to write such novels as* The Stochastic Man *and* Shadrach in the Furnace, *even so, because I was contractually bound to do them, and I have always honored my contracts. Waking up in the morning and saying, "Hi ho, I think I'll write a short story for somebody today!" —no, I stopped feeling such impulses decades ago. Only when some friend or colleague who was editing an anthology of new fiction asked me to contribute something could I push myself into tackling the job.*

But I have always responded to a good challenge, and the one that came from Barry Malzberg and Ed Ferman in the winter of 1972-73 was a beauty. They were editing a book called Final Stage: The Ultimate Science Fiction Anthology, *and each story in it was supposed to be the definitive statement of its theme—time travel, immortality, space exploration, robots and androids, the future of sex, etc. Malzberg and Ferman offered a list of themes to a select group of writers and asked them to pick the one that held the greatest personal appeal.*

Isaac Asimov, of course, took robots, and who would begrudge that choice to him? Harlan Ellison and Joanna Russ tackled the future of sex from very different viewpoints. I wanted time travel, but I think Philip K. Dick beat me to it, or else I simply opted right away for alternative universes and left the time-travel theme free for him; I don't quite remember. At any rate, I set about my task, which was to create close to a dozen alternative Californias in the space of some 12,000 words. And so I did, in March, 1973, with a profligacy of invention that would serve to fill a pair of trilogies today.

When the much-heralded "ultimate anthology" came out, I was appalled to discover that my story had been cut to shreds, the carefully calculated prose effects slashed, the elaborate historical backgrounds outrageously mutilated, three whole sections simply deleted. Harlan Ellison and Poul Anderson had had the same experience. I protested vociferously to editors Malzberg and Ferman, who replied that they hadn't been aware of the heavy-handed revisions and were as annoyed as I was. They took the matter up with the publisher. "Well," the publisher's editor said, "the book was a little long, so I cut parts of some of the stories." Without consulting the writers? "Yes," she replied. "I figured, it's only science fiction, so why would anyone care?" Back in those distant days before s-f routinely made best-seller lists, science-fiction writers were mere plantation hands, and we could be sold down the river without the slightest qualm. When the book was reprinted in paperback, the original texts were restored, but I carried a grudge against that editor—who eventually gave up editing and became a lawyer—to the end of her days. I suppose I carry it still. Sometimes I wonder which circle of Hell she's in now, the one for editors, or the one reserved for lawyers.

Does this path have a heart? All paths are the same: they lead nowhere. They are paths going through the bush, or into the bush. In my own life I could say I have traversed long, long paths, but I am not anywhere...Does this path have a heart? If it does, the path is good, if it doesn't, it is of no use. Both paths lead nowhere; but one has a heart, the other doesn't. One makes for a joyful journey; as long as you follow it, you are one with it. The other will make you curse your life.

THE TEACHINGS OF DON JUAN

1.

The second place you come to—the first having proved unsatisfactory, for one reason and another—is a city which could almost be San

Francisco. Perhaps it is, sitting out there on the peninsula between the ocean and the bay, white buildings clambering over improbably steep hills. It occupies the place in your psychic space that San Francisco has always occupied, although you don't really know yet what this city calls itself. Perhaps you'll find out before long.

You go forward. What you feel first is the strangeness of the familiar, and then the utter heartless familiarity of the strange. For example the automobiles, and there are plenty of them, are all halftracks: low sleek sexy sedans that have the flashy Detroit styling, the usual chrome, the usual streamlining, the low-raked windows all agleam, but there are only two wheels, both of them in front, with a pair of tread-belts circling endlessly in back. Is this good design for city use? Who knows? Somebody evidently thinks so, here. And then the newspapers: the format is the same, narrow columns, gaudy screaming headlines, miles of black type on coarse grayish-white paper, but the names and the places have been changed. You scan the front page of a newspaper in the window of a curbside vending machine. Big photo of Chairman DeGrasse, serving as host at a reception for the Patagonian Ambassador. An account of the tribal massacres in the highlands of Dzungaria. Details of the solitude epidemic that is devastating Persepolis. When the halftracks stall on the hillsides, which is often, the other drivers ring silvery chimes, politely venting their impatience. Men who look like Navahos chant what sound like sutras in the intersections. The traffic lights are blue and orange. Clothing tends toward the prosaic, grays and dark blues, but the cut and slope of men's jackets has an angular formal eighteenth-century look, verging on pomposity.

You pick up a bright coin that lies in the street; it is vaguely metallic but rubbery, as if you could compress it between your fingers, and its thick edges bear incuse lettering: TO GOD WE OWE OUR SWORDS. On the next block a squat two-story building is ablaze, and agitated clerks do a desperate dance. The fire engine is glossy green and its pump looks like a diabolical cannon embellished with sweeping flanges; it spouts a glistening yellow foam that eats the flames and, oxidizing, runs off down the gutter, a trickle of sluggish blue fluid. Everyone wears eyeglasses here, everyone. At a sidewalk cafe, pale waitresses offer mugs of boiling-hot milk into which the silent tight-faced patrons put cinnamon, mustard, and what seems to be Tabasco sauce. You offer your coin and try a sample, imitating what they do, and everyone bursts into laughter. The girl behind the counter pushes a thick stack of paper currency at you by way of change: UNITED FEDERAL COLUMBIAN REPUBLIC, each bill declares, GOOD FOR ONE EXCHANGE. Illegible signatures. Portrait of early leader of the republic, so famous that they give him no label of identification, bewigged, wall-eyed, ecstatic. You sip your milk, blowing gently. A light scum begins to form on its speckled surface. Sirens start to wail. About you, the other milk-drinkers stir uneasily. A parade is coming. Trumpets, drums, far-off chanting. Look! Four naked boys carry an open brocaded litter on which there sits an immense block of ice, a great frosted cube, mysterious, impenetrable. "Patagonia!" the onlookers cry sadly. The word is wrenched from them: "Patagonia!" Next, marching by himself, a mitered bishop advances, all in green, curtseying to the crowd, tossing hearty blessings as though they were flowers. "Forget your sins! Cancel your debts! All is made new! All is good!" You shiver and peer intently into his eyes as he passes you, hoping that he will single you out for an embrace. He is terribly tall but white-haired and fragile, somehow, despite his agility and energy. He reminds you of Norman, your wife's older brother, and perhaps he *is* Norman, the Norman of this place, and you wonder if he can give you news of Elizabeth, the Elizabeth of this place, but you say nothing and he goes by.

And then comes a tremendous wooden scaffold on wheels, a true juggernaut, at the summit of which rests a polished statue carved out of gleaming black stone: a human figure, male, plump, arms intricately folded, face complacent. The statue emanates a sense of vast Sumerian calm. The face is that of Chairman DeGrasse. "He'll die in the first blizzard," murmurs a man to your left. Another, turning suddenly, says with great force, "No, it's going to be done the proper way. He'll last until the time of the accidents, just as he's supposed to. I'll bet on that." Instantly they are nose to nose, glaring, and then they are wagering—a tense complicated ritual involving slapping of palms, interchanges of slips of paper, formal voiding of spittle, hysterical appeals to witnesses. The emotional climate here seems a trifle too intense. You decide to move along. Warily you leave the café, looking in all directions.

2.

Before you began your travels you were told how essential it was to define your intended role. Were you going to be a tourist, or an explorer, or an infiltrator? Those are the choices that confront anyone arriving at a new place. Each bears its special risks.

To opt for being a tourist is to choose the easiest but most contemptible path; ultimately it's the most dangerous one, too, in a certain sense. You have to accept the built-in epithets that go with the part: they will think of you as a *foolish* tourist, an *ignorant* tourist, a *vulgar* tourist, a *mere* tourist. Do you want to be considered mere? Are you able to accept that? Is that really your preferred self-image—baffled, bewildered, led about by the nose? You'll sign up for packaged tours, you'll carry guidebooks and cameras, you'll go to the cathedral and the museums and the marketplace, and you'll remain always on the outside of things, seeing a great deal, experiencing nothing. What a waste! You will be diminished by the very traveling that you thought would expand you. Tourism hollows and parches you. All places become one: a hotel, a smiling, swarthy, sunglassed guide, a bus, a plaza, a fountain, a marketplace, a museum, a cathedral. You are transformed into a feeble shriveled thing made out of glued-together travel folders; you are naked but for your visas; the sum of your life's adventures is a box of leftover small change from many indistinguishable lands.

To be an explorer is to make the macho choice. You swagger in, bent on conquest; for isn't any discovery a kind of conquest? Your existential position, like that of any mere tourist, lies outside the heart of things, but you are unashamed of that. And while tourists are essentially passive, the explorer's role is active: an explorer intends to grasp that heart, take possession, squeeze. In the explorer's role you consciously cloak yourself in the trappings of power: self-assurance, thick bankroll, stack of credit cards. You capitalize on the glamour of being a stranger. Your curiosity is invincible; you ask unabashed questions about the most intimate things, never for an instant relinquishing eye contact. You open locked doors and flash bright lights into curtained rooms. You are Magellan; you are Malinowski; you are Captain Cook. You will gain much, but—ah, here is the price!—you will always be feared and hated, you will never be permitted to attain the true core. Nor is superficiality the worst peril. Remember that Magellan and Captain Cook left their bones on tropic beaches. Sometimes the natives lose patience with explorers.

The infiltrator, though? His is at once the most difficult role and the most rewarding one. Will it be yours? Consider. You'll have to get right with it when you reach your destination, instantly learn the regulations, find your way around like an old hand, discover the location of shops and freeways and hotels, figure out the units of currency, the rules of social intercourse—all of this knowledge mastered surreptitiously, through observation alone, while moving about silently, camouflaged, never asking for help. You must become a part of the world you have entered, and the way to do it is to encourage a general assumption that you already are a part of it, have always been a part of it. Wherever you land, you need to recognize that life has been going on for millions of years, life goes on there steadily, with you or without you; you are the intrusive one, and if you don't want to feel intrusive you'd better learn fast how to fit in.

Of course, it isn't easy. The infiltrator doesn't have the privilege of buying stability by acting dumb. You won't be able to say, "How much does it cost to ride on the cable car?" You won't be able to say, "I'm from somewhere else, and this is the kind of money I carry, dollars quarters pennies halves nickels, is any of it legal tender here?" You don't dare identify yourself in any way as an outsider. If you don't get the idioms or the accent right, you can tell them you grew up out of town, but that's as much as you can reveal. The truth is your eternal secret, even when you're in trouble, *especially* when you're in trouble. When your back's to the wall you won't have time to say, "Look, I wasn't born in this universe at all, you see, I came zipping in from some other place, so pardon me, forgive me, excuse me, pity me." No, no, no, you can't do that. They won't believe you, and even if they do, they'll make it all the worse for you once they know. If you want to infiltrate, Cameron, you've got to fake it all the way. Jaunty smile; steely, even gaze. And you have to infiltrate. You know that, don't you? You don't really have any choice.

Infiltrating has its dangers, too. The rough part comes when they find you out, and they always will find you out. Then they'll react bitterly against your deception; they'll lash out in blind rage. If you're lucky, you'll be gone before they learn your sweaty little secret. Before they discover the discarded phrasebook hidden in the boarding-house room, before they stumble on the torn-off pages of your private journal. They'll find you out. They always do. But by then you'll be somewhere else, you hope, beyond the reach of their anger and their sorrow, beyond their reach.

3.

Suppose I show you, for Exhibit A, Cameron reacting to an extraordinary situation. You can test your own resilience by trying to picture yourself in his position. There has been a sensation in Cameron's mind very much like that of the extinction of the cosmos: a thunderclap, everything going black, a blankness, a total absence. Followed by the return of light, flowing inward upon him like high tide on the celestial shore, a surging stream of brightness moving with inexorable certainty. He stands flatfooted, dumbfounded, high on a bare hillside in warm early-hour sunlight. The house—redwood timbers, picture window, driftwood sculptures, paintings, books, records, refrigerator, gallon jugs of red wine, carpets, tiles, avocado plants in wooden tubs, carport, car, driveway—is gone. The neighboring houses are gone. The winding street is gone. The eucalyptus forest that ought to be behind him, rising toward the crest of the hill, is gone. Downslope there is no Oakland, there is no Berkeley, only a scattering of crude squatter's shacks running raggedly along unpaved switchbacks toward the pure blue bay. Across the water there is no Bay Bridge; on the far shore there is no San Francisco. The Golden Gate Bridge does not span the gap between the city and the Marin headland—Cameron is astonished, not that he didn't expect something like this, but that the transformation is so complete, so absolute. "If you don't want your world any more," the old man had said, "you can drop it, can't you? Let go of it, let it drop. Can't you? Of course you can."

And so Cameron has let go of it. He's in another place entirely, now. Wherever this place is, it isn't home. The sprawling Bay Area cities and towns aren't here, never were. Goodbye, San Leandro, San Mateo, El Cerrito, Walnut Creek. He sees a landscape of gentle bare hills, rolling meadows, the dry brown grass of summer; the scarring hand of man is evident only occasionally. He begins to adapt. This is what he must have wanted, after all; and though he has been jarred by the shock of transition, he is recovering quickly; he is settling in; he feels already that he could belong here. He will explore this unfamiliar world, and if he finds it good he will discover a niche for himself. The air is sweet. The sky is cloudless. Has he really gone to some new place, or is he still in the old place and has everything else that was there simply gone away? Easy. He has gone. Everything else has gone. The cosmos has entered into a transitional phase. Nothing's stable any more. From this moment onward, Cameron's existence is a conditional matter, subject to ready alteration. What did the old man say? *Go wherever you like. Define your world as you would like it to be, and go there, and if you discover that you don't care for this or don't need that, why, go somewhere else. It's all trips, this universe.* What else is there? There isn't anything but trips. Just trips. So here you are, friend. New frameworks! New patterns! New!

4.

There is a sound to his left, the crackling of dry brush underfoot, and Cameron turns, looking straight into the morning sun, and sees a man on horseback approaching him. He is tall, slender, about Cameron's own height and build, it seems, but perhaps a shade broader through the shoulders. His hair, like Cameron's, is golden, but it is much longer, descending in a straight flow to his shoulders and tumbling onto his chest. He has a soft, full curling beard, untrimmed but tidy. He wears a wide-brimmed hat, buckskin chaps, and a light fringed jacket of tawny leather. Because of the sunlight Cameron has difficulty at first making out his features, but after a moment his eyes adjust and he sees that the other's face is very much like his own: thin lips, jutting high-bridged nose, cleft chin, cool blue eyes below heavy brows. Of course. Your face is my face. You and I, I and you, drawn to the same place at the same time across the many worlds. Cameron had not expected this, but now that it has happened it seems to have been inevitable.

They look at each other. Neither speaks. During that silent moment Cameron invents a scene for them. He imagines the other dismounting, inspecting him in wonder, walking around him, peering into his face, studying it, frowning, shaking his head, finally grinning and saying:

—I'll be damned. I never knew I had a twin brother. But here you are. It's just like looking in the mirror.

—We aren't twins.

—We've got the same face. Same everything. Trim away a little hair and nobody could tell me from you, you from me. If we aren't twins, what are we?

—We're closer than brothers.

—I don't follow your meaning, friend.

—This is how it is: I'm you. You're me. One soul, one identity. What's your name?

—Cameron.

—Of course. First name?

—Kit.

—That's short for Christopher, isn't it? My name is Cameron too. Chris. Short for Christopher. I tell you, we're one and the same person, out of two different worlds. Closer than brothers. Closer than anything.

None of this is said, however. Instead, the man in the leather clothing rides slowly toward Cameron, pauses, gives him a long incurious stare, and says simply, "Morning. Nice day." And continues onward.

"Wait," Cameron says.

The man halts. Looks back. "What?"

Never ask for help. Fake it all the way. Jaunty smile; steely, even gaze.

Yes. Cameron remembers all that. Somehow, though, infiltration seems easier to bring off in a city. You can blend into the background there. More difficult here, exposed as you are against the stark, unpeopled landscape.

Cameron says, as casually as he can, using what he hopes is a colorless neutral accent, "I've been traveling out from inland. Came a long way."

"Umm. Didn't think you were from around here. Your clothes."

"Inland clothes."

"The way you talk. Different. So?"

"New to these parts. Wondered if you could tell me a place I could hire a room till I got settled."

"You come all this way on foot?"

"Had a mule. Lost him back in the valley. Lost everything I had with me."

"Umm. Indians cutting up again. You give them a little gin, they go crazy." The other smiles faintly; then the smile fades and he retreats into impassivity, sitting motionless with hands on thighs, face a mask of patience that seems merely to be a thin covering for impatience or worse.

—Indians?—

"They gave me a rough time," Cameron says, getting into the fantasy of it.

"Umm."

"Cleaned me out, let me go."

"Umm. Umm."

Cameron feels his sense of a shared identity with this man lessening. There is no way of engaging him. I am you, you are I, and yet you take no notice of the strange fact that I wear your face and body, you seem to show no interest in me at all. Or else you hide your interest amazingly well.

Cameron says, "You know where I can get lodging?"

"Nothing much around here. Not many settlers this side of the bay, I guess."

"I'm strong. I can do most any kind of work. Maybe you could use—"

"Umm. No." Cold dismissal glitters in the frosty eyes. Cameron wonders how often people in the world of his former life saw such a look in his own. A tug on the reins. Your time is up, stranger. The horse swings around and begins picking its way daintily along the path.

Desperately Cameron calls, "One thing more!"

"Umm?"

"Is your name Cameron?"

A flicker of interest. "Might be."

"Christopher Cameron. Kit. Chris. That you?"

"Kit." The other's eyes drill into his own. The mouth compresses until the lips are invisible: not a scowl but a speculative, pensive movement. There is tension in the way the other man grasps his reins. For the first time Cameron feels that he has made contact. "Kit Cameron, yes. Why?"

"Your wife," Cameron says. "Her name Elizabeth?"

The tension increases. The other Cameron is cloaked in explosive silence. Something terrible is building within him. Then, unexpectedly, the tension snaps. The other man spits, scowls, slumps in his saddle. "My woman's dead," he mutters. "Say, who the hell are you? What do you want with me?"

"I'm—I'm—" Cameron falters. He is overwhelmed by fear and pity. A bad start, a lamentable start. He trembles. He had not thought it would be anything like this. With an effort he masters himself. Fiercely he says, "I've got to know. Was her name Elizabeth?" For an answer the horseman whacks his heels savagely against his mount's ribs and gallops away, fleeing as though he has had an encounter with Satan.

5.

Go, the old man said. You know the score. This is how it is: everything's random, nothing's fixed unless we want it to be, and even then the system isn't as stable as we think it is. So go. Go. Go, he said, and, of course, hearing something like that, Cameron went. What else could he do, once he had his freedom, but abandon his native universe and try a different one? Notice that I didn't say a better one, just a different one. Or two or three or five different ones. It was a gamble, certainly. He might lose everything that mattered to him, and gain nothing worth having. But what of it? Every day is full of gambles like that: you stake your life whenever you open a door. You never know what's heading your way, not ever, and still you choose to play the game. How can a man be expected to become all he's capable of becoming if he spends his whole life pacing up and down the same courtyard? Go. Make your voyages. Time forks, again and again and again. New universes split off at each instant of decision. Left turn, right turn, honk your horn, jump the traffic light, hit your gas, hit your brake, every action spawns whole galaxies of possibility. We move through a soup of infinities. If repressing a sneeze generates an alternative continuum, what, then, are the consequences of the truly major acts, the assassinations and inseminations, the conversions, the renunciations? Go. And as you travel, mull these thoughts constantly. Part of the game is discerning the precipitating factors that shaped the worlds you visit. What's the story here? Dirt roads, donkey-carts, hand-sewn clothes. No Industrial Revolution, is that it? The steam-engine man—what was his name, Savery, Newcomen Watt?—smothered in his cradle? No mines, no factories, no assembly lines, no dark satanic mills. That must be it. The air is so pure here: you can tell by that, it's a simpler era. Very good, Cameron. You see the patterns swiftly. But now try somewhere else. Your own self has rejected you here; besides, this place has no Elizabeth. Close your eyes. Summon the lightning.

6.

The parade has reached a disturbing level of frenzy. Marchers and floats now occupy the side streets as well as the main boulevard, and there is no way to escape from their demonic enthusiasm. Streamers cascade from office windows, and gigantic photographs of Chairman DeGrasse have sprouted on every wall, suddenly, like dark infestations of lichen. A boy presses close against Cameron, extends a clenched fist, opens his fingers: on his palm rests a glittering jeweled case, egg-shaped, thumbnail-sized, "Spores from Patagonia," he says. "Let me have ten exchanges and they're yours." Politely Cameron declines. A woman in a blue and orange frock tugs at his arm and says urgently, "All the rumors are true, you know. They've just been confirmed. What are you going to do about that? What are you going to do?" Cameron shrugs and smiles and disengages himself. A man with gleaming buttons asks, "Are you enjoying the festival? I've sold everything, and I'm going to move to the highway next Godsday." Cameron nods and murmurs congratulations, hoping congratulations are in order. He turns a corner and confronts, once more, the bishop who looks like Elizabeth's brother, who is, he concludes, indeed Elizabeth's brother. "Forget your sins!" he is crying still. "Cancel your debts!" Cameron thrusts his head between two plump girls at the curb and attempts to call to him, but his voice fails, nothing coming forth but a hoarse wordless rasp, and the bishop moves on. Moving on is a good idea, Cameron tells himself. This place exhausts him. He has come to it too soon, and its manic tonality is more than he wants to handle. He finds a quiet alleyway, presses his cheek against a cool brick wall, and stands there breathing deeply until he is calm enough to depart. All right. Onward.

7.

Empty grasslands spread to the horizon. This could be the Gobi steppe. Cameron sees neither cities nor towns nor even villages, just six or seven squat black tents pitched in a loose circle in the saddle between two low gray-green hummocks, a few hundred yards from where he stands. He looks beyond, across the gently folded land, and spies dark animal figures at the limits of his range of vision: about a dozen horses, close together, muzzle to muzzle, flank to flank, horses with riders. Or perhaps they are a congregation of centaurs. Anything is possible. He decides, though, that they are Indians, a war party of young braves, maybe, camping in these desolate plains. They see him. Quite likely they saw him some while before he noticed them. Casually they break out of their grouping, wheel, ride in his direction.

He awaits them. Why should he flee? Where could he hide? Their pace accelerates from trot to canter, from canter to wild gallop; now they plunge toward him with fluid ferocity and a terrifying eagerness. They wear open leather jackets and rough rawhide leggings; they carry lances, bows, battle-axes, long curved swords; they ride small, agile horses, hardly more than ponies, tireless packets of energy. They surround him, pulling up, the fierce little steeds rearing and whinnying; they peer at him, point, laugh, exchange harsh derisive comments in a mysterious language. Then, solemnly, they begin to ride slowly in a wide circle around him. They are flat-faced, small-nosed, bearded, with broad, prominent cheekbones; the crowns of their heads are shaven but long black hair streams down over their ears and the napes of their necks. Heavy folds in the upper lids give their eyes a slanted look. Their skins are copper-colored but with an underlying golden tinge, as though these are not Indians at all, but—what? Japanese? A samurai corps? No, probably not Japanese. But not Indians either.

They continue to circle him, gradually moving more swiftly. They chatter to one another and occasionally hurl what sound like questions at him. They seem fascinated by him, but also contemptuous. In a sudden demonstration of horsemanship one of them cuts from the circular formation and, goading his horse to an instant gallop, streaks past Cameron, leaning down to jab a finger into his forearm. Then another does it, and another, streaking back and forth across the circle, poking him, plucking at his hair, tweaking him, nearly running him down. They draw their swords and swish them through the air just above his head. They menace him, or pretend to, with their lances. Throughout it all they laugh. He stands perfectly still. This ordeal, he suspects, is a test of his courage. Which he passes, eventually. The lunatic galloping ceases; they rein in, and several of them dismount.

They are little men, chest-high to him but thicker through the chest and shoulders than he is. One unships a leather pouch and offers it to him with an unmistakable gesture: take, drink. Cameron sips cautiously. It is a thick grayish fluid, both sweet and sour. Fermented milk? He gags, winces, forces himself to sip again; they watch him closely. The second taste isn't so bad. He takes a third more willingly and gravely returns the pouch. The warriors laugh, not derisively now but more in applause, and the man who had given him the pouch slaps Cameron's shoulder admiringly. He tosses the pouch back to Cameron. Then he leaps to his saddle, and abruptly they all take off. Mongols, Cameron realizes. The sons of Genghis Khan, riding to the horizon. A worldwide empire? Yes, and this must be the wild west for them, the frontier, where the young men enact their rites of passage. Back in Europe, after seven centuries of Mongol dominance, they have become citified, domesticated, sippers of wine, theatregoers, cultivators of gardens, but here they follow the ways of their all-conquering forefathers. Cameron shrugs. Nothing for him here. He takes a last sip of the milk and drops the pouch into the tall grass. Onward.

8.

No grass here. He sees the stumps of buildings, the blackened trunks of dead trees, mounds of broken tile and brick. The smell of death is in the air. All the bridges are down. Fog rolls in off the bay, dense and greasy, and becomes a screen on which images come alive. These ruins are inhabited. Figures move about. They are the living dead. Looking into the thick mist he sees a vision of the shock wave, he recoils as alpha particles shower his skin. He beholds the survivors emerging from their shattered houses, straggling into the smoldering streets, naked, stunned, their bodies charred, their eyes glazed, some of them with their hair on fire. The walking dead. No one speaks. No one asks why this has happened. He is watching a silent movie. The apocalyptic fire has touched the ground here; the land itself is burning. Blue phosphorescent flames rise from the earth. The final judgment, the day of wrath.

Now he hears a dread music beginning, a death march, all cellos and basses, the dark notes coming at wide intervals: ooom ooom ooom ooom ooom. And then the tempo picks up, the music becomes a danse macabre, syncopated, lively, the timbre still dark, the rhythms funereal: ooom ooom ooom-de-ooom de-ooom de-ooom de-ooom-de-ooom, jerky, chaotic, wildly gay. The distorted melody of the Ode to Joy lurks somewhere in the ragged strands of sound. The dying victims stretch their fleshless hands toward him. He shakes his head. What service can I do for you? Guilt assails him. He is a tourist in the land of their grief. Their eyes reproach him. He would embrace them, but he fears they will crumble at his touch, and he lets the procession go past him without doing anything to cross the gulf between himself and them. "Elizabeth?" he murmurs. "Norman?" They have no faces, only eyes. "What can I do? I can't do anything for you." Not even tears will come. He looks away. Though I speak with the tongues of men and of angels, and have not charity, I am become as sounding brass or a tinkling cymbal. And though I have the gift of prophecy, and understand all mysteries, and all knowledge; and though I have all faith, so that I could remove mountains, and have not charity, I am nothing. But this world is beyond the reach of love. He looks away. The sun appears. The fog burns off. The visions fade. He sees only the dead land, the ashes, the ruins. All right. Here we have no continuing city, but we seek one to come. Onward. Onward.

9.

And now, after this series of brief, disconcerting intermediate stops, Cameron has come to a city that is San Francisco beyond doubt, not some other city on San Francisco's site but a true San Francisco, a recognizable San Francisco. He pops into it atop Russian Hill, at the very crest, on a dazzling, brilliant, cloudless day. To his left, below, lies Fisherman's Wharf; ahead of him rises the Coit Tower; yes, and he can see the Ferry Building and the Bay Bridge. Familiar landmarks—but how strange all the rest seems! Where is the eye-stabbing Transamerica pyramid? Where is the colossal somber stalk of the Bank of America? The strangeness, he realizes, derives not so much from substitutions as from absences. The big Embarcadero developments are not there, nor the Chinatown Holiday Inn, nor the miserable tentacles of the elevated freeways, nor, apparently, anything else that was constructed in the last twenty years. This is the old short-shanked San Francisco of his boyhood, a sparkling miniature city, unManhattanized, skylineless. Surely he has returned to the place he knew in the sleepy 1950s, the tranquil Eisenhower years.

He heads downhill, searching for a newspaper box. He finds one at the corner of Hyde and North Point, a bright-yellow metal rectangle. *San Francisco Chronicle,* ten cents? Is that the right price for 1954? One Roosevelt dime goes into the slot. The paper, he finds, is dated Tuesday, August 19, 1975. In what Cameron still thinks of, with some irony now, as the real world, the world that has been receding rapidly from him all day in a series of discontinuous jumps, it is also Tuesday, the 19th of August, 1975. So he has not gone backward in time at all; he has come to a San Francisco where time had seemingly been standing still. Why? In vertigo he eyes the front page. A three-column headline declares:

FUEHRER ARRIVES IN WASHINGTON

Under it, to the left, a photograph of three men, smiling broadly, positively beaming at one another. The caption identifies them as President Kennedy, Fuehrer Goering, and Ambassador Togarashi of Japan, meeting in the White House Rose Garden. Cameron closes his eyes. Using no data other than the headline and the caption, he attempts to concoct a plausible speculation. This is a world, he decides, in which the Axis must have won the war. The United States is a

German fiefdom. There are no high rise buildings in San Francisco because the American economy, shattered by defeat, has not yet in thirty years of peace returned to a level where it can afford to erect them, or perhaps because American venture capital, prodded by the financial ministers of the Third Reich (Hjalmar Schacht? The name drifts out of the swampy recesses of memory) now tends to flow toward Europe. But how could it have happened? Cameron remembers the war years clearly, the tremendous surge of patriotism, the vast mobilization, the great national effort. *Rosie the Riveter. Lucky Strike Green Goes to War. Let's Remember Pearl Harbor, As We Did the Alamo.* He doesn't see any way the Germans might have brought America to her knees. Except one. The bomb, he thinks, the bomb, the Nazis get the bomb in 1940 and Wernher von Braun invents a transatlantic rocket, and New York and Washington are nuked one night and that's it, we've been pushed beyond the resources of patriotism; we cave in and surrender within a week. And so—

He studies the photograph. President Kennedy, grinning, standing between Reichsfuehrer Goering and a suave youthful-looking Japanese. Kennedy? Ted? No, this is Jack, the very same Jack who, looking jowly, heavy bags under his eyes, deep creases in his face—he must be almost sixty years old, nearing the end of what is probably his second term of office. Jacqueline waiting none too patiently for him upstairs. Get done with your Japs and Nazis, love, and let's have a few drinkies together before the concert. Yes. John-John and Caroline are somewhere on the premises too, the nation's darlings, models for young people everywhere. Yes. And Goering? Indeed, the very same Goering. Well into his eighties, monstrously fat, chin upon chin, multitudes of chins, vast bemedaled bosom, little mischievous eyes glittering with a long lifetime's cheery recollections of gratified lusts. How happy he looks! And how amiable! It was always impossible to hate Goering the way one loathed Goebbels, say, or Himmler or Streicher; Goering had charm, the outrageous charm of a *monstre sacré,* of a Nero, of a Caligula, and here he is alive in the 1970s, a mountain of immoral flesh, having survived Adolf to become—Cameron assumes—second Fuehrer and to be received in pomp at the White House, no less. Perhaps a state banquet tomorrow night, rollmops, sauerbraten, kassler rippchen, koenigsberger klopse, washed down with flagons of Bernkasteler Doktor '69, Schloss Johannisberg '71, or does the Fuehrer prefer beer? We have the finest lagers on tap, Löwenbrau, Würzburger Hofbrau—

But wait. Something rings false in Cameron's historical construct. He is unable to find in John F. Kennedy those depths of opportunism that would allow him to serve as puppet President of a Nazi-ruled America, taking orders from some slick-haired hard-eyed gauleiter and hopping obediently when the Fuehrer comes to town. Bomb or no bomb, there would have been a diehard underground resistance movement, decades of guerrilla warfare, bitter hatred of the German oppressor and of all collaborators. No surrender, then. The Axis has won the war, but the United States has retained its autonomy. Cameron revises his speculations. Suppose, he tells himself, Hitler in this universe did not break his pact with Stalin and invade Russia in the summer of 1941, but led his forces across the Channel instead to wipe out Britain. And the Japanese left Pearl Harbor alone, so the United States never was drawn into the war, which was over in fairly short order—say, by September of 1942. The Germans now rule Europe from Cornwall to the Urals and the Japanese have the whole Pacific, west of Hawaii; the United States, lost in dreamy neutrality, is an isolated nation, a giant Portugal, economically stagnant, largely cut off from world trade. There are no skyscrapers in San Francisco because no one sees reason to build anything in this country. Yes? Is this how it is?

He seats himself on the stoop of a house and explores his newspaper. This world has a stock market, albeit a sluggish one: the Dow-Jones Industrials stand at 354.61. Some of the listings are familiar—IBM, AT&T, General Motors—but many are not. Litton, Syntex, and Polaroid all are missing; so is Xerox, but he finds its primordial predecessor, Haloid, in the quotations. There are two baseball leagues, each with eight clubs; the Boston Braves have moved to Milwaukee but otherwise the table of teams could have come straight out of the 1940s. Brooklyn is leading in the National League, Philadelphia in the American. In the news section he finds recognizable names: New York has a Senator Rockefeller, Massachusetts has a Senator Kennedy. (Robert, apparently. He is currently in Italy. Yesterday he toured the majestic Tomb of Mussolini near the Colosseum, today he has an audience with Pope Benedict.) An airline advertisement invites San Franciscans to go to New York via TWA's glorious new Starliners, now only twelve hours with only a brief stop in Chicago. The accompanying sketch indicates that they have about reached the DC-4 level here, or is that a DC-6, with all those propellers?

The foreign news is tame and sketchy: not a word about Israel vs. the Arabs, the squabbling republics of Africa, the People's Republic of China, or the war in South America. Cameron assumes that the only surviving Jews are those of New York and Los Angeles, that Africa is one immense German colonial tract with a few patches under Italian rule, that China is governed by the Japanese, not by the heirs of Chairman Mao, and that the South American nations are torpid and unaggressive. Yes? Reading this newspaper is the strangest experience this voyage has given him so far, for the pages *look* right, the tone of the writing *feels* right, there is the insistent texture of unarguable reality about the whole paper, and yet everything is subtly off, everything has undergone a slight shift along the spectrum of events. The newspaper has the quality of a dream, but he has never known a dream to have such overwhelming substantive density.

He folds the paper under his arm and strolls toward the bay. A block from the waterfront he finds a branch of the Bank of America—some things withstand all permutations—and goes inside to change some money. There are risks, but he is curious. The teller unhesitatingly takes his five-dollar bill and hands him four singles and a little stack of coins. The singles are unremarkable, and Lincoln, Jefferson, and Washington occupy their familiar places on the cent, nickel, and quarter; but the dime shows Ben Franklin and the fifty-cent piece bears the features of a hearty-looking man, youngish, full-faced, bushy-haired, whom Cameron is unable to identify at all.

On the next corner eastward he comes to a public library. Now he can confirm his guesses. An almanac! Yes, and how odd the list of Presidents looks. Roosevelt, he learns, retired in poor health in 1940, and that, so far as he can discover, is the point of divergence between this world and his. The rest follows predictably enough. Wendell Willkie, defeating John Nance Garner in the 1940 election, maintains a policy of strict neutrality while—yes, it was as he imagined—the Germans and Japanese quickly conquer most of the world. Willkie dies in office during the 1944 Presidential campaign—Aha! That's Willkie on the half dollar!—and is briefly succeeded by Vice President McNary, who does not want the Presidency; a hastily recalled Republican convention nominates Robert Taft. Two terms then for Taft, who beats James Byrnes, and two for Thomas Dewey, and then in 1960 the long Republican era is ended at last by Senator Lyndon Johnson of Texas. Johnson's running mate—it is an amusing reversal, Cameron thinks—

is Senator John F. Kennedy of Massachusetts. After the traditional two terms, Johnson steps down and Vice President Kennedy wins the 1968 Presidential election. He has been re-elected in 1972, naturally; in this placid world incumbents always win. There is, of course, no UN here, there has been no Korean War, no movement of colonial liberation, no exploration of space. The almanac tells Cameron that Hitler lived until 1960, Mussolini until 1958. The world seems to have adapted remarkably readily to Axis rule, although a German army of occupation is still stationed in England.

He is tempted to go on and on, comparing histories, learning the transmuted destinies of such figures as Hubert Humphrey, Dwight Eisenhower, Harry Truman, Nikita Khrushchev, Lee Harvey Oswald, Juan Peron. But suddenly a more intimate curiosity flowers in him. In a hallway alcove he consults the telephone book. There is one directory covering both Alameda and Contra Costa counties, and it is a much more slender volume than the directory which in his world covers Oakland alone. There are two dozen Cameron listings, but none at his address, and no Christophers or Elizabeths or any plausible permutations of those names. On a hunch he looks in the San Francisco book. Nothing promising there either; but then he checks Elizabeth under her maiden name, Dudley, and yes, there is an Elizabeth Dudley at the familiar old address on Laguna. The discovery causes him to tremble. He rummages in his pocket, finds his Ben Franklin dime, drops it in the slot. He listens. There's the dial tone. He makes the call.

10.

The apartment, what he can see of it by peering past her shoulder, looks much as he remembers it: well-worn couches and chairs upholstered in burgundy and dark green, stark whitewashed walls, elaborate sculptures—her own—of gray driftwood, huge ferns in hanging containers. To behold these objects in these surroundings wrenches powerfully at his sense of time and place and afflicts him with an almost unbearable nostalgia. The last time he was here, if indeed he has ever been "here" in any sense, was in 1969; but the memories are vivid, and what he sees corresponds so closely to what he recalls that he feels transported to that earlier era. She stands in the doorway, studying him with cool curiosity tinged with unmistakable suspicion. She wears unexpectedly ordinary clothes, a loose-fitting embroidered white blouse and a short, pleated blue skirt, and her golden hair looks dull and carelessly combed, but surely she is the same woman from whom he parted this morning, the same woman with whom he has shared his life these past seven years, a beautiful woman, a tall woman, nearly as tall as he—on some occasions taller, it has seemed—with a serene smile and steady green eyes and smooth, taut skin. "Yes?" she says uncertainly. "Are you the man who phoned?"

"Yes. Chris Cameron." He searches her face for some flicker of recognition. "You don't know me? Not at all?"

"Not at all. Should I know you?"

"Perhaps. Probably not. It's hard to say."

"Have we once met? Is that it?"

"I'm not sure how I'm going to explain my relationship to you."

"So you said when you called. Your *relationship* to me? How can strangers have had a relationship?"

"It's complicated. May I come in?"

She laughs nervously, as though caught in some embarrassing faux pas. "Of course," she says, not without giving him a quick appraisal, making a rapid estimate of risk. The apartment is in fact almost exactly as he knew it, except that there is no stereo phonograph, only a bulky archaic Victrola, and her record collection is surprisingly scanty, and there are rather fewer books than his Elizabeth would have had. They confront one another stiffly. He is as uneasy over this encounter as she is, and finally it is she who seeks some kind of social lubricant, suggesting that they have a little wine. She offers him red or white.

"Red, please," he says.

She goes to a low sideboard and takes out two cheap, clumsy-looking tumblers. Then, effortlessly she lifts a gallon jug of wine from the floor and begins to unscrew its cap. "You were awfully mysterious on the phone," she says, "and you're still being mysterious now. What brings you here? Do we have mutual friends?"

"I think it wouldn't be untruthful to say that we do. At least in a manner of speaking."

"Your own manner of speaking is remarkably round-about, Mr Cameron."

"I can't help that right now. And call me Chris, please." As she pours the wine he watches her closely, thinking of that other Elizabeth, *his* Elizabeth, thinking how well he knows her body, the supple play of muscles in her back, the sleek texture of her skin, the firmness of her flesh, and he flashes instantly to their strange, absurdly romantic meeting years ago, that June when he had gone off alone into the Sierra high country for a week of backpacking and, following heaps of stones that he had wrongly taken to be trail markers, had come to a place well off the path, a private place, a cool dark glacial lake rimmed by brilliant patches of late-lying snow, and had begun to make camp, and had become suddenly aware of someone else's pack thirty yards away, and a pile of discarded clothing on the shore, and then had seen her, swimming just beyond a pine-tipped point, heading toward land, rising like Venus from the water, naked, noticing him, startled by his presence, apprehensive for a moment but then immediately making the best of it, relaxing, smiling, standing unashamed shin-deep in the chilly shallows and inviting him to join her for a swim.

These recollections of that first contact and all that ensued excite him terribly, for this person before him is at once the Elizabeth he loves, familiar, joined to him by the bond of shared experience, and also someone new, a complete stranger, from whom he can draw fresh inputs, that jolting gift of novelty which his Elizabeth can never again offer him. He stares at her shoulders and back with fierce, intense hunger; she turns toward him with the glasses of wine in her hands, and, before he can mask that wild gleam of desire, she receives it with full force. The impact is immediate. She recoils. She is not the Elizabeth of the Sierra lake; she seems unable to handle such a level of unexpected erotic voltage. Jerkily she thrusts the wine at him, her hands shaking so that she spills a little on her sleeve. He takes the glass and backs away, a bit dazed by his own frenzied upwelling of emotion. With an effort he calms himself. There is a long moment of awkward silence while they drink. The psychic atmosphere grows less torrid; a certain mood of remote, businesslike courtesy develops between them.

After the second glass of wine she says, "Now. How do you know me and what do you want from me?"

Briefly he closes his eyes. What can he tell her? How can he explain? He has rehearsed no strategies. Already he has managed to alarm her with a single unguarded glance; what effect would a confession of apparent madness have? But he has never used strategies with Elizabeth, has never resorted to any tactics except the tactic of utter candidness. And this is Elizabeth. Slowly he says, "In another existence you and I are married, Elizabeth. We live in the Oakland hills and we're extraordinarily happy together."

"Another existence?"

"In a world apart from this, a world where history took a different course a generation ago, where the Axis lost the war, where John Kennedy was President in 1963 and was killed by an assassin, where you and I met beside a lake in the Sierras and fell in love. There's an infinity of worlds, Elizabeth, side by side, worlds in which all possible variations of every possible event take place. Worlds in which you and I are married happily, in which you and I have been married and divorced, in which you and I don't exist, in which you exist and I don't, in which we meet and loathe one another, in which—in which—do you see, Elizabeth, there's a world for everything, and I've been traveling from world to world. I've seen nothing but wilderness where San Francisco ought to be, and I've met Mongol horsemen in the East Bay hills, and I've seen this whole area devastated by atomic warfare, and—does this sound insane to you, Elizabeth?"

"Just a little." She smiles. The old Elizabeth, cool, judicious, performing one of her specialities, the conditional acceptance of the unbelievable for the sake of some amusing conversation. "But go on. You've been jumping from world to world. I won't even bother to ask you how. What are you running away from?"

"I've never seen it that way. I'm running *toward.*"

"Toward what?"

"An infinity of worlds. An endless range of possible experience."

"That's a lot to swallow. Isn't one world enough for you to explore?"

"Evidently not."

"You had all infinity," she says. "Yet you chose to come to me. Presumably I'm the one point of familiarity for you in this otherwise strange world. Why come here? What's the point of your wanderings, if you seek the familiar? If all you wanted to do was find your way back to your Elizabeth, why did you leave her in the first place? Are you as happy with her as you claim to be?"

"I can be happy with her and still desire her in other guises."

"You sound driven."

"No," he says. "No more driven than Faust. I believe in searching as a way of life. Not searching *for,* just searching. And it's impossible to stop. To stop is to die, Elizabeth. Look at Faust, going on and on, going to Helen of Troy herself, experiencing everything the world has to offer, and always seeking more. When Faust finally cries out, *This is it, this is what I've been looking for, this is where I choose to stop,* Mephistopheles wins his bet."

"But that was Faust's moment of supreme happiness."

"True. When he attains it, though, he loses his soul to the devil, remember?"

"So you go on, on and on, world after world, seeking you know not what, just seeking, unable to stop. And yet you claim you're not driven."

He shakes his head. "Machines are driven. Animals are driven. I'm an autonomous human being operating out of free will. I don't make this journey because I have to, but because I want to."

"Or because you think you ought to want to."

"I'm motivated by feelings, not by intellectual calculations and preconceptions."

"That sounds very carefully thought out," she tells him. He is stung by her words, and looks away, down into his empty glass. She indicates that he should help himself to the wine. "I'm sorry," she says, her tone softening a little.

He says, "At any rate, I was in the library and there was a telephone directory and I found you. This is where you used to live in my world too, before we were married." He hesitates. "Do you mind if I ask—"

"What?"

"You're not married?"

"No. I live alone. And like it."

"You always were independent-minded."

"You talk as though you know me so well."

"I've been married to you for seven years."

"No. Not to me. Never to me. You don't know me at all."

He nods. "You're right. I don't really know you, Elizabeth, however much I think I do. But I want to. I feel drawn to you as strongly as I was to the other Elizabeth, that day in the mountains. It's always best right at the beginning, when two strangers reach toward one another, when the spark leaps the gap—" Tenderly he says, "May I spend the night here?"

"No."

Somehow the refusal comes as no surprise. He says, "You once gave me a different answer when I asked you that."

"Not I. Someone else."

"I'm sorry. It's so hard for me to keep you and her distinct in my mind, Elizabeth. But please don't turn me away. I've come so far to be with you."

"You came uninvited. Besides, I'd feel so strange with you—knowing you were thinking of her, comparing me with her, measuring our differences, our points of similarities—"

"What makes you think I would?"

"You would."

"I don't think that's sufficient reason for sending me away."

"I'll give you another," she says. Her eyes sparkle mischievously. "I never let myself get involved with married men."

She is teasing him now. He says, laughing, confident that she is beginning to yield. "That's the damnedest far-fetched excuse I've ever heard, Elizabeth!"

"Is it? I feel a great kinship with her. She has all my sympathies. Why should I help you deceive her?"

"Deceive? What an old-fashioned word! Do you think she'd object? She never expected me to be chaste on this trip. She'd be flattered and delighted to know that I went looking for you here. She'd be eager to hear about everything that went on between us. How could she possibly be hurt by knowing that I had been with you, when you and she are—"

"Nevertheless, I'd like you to leave. Please."

"You haven't given me one convincing reason."

"I don't need to."

"I love you. I want to spend the night with you."

"You love someone else who resembles me," she replies. "I keep telling you that. In any case, I don't love you. I don't find you attractive, I'm afraid."

"Oh. She does, but you—don't. I see. How do you find me then? Ugly? Overbearing? Repellent?"

"I find you disturbing," she says. "A little frightening. Much too intense, much too controlled, perhaps dangerous. You aren't my type. I'm probably not yours. Remember, I'm not the Elizabeth you met by that mountain lake. Perhaps I'd be happier if I were, but I'm not. I wish you had never come here. Now please go. Please."

11.

Onward. This place is all gleaming towers and airy bridges, a glistening fantasy of a city. High overhead float glassy bubbles, silent airborne passenger vehicles, containing two or three people apiece who sprawl in postures of elegant relaxation. Bronzed young boys and girls lie naked beside soaring fountains spewing turquoise-and-scarlet foam. Giant orchids burst in tropical voluptuousness from the walls of colossal hotels. Small mechanical birds wheel and dart in the soft air like golden bullets, emitting sweet pinging sounds. From the tips of the tallest buildings comes a darker music, a ground bass of swelling hundred-cycle notes oscillating around an insistent central rumble. This is a world two centuries ahead of his, at the least. He could never infiltrate here. He could never even be a tourist. The only role available to him is that of visiting savage. Jemmy Button among the Londoners, and what, after all, was Jemmy Button's fate? Not a happy one. Patagonia! Patagonia! Thees ticket eet ees no longer good here, sor. Colored rays dance in the sky, red, green, blue, exploding, showering the city with transcendental images. Cameron smiles. He will not let himself be overwhelmed, though this place is more confusing than the world of the halftrack automobiles. Jauntily he plants himself at the center of a small park between two lanes of flowing, noiseless traffic. It is a formal garden lush with toothy orange-fronded ferns and thorny skyrockets of looping cactus. Lovers stroll past him arm in arm, offering one another swigs from glossy sweat-beaded green flasks that look like tubes of polished jade. Delicately they dangle blue grapes before each other's lips; playfully they smile, arch their necks, take the bait with eager pounces; then they laugh, embrace, tumble into the dense moist grass, which stirs and sways and emits gentle thrumming melodies. This place pleases him. He wanders through the garden, thinking of Elizabeth, thinking of springtime, and, coming ultimately to a sinuous brook in which the city's tallest towers are reflected as inverted needles, he kneels to drink. The water is cool, sweet, tart, much like young wine. A moment after it touches his lips a mechanism rises from the spongy earth, five slender brassy columns, three with eye-sensors sprouting on all sides, one marked with a pattern of dark gridwork, one bearing an arrangement of winking colored lights. Out of the gridwork come ominous words in an unfathomable language. This is some kind of police machine, demanding his credentials: that much is clear. "I'm sorry," he says. "I can't understand what you're saying." Other machines are extruding themselves from trees, from the bed of the stream, from the hearts of the sturdiest ferns. "It's all right," he says. "I don't mean any harm. Just give me a chance to learn the language and I promise to become a useful citizen." One of the machines sprays him with a fine azure mist. Another drives a tiny needle into his forearm and extracts a droplet of blood. A crowd is gathering. They point, snicker, wink. The music of the building tops has become higher in pitch, more sinister in texture, it shakes the balmy air and threatens him in a personal way. "Let me stay," Cameron begs, but the music is shoving him, pushing him with a flat irresistible hand, inexorably squeezing him out of this world. He is too primitive for them. He is too coarse; he carries too many obsolete microbes. Very well. If that's what they want, he'll leave, not out of courtesy alone. In a flamboyant way he bids them farewell, bowing with a flourish worthy of Raleigh, blowing a kiss to the five-columned machine, smiling, even doing a little dance. Farewell. Farewell. The music rises to a wild crescendo. He hears celestial trumpets and distant thunder. Farewell. Onward.

12.

Here some kind of oriental marketplace has sprung up, foul-smelling, cluttered, medieval. Swarthy old men, white-bearded, in thick gray robes, sit patiently behind open burlap sacks of spices and grains. Lepers and cripples roam everywhere, begging importunately. Slender long-legged men wearing only tight loincloths and jingling dangling earrings of bright copper stalk through the crowd on solitary orbits, buying nothing, saying nothing; their skins are dark red; their faces are gaunt; their solemn features are finely modeled. They carry themselves like Inca princes. Perhaps they are Inca princes. In the haggle and babble of the market Cameron hears no recognizable tongue spoken. He sees the flash of gold as transactions are completed. The women balance immense burdens on their heads and show brilliant teeth when they smile. They favor patchwork skirts that cover their ankles, but they leave their breasts bare. Several of them glance provocatively at Cameron but he dares not return their quick dazzling probes until he knows what is permissible here. On the far side of the squalid plaza he catches sight of a woman who might well be Elizabeth; her back is to him, but he would know those strong shoulders anywhere, that erect stance, that cascade of unbound golden hair. He starts toward her, sliding with difficulty between the close-packed marketgoers. When he is still halfway across the marketplace from her he notices a man at her side, tall, a man of his own height and build. He wears a loose black robe and a dark scarf covers the lower half of his face. His eyes are grim and sullen and a terrible cicatrice, wide and glaringly cross-hatched with stitch marks, runs along his left cheek up to his hairline. The man whispers something to the woman who might be Elizabeth; she nods and turns, so that Cameron now is able to see her face, and yes, the woman does seem to be Elizabeth, but she bears a matching scar, angry and hideous, up the right side of her face. Cameron gasps. The scar-faced man suddenly points and shouts. Cameron senses motion to one side, and swings around just in time to see a short thickbodied man come rushing toward him wildly waving a scimitar. For an instant Cameron sees the scene as though in a photograph: he has time to make a leisurely examination of his attacker's oily beard, his hooked hairy-nostriled nose, his yellowed teeth, the cheap glassy-looking inlaid stones on the haft of the scimitar. Then the frightful blade descends, while the assassin screams abuse at Cameron in what might be Arabic. It is a sorry welcome. Cameron cannot prolong this investigation. An instant before the scimitar cuts him in two he takes himself elsewhere, with regret.

13.

Onward. To a place where there is no solidity, where the planet itself has vanished, so that he swims through space, falling peacefully, going from nowhere to nowhere. He is surrounded by a brilliant green light that emanates from every point at once, like a message from the fabric of the universe. In great tranquillity he drops through this cheerful glow for days on end, or what seems like days on end, drifting, banking, checking his course with small motions of his elbows or knees. It makes no difference where he goes; everything here is like everything else here. The green glow supports and sustains and nourishes him, but it makes him restless. He plays with it. Out of its lambent substance he succeeds in shaping images, faces, abstract patterns; he conjures up Elizabeth for himself, he evokes his own sharp features, he fills the heavens with a legion of marching Chinese in tapered straw hats, he obliterates them with forceful diagonal lines, he causes a river of silver to stream across the firmament and discharge its glittering burden down a mountainside a thousand miles high. He spins. He floats. He glides. He releases all his fantasies. This is total freedom, here in this unworldly place. But it is not enough. He grows weary of emptiness. He grows weary of serenity. He has drained this place of all it has to offer, too soon, too soon. He is not sure whether the failure is in himself or in the place, but he feels he must leave. Therefore: onward.

14.

Terrified peasants run shrieking as he materializes in their midst. This is some sort of farming village along the eastern shore of the bay: neat green fields, a cluster of low wicker huts radiating from a central plaza, naked children toddling and crying, a busy sub-population of goats and geese and chickens. It is midday; Cameron sees the bright gleam of water in the irrigation ditches. These people work hard. They have scattered at his approach, but now they creep back warily, crouching, ready to take off again if he performs any more miracles. This is another of those bucolic worlds in which San Francisco has not happened, but he is unable to identify these settlers, nor can he isolate the chain of events that brought them here. They are not Indians, nor Chinese, nor Peruvians; they have a European look about them, somehow Slavic, but what would Slavs be doing in California? Russian farmers, maybe, colonizing by way of Siberia? There is some plausibility in that—their dark complexions, their heavy facial structure, their squat powerful bodies—but they seem oddly primitive, half-naked, in furry leggings or less, as though they are no subjects of the Tsar but rather Scythians or Cimmerians transplanted from the prehistoric marshes of the Vistula.

"Don't be frightened," he tells them, holding his upraised outspread arms toward them. They do seem less fearful of him now, timidly approaching, staring with big dark eyes. "I won't harm you. I'd just like to visit with you." They murmur. A woman boldly shoves a child forward, a girl of about five, bare, with black greasy ringlets, and Cameron scoops her up, caresses her, tickles her, lightly sets her down. Instantly the whole tribe is around him, no longer afraid; they touch his arm, they kneel, they stroke his shins. A boy brings him a wooden bowl of porridge. An old woman gives him a mug of sweet wine, a kind of mead. A slender girl drapes a stole of auburn fur over his shoulders. They dance; they chant; their fear has turned into love; he is their honored guest. He is more than that: he is a god. They take him to an unoccupied hut, the largest in the village. Piously they bring him offerings of incense and acorns. When it grows dark they build an immense bonfire in the plaza, so that he wonders in vague concern if they will feast on him when they are done honoring him, but they feast on slaughtered cattle instead, and yield to him the choicest pieces, and afterward they stand by his door, singing discordant, energetic hymns. That night three girls of the tribe, no doubt the fairest virgins available, are sent to him, and in the morning he finds his threshold heaped with newly plucked blossoms. Later two tribal artisans, one lame and the other blind, set to work with stone adzes and chisels, hewing an immense and remarkably accurate likeness of him out of a redwood stump that has been mounted at the plaza's center.

So he has been deified. He has a quick Faustian vision of himself living among these diligent people, teaching them advanced methods of agriculture, leading them eventually into technology, into modern hygiene, into all the contemporary advantages without the contemporary abominations. Guiding them toward the light, molding them, creating them. This world, this village, would be a good place for him to stop his transit of the infinities, if stopping were desirable: god, prophet, king of a placid realm, teacher, inculcator of civilization, a purpose to his existence at last. But there is no place to stop. He knows that. Transforming happy primitive farmers into sophisticated twentieth-century agriculturalists is ultimately as useless a pastime as training fleas to jump through hoops. It is tempting to live as a god, but even divinity will pall, and it is dangerous to become attached to an unreal satisfaction, dangerous to become attached at all. The journey, not the arrival, matters. Always.

So Cameron does godhood for a little while. He finds it pleasant and fulfilling. He savors the rewards until he senses that the rewards are becoming too important to him. He makes his formal renunciation of his godhead. Then: onward.

15.

And this place he recognizes. His street, his house, his garden, his green car in the carport, Elizabeth's yellow one parked out front. Home again, so soon? He hadn't expected that; but every leap he has made, he knows, must in some way have been a product of deliberate choice, and evidently whatever hidden mechanism within him that has directed these voyages has chosen to bring him home again. All right, touch base. Digest your travels, examine them, allow your experiences to work their alchemy on you: you need to stand still a moment for that. Afterward you can always leave again. He slides his key into the door.

Elizabeth has one of the Mozart quartets on the phonograph. She sits curled up in the living-room window seat, leafing through a magazine. It is late afternoon, and the San Francisco skyline, clearly visible across the bay through the big window, is haloed by the brilliant retreating sunlight. There are freshly cut flowers in the little crystal bowl on the redwood-burl table; the fragrance of gardenias and jasmine dances past him. Unhurriedly she looks up, brings her eyes into line with his, dazzles him with the warmth of her smile, and says, "Well, hello!"

"Hello, Elizabeth."

She comes to him. "I didn't expect you back this quickly, Chris, I don't know if I expected you to come back at all, as a matter of fact."

"This quickly? How long have I been gone, for you?"

"Tuesday morning to Thursday afternoon. Two and a half days." She eyes his coarse new beard, his ragged, sun-bleached shirt. "It's been longer for you, hasn't it?"

"Weeks and weeks. I'm not sure how long. I was in eight or nine different places, and I stayed in the last one quite some time. They were villagers, farmers, some primitive Slavonic tribe living down by the bay. I was their god, but I got bored with it."

"You always did get bored so easily," she says, and laughs, and takes his hands in hers and pulls him toward her. She brushes her lips lightly against him, a peck, a play-kiss, their usual first greeting, and then they kiss more passionately, bodies pressing close, tongue seeking tongue. He feels a pounding in his chest, the old inextinguishable throb. When they release each other he steps back, a little dizzied, and says, "I missed you, Elizabeth. I didn't know how much I'd miss you until I was somewhere else and aware that I might never find you again."

"Did you seriously worry about that?"

"Very much."

"I never doubted we'd be together again, one way or another. Infinity's such a big place, darling. You'd find your way back to me, or to someone very much like me. And someone very much like you would find his way to me, if you didn't. How many Chris Camerons do you think there are, on the move between worlds right now? A thousand?

A trillion trillion?" She turns toward the sideboard and says, without breaking the flow of her words, "Would you like some wine?" and begins to pour from a half-empty jug of red. "Tell me where you've been," she says.

He comes up behind her and rests his hands on her shoulders, and draws them down the back of her silk blouse to her waist, holding her there, kissing the nape of her neck. He says, "To a world where there was an atomic war here, and to one where there still were Indian raiders out by Livermore, and one that was all fantastic robots and futuristic helicopters, and one where Johnson was President before Kennedy and Kennedy is alive and President now, and one where—oh, I'll give you all the details later. I need a chance to unwind first." He releases her and kisses the tip of her earlobe and takes one of the glasses from her, and they salute each other and drink, draining the wine quickly. "It's so good to be home," he says softly. "Good to have gone where I went, good to be back." She fills his glass again. The familiar domestic ritual: red wine is their special drink, cheap red wine out of gallon jugs. A sacrament, more dear to him than the burnt offerings of his recent subjects. Halfway through the second glass he says, "Come. Let's go inside."

The bed has fresh linens on it, cool, inviting. There are three thick books on the night table: she's set up for some heavy reading in his absence. Cut flowers in here, too, fragrance everywhere. Their clothes drop away. She touches his beard and chuckles at the roughness, and he kisses the smooth cool place along the inside of her thigh and draws his cheek lightly across it, sandpapering her lovingly, and then she pulls him to her and their bodies slide together and he enters her. Everything thereafter happens quickly, much too quickly; he has been long absent from her, if not she from him, and now her presence excites him, there is a strangeness about her body, her movements, and it hastens him to his ecstasy. He feels a mild pang of regret, but no more: he'll make it up to her soon enough, they both know that. They drift into a sleepy embrace, neither of them speaking, and eventually uncoil into tender new passion, and this time all is as it should be. Afterward they doze. A spectacular sunset blazes over the city when he opens his eyes. They rise, they take a shower together, much giggling, much playfulness. "Let's go across the bay for a fancy dinner tonight," he suggests. "Trianon, Blue Fox, Ernie's, anywhere. You name it. I feel like celebrating."

"So do I, Chris."

"It's good to be home again."

"It's good to have you here," she tells him. She looks for her purse. "How soon do you think you'll be heading out again? Not that I mean to rush you, but—"

"You know I'm not going to be staying?"

"Of course I know."

"Yes. You would." She had never questioned his going. They both tried to be responsive to each other's needs; they had always regarded one another as equal partners, free to do as they wished. "I can't say how long I'll stay. Probably not long. Coming home this soon was really an accident, you know. I just planned to go on and on and on, world after world, and I never programmed my next jump, at least not consciously. I simply leaped. And the last leap deposited me on my own doorstep, somehow, so I let myself into the house. And there you were to welcome me home."

She presses his hand between hers. Almost sadly she says, "You aren't home, Chris."

"What?"

He hears the sound of the front door opening. Footsteps in the hallway.

"You aren't home," she says.

Confusion seizes him. He thinks of all that has passed between them this evening.

"Elizabeth?" calls a deep voice from the living room.

"In here, darling. I have company!"

"Oh? Who?" A man enters the bedroom, halts, grins. He is clean-shaven and dressed in the clothes Cameron had worn on Tuesday; otherwise they could be twins. "Hey, hello!" he says warmly, extending his hand.

Elizabeth says, "He comes from a place that must be very much like this one. He's been here since five o'clock, and we were just going out for dinner. Have you been having an interesting time?"

"Very," the other Cameron says. "I'll tell you all about it later. Go on, don't let me keep you."

"You could join us for dinner," Cameron suggests helplessly.

"That's all right. I've just eaten. Breast of passenger pigeon—they aren't extinct everywhere. I wish I could have brought some home for the freezer. So you two go and enjoy. I'll see you later. Both of you, I hope. Will you be staying with us? We've got notes to compare, you and I."

16.

He rises just before dawn, in a marvelous foggy stillness. The Camerons have been wonderfully hospitable, but he must be moving along. He scrawls a thank-you note and slips it under their bedroom door. Let's get together again someday. Somewhere. Somehow. They wanted him as a house guest for a week or two, but no, he feels like a bit of an intruder here, and anyway the universe is waiting for him. He has to go. The journey, not the arrival, matters, for what else is there but trips? Departing is unexpectedly painful, but he knows the mood will pass. He closes his eyes. He breaks his moorings. He gives himself up to his sublime restlessness. Onward. Onward. *Goodbye, Elizabeth. Goodbye, Chris. I'll see you both again.* Onward.

BORN WITH THE DEAD

For most of its half-century-plus of existence the magazine that is formally known as The Magazine of Fantasy and Science Fiction, *but more usually* F&SF, *has been a bastion of civilized and cultivated material. That was true under its founding editors, Anthony Boucher and J. Francis McComas, and under such succeeding editors as Robert P. Mills and Avram Davidson. By the 1970s, editorial control had passed into the hands of Edward L. Ferman, who also happened to be the publisher of the magazine, and who functioned in admirable fashion in both capacities for many years thereafter.*

My fiction had been appearing on and off in F&SF *since the days of the Boucher-McComas administration; but it was Ed Ferman who turned me into a steady contributor. He published a flock of my short stories in the magazine in the 1960s, of which the best known was the much-anthologized "Sundance," and then, as I began to turn away from shorter fiction in favor of novellas and novels, Ferman let me know that he would be interested in publishing some of my longer work also.*

In December, 1972, just after the publication of my novel Dying Inside, *I got a note from Ferman that mentioned that he had just received a review copy of that book. "I simply wanted to tell you what a fine and moving and painful experience it was to read it," he wrote, going on to compare the novel favorably to recent works by Bernard Malamud and Chaim Potok. And he added in a postscript, "The editor in me has just popped up, and I can't help asking what I have to do to see your next novel. If it's anything near the quality of* Dying Inside, *I'll go higher than our top rate."*

I wasn't planning to write another novel just then—1972 was a particularly turbulent year for me, involving, among other things, the reverberations involved in my recent transplantation from New York to California, and I was unwilling to commit myself to any very lengthy work until things had settled down a little in my life. And I was already working on a longish short story called "Trips" for an anthology Ferman was editing in collaboration with Barry Malzberg. But I did tell him that I had another long story in mind to write after that, one that would probably run to novella length, and it was his if he wanted it. Ferman replied at once that he did, and early in April of 1973 wrote me to say, "I don't recall if I've mentioned length, but with the added pages I can take as much as 30,000 words. I don't expect that long a story, but if it develops that way I'd be happy to have it."

The story was Born With the Dead, and it did develop that way.

It had the feel of a major story from the moment I conceived it. I had played with the idea of the resuscitation of the dead in fiction since my 1957 novel Recalled to Life, and now, I felt, I was ready to return to it with a kind of culminating statement on the subject. I let Ferman know that I was already at work on it, and that it was going to be a big one. To which he replied on April 16, 1973 that he proposed to make the story the centerpiece of a special Robert Silverberg issue of the magazine.

That had real impact on me. Over the years F&SF had done a handful of special issues honoring its favorite contributors—for Theodore Sturgeon, Ray Bradbury, Fritz Leiber, Poul Anderson, James Blish, and one or two others. Each special issue featured a portrait of the writer on the cover, a major new story by him, several critical essays, and a bibliography. All of the writers chosen had been favorites of mine since my days as an avid adolescent reader; and now, suddenly, in my mid-thirties and just reaching the peak of my career, I found myself chosen to join their company. It gave me a nice shiver down the spine.

But of course I had to write a story worthy of that company—and this at a time when my private life was in chaos and the world about me, there in the apocalyptic days of the late Nixon era, was pretty chaotic too. So every day's work was an ordeal. Sometimes I managed no more than a couple of paragraphs. The weeks dragged by; I entered the second month of the project with more than half the story still to tell. (By way of comparison: Dying Inside, also a difficult thing to write and three times as long, took me just nine weeks.) And now it was the middle of May; I had begun the story in late March. But somehow, finally, I regained my stride in early June, and the closing scenes, grim as their content was, were much easier to *write than those that had gone before. One night in early June I was at the movies—Marlon Brando's* Last Tango in Paris, *it was—when the closing paragraphs of the story began to form in my mind. I turned to my wife and asked her for the notebook she always carried, and began to scribble sentences in the dark during the final minutes of the film. The movie ended; the lights came on; the theater emptied; and there I sat, still writing. "Are you a movie critic?" an usher asked me. I shook my head and went on writing.*

So the thing was done, and I knew that I had hooked me a big fish. The next day I typed out what I had written in the theater, and set about preparing a final draft for Ed Ferman, and on June 16, 1973 I sent it to him with a note that said, "Here It Is. I feel exhausted, drained, relieved, pleased, proud, etc. I hope the thing is worthy of all the sweat that went into it. What I'm going to do tomorrow is don my backpack and head for the Sierra for a week in the back country at 10,000 feet, a kind of rite of purification after all these months of crazy intense typing."

"I could not be more pleased with Born With the Dead," *Ferman replied four days later. (E-mail was mere science fiction in those days.) "It seems to me that it brings to a peak the kind of thing you've been doing with* Book of Skulls *and* Dying Inside." *(I had not noticed until that moment the string of death-images running through the titles of those three practically consecutive works of mine.) "I don't think there is a wrong move in this story, and it comes together beautifully in the ending, which I found perfect and quite moving."*

The story appeared in the April, 1974 F&SF, *which was indeed the special Robert Silverberg issue, with an Ed Emshwiller portrait of me on the cover in my best long-haired 1970s psychedelic mode, and essays about me within by Barry Malzberg and Tom Clareson, along with a Silverberg bibliography in very small type (so it didn't fill half the issue.)* Born With the Dead *went on to win the Nebula award in 1975 and the Locus award as well, and finished a close second in the Hugo voting. Since then it has been reprinted in innumerable anthologies, translated into ten foreign languages, and—just last week, as a matter of fact—optioned for motion picture production. I have rarely had so much difficulty writing a story as I had with this one; but the anguish and trauma that it cost me now lie more than thirty years behind me, and the story is still here, to my great delight as its creator and, I hope, to yours as reader.*

One

And what the dead had no speech for, when living,
They can tell you, being dead: the communication
Of the dead is tongued with fire beyond the language of the living.

T.S. Eliot: *Little Gidding*

Supposedly his late wife Sybille was on her way to Zanzibar. That was what they told him, and he believed it. Jorge Klein was at that stage in his search when he would believe anything, if belief would only lead him to Sybille. Anyway, it wasn't so absurd that she would go to Zanzibar. Sybille had always wanted to go there. In some unfathomable obsessive way the place had seized the center of her consciousness long ago. When she was alive it hadn't been possible for her to go there, but now, loosed from all bonds, she would be drawn toward Zanzibar like a bird to its nest, like Ulysses to Ithaca, like a moth to a flame.

The plane, a small Air Zanzibar Havilland FP-803, took off more than half empty from Dar es Salaam at 0915 on a mild bright morning, gaily circled above the dense masses of mango trees, red-flowering flamboyants, and tall coconut palms along the aquamarine shores of the Indian Ocean, and headed northward on the short hop across the strait to Zanzibar. This day—Tuesday, the ninth of March, 1993—would be an unusual one for Zanzibar: five deads were aboard the plane, the first of their kind ever to visit that fragrant isle. Daud Mahmoud Barwani, the health officer on duty that morning at Zanzibar's Karume Airport, had been warned of this by the emigration officials on the mainland. He had no idea how he was going to handle the situation, and he was apprehensive: these were tense times in Zanzibar. Times are always tense in Zanzibar. Should he refuse them entry? Did deads pose any threat to Zanzibar's ever-precarious political stability? What about subtler menaces? Deads might be carriers of dangerous spiritual maladies. Was there anything in the Revised Administrative Code about refusing visas on grounds of suspected contagions of the spirit? Daud Mahmoud Barwani nibbled moodily at his breakfast—a cold chapatti, a mound of cold curried potato—and waited without eagerness for the arrival of the deads.

Almost two and a half years had passed since Jorge Klein had last seen Sybille: the afternoon of Saturday, October 13, 1990, the day of her funeral. That day she lay in her casket as though merely asleep, her beauty altogether unmarred by her final ordeal: pale skin, dark lustrous hair, delicate nostrils, full lips. Iridescent gold and violet fabric enfolded her serene body; a shimmering electrostatic haze, faintly perfumed with a jasmine fragrance, protected her from decay. For five hours she floated on the dais while the rites of parting were read and the condolences were offered—offered almost furtively, as if her death were a thing too monstrous to acknowledge with a show of strong feeling; then, when only a few people remained, the inner core of their circle of friends, Klein kissed her lightly on the lips and surrendered her to the silent dark-clad men whom the Cold Town had sent. She had asked in her will to be rekindled; they took her away in a black van to work their magic on her corpse. The casket, retreating on their broad shoulders, seemed to Klein to be disappearing into a throbbing gray vortex that he was helpless to penetrate. Presumably he would never hear from her again. In those days the deads kept strictly to themselves, sequestered behind the walls of their self-imposed ghettos; it was rare ever to see one outside the Cold Towns, rare even for one of them to make oblique contact with the world of the living.

So a redefinition of their relationship was forced on him. For nine years it had been Jorge and Sybille, Sybille and Jorge, I and thou forming *we*, above all *we*, a transcendental *we*. He had loved her with almost painful intensity. In life they had gone everywhere together, had done everything together, shared research tasks and classroom assignments, thought interchangeable thoughts, expressed tastes that were nearly always identical, so completely had each permeated the other. She was a part of him, he of her, and until the moment of her unexpected death he had assumed it would be like that forever. They were still young, he thirty-eight, she thirty-four, decades to look forward to. Then she was gone. And now they were mere anonymities to one another, she not Sybille but only a dead, he not Jorge but only a warm. She was somewhere on the North American continent, walking about, talking, eating, reading, and yet she was gone, lost to him, and it behooved him to accept that alteration in his life, and outwardly he did accept it, but yet, though he knew he could never again have things as they once had been, he allowed himself the indulgence of a lingering wistful hope of regaining her.

Shortly the plane was in view, dark against the brightness of the sky, a suspended mote, an irritating fleck in Barwani's eye, growing larger, causing him to blink and sneeze. Barwani was not ready for it. When Ameri Kombo, the flight controller in the cubicle next door, phoned him with the routine announcement of the landing, Barwani replied, "Notify the pilot that no one is to debark until I have given clearance. I must consult the regulations. There is possibly a peril to public health." For twenty minutes he let the plane sit, all hatches sealed, on the quiet runway. Wandering goats emerged from the shrubbery and inspected it. Barwani consulted no regulations. He finished his modest meal; then he folded his arms and sought to attain the proper state of tranquility. These deads, he told himself, could do no harm. They were people like all other people, except that they had undergone extraordinary medical treatment. He must overcome his superstitious fear of them: he was no peasant, no silly clovepicker, nor was Zanzibar an abode of primitives. He would admit them, he would give them their anti-malaria tablets as though they were ordinary tourists, he would send them on their way. Very well. Now he was ready. He phoned Ameri Kombo. "There is no danger," he said. "The passengers may exit."

There were nine altogether, a sparse load. The four warms emerged first, looking somber and a little congealed, like people who had had to travel with a party of uncaged cobras. Barwani knew them all: the German consul's wife, the merchant Chowdhary's son, and two Chinese engineers, all returning from brief holidays in Dar. He waved them through the gate without formalities. Then came the deads, after an interval of half a minute: probably they had been sitting together at one end of the nearly empty plane and the others had been at the other. There were two women, three men, all of them tall and surprisingly robust-looking. He had expected them to shamble, to shuffle, to limp, to falter, but they moved with aggressive strides, as if they were in better health now than when they had been alive. When they reached the gate, Barwani stepped forward to greet them, saying softly, "Health regulations, come this way, kindly." They were breathing, undoubtedly breathing: he tasted an emanation of liquor from the big red-haired man, a mysterious and pleasant sweet flavor, perhaps anise, from the dark-haired woman. It seemed to Barwani that their skins had an odd waxy texture, an unreal glossiness, but possibly that was his imagination; white skins had always looked artificial to him. The only certain difference he could detect about the deads was in their eyes, a way they had of remaining unnervingly fixed in a single intense gaze for many seconds before shifting. Those were the eyes, Barwani thought, of people who had looked upon the Emptiness without having been swallowed into it. A turbulence of questions erupted within him: What is it like, how do you feel, what do you remember, where did you go? He left them unspoken. Politely he said, "Welcome to the isle of cloves. We ask you to observe that malaria has been wholly eradicated here through extensive precautionary measures, and to prevent recurrence of unwanted disease we require of you that you take these tablets before proceeding further: Tourists often objected to that; these people swallowed their pills without a word of protest. Again Barwani yearned to reach toward them, to achieve some sort of contact that might perhaps help him to transcend the leaden weight of being. But an aura, a shield of strangeness, surrounded these five, and though he was an amiable man who tended to fall into conversations easily with strangers, he passed them on in silence to Mponda the immigration man.

Mponda's high forehead was shiny with sweat, and he chewed at his lower lip; evidently he was as disturbed by the deads as Barwani. He fumbled forms, he stamped a visa in the wrong place, he stammered while telling the deads that he must keep their passports overnight. "I shall post them by messenger to your hotel in the morning," Mponda promised them, and sent the visitors onward to the baggage pickup area with undue haste.

Klein had only one friend with whom he dared talk about it, a colleague of his at UCLA, a sleek supple Parsee sociologist from Bombay named Framji Jijibhoi, who was as deep into the elaborate new subculture of the deads as a warm could get. "How can I accept this?" Klein demanded. "I can't accept it at all. She's out there somewhere, she's alive, she's—"

Jijibhoi cut him off with a quick flick of his fingertips. "No, dear friend," he said sadly, "not alive, not alive at all, merely rekindled. You must learn to grasp the distinction."

Klein could not learn to grasp the distinction. Klein could not learn to grasp anything having to do with Sybille's death. He could not bear to think that she had passed into another existence from which he was totally excluded. To find her, to speak with her, to participate in her experience of death and whatever lay beyond death, became his only purpose. He was inextricably bound to her, as though she were still his wife, as though Jorge-and-Sybille still existed in any way.

He waited for letters from her, but none came. After a few months he began trying to trace her, embarrassed by his own compulsiveness and by his increasingly open breaches of the etiquette of this sort of widowerhood. He traveled from one Cold Town to another—Sacramento, Boise, Ann Arbor, Louisville—but none would admit him, none would even answer his questions. Friends passed on rumors to him, that she was living among the deads of Tucson, of Roanoke, of Rochester, of San Diego, but nothing came of these tales; then Jijibhoi, who had tentacles into the world of the rekindled in many places, and who was aiding Klein in his quest even though he disapproved of its goal, brought him an authoritative-sounding report that she was at Zion Cold Town in southeastern Utah. They turned him away there too, but not entirely cruelly, for he did manage to secure plausible evidence that that was where Sybille really was.

In the summer of '92 Jijibhoi told him that Sybille had emerged from Cold Town seclusion. She had been seen, he said, in Newark, Ohio, touring the municipal golf course at Octagon State Memorial in the company of a swaggering red-haired archeologist named Kent Zacharias, also a dead, formerly a specialist in the mound-building Hopewellian cultures of the Ohio Valley. "It is a new phase," said Jijibhoi, "not unanticipated. The deads are beginning to abandon their early philosophy of total separatism. We have started to observe them as tourists visiting our world—exploring the life-death interface, as they like to term it. It will be very interesting, dear friend." Klein flew at once to Ohio and without ever actually seeing her, tracked her from Newark to Chillicothe, from Chillicothe to Marietta, from Marietta into West Virginia, where he lost her trail somewhere between Moundsville and Wheeling. Two months later she was said to be in London, then in Cairo, then Addis Ababa. Early in '93 Klein learned, via the scholarly grapevine—an ex-Californian now at Nyerere University in Arusha—that Sybille was on safari in Tanzania and was planning to go, in a few weeks, across to Zanzibar.

Of course. For ten years she had been working on a doctoral thesis on the establishment of the Arab Sultanate in Zanzibar in the early nineteenth century—studies unavoidably interrupted by other academic chores, by love affairs, by marriage, by financial reverses, by illnesses, death, and other responsibilities—and she had never actually been able to visit the island that was so central to her. Now she was free of all entanglements. Why shouldn't she go to Zanzibar at last? Why not? Of course: she was heading for Zanzibar. And so Klein would go to Zanzibar too, to wait for her.

As the five disappeared into taxis, something occurred to Barwani. He asked Mponda for the passports and scrutinized the names. Such strange ones: Kent Zacharias, Nerita Tracy, Sybille Klein, Anthony Gracchus, Laurence Mortimer. He had never grown accustomed to the names of Europeans. Without the photographs he would be unable to tell which were the women, which the men. Zacharias, Tracy, Klein…ah. *Klein.* He checked a memo, two weeks old, tacked to his desk. Klein, yes. Barwani telephoned the Shirazi Hotel—a project that consumed several minutes—and asked to speak with the American who had arrived ten days before, that slender man whose lips had been pressed tight in tension, whose eyes had glittered with fatigue, the one who had asked a little service of Barwani, a special favor, and had dashed him a much-needed hundred shillings as payment in advance. There was a lengthy delay, no doubt while porters searched the hotel, looking in the men's room, the bar, the lounge, the garden, and then the American was on the line. "The person about whom you inquired has just arrived sir," Barwani told him.

Two

The dance begins. Worms underneath fingertips, lips beginning to pulse, heartache and throat-catch. All slightly out of step and out of key, each its own tempo and rhythm. Slowly, connections. Lip to lip, heart to heart, finding self in other, dreadfully, tentatively, burning…notes finding themselves in chords, chords in sequence, cacophony turning to polyphonous contrapuntal chorus, a diapason of celebration.

R.D. Laing: *The Bird of Paradise*

Sybille stands timidly at the edge of the municipal golf course at Octagon State Memorial in Newark, Ohio, holding her sandals in her hand and surreptitiously working her toes into the lush, immaculate carpet of dense, close-cropped lime-green grass. It is a summer afternoon in 1992, very hot; the air, beautifully translucent, has that timeless midwestern shimmer, and the droplets of water from the morning sprinkling have not yet burned off the lawn. Such extraordinary grass! She hadn't often seen grass like that in California, and certainly not at Zion Cold Town in thirsty Utah. Kent Zacharias, towering beside her, shakes his head sadly. "A golf course!" he mutters. "One of the most important prehistoric sites in North America and they make a golf course out of it! Well, I suppose it could have been worse. They might have bulldozed the whole thing and turned it into a municipal parking lot. Look, there, do you see the earthworks?"

She is trembling. This is her first extended journey outside the Cold Town, her first venture into the world of the warms since her rekindling, and she is picking up threatening vibrations from all the life that burgeons about her. The park is surrounded by pleasant little houses, well kept. Children on bicycles rocket through the streets. In front of her, golfers are merrily slamming away. Little yellow golf carts clamber with lunatic energy over the rises and dips of the course. There are platoons of tourists who, like herself and Zacharias, have come to see the Indian mounds. There are dogs running free. All this seems menacing to her. Even the vegetation—the thick grass, the manicured shrubs, the heavy-leafed trees with low-hanging boughs—disturbs her. Nor is the nearness of Zacharias reassuring, for he too seems inflamed with undeadlike vitality; his face is florid, his gestures are broad and overanimated, as he points out the low flat-topped mounds, the grassy bumps and ridges making up the giant joined circle and octagon of the ancient monument. Of course, these mounds are the mainspring of his being, even now, five years post mortem. Ohio is his Zanzibar.

"—once covered four square miles. A grand ceremonial center, the Hopewellian equivalent of Chichén Itzá, of Luxor, of—" He pauses. Awareness of her distress has finally filtered through the intensity of his archeological zeal. "How are you doing?" he asks gently.

She smiles a brave smile. Moistens her lips. Inclines her head toward the golfers, toward the tourists, toward the row of darling little houses outside the rim of the park. Shudders.

"Too cheery for you, is it?"

"Much," she says.

Cheery. Yes. A cheery little town, a magazine-cover town, a chamber-of-commerce town. Newark lies becalmed on the breast of the sea of time: but for the look of the automobiles, this could be 1980 or 1960 or perhaps 1940. Yes. Motherhood, baseball, apple pie, church every Sunday. Yes. Zacharias nods and makes one of the signs of comfort at her. "Come," he whispers. "Let's go toward the heart of the complex. We'll lose the twentieth century along the way."

With brutal imperial strides he plunges into the golf course. Long-legged Sybille must work hard to keep up with him. In a moment they are within the embankment, they have entered the sacred octagon, they have penetrated the vault of the past, and at once Sybille feels they have achieved a successful crossing of the interface between life and death. How still it is here! She senses the powerful presence of the forces of death, and those dark spirits heal her unease. The encroachments of the world of the living on these precincts of the dead become insignificant: the houses outside the park are no longer in view, the golfers are mere foolish incorporeal shadows, the bustling yellow golf carts become beetles, the wandering tourists are invisible.

She is overwhelmed by the size and symmetry of the ancient site. What spirits sleep here? Zacharias conjures them, waving his hands like a magician. She has heard so much from him already about these people, these Hopewellians—What did they call themselves? How can we ever know?—who heaped up these ramparts of earth twenty centuries ago. Now he brings them to life for her with gestures and low urgent words. He whispers fiercely:

—Do you see them?

And she does see them. Mists descend. The mounds reawaken; the mound-builders appear. Tall, slender, swarthy, nearly naked, clad in shining copper breastplates, in necklaces of flint disks, in bangles of bone and mica and tortoise shell, in heavy chains of bright lumpy pearls, in rings of stone and terra cotta, in armlets of bears' teeth and panthers' teeth, in spool-shaped metal ear-ornaments, in furry loin-cloths. Here are priests in intricately woven robes and awesome masks. Here are chieftains with crowns of copper rods, moving in frosty dignity along the long earthen-walled avenue. The eyes of these people glow with energy. What an enormously vital, enormously profligate culture they sustain here! Yet Sybille is not alienated by their throbbing vigor, for it is the vigor of the dead, the vitality of the vanished.

Look, now. Their painted faces, their unblinking gazes. This is a funeral procession. The Indians have come to these intricate geometrical enclosures to perform their acts of worship, and now, solemnly parading along the perimeters of the circle and the octagon, they pass onward, toward the mortuary zone beyond. Zacharias and Sybille are left alone in the middle of the field. He murmurs to her:

—Come. We'll follow them.

He makes it real for her. Through his cunning craft she has access to this community of the dead. How easily she has drifted backward across time! She learns here that she can affix herself to the sealed past at any point; it's only the present, open-ended and unpredictable, that is troublesome. She and Zacharias float through the misty meadow, no sensation of feet touching ground; leaving the octagon, they travel now down a long grassy causeway to the place of the burial mounds, at the edge of a dark forest of wide-crowned oaks. They enter a vast clearing. In the center the ground has been plastered with clay, then covered lightly with sand and fine gravel; on this base the mortuary house, a roofless four-sided structure with walls consisting of rows of wooden palisades, has been erected. Within this is a low clay platform topped by a rectangular tomb of log cribbing, in which two bodies can be seen: a young man, a young woman, side by side, bodies fully extended, beautiful even in death. They wear copper breastplates, copper ear ornaments, copper bracelets, necklaces of gleaming yellowish bears' teeth.

Four priests station themselves at the corners of the mortuary house. Their faces are covered by grotesque wooden masks topped by great antlers, and they carry wands two feet long, effigies of the death-cup mushroom in wood sheathed with copper. One priest commences a harsh, percussive chant. All four lift their wands and abruptly bring them down. It is a signal; the depositing of grave-goods begins. Lines of mourners owed under heavy sacks approach the mortuary house. They are unweeping, even joyful, faces ecstatic, eyes shining, for these people know what later cultures will forget, that death is no termination but rather a natural continuation of life. Their departed friends are to be envied. They are honored with lavish gifts, so that they may live like royalty in the next world: out of the sacks come nuggets of copper, meteoric iron, and silver, thousands of pearls, shell beads, beads of copper and iron, buttons of wood and stone, heaps of metal ear-spools, chunks and chips of obsidian, animal effigies carved from slate and bone and tortoise shell, ceremonial copper axes and knives, scrolls cut from mica, human jawbones inlaid with turquoise, dark coarse pottery, needles of bone, sheets of woven cloth, coiled serpents fashioned from dark stone, a torrent of offerings, heaped up around and even upon the two bodies.

At length the tomb is choked with gifts. Again there is a signal from the priests. They elevate their wands and the mourners, drawing back to the borders of the clearing, form a circle and begin to sing a somber, throbbing funeral hymn. Zacharias, after a moment, sings with them, wordlessly embellishing the melody with heavy melismas. His voice is a rich *basso cantante,* so unexpectedly beautiful that Sybille is moved almost to confusion by it, and looks at him in awe. Abruptly he breaks off, turns to her, touches her arm, leans down to say:

—You sing too.

Sybille nods hesitantly. She joins the song, falteringly at first, her throat constricted by self-consciousness; then she finds herself becoming part of the rite, somehow, and her tone becomes more confident. Her high clear soprano soars brilliantly above the other voices.

Now another kind of offering is made: boys cover the mortuary house with heaps of kindling—twigs, dead branches, thick boughs, all sorts of combustible debris—until it is quite hidden from sight, and the priests cry a halt. Then, from the forest, comes a woman bearing a blazing firebrand, a girl, actually, entirely naked, her sleek fair-skinned body painted with bizarre horizontal stripes of red and green on breasts and buttocks and thighs, her long glossy black hair flowing like a cape behind her as she runs. Up to the mortuary house she sprints; breathlessly she touches the firebrand to the kindling, here, here, here, performing a wild dance as she goes, and hurls the torch into the center of the pyre. Skyward leap the flames in a ferocious rush. Sybille feels seared by the blast of heat. Swiftly the house and tomb are consumed.

While the embers still glow, the bringing of earth gets under way. Except for the priests, who remain rigid at the cardinal points of the site, and the girl who wielded the torch, who lies like discarded clothing at the edge of the clearing, the whole community takes part. There is an open pit behind a screen of nearby trees; the worshipers, forming lines, go to it and scoop up soil, carrying it to the burned mortuary house in baskets, in buckskin aprons, in big moist clods held in their bare hands. Silently they dump their burdens on the ashes and go back for more.

Sybille glances at Zacharias; he nods; they join the line. She goes down into the pit, gouges a lump of moist black clayey soil from its side, takes it to the growing mound. Back for another, back for another. The mound rises rapidly, two feet above ground level now, three, four, a swelling circular blister, its outlines governed by the unchanging positions of the four priests, its tapering contours formed by the tamping of scores of bare feet. Yes, Sybille thinks, this is a valid way of celebrating death, this is a fitting rite. Sweat runs down her body, her clothes become stained and muddy, and still she runs to the earth-quarry, runs from there to the mound, runs to the quarry, runs to the mound, runs, runs, transfigured, ecstatic.

Then the spell breaks. Something goes wrong, she does not know what, and the mists clear, the sun dazzles her eyes, the priests and the mound-builders and the unfinished mound disappear. She and Zacharias are once again in the octagon, golf carts roaring past them on every side. Three children and their parents stand just a few feet from her, staring, staring, and a boy about ten years old points to Sybille and says in a voice that reverberates through half of Ohio, "Dad, what's wrong with those people? Why do they look so weird?"

Mother gasps and cries, "*Quiet,* Tommy, don't you have any manners?" Dad, looking furious, gives the boy a stinging blow across the face with the tips of his fingers, seizes him by the wrist, tugs him toward the other side of the park, the whole family following in their wake.

Sybille shivers convulsively. She turns away, clasping her hands to her betraying eyes. Zacharias embraces her. "It's all right," he says tenderly. "The boy didn't know any better. It's all right."

"Take me away from here!"

"I want to show you—"

"Some other time. Take me away. To the motel. I don't want to see anything. I don't want anybody to see me."

He takes her to the motel. For an hour she lies face down on the bed, racked by dry sobs. Several times she tells Zacharias she is unready for this tour, she wants to go back to the Cold Town, but he says nothing, simply strokes the tense muscles of her back, and after a while the mood passes. She turns to him and their eyes meet and he touches her and they make love in the fashion of the deads.

Three

> *Newness is renewal:* ad hoc enim venit, ut renovemur in illo*; making it new again, as on the first day;* herrlich wie am ersten Tag. *Reformation, or renaissance; rebirth. Life is Phoenix-like, always being born again out of its own death. The true nature of life is resurrection; all life is life after death, a second life, reincarnation.* Totus hic ordo revolubilis testatio est resurrectionis mortuorum. *The universal pattern of recurrence bears witness to the resurrection of the dead.*
>
> Norman O. Brown: *Love's Body*

"The rains shall be commencing shortly, gentleman and lady," the taxi driver said, speeding along the narrow highway to Zanzibar Town. He had been chattering steadily, wholly unafraid of his passengers. He must not know what we are, Sybille decided. "Perhaps in a week or two they begin. These shall be the long rains. The short rains come in the last of November and December:"

"Yes, I know," Sybille said.

"Ah, you have been to Zanzibar before?"

"In a sense," she replied. In a sense she had been to Zanzibar many times, and how calmly she was taking it, now that the true Zanzibar was beginning to superimpose itself on the template in her mind, on that dream-Zanzibar she had carried about so long! She took everything calmly now: nothing excited her, nothing aroused her. In her former life the delay at the airport would have driven her into a fury: a ten-minute flight, and then to be trapped on the runway twice as long! But she had remained tranquil throughout it all, sitting almost immobile, listening vaguely to what Zacharias was saying and occasionally replying as if sending messages from some other planet. And now Zanzibar, so placidly accepted. In the old days she had felt a sort of paradoxical amazement whenever some landmark familiar from childhood geography lessons or the movies or travel posters—the Grand Canyon, the Manhattan skyline, Taos Pueblo—turned out in reality to look exactly as she imagined it would; but now here was Zanzibar, unfolding predictably and unsurprisingly before her, and she observed it with a camera's cool eye, unmoved, unresponsive.

The soft, steamy air was heavy with a burden of perfumes, not only the expected pungent scent of cloves but also creamier fragrances which perhaps were those of hibiscus, frangipani, jacaranda, bougainvillaea, penetrating the cab's open window like probing tendrils. The imminence of the long rains was a tangible pressure, a presence, a heaviness in the atmosphere: at any moment a curtain might be drawn aside and the torrents would start. The highway was lined by two shaggy green walls of palms broken by tin-roofed shacks; behind the palms were mysterious dark groves, dense and alien. Along the edge of the road was the usual tropical array of obstacles: chickens, goats, naked children, old women with shrunken, toothless faces, all wandering around untroubled by the taxi's encroachment on their right-of-way. On through the rolling flatlands the cab sped, out onto the peninsula on which Zanzibar Town sits. The temperature seemed to be rising perceptibly minute by minute; a fist of humid heat was clamping tight over the island. "Here is the waterfront, gentleman and lady," the driver said. His voice was an intrusive hoarse purr, patronizing, disturbing. The sand was glaringly white, the water a dazzling glassy blue; a couple of dhows moved sleepily across the mouth of the harbor, their lateen sails bellying slightly as the gentle sea breeze caught them. "On this side, please—" An enormous white wooden building, four stories high, a wedding cake of long verandahs and cast-iron railings, topped by a vast cupola. Sybille, recognizing it, anticipated the driver's spiel, hearing it like a subliminal pre-echo: "Beit al-Ajaib, the House of Wonders, former government house. Here the Sultan was often make great banquets, here the famous of all Africa came homaging. No longer in use. Next door the old Sultan's Palace, now Palace of People. You wish to go in House of Wonders? Is open: we stop, I take you now."

"Another time," Sybille said faintly. "We'll be here awhile."

"You not here just a day like most?"

"No, a week or more. I've come to study the history of your island. I'll surely visit the Bett al-Ajaib. But not today."

"Not today, no. Very well: you call me, I take you anywhere. I am Ibuni." He gave her a gallant toothy grin over his shoulder and swung the cab inland with a ferocious lurch, into the labyrinth of winding streets and narrow alleys that was Stonetown, the ancient Arab quarter.

All was silent here. The massive white stone buildings presented blank faces to the streets. The windows, mere slits, were shuttered. Most doors—the famous paneled doors of Stonetown, richly carved, studded with brass, cunningly inlaid, each door an ornate Islamic masterpiece—were closed and seemed to be locked. The shops looked shabby, and the small display windows were speckled with dust. Most of the signs were so faded Sybille could barely make them out:

PREMCHAND'S EMPORIUM
MONJI'S CURIOS
ABDULLAH'S BROTHERHOOD STORE
MOTILAL'S BAZAAR

The Arabs were long since gone from Zanzibar. So were most of the Indians, though they were said to be creeping back. Occasionally, as it pursued its intricate course through the maze of Stonetown, the taxi passed elongated black limousines, probably of Russian or Chinese make, chauffeur-driven, occupied by dignified self-contained dark-skinned men in white robes. Legislators, so she supposed them to be, en route to meetings of state. There were no other vehicles in sight, and no pedestrians except for a few women, robed entirely in black, hurrying on solitary errands. Stonetown had none of the vitality of the countryside; it was a place of ghosts, she thought, a fitting place for vacationing deads. She glanced at Zacharias, who nodded and smiled, a quick quirky smile that acknowledged her perception and told her that he too had had it. Communication was swift among the deads and the obvious rarely needed voicing.

The route to the hotel seemed extraordinarily involuted, and the driver halted frequently in front of shops, saying hopefully, "You want brass chests, copper pots, silver curios, gold chains from China?" Though Sybille gently declined his suggestions, he continued to point out bazaars and emporiums, offering earnest recommendations of quality and moderate price, and gradually she realized, getting her bearings in the town, that they had passed certain corners more than once. Of course: the driver must be in the pay of shopkeepers who hired him to lure tourists.

"Please take us to our hotel," Sybille said, and when he persisted in his huckstering—"Best ivory here, best lace"—she said it more firmly, but she kept her temper. Jorge would have been pleased by her transformation, she thought; he had all too often been the immediate victim of her fiery impatience. She did not know the specific cause of the change. Some metabolic side-effect of the rekindling process, maybe, or maybe her two years of communion with Guidefather at the Cold Town, or was it, perhaps, nothing more than the new knowledge that all of time was hers, that to let oneself feel hurried now was absurd?

"Your hotel is this," Ibuni said at last.

It was an old Arab mansion—high arches, innumerable balconies, musty air, electric fans turning sluggishly in the dark hallways. Sybille and Zacharias were given a sprawling suite on the third floor, overlooking a courtyard lush with palms, vermilion nandi, kapok trees, poinsettia, and agapanthus. Mortimer, Gracchus, and Nerita had long since arrived in the other cab and were in an identical suite one floor below. "I'll have a bath," Sybille told Zacharias. "Will you be in the bar?"

"Very likely. Or strolling in the garden."

He went out. Sybille quickly shed her travel-sweaty clothes. The bathroom was a Byzantine marvel, elaborate swirls of colored tile, an immense yellow tub standing high on bronze eagle-claw-and-globe legs. Lukewarm water dribbled in slowly when she turned the tap. She smiled at her reflection in the tall oval mirror. There had been a mirror somewhat like it at the rekindling house. On the morning after her awakening, five or six deads had come into her room to celebrate with her her successful transition across the interface, and they had had that big mirror with them; delicately, with great ceremoniousness, they had drawn the coverlet down to show herself to her in it, naked, slender, narrow-waisted, high-breasted, the beauty of her body unchanged, marred neither by dying nor by rekindling, indeed enhanced by it, so that she had become more youthful-looking and even radiant in her passage across that terrible gulf.

—You're a very beautiful woman.

That was Pablo. She would learn his name and all the other names later.

—I feel such a flood of relief. I was afraid I'd wake up and find myself a shriveled ruin.

—That could not have happened, Pablo said.

—And never will happen, said a young woman. Nerita, she was.

—But deads do age, don't they?

—Oh, yes, we age, just as the warms do. But not *just* as.

—More slowly?

—Very much more slowly. And differently. All our biological processes operate more slowly, except the functions of the brain, which tend to be quicker than they were in life.

—Quicker?

—You'll see.

—It all sounds ideal.

—We are extremely fortunate. Life has been kind to us. Our situation is, yes, ideal. We are the new aristocracy.

—The new aristocracy—

Sybille slipped slowly into the tub, leaning back against the cool porcelain, wriggling a little, letting the tepid water slide up as far as her throat. She closed her eyes and drifted peacefully. All of Zanzibar was waiting for her. *Streets I never thought I should visit.* Let Zanzibar wait. Let Zanzibar wait. *Words I never thought to speak. When I left my body on a distant shore.* Time for everything, everything in its due time.

—*You're a very beautiful woman,* Pablo had told her, not meaning to flatter.

Yes. She had wanted to explain to them, that first morning, that she didn't really care all that much about the appearance of her body, that her real priorities lay elsewhere, were "higher," but there hadn't been any need to tell them that. They understood. They understood everything. Besides, she did care about her body. Being beautiful was less important to her than it was to those women for whom physical beauty was their only natural advantage, but her appearance mattered to her; her body pleased her and she knew it was pleasing to others, it gave her access to people, it was a means of making connections, and she had always been grateful for that. In her other existence her delight in her body had been flawed by the awareness of the inevitability of its slow steady decay, the certainty of the loss of that accidental power that beauty gave her, but now she had been granted exemption from that: she would change with time but she would not have to feel, as warms must feel, that she was gradually falling apart. Her rekindled body would not betray her by turning ugly. No.

—*We are the new aristocracy*—

After her bath she stood a few minutes by the open window, naked to the humid breeze. Sounds came to her: distant bells, the bright chatter of tropical birds, the voices of children singing in a language she could not identify. Zanzibar! Sultans and spices, Livingstone and Stanley, Tippu Tib the slaver, Sir Richard Burton spending a night in this very hotel room, perhaps. There was a dryness in her throat, a throbbing in her chest: a little excitement coming alive in her after all. She felt anticipation, even eagerness. All Zanzibar lay before her. Very well. Get moving, Sybille, put some clothes on, let's have lunch, a look at the town.

She took a light blouse and shorts from her suitcase. Just then Zacharias returned to the room, and she said, not looking up, "Kent, do you think it's all right for me to wear these shorts here? They're—" A glance at his face and her voice trailed off. "What's wrong?"

"I've just been talking to your husband:"

"He's *here*?"

"He came up to me in the lobby. Knew my name. 'You're Zacharias,' he said, with a Bogarty little edge to his voice, like a deceived movie husband confronting the Other Man. 'Where is she? I have to see her.'"

"Oh, no, Kent."

"I asked him what he wanted with you. 'I'm her husband,' he said, and I told him, 'Maybe you were her husband once, but things have changed,' and then—"

"I can't imagine Jorge talking tough. He's such a *gentle* man, Kent! How did he look?"

"Schizoid," Zacharias said. "Glassy eyes, muscles bunching in his jaws, signs of terrific pressure all over him. He knows he's not supposed to do things like this, doesn't he?"

"Jorge knows exactly how he's supposed to behave. Oh, Kent, what a stupid mess! Where is he now?"

"Still downstairs. Nerita and Laurence are talking to him. You don't want to see him, do you?"

"Of course not."

"Write him a note to that effect and I'll take it down to him. Tell him to clear off."

Sybille shook her head. "I don't want to hurt him."

"Hurt him? He's followed you halfway around the world like a lovesick boy, he's tried to violate your privacy, he's disrupted an important trip, he's refused to abide by the conventions that govern the relationships of warms and deads, and you—"

"He loves me, Kent."

"He loved you. All right, I concede that. But the person he loved doesn't exist any more. He has to be made to realize that."

Sybille closed her eyes. "I don't want to hurt him. I don't want you to hurt him either."

"I won't hurt him. Are you going to see him?"

"No," she said. She grunted in annoyance and threw her shorts and blouse into a chair. There was a fierce pounding at her temples, a sensation of being challenged, of being threatened, that she had not felt since that awful day at the Newark mounds. She strode to the window and looked out, half expecting to see Jorge arguing with Nerita and Laurence in the courtyard. But there was no one down there except a houseboy who looked up as if her bare breasts were beacons and gave her a broad dazzling smile. Sybille turned her back to him and said dully, "Go back down. Tell him that it's impossible for me to see him. Use that word. Not that I *won't* see him, not that I *don't want to* see him, not that it isn't *right* for me to see him, just that it's impossible. And then phone the airport. I want to go back to Dar on the evening plane."

"But we've only just arrived!"

"No matter. We'll come back some other time. Jorge is very persistent; he won't accept anything but a brutal rebuff, and I can't do that to him. So we'll leave."

Klein had never seen deads at close range before. Cautiously, uneasily, he stole quick intense looks at Kent Zacharias as they sat side by side on rattan chairs among the potted palms in the lobby of the hotel. Jijibhoi had told him that it hardly showed, that you perceived it more subliminally than by any outward manifestation, and that was true; there was a certain look about the eyes, of course, the famous fixity of the deads, and there was something oddly pallid about Zacharias' skin *beneath* the florid complexion, but if Klein had not known what Zacharias was, he might not have guessed it. He tried to imagine this man, this red-haired red-faced dead archeologist, this digger of dirt mounds, in bed with Sybille. Doing with her whatever it was that the deads did in their couplings. Even Jijibhoi wasn't sure. Something with hands, with eyes, with whispers and smiles, not at all genital—so Jijibhoi believed. *This is Sybille's lover I'm talking to. This is Sybille's lover.* How strange that it bothered him so. She had had affairs when she was living; so had he; so had everyone; it was the way of life. But he felt threatened, overwhelmed, defeated, by this walking corpse of a lover.

Klein said, "Impossible?"

"That was the word she used."

"Can't I have ten minutes with her?"

"Impossible."

"Would you let me see her for a few moments, at least? I'd just like to find out how she looks."

"Don't you find it humiliating, doing all this scratching around just for a glimpse of her?"

"Yes."

"And you still want it?"

"Yes."

Zacharias sighed. "There's nothing I can do for you. I'm sorry."

"Perhaps Sybille is tired from having done so much traveling. Do you think she might be in a more receptive mood tomorrow?"

"Maybe," Zacharias said. "Why don't you come back then?"

"You've been very kind."

"De nada."

"Can I buy you a drink?"

"Thanks, no," Zacharias said. "I don't indulge any more. Not since—" He smiled.

Klein could smell whiskey on Zacharias' breath. All right, though. All right. He would go away. A driver waiting outside the hotel grounds poked his head out of his cab window and said hopefully, "Tour of the island, gentleman? See the clove plantations, see the athlete stadium?"

"I've seen them already," Klein said. He shrugged. "Take me to the beach."

He spent the afternoon watching turquoise wavelets lapping pink sand. The next morning he returned to Sybille's hotel, but they were gone, all five of them, gone on last night's flight to Dar, said the apologetic desk clerk. Klein asked if he could make a telephone call, and the clerk showed him an ancient instrument in an alcove near the bar. He phoned Barwani. "What's going on?" he demanded. "You told me they'd be staying at least a week!"

"Oh, sir, things change," Barwani said softly.

Four

What portends? What will the future bring? I do not know, I have no presentiment. When a spider hurls itself down from some fixed point, consistently with its nature, it always sees before it only an empty space wherein it can find no foothold however much it sprawls. And so it is with me: always before me an empty space; what drives me forward is a consistency which lies behind me. This life is topsy-turvy and terrible, not to be endured.

Søren Kierkegaard: *Either/Or*

Jijibhoi said, "In the entire question of death who is to say what is right, dear friend? When I was a boy in Bombay it was not unusual for our Hindu neighbors to practice the rite of suttee, that is, the burning of the widow on her husband's funeral pyre, and by what presumption may we call them barbarians? Of course"—his dark eyes flashed mischievously—"we did call them barbarians, though never when they might hear us. Will you have more curry?"

Klein repressed a sigh. He was getting full, and the curry was fiery stuff, of an incandescence far beyond his usual level of tolerance; but Jijibhoi's hospitality, unobtrusively insistent, had a certain hieratic quality about it that made Klein feel like a blasphemer whenever he refused anything in his home. He smiled and nodded, and Jijibhoi, rising, spooned a mound of rice into Klein's plate, buried it under curried lamb, bedecked it with chutneys and sambals. Silently, unbidden, Jijibhoi's wife went to the kitchen and returned with a cold bottle of Heinekens. She gave Klein a shy grin as she set it down before him. They worked well together, these two Parsees, his hosts.

They were an elegant couple—striking, even. Jijibhoi was a tall, erect man with a forceful aquiline nose, dark Levantine skin, jet-black hair, a formidable mustache. His hands and feet were extraordinarily small; his manner was polite and reserved; he moved with a quickness of action bordering on nervousness. Klein guessed that he was in his early forties, though he suspected his estimate could easily be off by ten years in either direction. His wife—strangely, Klein had never been told her name—was younger than her husband, nearly as tall, fair of complexion—a light-olive tone—and voluptuous of figure. She dressed invariably in flowing silken saris; Jijibhoi affected western business dress, suits and ties in a style twenty years out of date. Klein had never seen either of them bareheaded: she wore a kerchief of white linen, he a brocaded skullcap that might lead people to mistake him for an Oriental Jew. They were childless and self-sufficient, forming a closed dyad, a perfect unit, two segments of the same entity, conjoined and indivisible, as Klein and Sybille once had been. Their harmonious interplay of thought and gesture made them a trifle disconcerting, even intimidating, to others. As Klein and Sybille once had been.

Klein said, "Among your people—"

"Oh, very different, very different, quite unique. You know of our funeral custom?"

"Exposure of the dead, isn't it?"

Jijibhoi's wife giggled. "A very ancient recycling scheme!"

"The Towers of Silence," Jijibhoi said. He went to the dining room's vast window and stood with his back to Klein, staring out at the dazzling lights of Los Angeles. The Jijibhois' house, all redwood and glass, perched precariously on stilts near the crest of Benedict Canyon, just below Mulholland: the view took in everything from Hollywood to Santa Monica. "There are five of them in Bombay," said Jijibhoi, "on Malabar Hill, a rocky ridge overlooking the Arabian Sea. They are centuries old, each one circular, several hundred feet in circumference, surrounded by a stone wall twenty or thirty feet high. When a Parsee dies—do you know of this?"

"Not as much as I'd like to know."

"When a Parsee dies, he is carried to the Towers on an iron bier by professional corpse-bearers; the mourners follow in procession, two by two, joined hand to hand by holding a white handkerchief between them. A beautiful scene, dear Jorge. There is a doorway in the stone wall through which the corpse-bearers pass, carrying their burden. No one else may enter the Tower. Within is a circular platform paved with large stone slabs and divided into three rows of shallow, open receptacles. The outer row is used for the bodies of males, the next for those of females, the innermost one for children. The dead one is given a resting-place; vultures rise from the lofty palms in the gardens adjoining the Towers; within an hour or two, only bones remain. Later, the bare, sun-dried skeleton is cast into a pit at the center of the Tower. Rich and poor crumble together there into dust."

"And all Parsees are—ah—buried in this way?"

"Oh, no, no, by no means," Jijibhoi said heartily. "All ancient traditions are in disrepair nowadays, do you not know? Our younger people advocate cremation or even conventional interment. Still, many of us continue to see the beauty of our way."

"—beauty?—"

Jijibhoi's wife said in a quiet voice, "To bury the dead in the ground, in a moist tropical land where diseases are highly contagious, seems not sanitary to us. And to burn a body is to waste its substance. But to give the bodies of the dead to the efficient hungry birds—quickly, cleanly, without fuss—is to us a way of celebrating the economy of nature. To have one's bones mingle in the pit with the bones of the entire community is, to us, the ultimate democracy."

"And the vultures spread no contagions themselves, feeding as they do on the bodies of—"

"Never," said Jijibhoi firmly. "Nor do they contract our ills."

"And I gather that you both intend to have your bodies returned to Bombay when you—" Aghast, Klein paused, shook his head, coughed in embarrassment, forced a weak smile. "You see what this radioactive curry of yours has done to my manners? Forgive me. Here I sit, a guest at your dinner table, quizzing you about your funeral plans!"

Jijibhoi chuckled. "Death is not frightening to us, dear friend. It is—one hardly needs say it, does one?—it is a natural event. For a time we are here, and then we go. When our time ends, yes, she and I will give ourselves to the Towers of Silence."

His wife added sharply, "Better there than the Cold Towns! Much better!"

Klein had never observed such vehemence in her before.

Jijibhoi swung back from the window and glared at her. Klein had never seen that before either. It seemed as if the fragile web of elaborate courtesy that he and these two had been spinning all evening was suddenly unraveling, and that even the bonds between Jijibhoi and his wife were undergoing strain. Agitated now, fluttery, Jijibhoi began to collect the empty dishes, and after a long awkward moment said, "She did not mean to give offense."

"Why should I be offended?"

"A person you love chose to go to the Cold Towns. You might think there was implied criticism of her in my wife's expression of distaste for—"

Klein shrugged. "She's entitled to her feelings about rekindling. I wonder, though—"

He halted, uneasy, fearing to probe too deeply.

"Yes?"

"It was irrelevant."

"Please," Jijibhoi said. "We are old friends."

"I was wondering," said Klein slowly, "if it doesn't make things hard for you, spending all your time among deads, studying them, mastering their ways, devoting your whole career to them, when your wife evidently despises the Cold Towns and everything that goes on in them. If the theme of your work repels her, you must not be able to share it with her."

"Oh," Jijibhoi said, tension visibly going from him, "if it comes to that, I have even less liking for the entire rekindling phenomenon than she."

"You do?" This was a side of Jijibhoi that Klein had never suspected. "It repels you? Then why did you choose to make such an intensive survey of it?"

Jijibhoi looked genuinely amazed. "What? Are you saying one must have personal allegiance to the subject of one's field of scholarship?" He laughed. "You are of Jewish birth, I think, and yet your doctoral thesis was concerned, was it not, with the early phases of the Third Reich?"

Klein winced. "Touché!"

"I find the subculture of the deads irresistible, as a sociologist," Jijibhoi went on. "To have such a radical new aspect of human existence erupt during one's career is an incredible gift. There is no more fertile field for me to investigate. Yet I have no wish, none at all, ever to deliver myself up for rekindling. For me, my wife, it will be the Towers of Silence, the hot sun, the obliging vultures—and finis, the end, no more, terminus."

"I had no idea you felt this way. I suppose if I'd known more about Parsee theology, I might have realized—"

"You misunderstand. Our objections are not theological. It is that we share a wish, an idiosyncratic whim, not to continue beyond the allotted time. But also I have serious reservations about the impact of rekindling on our society. I feel a profound distress at the presence among us of these deads, I feel a purely private fear of these people and the culture they are creating, I feel even an abhorrence for—" Jijibhoi cut himself short. "Your pardon. That was perhaps too strong a word. You see how complex my attitudes are toward this subject, my mixture of fascination and repulsion? I exist in constant tension between those poles. But why do I tell you all this, which if it does not disturb you, must surely bore you? Let us hear about your journey to Zanzibar."

"What can I say? I went, I waited a couple of weeks for her to show up, I wasn't able to get near her at all, and I came home. All the way to Africa and I never even had a glimpse of her."

"What a frustration, dear Jorge!"

"She stayed in her hotel room. They wouldn't let me go upstairs to her."

"They?"

"Her entourage," Klein said. "She was traveling with four other deads, a woman and three men. Sharing her room with the archeologist, Zacharias. He was the one who shielded her from me, and did it very cleverly, too. He acts as though he owns her. Perhaps he does. What can you tell me, Framji? Do the deads marry? Is Zacharias her new husband?"

"It is very doubtful. The terms 'wife' and 'husband' are not in use among the deads. They form relationships, yes, but pair-bonding seems to be uncommon among them, possibly altogether unknown. Instead they tend to create supportive pseudo-familial groupings, of three or four or even more individuals, who—"

"Do you mean that all four of her companions in Zanzibar are her lovers?"

Jijibhoi gestured eloquently. "Who can say? If you mean in a physical sense, I doubt it, but one can never be sure. Zacharias seems to be her special companion, at any rate. Several of the others may be part of her pseudo-family also, or all, or none. I have reason to think that at certain times every dead may claim a familial relationship to all others of his kind. Who can say? We perceive the doings of these people, as they say, through a glass, darkly."

"I don't see Sybille even that well. I don't even know what she looks like now."

"She has lost none of her beauty."

"So you've told me before. But I want to see her myself. You can't really comprehend, Framji, how much I want to see her. The pain I feel, not able—"

"Would you like to see her right now?"

Klein shook in a convulsion of amazement. "What? What do you mean? Is she—"

"Hiding in the next room? No, no, nothing like that. But I do have a small surprise for you. Come into the library." Smiling expansively, Jijibhoi led the way from the dining room to the small study adjoining it, a room densely packed from floor to ceiling with books in an astonishing range of languages—not merely English, French, and German, but also Sanskrit, Hindi, Gujerati, Farsi, the tongues of Jijibhoi's polyglot upbringing among the tiny Parsee colony of Bombay, a community in which no language once cherished was ever discarded. Pushing aside a stack of dog-eared professional journals, he drew forth a glistening picture-cube, activated its inner light with a touch of his thumb, and handed it to Klein.

The sharp, dazzling holographic image showed three figures to a broad grassy plain that seemed to have no limits and was without trees, boulders, or other visual interruptions, an endlessly unrolling green carpet under a blank death-blue sky. Zacharias stood at the left, his face averted from the camera; he was looking down, tinkering with the action of an enormous rifle. At the far right stood a stocky, powerful-looking dark-haired man whose pale, harsh-featured face seemed all beard and nostrils. Klein recognized him: Anthony Gracchus, one of the deads who had accompanied Sybille to Zanzibar. Sybille stood beside him, clad in khaki slacks and a crisp white blouse. Gracchus' arm was extended; evidently he had just pointed out a target to her, and she was intently aiming a gun nearly as big as Zacharias'.

Klein shifted the cube about, studying her face from various angles, and the sight of her made his fingers grow thick and clumsy, his eyelids to quiver. Jijibhoi had spoken truly: she had lost none of her beauty. Yet she was not at all the Sybille he had known. When he had last seen her, lying in her casket, she had seemed to be a flawless marble image of herself, and she had that same surreal statuary appearance now. Her face was an expressionless mask, calm, remote, aloof; her eyes were glossy mysteries; her lips registered a faint, enigmatic, barely perceptible smile. It frightened him to behold her this way, so alien, so unfamiliar. Perhaps it was the intensity of her concentration that gave her that forbidding marmoreal look, for she seemed to be pouring her entire being into the task of taking aim. By tilting the cube more extremely, Klein was able to see what she was aiming at: a strange awkward bird moving through the grass at the lower left, a bird larger than a turkey, round as a sack, with ash-gray plumage, a whitish breast and tail, yellow-white wings, and short, comical yellow legs. Its head was immense and its black bill ended in a great snubbed hook. The creature seemed solemn, rather dignified, and faintly absurd; it showed no awareness that its doom was upon it. How odd that Sybille should be about to kill it, she who had always detested the taking of life: Sybille the huntress now, Sybille the lunar goddess, Sybille-Diana!

Shaken, Klein looked up at Jijibhoi and said, "Where was this taken? On that safari in Tanzania, I suppose."

"Yes. In February. This man is the guide, the white hunter."

"I saw him in Zanzibar. Gracchus, his name is. He was one of the deads traveling with Sybille."

"He operates a hunting preserve not far from Kilimanjaro," Jijibhoi said, "that is set aside exclusively for the use of the deads. One of the more bizarre manifestations of their subculture, actually. They hunt only those animals which—"

Klein said impatiently, "How did you get this picture?"

"It was taken by Nerita Tracy, who is one of your wife's companions."

"I met her in Zanzibar too. But how—"

"A friend of hers is an acquaintance of mine, one of my informants, in fact, a valuable connection in my researches. Some months ago I asked him if he could obtain something like this for me. I did not tell him, of course, that I meant it for you." Jijibhoi looked close. "You seem troubled, dear friend."

Klein nodded. He shut his eyes as though to protect them from the glaring surfaces of Sybille's photograph. Eventually he said in a flat, toneless voice, "I have to get to see her."

"Perhaps it would be better for you if you would abandon—"

"No."

"Is there no way I can convince you that it is dangerous for you to pursue your fantasy of—"

"No," Klein said. "Don't even try: It's necessary for me to reach her. Necessary."

"How will you accomplish this, then?"

Klein said mechanically, "By going to Zion Cold Town."

"You have already done that. They would not admit you."

"This time they will. They don't turn away deads."

The Parsee's eyes widened. "You will surrender your own life? Is this your plan? What are you saying, Jorge?"

Klein, laughing, said, "That isn't what I meant at all."

"I am bewildered."

"I intend to infiltrate. I'll disguise myself as one of them. I'll slip into the Cold Town the way an infidel slips into Mecca." He seized Jijibhoi's wrist. "Can you help me? Coach me in their ways, teach me their jargon?"

"They'll find you out instantly."

"Maybe not. Maybe I'll get to Sybille before they do."

"This is insanity," Jijibhoi said quietly.

"Nevertheless. You have the knowledge. Will you help me?"

Gently Jijibhoi withdrew his arm from Klein's grasp. He crossed the room and busied himself with an untidy bookshelf for some moments, fussily arranging and rearranging. At length he said, "There is little I can do for you myself. My knowledge is broad but not deep, not deep enough. But if you insist on going through with this, Jorge, I can introduce you to someone who may be able to assist you. He is one of my informants, a dead, a man who has rejected the authority of the Guidefathers, a person who is *of* the deads but not with them. Possibly he can instruct you in what you would need to know."

"Call him," Klein said.

"I must warn you he is unpredictable, turbulent, perhaps even treacherous. Ordinary human values are without meaning to him in his present state."

"Call him."

"If only I could discourage you from—"

"Call him."

Five

Quarreling brings trouble. These days lions roar a great deal. Joy follows grief. It is not good to beat children much. You had better go away now and go home. It is impossible to work today. You should go to school every day. It is not advisable to follow this path, there is water in the way. Never mind, I shall be able to pass. We had better go back quickly. These lamps use a lot of oil. There are no mosquitoes in Nairobi. There are no lions here. There are people here, looking for eggs. Is there water in the well? No, there is none. If there are only three people, work will be impossible today.

D.V. Perrott: *Teach Yourself Swahili*

Gracchus signals furiously to the porters and bellows, "*Shika njia hii hii!*" Three turn, two keep trudging along. "*Ninyi nyote!*" he calls. "*Fanga karma hivi!*" He shakes his head, spits, flicks sweat from his forehead. He adds, speaking in a lower voice and in English, taking care that they will not hear him, "Do as I say, you malevolent black bastards, or you'll be deader than I am before sunset!"

Sybille laughs nervously. "Do you always talk to them like that?"

"I try to be easy on them. But what good does it do, what good does any of it do? Come on, let's keep up with them."

It is less than an hour after dawn, but already the sun is very hot, here in the flat dry country between Kilimanjaro and Serengeti. Gracchus is leading the party northward across the high grass, following the spoor of what he thinks is a quagga, but breaking a trail in the high grass is hard work and the porters keep veering away toward a ravine that offers the tempting shade of a thicket of thorn trees, and he constantly has to harass them in order to hold them to the route he wants. Sybille has noticed that Gracchus shouts fiercely to his blacks, as if they were no more than recalcitrant beasts, and speaks of them behind their backs with a rough contempt, but it all seems done for show, all part of his white-hunter role: she has also noticed, at times when she was not supposed to notice, that privately Gracchus is in fact gentle, tender, even loving among the porters, teasing them—she supposes—with affectionate Swahili banter and playful mock-punches. The porters are role-players too: they behave in the traditional manner of their profession, alternately deferential and patronizing to the clients, alternately posing as all-knowing repositories of the lore of the bush and as simple, guileless savages fit only for carrying burdens. But the clients they serve are not quite like the sportsmen of Hemingway's time, since they are deads, and secretly the porters are terrified of the strange beings whom they serve. Sybille has seen them muttering prayers and fondling amulets whenever they accidentally touch one of the deads, and has occasionally detected an unguarded glance conveying unalloyed fear, possibly revulsion. Gracchus is no friend of theirs, however jolly he may get with them: they appear to regard him as some sort of monstrous sorcerer and the clients as fiends made manifest.

Sweating, saying little, the hunters move in single file, first the porters with the guns and supplies, then Gracchus, Zacharias, Sybille, Nerita constantly clicking her camera, and Mortimer. Patches of white cloud drift slowly across the immense arch of the sky. The grass is lush and thick, for the short rains were unusually heavy in December. Small animals scurry through it, visible only in quick flashes, squirrels and jackals and guinea-fowl. Now and then larger creatures can be seen: three haughty ostriches, a pair of snuffling hyenas, a band of Thomson gazelles flowing like a tawny river across the plain. Yesterday Sybille spied two wart hogs, some giraffes, and a serval, an elegant big-eared wildcat that slithered along like a miniature cheetah. None of these beasts may be hunted, but only those special ones that the operators of the preserve have introduced for the special needs of their clients; anything considered native African wildlife, which is to say anything that was living here before the deads leased this tract from the Masai, is protected by government decree. The Masai themselves are allowed to do some lion-hunting, since this is their reservation, but there are so few Masai left that they can do little harm. Yesterday, after the wart hogs and before the giraffes, Sybille saw her first Masai, five lean, handsome, long-bodied men, naked under skimpy red robes, drifting silently through the bush, pausing frequently to stand thoughtfully on one leg, propped against their spears. At close range they were less handsome—toothless, fly-specked, herniated. They offered to sell their spears and their beaded collars for a few shillings, but the safarigoers had already stocked up on Masai artifacts in Nairobi's curio shops, at astonishingly higher prices.

All through the morning they stalk the quagga, Gracchus pointing out hoofprints here, fresh dung there. It is Zacharias who has asked to shoot a quagga. "How can you tell we're not following a zebra?" he asks peevishly.

Gracchus winks. "Trust me. We'll find zebras up ahead too. But you'll get your quagga. I guarantee it."

Ngiri, the head porter, turns and grins. *"Piga guagga m'uzuri bwana,"* he says to Zacharias, and winks also, and then—Sybille sees it plainly—his jovial confident smile fades as though he has had the courage to sustain it only for an instant, and a veil of dread covers his dark glossy face.

"What did he say?" Zacharias asks.

"That you'll shoot a fine quagga," Gracchus replies.

Quaggas. The last wild one was killed about 1870, leaving only three in the world, all females, in European zoos. The Boers had hunted them to the edge of extinction in order to feed their tender meat to Hottentot slaves and to make from their striped hides sacks for Boer grain, leather *veldschoen* for Boer feet. The quagga of the London zoo died in 1872, that in Berlin in 1875, the Amsterdam quagga in 1883, and none was seen alive again until the artificial revival of the species through breedback selection and genetic manipulation in 1990, when this hunting preserve was opened to a limited and special clientele.

It is nearly noon, now, and not a shot has been fired all morning. The animals have begun heading for cover; they will not emerge until the shadows lengthen. Time to halt, pitch camp, break out the beer and sandwiches, tell tall tales of harrowing adventures with maddened buffaloes and edgy elephants. But not quite yet. The marchers come over a low hill and see, in the long sloping hollow beyond, a flock of ostriches and several hundred grazing zebras. As the humans appear, the ostriches begin slowly and warily to move off, but the zebras, altogether unafraid, continue to graze. Ngiri points and says, *"Piga quagga, bwana."*

"Just a bunch of zebras," Zacharias says.

Gracchus shakes his head. "No. Listen. You hear the sound?"

At first no one perceives anything unusual. But then, yes, Sybille hears it: a shrill barking neigh, very strange, a sound out of lost time, the cry of some beast she has never known. It is a song of the dead. Nerita hears it too, and Mortimer, and finally Zacharias. Gracchus nods toward the far side of the hollow. There, among the zebras, are half a dozen animals that might almost be zebras, but are not—unfinished zebras, striped only on their heads and foreparts; the rest of their bodies are yellowish brown, their legs are white, their manes are dark-brown with pale stripes. Their coats sparkle like mica in the sunshine. Now and again they lift their heads, emit that weird percussive whistling snort, and bend to the grass again. Quaggas. Strays out of the past, relicts, rekindled specters. Gracchus signals and the party fans out along the peak of the hill. Ngiri hands Zacharias his colossal gun. Zacharias kneels, sights.

"No hurry," Gracchus murmurs. "We have all afternoon."

"Do I seem to be hurrying?" Zacharias asks. The zebras now block the little group of quaggas from his view, almost as if by design. He must not shoot a zebra, of course, or there will be trouble with the rangers. Minutes go by. Then the screen of zebras abruptly parts and Zacharias squeezes his trigger. There is a vast explosion; zebras bolt in ten directions, so that the eye is bombarded with dizzying stroboscopic waves of black and white; when the convulsive confusion passes, one of the quaggas is lying on its side, alone in the field, having made the transition across the interface. Sybille regards it calmly. Death once dismayed her, death of any kind, but no longer.

"Piga m'uzuri!" the porters cry exultantly.

"Kufa," Gracchus says. "Dead. A neat shot. You have your trophy."

Ngiri is quick with the skinning-knife. That night, camping below Kilimanjaro's broad flank, they dine on roast quagga, deads and porters alike. The meat is juicy, robust, faintly tangy.

* * *

Late the following afternoon, as they pass through cooler stream-broken country thick with tall, scrubby gray-green vase-shaped trees, they come upon a monstrosity, a shaggy shambling thing twelve or fifteen feet high, standing upright on ponderous hind legs and balancing itself on an incredibly thick, heavy tail. It leans against a tree, pulling at its top branches with long forelimbs that are tipped with ferocious claws like a row of sickles; it munches voraciously on leaves and twigs. Briefly it notices them, and looks around, studying them with small stupid yellow eyes; then it returns to its meal.

"A rarity," Gracchus says. "I know hunters who have been all over this park without ever running into one. Have you ever seen anything so ugly?"

"What is it?" Sybille asks.

"Megatherium. Giant ground sloth. South American, really, but we weren't fussy about geography when we were stocking this place. We have only four of them, and it costs God knows how many thousands of dollars to shoot one. Nobody's signed up for a ground sloth yet. I doubt anyone will."

Sybille wonders where the beast might be vulnerable to a bullet: surely not in its dim peanut-sized brain. She wonders, too, what sort of sportsman would find pleasure in killing such a thing. For a while they watch as the sluggish monster tears the tree apart. Then they move on.

* * *

Gracchus shows them another prodigy at sundown: a pale dome, like some huge melon, nestling in a mound of dense grass beside a stream. "Ostrich egg?" Mortimer guesses.

"Close. Very close. It's a moa egg. World's biggest bird. From New Zealand, extinct since about the eighteenth century."

Nerita crouches and lightly taps the egg. "What an omelet we could make!"

"There's enough there to feed seventy-five of us," Gracchus says. "Two gallons of fluid, easy. But of course we mustn't meddle with it. Natural increase is very important in keeping this park stocked."

"And where's mama moa?" Sybille asks. "Should she have abandoned the egg?"

"Moas aren't very bright," Gracchus answers. "That's one good reason why they became extinct. She must have wandered off to find some dinner. And—"

"Good God," Zacharias blurts.

The moa has returned, emerging suddenly from a thicket. She stands like a feathered mountain above them, limned by the deep-blue of twilight: an ostrich, more or less, but a magnified ostrich, an ultimate ostrich, a bird a dozen feet high, with a heavy rounded body and a great thick hose of a neck and taloned legs sturdy as saplings. Surely this is Sinbad's rukh, that can fly off with elephants in its grasp! The bird peers at them, sadly contemplating the band of small beings clustered about her egg; she arches her neck as though readying for an attack, and Zacharias reaches for one of the rifles, but Gracchus checks his hand, for the moa is merely rearing back to protest. It utters a deep mournful mooing sound and does not move. "Just back slowly away," Gracchus tells them. "It won't attack. But keep away from the feet; one kick can kill you."

"I was going to apply for a license on a moa," Mortimer says.

"Killing them's a bore," Gracchus tells him. "They just stand there and let you shoot. You're better off with what you signed up for."

What Mortimer has signed up for is an aurochs, the vanished wild ox of the European forests, known to Caesar, known to Pliny, hunted by the hero Siegfried, altogether exterminated by the year 1627. The plains of East Africa are not a comfortable environment for the aurochs and the herd that has been conjured by the genetic necromancers keeps to itself in the wooded highlands, several days' journey from the haunts of quaggas and ground sloths. In this dark grove the hunters come upon troops of chattering baboons and solitary big-eared elephants and, in a place of broken sunlight and shadow, a splendid antelope, a bull bongo with a fine curving pair of horns. Gracchus leads them onward, deeper in. He seems tense: there is peril here. The porters slip through the forest like black wraiths, spreading out in arching crab-claw patterns, communicating with one another and with Gracchus by whistling. Everyone keeps weapons ready in here. Sybille half expects to see leopards draped on overhanging branches, cobras slithering through the undergrowth. But she feels no fear.

They approach a clearing.

"Aurochs," Gracchus says.

A dozen of them are cropping the shrubbery: big short-haired long-horned cattle, muscular and alert. Picking up the scent of the intruders, they lift their heavy heads, sniff, glare. Gracchus and Ngiri confer with eyebrows. Nodding, Gracchus mutters to Mortimer, "Too many of them. Wait for them to thin off." Mortimer smiles. He looks a little nervous. The aurochs has a reputation for attacking without warning. Four, five, six of the beasts slip away, and the others withdraw to the edge of the clearing, as if to plan strategy; but one big bull, sour-eyed and grim, stands his ground, glowering. Gracchus rolls on the balls of his feet. His burly body seems, to Sybille, a study in mobility, in preparedness.

"Now," he says.

In the same moment the bull aurochs charges, moving with extraordinary swiftness, head lowered, horns extended like spears. Mortimer fires. The bullet strikes with a loud whonking sound, crashing into the shoulder of the aurochs, a perfect shot, but the animal does not fall, and Mortimer shoots again, less gracefully ripping into the belly, and then Gracchus and Ngiri are firing also, not at Mortimer's aurochs but over the heads of the others, to drive them away, and the risky tactic works, for the other animals go stampeding off into the woods. The one Mortimer has shot continues toward him, staggering now, losing momentum, and falls practically at his feet, rolling over, knifing the forest floor with its hooves.

"Kufa," Ngiri says. *"Piga nyati m'uzuri, bwana."*

Mortimer grins. *"Piga,"* he says.

Gracchus salutes him. "More exciting than moa," he says.

"And these are mine," says Nerita three hours later, indicating a tree at the outer rim of the forest. Several hundred large pigeons nest in its boughs, so many of them that the tree seems to be sprouting birds rather than leaves. The females are plain—light-brown above, gray below—but the males are flamboyant, with rich, glossy blue plumage on their wings and backs, breasts of a wine-red chestnut color, iridescent spots of bronze and green on their necks, and weird, vivid eyes of a bright, fiery orange. Gracchus says, "Right. You've found your passenger pigeons."

"Where's the thrill in shooting pigeons out of a tree?" Mortimer asks.

Nerita gives him a withering look. "Where's the thrill in gunning down a charging bull?" She signals to Ngiri, who fires a shot into the air. The startled pigeons burst from their perches and fly in low circles. In the old days, a century and a half ago in the forests of North America, no one troubled to shoot passenger pigeons on the wing: the pigeons were food, not sport, and it was simpler to blast them as they sat, for that way a single hunter might kill thousands of birds in one day. Thus it took only fifty years to reduce the passenger pigeon population from uncountable sky-blackening billions to zero. Nerita is more sporting. This is a test of her skill, after all. She aims her shotgun, shoots, pumps, shoots, pumps. Stunned birds drop to the ground. She and her gun are a single entity, sharing one purpose. In moments it is all over. The porters retrieve the fallen birds and snap their necks. Nerita has the dozen pigeons her license allows: a pair to mount, the rest for tonight's dinner. The survivors have returned to their tree and stare placidly, unreproachfully, at the hunters.

"They breed so damned fast," Gracchus mutters. "If we aren't careful, they'll be getting out of the preserve and taking over all of Africa."

Sybille laughs. "Don't worry. We'll cope. We wiped them out once and we can do it again, if we have to."

Sybille's prey is a dodo. In Dar, when they were applying for their licenses, the others mocked her choice: a fat flightless bird, unable to run or fight, so feeble of wit that it fears nothing. She ignored them. She wants a dodo because to her it is the essence of extinction, the prototype of all that is dead and vanished. That there is no sport in shooting foolish dodos means little to Sybille. Hunting itself is meaningless for her.

Through this vast park she wanders as in a dream. She sees ground sloths, great auks, quaggas, moas, heath hens, Javan rhinos, giant armadillos, and many other rarities. The place is an abode of ghosts. The ingenuities of the genetic craftsmen are limitless; someday, perhaps, the preserve will offer trilobites, tyrannosaurs, mastodons, saber-toothed cats, baluchitheria, even—why not?—packs of Australopithecines, tribes of Neanderthals. For the amusement of the deads, whose games tend to be somber. Sybille wonders whether it can really be considered killing, this slaughter of laboratory-spawned novelties. Are these animals real or artificial? Living things, or cleverly animated constructs? Real, she decides. Living. They eat, they metabolize, they reproduce. They must seem real to themselves, and so they are real, realer, maybe, than dead human beings who walk again in their own cast-off bodies.

"Shotgun," Sybille says to the closest porter.

There is the bird, ugly, ridiculous, waddling laboriously through the tall grass. Sybille accepts a weapon and sights along its barrel. "Wait," Nerita says. "I'd like to get a picture of this." She moves slantwise around the group, taking exaggerated care not to frighten the dodo, but the dodo does not seem to be aware of any of them. Like an emissary from the realm of darkness, carrying good news of death to those creatures not yet extinct, it plods diligently across their path. "Fine," Nerita says. "Anthony, point at the dodo, will you, as if you've just noticed it? Kent, I'd like you to look down at your gun, study its bolt or something. Fine. And Sybille, just hold that pose—aiming—yes—"

Nerita takes the picture.

Calmly Sybille pulls the trigger.

"*Kazi imekwisha,*" Gracchus says. "The work is finished."

Six

Although to be driven back upon oneself is an uneasy affair at best, rather like trying to cross a border with borrowed credentials, it seems to be now the one condition necessary to the beginnings of real self-respect. Most of our platitudes notwithstanding, self-deception remains the most difficult deception. The tricks that work on others count for nothing in that very well-lit back alley where one keeps assignations with oneself: no winning smiles will do here, no prettily drawn lists of good intentions.

Joan Didion: *On Self-Respect*

"You better believe what Jeej is trying to tell you," Dolorosa said. "Ten minutes inside the Cold Town, they'll have your number. Five minutes."

Jijibhoi's man was small, rumpled-looking, forty or fifty years old, with untidy long dark hair and wide-set smoldering eyes. His skin was sallow and his face was gaunt. Such other deads as Klein had seen at close range had about them an air of unearthly serenity, but not this one: Dolorosa was tense, fidgety, a knuckle-cracker, a lip-gnawer. Yet somehow there could be no doubt he was a dead, as much a dead as Zacharias, as Gracchus, as Mortimer.

"They'll have my what?" Klein asked.

"Your number. Your number. They'll know you aren't a dead, because it can't be faked. Jesus, don't you even speak English? Jorge, that's a foreign name. I should have known. Where are you from?"

"Argentina, as a matter of fact, but I was brought to California when I was a small boy. In 1955. Look, if they catch me, they catch me. I just want to get in there and spend half an hour talking with my wife."

"Mister, you don't have any wife any more."

"With Sybille," Klein said, exasperated. "To talk with Sybille, my—my former wife."

"All right. I'll get you inside."

"What will it cost?"

"Never mind that," Dolorosa said. "I owe Jeej here a few favors. More than a few. So I'll get you the drug—"

"Drug?"

"The drug the Treasury agents use when they infiltrate the Cold Towns. It narrows the pupils, contracts the capillaries, gives you that good old zombie look. The agents always get caught and thrown out, and so will you, but at least you'll go in there feeling that you've got a convincing disguise. Little oily capsule, one every morning before breakfast."

Klein looked at Jijibhoi. "Why do Treasury agents infiltrate the Cold Towns?"

"For the same reasons they infiltrate anywhere else," Jijibhoi said. "To spy. They are trying to compile dossiers on the financial dealings of the deads, you see, and until proper life-defining legislation is approved by Congress there is no precise way of compelling a person who is deemed legally dead to divulge—"

Dolorosa said, "Next, the background. I can get you a card of residence from Albany Cold Town in New York. You died last December, okay, and they rekindled you back east because—let's see—"

"I could have been attending the annual meeting of the American Historical Association in New York," Klein suggested. "That's what I do, you understand, professor of contemporary history at UCLA. Because of the Christmas holiday my body couldn't be shipped back to

California, no room on any flight, and so they took me to Albany. How does that sound?"

Dolorosa smiled. "You really enjoy making up lies, Professor, don't you? I can dig that quality in you. Okay, Albany Cold Town, and this is your first trip out of there, your drying-off trip—that's what it's called, drying-off—you come out of the Cold Town like a new butterfly just out of its cocoon, all soft and damp, and you're on your own in a strange place. Now, there's a lot of stuff you'll need to know about how to behave, little mannerisms, social graces, that kind of crap, and I'll work on that with you tomorrow and Wednesday, and Friday, three sessions; that ought to be enough. Meanwhile let me give you the basics. There are only three things you really have to remember while you're inside:

"(1) Never ask a direct question.

"(2) Never lean on anybody's arm. You know what I mean?

"(3) Keep in mind that to a dead the whole universe is plastic, nothing's real, nothing matters a hell of a lot, it's all only a joke. Only a joke, friend, only a joke."

Early in April he flew to Salt Lake City, rented a car, and drove out past Moab into the high plateau rimmed by red-rock mountains where the deads had built Zion Cold Town. This was Klein's second visit to the necropolis. The other had been in the late summer of '91, a hot, parched season when the sun filled half the sky and even the gnarled junipers looked dazed from thirst; but now it was a frosty afternoon, with faint pale light streaming out of the wintry western hills and occasional gusts of light snow whirling through the iron-blue air. Jijibhoi's route instructions pulsed from the memo screen on his dashboard. Fourteen miles from town, yes, narrow paved lane turns off highway, yes, discreet little sign announcing PRIVATE ROAD, NO ADMITTANCE, yes, a second sign a thousand yards in, ZION COLD TOWN, MEMBERS ONLY, yes, and then just beyond that the barrier of green light across the road, the scanner system, the roadblocks sliding like scythes out of the underground installations, a voice on an invisible loudspeaker saying, "If you have a permit to enter Zion Cold Town, please place it under your left-hand windshield wiper."

That other time he had had no permit, and he had gone no farther than this, though at least he had managed a little colloquy with the unseen gatekeeper out of which he had squeezed the information that Sybille was indeed living in that particular Cold Town. This time he affixed Dolorosa's forged card of residence to his windshield, and waited tensely, and in thirty seconds the roadblocks slid from sight. He drove on, along a winding road that followed the natural contours of a dense forest of scrubby conifers, and came at last to a brick wall that curved away into the trees as though it encircled the entire town. Probably it did. Klein had an overpowering sense of the Cold Town as a hermetic city, ponderous and sealed as old Egypt. There was a metal gate in the brick wall; green electronic eyes surveyed him, signaled their approval, and the wall rolled open.

He drove slowly toward the center of town, passing through a zone of what he supposed were utility buildings—storage depots, a power substation, the municipal waterworks, whatever, a bunch of grim windowless one-story cinderblock affairs—and then into the residential district, which was not much lovelier. The streets were laid out on a rectangular grid; the buildings were squat, dreary, impersonal, homogeneous. There was practically no automobile traffic, and in a dozen blocks he saw no more than ten pedestrians, who did not even glance at him. So this was the environment in which the deads chose to spend their second lives. But why such deliberate bleakness? "You will never understand us," Dolorosa had warned. Dolorosa was right. Jijibhoi had told him that Cold Towns were something less than charming, but Klein had not been prepared for this. There was a glacial quality about the place, as though it were wholly entombed in a block of clear ice: silence, sterility, a mortuary calm. Cold Town, yes, aptly named. Architecturally, the town looked like the worst of all possible cheap-and-sleazy tract developments, but the psychic texture it projected was even more depressing, more like that of one of those ghastly retirement communities, one of the innumerable Leisure Worlds or Sun Manors, those childless joyless retreats where colonies of that other kind of living dead collected to await the last trumpet. Klein shivered.

✹

At last, another few minutes deeper into the town, a sign of activity, if not exactly of life: a shopping center, flat-topped brown stucco buildings around a U-shaped courtyard, a steady flow of shoppers moving about. All right. His first test was about to commence. He parked his car near the mouth of the U and strolled uneasily inward. He felt as if his forehead were a beacon, flashing glowing betrayals at rhythmic intervals:

FRAUD INTRUDER INTERLOPER SPY

Go ahead, he thought, seize me, seize the impostor, get it over with, throw me out, string me up, crucify me. But no one seemed to pick up the signals. He was altogether ignored. Out of courtesy? Or just contempt? He stole what he hoped were covert glances at the shoppers, half expecting to run across Sybille right away. They all looked like sleepwalkers, moving in glazed silence about their errands. No smiles, no chatter: the icy aloofness of these self-contained people heightened the familiar suburban atmosphere of the shopping center into surrealist intensity, Norman Rockwell with an overlay of Dali or De Chirico. The shopping center looked like all other shopping centers: clothing stores, a bank, a record shop, snack bars, a florist, a TV stereo outlet, a theater, a five-and-dime. One difference, though, became apparent as Klein wandered from shop to shop: the whole place was automated. There were no clerks anywhere, only the ubiquitous data screens, and no doubt a battery of hidden scanners to discourage shoplifters. (Or did the impulse toward petty theft perish with the body's first death?) The customers selected all the merchandise themselves, checked it out via data screens, touched their thumbs to chargeplates to debit their accounts. Of course. No one was going to waste his precious rekindled existence standing behind a counter to sell tennis shoes or cotton candy. Nor were the dwellers in the Cold Towns likely to dilute their isolation by hiring a labor force of imported warms. Somebody here had to do a little work, obviously—how did the merchandise get into the stores?—but, in general, Klein realized, what could not be done here by machines would not be done at all.

For ten minutes he prowled the center. Just when he was beginning to think he must be entirely invisible to these people, a short, broad-shouldered man, bald but with oddly youthful features, paused in front of him and said, "I am Pablo. I welcome you to Zion Cold Town." This unexpected puncturing of the silence so startled Klein that he had to fight to retain appropriate deadlike imperturbability. Pablo smiled warmly and touched both his hands to Klein's in friendly greeting, but his eyes were frigid, hostile, remote, a terrifying contradiction. "I've been sent to bring you to the lodging-place. Come: your car."

Other than to give directions, Pablo spoke only three times during the five-minute drive. "Here is the rekindling house," he said. A five-story building, as inviting as a hospital, with walls of dark bronze and windows black as onyx. "This is Guidefather's house," Pablo said a moment later. A modest brick building, like a rectory, at the edge of a small park. And, finally: "This is where you will stay. Enjoy your visit." Abruptly he got out of the car and walked rapidly away.

This was the house of strangers, the hotel for visiting deads, a long low cinderblock structure, functional and unglamorous, one of the least seductive buildings in this city of stark disagreeable buildings. However else it might be with the deads, they clearly had no craving for fancy architecture. A voice out of a data screen in the spartan lobby assigned him to a room: a white-walled box, square, high of ceiling. He had his own toilet, his own data screen, a narrow bed, a chest of drawers, a modest closet, a small window that gave him a view of a neighboring building just as drab as this. Nothing had been said about rental; perhaps he was a guest of the city. Nothing had been said about anything. It seemed that he had been accepted. So much for Jijibhoi's gloomy assurance that he would instantly be found out, so much for Dolorosa's insistence that they would have his number in ten minutes or less. He had been in Zion Cold Town for half an hour. Did they have his number?

"Eating isn't important among us," Dolorosa had said.

"But you do eat?"

"Of course we eat. It just isn't *important*."

It was important to Klein, though. Not haute cuisine, necessarily, but some sort of food, preferably three times a day. He was getting hungry now. Ring for room service? There were no servants in this city. He turned to the data screen. Dolorosa's first rule: *Never ask a direct question*. Surely that didn't apply to the data screen, only to his fellow deads. He didn't have to observe the niceties of etiquette when talking to a computer. Still, the voice behind the screen might not be that of a computer after all, so he tried to employ the oblique, elliptical conversational style that Dolorosa said the deeds favored among themselves:

"Dinner?"

"Commissary."

"Where?"

"Central Four," said the screen.

Central Four? All right. He would find the way. He changed into fresh clothing and went down the long vinyl-floored hallway to the lobby. Night had come; street lamps were glowing; under cloak of darkness the city's ugliness was no longer so obtrusive, and there was even a kind of controlled beauty about the brutal regularity of its streets.

The streets were unmarked, though, and deserted. Klein walked at random for ten minutes, hoping to meet someone heading for the Central Four commissary. But when he did come upon someone, a tall and regal woman well advanced in years, he found himself incapable of approaching her. *(Never ask a direct question. Never lean on anybody's arm.)* He walked alongside her, in silence and at a distance, until she turned suddenly to enter a house. For ten minutes more he wandered alone again. This is ridiculous, he thought: dead or warm, I'm a stranger in town, I should be entitled to a little assistance. Maybe Dolorosa was just trying to complicate things. On the next corner, when Klein caught sight of a man hunched away from the wind, lighting a cigarette, he went boldly over to him. "Excuse me, but—"

The other looked up. "Klein?" he said. "Yes. Of course. Well, so you've made the crossing too!"

He was one of Sybille's Zanzibar companions, Klein realized. The quick-eyed, sharp-edged one—Mortimer. A member of her pseudo-familial grouping, whatever that might be. Klein stared sullenly at him. This had to be the moment when his imposture would be exposed, for only some six weeks had passed since he had argued with Mortimer in the gardens of Sybille's Zanzibar hotel, not nearly enough time for someone to have died and been rekindled and gone through his drying-off. But a moment passed and Mortimer said nothing. At length Klein said, "I just got here. Pablo showed me to the house of strangers and now I'm looking for the commissary."

"Central Four? I'm going there myself. How lucky for you." No sign of suspicion in Mortimer's face. Perhaps an elusive smile revealed his awareness that Klein could not be what he claimed to be. *Keep in mind that to a dead the whole universe is plastic, it's all only a joke.* "I'm waiting for Nerita," Mortimer said. "We can all eat together."

Klein said heavily, "I was rekindled in Albany Cold Town. I've just emerged."

"How nice," Mortimer said.

Nerita Tracy stepped out of a building just beyond the corner—a slim, athletic-looking woman, about forty, with short reddish-brown hair. As she swept toward them, Mortimer said, "Here's Klein, who we met in Zanzibar, just rekindled, out of Albany."

"Sybille will be amused."

"Is she in town?" Klein blurted.

Mortimer and Nerita exchanged sly glances. Klein felt abashed. *Never ask a direct question.* Damn Dolorosa!

Nerita said, "You'll see her before long. Shall we go to dinner?"

The commissary was less austere than Klein had expected: actually quite an inviting restaurant, elaborately constructed on five or six levels divided by lustrous dark hangings into small, secluded dining areas. It had the warm, rich look of a tropical resort.

But the food, which came automat-style out of revolving dispensers, was prefabricated and cheerless—another jarring contradiction. *Only a joke, friend, only a joke.* In any case he was less hungry than he had imagined at the hotel. He sat with Mortimer and Nerita, picking at his meal, while their conversation flowed past him at several times the speed of thought. They spoke in fragments and ellipses, in periphrastics and aposiopeses, in a style abundant in chiasmus, metonymy, meiosis, oxymoron, and zeugma; their dazzling rhetorical techniques left him baffled and uncomfortable, which beyond much doubt was their intention. Now and again they would dart from a thicket of indirection to skewer him with a quick corroborative stab: Isn't that so, they would say, and he would smile and nod, nod and smile, saying, Yes, yes, absolutely. Did they know he was a fake, and were they merely playing with him, or had they, somehow, impossibly, accepted him as one of them? So subtle was their style that he could not tell. A very new member of the society of the rekindled, he told himself, would be nearly as much at sea here as a warm in deadface.

Then Nerita said—no verbal games, this time—"You still miss her terribly, don't you?"

"I do. Some things evidently never perish."

"Everything perishes," Mortimer said. "The dodo, the aurochs, the Holy Roman Empire, the T'ang Dynasty, the walls of Byzantium, the language of Mohenjo-daro."

"But not the Great Pyramid, the Yangtze, the coelacanth, or the skullcap of Pithecanthropus," Klein countered. "Some things persist and endure. And some can be regenerated. Lost languages have been deciphered. I believe the dodo and the aurochs are hunted in a certain African park in this very era."

"Replicas," Mortimer said.

"Convincing replicas. Simulations as good as the original."

"Is that what you want?" Nerita asked.

"I want what's possible to have."

"A convincing replica of lost love?"

"I might be willing to settle for five minutes of conversation with her."

"You'll have it. Not tonight. See? There she is. But don't bother her now." Nerita nodded across the gulf in the center of the restaurant; on the far side, three levels up from where they sat, Sybille and Kent Zacharias had appeared. They stood for a brief while at the edge of their dining alcove, staring blandly and emotionlessly into the restaurant's central well. Klein felt a muscle jerking uncontrollably in his cheek, a damning revelation of undeadlike uncoolness, and pressed his hand over it, so that it twanged and throbbed against his palm. She was like a goddess up there, manifesting herself in her sanctum to her worshipers, a pale shimmering figure, more beautiful even than she had become to him through the anguished enhancements of memory, and it seemed impossible to him that that being had ever been his wife, that he had known her when her eyes were puffy and reddened from a night of study, that he had looked down at her face as they made love and had seen her lips pull back in that spasm of ecstasy that is so close to a grimace of pain, that he had known her crochety and unkind in her illness, short-tempered and impatient in health, a person of flaws and weaknesses, of odors and blemishes, in short a human being, this goddess, this unreal rekindled creature, this object of his quest, this Sybille. Serenely she turned, serenely she vanished into her cloaked alcove. "She knows you're here," Nerita told him. "You'll see her.

Perhaps tomorrow." Then Mortimer said something maddeningly oblique, and Nerita replied with the same off-center mystification, and Klein once more was plunged into the river of their easy dancing word-play, down into it, down and down and down, and as he struggled to keep from drowning, as he fought to comprehend their interchanges, he never once looked toward the place where Sybille sat, not even once, and congratulated himself on having accomplished that much at least in his masquerade.

That night, lying alone in his room at the house of strangers, he wonders what he will say to Sybille when they finally meet, and what she will say to him. Will he dare bluntly to ask her to describe to him the quality of her new existence? That is all that he wants from her, really, that knowledge, that opening of an aperture into her transfigured self; that is as much as he hopes to get from her, knowing as he does that there is scarcely a chance of regaining her, but will he dare to ask, will he dare even that? Of course his asking such things will reveal to her that he is still a warm, too dense and gross of perception to comprehend the life of a dead; but he is certain she will sense that anyway, instantly. What will he say, what will he say? He plays out an imagined script of their conversation in the theater of his mind:

—Tell me what it's like, Sybille, to be the way you are now.

—Like swimming under a sheet of glass.

—I don't follow.

—Everything is quiet where I am, Jorge. There's a peace that passeth all understanding. I used to feel sometimes that I was caught up in a great storm, that I was being buffeted by every breeze, that my life was being consumed by agitations and frenzies, but now, now, I'm at the eye of the storm, at the place where everything is always calm. I observe rather than let myself be acted upon.

—But isn't there a loss of feeling that way? Don't you feel that you're wrapped in an insulating layer? Like swimming, under glass, you say—that conveys being insulate, being cut off, being almost numb.

—I suppose you might think so. The way it is, is that one no longer is affected by the unnecessary.

—It sounds to me like a limited existence.

—Less limited than the grave, Jorge.

—I never understood why you wanted rekindling. You were such a world-devourer, Sybille, you lived with such intensity, such passion. To settle for the kind of existence you have now, to be only half-alive—

—Don't be a fool, Jorge. To be half-alive is better than to be rotting in the ground. I was so young. There was so much else still to see and do.

—But to see it and do it half-alive?

—Those were your words, not mine. I'm not alive at all. I'm neither less nor more than the person you knew. I'm another kind of being altogether. Neither less nor more, only different.

—Are all your perceptions different?

—Very much so. My perspective is broader. Little things stand revealed as little things.

—Give me an example, Sybille.

—I'd rather not. How could I make anything clear to you? Die and be with us, and you'll understand.

—You know I'm not dead?

—Oh, Jorge, how funny you are!

—How nice that I can still amuse you.

—You look so hurt, so tragic. I could almost feel sorry for you. Come: ask me anything.

—Could you leave your companions and live in the world again?

—I've never considered that.

—Could you?

—I suppose I could. But why should I? This is my world now.

—This ghetto.

—Is that how it seems to you?

—You lock yourselves into a closed society of your peers, a tight subculture. Your own jargon, your own wall of etiquette and idiosyncrasy. Designed, I think, mainly to keep the outsiders off balance, to keep them feeling like outsiders. It's a defensive thing. The hippies, the blacks, the gays, the deads—same mechanism, same process.

—The Jews, too. Don't forget the Jews.

—All right, Sybille, the Jews. With their little tribal jokes, their special holidays, their own mysterious language, yes, a good case in point.

—So I've joined a new tribe. What's wrong with that?

—Did you need to be part of a tribe?

—What did I have before? The tribe of Californians? The tribe of academics?

—The tribe of Jorge and Sybille Klein.

—Too narrow. Anyway, I've been expelled from that tribe. I needed to join another one.

—Expelled?

—By death. After that there's no going back.

—You could go back. Any time.

—Oh, no, no, no, Jorge, I can't; I can't, I'm not Sybille Klein any more, I never will be again. How can I explain it to you? There's no way. Death brings on changes. Die and see, Jorge. Die and see.

Nerita said, "She's waiting for you in the lounge."

It was a big, coldly furnished room at the far end of the other wing of the house of strangers. Sybille stood by a window through which pale, chilly morning light was streaming. Mortimer was with her, and also Kent Zacharias. The two men favored Klein with mysterious oblique smiles—courteous or derisive, he could not tell which. "Do you like our town?" Zacharias asked. "Have you been seeing the sights?" Klein chose not to reply. He acknowledged the question with a faint nod and turned to Sybille. Strangely, he felt altogether calm at this moment of attaining a years-old desire: he felt nothing at all in her presence, no panic, no yearning, no dismay, no nostalgia, nothing, nothing. As though he were truly a dead. He knew it was the tranquility of utter terror.

"We'll leave you two alone," Zacharias said. "You must have so much to tell each other." He went out, with Nerita and Mortimer. Klein's eyes met Sybille's and lingered there. She was looking at him coolly, in a kind of impersonal appraisal. That damnable smile of hers, Klein thought: dying turns them all into Mona Lisas.

She said, "Do you plan to stay here long?"

"Probably not. A few days, maybe a week." He moistened his lips. "How have you been, Sybille? How has it been going?"

"It's all been about as I expected."

What do you mean by that? Can you give me some details? Are you at all disappointed? Have there been any surprises? What has it been like for you, Sybille? Oh, Jesus—

—Never ask a direct question—

He said, "I wish you had let me visit with you in Zanzibar."

"That wasn't possible. Let's not talk about it now." She dismissed the episode with a casual wave. After a moment she said, "Would you like to hear a fascinating story I've uncovered about the early days of Omani influence in Zanzibar?"

The impersonality of the question startled him. How could she display such absolute lack of curiosity about his presence in Zion Cold Town, his claim to be a dead, his reasons for wanting to see her? How could she plunge so quickly, so coldly, into a discussion of archaic political events in Zanzibar?

"I suppose so," he said weakly.

"It's a sort of Arabian Nights story, really. It's the story of how Ahmad the Sly overthrew Abdullah ibn Muhammad Alawi."

The names were strange to him. He had indeed taken some small part in her historical researches, but it was years since he had worked with her, and everything had drifted about in his mind, leaving a jumbled residue of Ahmads and Hasans and Abdullahs. "I'm sorry," he said. "I don't recall who they were."

Unperturbed, Sybille said, "Certainly you remember that in the eighteenth and early nineteenth centuries the chief power in the Indian Ocean was the Arab state of Oman, ruled from Muscat on the Persian Gulf. Under the Busaidi dynasty, founded in 1744 by Ahmad ibn Said al-Busaidi, the Omani extended their power to East Africa. The logical capital for their African empire was the port of Mombasa, but they were unable to evict a rival dynasty reigning there, so the Busaidi looked toward nearby Zanzibar—a cosmopolitan island of mixed Arab, Indian, and African population. Zanzibar's strategic placement on the coast and its spacious and well-protected harbor made it an ideal base for the East African slave trade that the Busaidi of Oman intended to dominate."

"It comes back to me now, I think."

"Very well. The founder of the Omani Sultanate of Zanzibar was Ahmad ibn Majid the Sly, who came to the throne of Oman in 1811—do you remember?—upon the death of his uncle Abd-er-Rahman al-Busatdi."

"The names sound familiar," Klein said doubtfully.

"Seven years later," Sybille continued, "seeking to conquer Zanzibar without the use of force, Ahmad the Sly shaved his beard and mustache and visited the island disguised as a soothsayer, wearing yellow robes and a costly emerald in his turban. At that time most of Zanzibar was governed by a native ruler of mixed Arab and African blood, Abdullah ibn Muhammad Alawi, whose hereditary title was Mwenyi Mkuu. The Mwenyi Mkuu's subjects were mainly Africans, members of a tribe called the Hadimu. Sultan Ahmad, arriving in Zanzibar Town, gave a demonstration of his soothsaying skills on the waterfront and attracted so much attention that he speedily gained an audience at the court of the Mwenyi Mkuu. Ahmad predicted a glowing future for Abdullah, declaring that a powerful prince famed throughout the world would come to Zanzibar, make the Mwenyi Mkuu his high lieutenant, and confirm him and his descendants as lords of Zanzibar forever.

"'How do you know these things?' asked the Mwenyi Mkuu.

"'There is a potion I drink,' Sultan Ahmad replied, 'that enables me to see what is to come. Do you wish to taste of it?'

"'Most surely I do,' Abdullah said, and Ahmad thereupon gave him a drug that sent him into rapturous transports and showed him visions of paradise. Looking down from his place near the footstool of Allah, the Mwenyi Mkuu saw a rich and happy Zanzibar governed by his children's children's children. For hours he wandered in fantasies of almighty power.

"Ahmad then departed, and let his beard and mustache grow again, and returned to Zanzibar ten weeks later in his full regalia as Sultan of Oman, at the head of an imposing and powerful armada. He went at once to the court of the Mwenyi Mkuu and proposed, just as the soothsayer had prophesied, that Oman and Zanzibar enter into a treaty of alliance under which Oman would assume responsibility for much of Zanzibar's external relations—including the slave trade—while guaranteeing the authority of the Mwenyi Mkuu over domestic affairs. In return for his partial abdication of authority, the Mwenyi Mkuu would receive financial compensation from Oman. Remembering the vision the soothsayer had revealed to him, Abdullah at once signed the treaty, thereby legitimizing what was, in effect, the Omani conquest of Zanzibar. A great feast was held to celebrate the treaty, and, as a mark of honor, the Mwenyi Mkuu offered Sultan Ahmad a rare drug used locally, known as *borqash,* or 'the flower of truth.' Ahmad only pretended to put the pipe to his lips, for he loathed all mind-altering drugs, but Abdullah, as the flower of truth possessed him, looked at Ahmad and recognized the outlines of the soothsayer's face behind the Sultan's new beard. Realizing that he had been deceived, the Mwenyi Mkuu thrust his dagger, the tip of which was poisoned, deep into the Sultan's side and fled the banquet hall, taking up residence on the neighboring island of Pemba. Ahmad ibn Majid survived, but the poison consumed his vital organs and the remaining ten years of his life were spent in constant agony. As for the Mwenyi Mkuu, the Sultan's men hunted him down and put him to death along with ninety members of his family, and native rule in Zanzibar was therewith extinguished."

Sybille paused. "Is that not a gaudy and wonderful story?" she asked at last.

"Fascinating," Klein said. "Where did you find it?"

"Unpublished memoirs of Claude Richburn of the East India Company. Buried deep in the London archives. Strange that no historian ever came upon it before, isn't it? The standard texts simply say that Ahmad used his navy to bully Abdullah into signing the treaty, and then had the Mwenyi Mkuu assassinated at the first convenient moment."

"Very strange," Klein agreed. But he had not come here to listen to romantic tales of visionary potions and royal treacheries. He groped for some way to bring the conversation to a more personal level. Fragments of his imaginary dialogue with Sybille floated through his mind. *Everything is quiet where I am, Jorge. There's a peace that passeth all understanding. Like swimming under a sheet of glass. The way it is, is that one no longer is affected by the unnecessary. Little things stand revealed as little things. Die and be with us, and you'll understand.* Yes. Perhaps. But did she really believe any of that? He had put all the words in her mouth; everything he had imagined her to say was his own construct, worthless as a key to the true Sybille. Where would he find the key, though?

She gave him no chance. "I will be going back to Zanzibar soon," she said. "There's much I want to learn about this incident from the people in the back country—old legends about the last days of the Mwenyi Mkuu, perhaps variants on the basic story—"

"May I accompany you?"

"Don't you have your own research to resume, Jorge?" she asked, and did not wait for an answer. She walked briskly toward the door of the lounge and went out, and he was alone.

Seven

I mean what they and their hired psychiatrists call "delusional systems." Needless to say, "delusions" are always officially defined. We don't have to worry about questions of real or unreal. They only talk out of expediency. It's the system that matters. How the data arrange themselves inside it. Some are consistent, others fall apart.

Thomas Pynchon: *Gravity's Rainbow*

Once more the deads, this time only three of them, coming over on the morning flight from Dar. Three was better than five, Daud Mahmoud Barwani supposed, but three was still more than a sufficiency. Not that those others, two months back, had caused any trouble, staying just the one day and flitting off to the mainland again, but it made him uncomfortable to think of such creatures on the same small island as himself. With all the world to choose, why did they keep coming to Zanzibar?

"The plane is here," said the flight controller.

Thirteen passengers. The health officer let the local people through the gate first—two newspapermen and four legislators coming back from the Pan-African Conference in Capetown—and then processed a party of four Japanese tourists, unsmiling owlish men festooned with cameras. And then the deads: and Barwani was surprised to discover that they were the same ones as before, the red-haired man, the brown-haired man without the beard, the black-haired woman. Did deads have so much money that they could fly from America to Zanzibar every few months? Barwani had heard a tale to the effect that each new dead, when he rose from his coffin, was presented with bars of gold equal to his own weight, and now he thought he believed it. No good will come of having such beings loose in the world, he told himself, and certainly none from letting them into Zanzibar. Yet he had no choice. "Welcome once again to the isle of cloves," he said unctuously, and smiled a bureaucratic smile, and wondered, not for the first time, what would become of Daud Mahmoud Barwani once his days on earth had reached their end.

"—Ahmad the Sly versus Abdullah Something," Klein said. "That's all she would talk about. The history of Zanzibar." He was in Jijibhoi's study. The night was warm and a late-season rain was falling, blurring the million sparkling lights of the Los Angeles basin. "It would have been, you know, gauche to ask her any direct questions. Gauche. I haven't felt so gauche since I was fourteen. I was helpless among them, a foreigner, a child."

"Do you think they saw through your disguise?" Jijibhoi asked.

"I can't tell. They seemed to be toying with me, to be having sport with me, but that may just have been their general style with any newcomer. Nobody challenged me. Nobody hinted I might be an impostor. Nobody seemed to care very much about me or what I was doing there or how I had happened to become a dead. Sybille and I stood face to face, and I wanted to reach out to her, I wanted her to reach out to me, and there was no contact, none, none at all, it was as though we had just met at some academic cocktail party and the only thing on her mind was the new nugget of obscure history she had just unearthed, and so she told me all about how Sultan Ahmad outfoxed Abdullah and Abdullah stabbed the Sultan." Klein caught sight of a set of familiar books on Jijibhoi's crowded shelves—Oliver and Mathew, *History of East Africa,* books that had traveled everywhere with Sybille in the years of their marriage. He pulled forth Volume I, saying, "She claimed that the standard histories give a sketchy and inaccurate description of the incident and that she's only now discovered the true story. For all I know, she was just playing a game with me, telling me a piece of established history as though it were something nobody knew till last week. Let me see—Ahmad, Ahmad, Ahmad—"

He examined the index. Five Ahmads were listed, but there was no entry for a Sultan Ahmad ibn Majid the Sly. Indeed, an Ahmad ibn Majid was cited, but he was mentioned only in a footnote and appeared to be an Arab chronicler. Klein found three Abdullahs, none of them a man of Zanzibar. "Something's wrong," he murmured.

"It does not matter, dear Jorge," Jijibhoi said mildly.

"It does. Wait a minute." He prowled the listings. Under *Zanzibar, Rulers,* he found no Ahmads, no Abdullahs; he did discover a Majid ibn Said, but when he checked the reference he found that he had reigned somewhere in the second half of the nineteenth century. Desperately Klein flipped pages, skimming, turning back, searching. Eventually he looked up and said, "It's all wrong!"

"The Oxford *History of East Africa*?"

"The details of Sybille's story. Look, she said this Ahmad the Sly gained the throne of Oman in 1811, and seized Zanzibar seven years later. But the book says that a certain Seyyid Said al-Busaidi became Sultan of Oman in 1806, and ruled for *fifty years.* He was the one, not this nonexistent Ahmad the Sly, who grabbed Zanzibar, but he did it in 1828, and the ruler he compelled to sign a treaty with him, the Mwenyi

Mkuu, was named Hasan ibn Ahmad Alawi, and—" Klein shook his head. "It's an altogether different cast of characters. No stabbings, no assassinations, the dates are entirely different, the whole thing—"

Jijibhoi smiled sadly. "The deads are often mischievous."

"But why would she invent a complete fantasy and palm it off as a sensational new discovery? Sybille was the most scrupulous scholar I ever knew! She would never—"

"That was the Sybille you knew, dear friend. I keep urging you to realize that this is another person, a new person, within her body."

"A person who would lie about history?"

"A person who would tease," Jijibhoi said.

"Yes," Klein muttered. "Who would tease." *Keep in mind that to a dead the whole universe is plastic, nothing's real, nothing matters a hell of a lot.* "Who would tease a stupid, boring, annoyingly persistent ex-husband who has shown up in her Cold Town, wearing a transparent disguise and pretending to be a dead. Who would invent not only an anecdote but even its principals, as a joke, a game, a *jeu d'esprit.* Oh, God. Oh, God, how cruel she is, how foolish I was! It was her way of telling me she knew I was a phony dead. Quid pro quo, fraud for fraud!"

"What will you do?"

"I don't know," Klein said.

✹

What he did, against Jijibhoi's strong advice and his own better judgment, was to get more pills from Dolorosa and return to Zion Cold Town. There would be a fitful joy, like that of probing the socket of a missing tooth, in confronting Sybille with the evidence of her fictional Ahmad, her imaginary Abdullah. Let there be no more games between us, he would say. Tell me what I need to know, Sybille, and then let me go away; but tell me only truth. All the way to Utah he rehearsed his speech, polishing and embellishing. There was no need for it, though, since this time the gate of Zion Cold Town would not open for him. The scanners scanned his forged Albany card and the loudspeaker said, "Your credentials are invalid."

Which could have ended it. He might have returned to Los Angeles and picked up the pieces of his life. All this semester he had been on sabbatical leave, but the summer term was coming and there was work to do. He did return to Los Angeles, but only long enough to pack a somewhat larger suitcase, find his passport, and drive to the airport. On a sweet May evening a BOAC jet took him over the Pole to London, where, barely pausing for coffee and buns at an airport shop, he boarded another plane that carried him southeast toward Africa. More asleep than awake, he watched the dreamy landmarks drifting past: the Mediterranean, coming and going with surprising rapidity, and the tawny carpet of the Libyan Desert, and the mighty Nile, reduced to a brown thread's thickness when viewed from a height of ten miles. Suddenly Kilimanjaro, mist-wrapped, snow-bound, loomed like a giant double-headed blister to his right, far below, and he thought he could make out to his left the distant glare of the sun on the Indian Ocean. Then the big needle-nosed plane began its abrupt swooping descent, and he found himself, soon after, stepping out into the warm humid air and dazzling sunlight of Dar es Salaam.

Too soon, too soon. He felt unready to go on to Zanzibar. A day or two of rest, perhaps: he picked a Dar hotel at random, the Agip, liking the strange sound of its name, and hired a taxi. The hotel was sleek and clean, a streamlined affair in the glossy 1960's style, much cheaper than the Kilimanjaro, where he had stayed briefly on the other trip, and located in a pleasant leafy quarter of the city, near the ocean. He strolled about for a short while, discovered that he was altogether exhausted, returned to his room for a nap that stretched on for nearly five hours, and awakening groggy, showered and dressed for dinner. The hotel's dining room was full of beefy red-faced fair-haired men, jacketless and wearing open-throated white shirts, all of whom reminded him disturbingly of Kent Zacharias; but these were warms, Britishers from their accents, engineers, he suspected, from their conversation. They were building a dam and a power plant somewhere up the coast, it seemed, or perhaps a power plant without a dam; it was hard to follow what they said. They drank a good deal of gin and spoke in hearty booming shouts. There were also a good many Japanese businessmen, of course, looking trim and restrained in dark-blue suits and narrow ties, and at the table next to Klein's were five tanned curly-haired men talking in rapid Hebrew—Israelis, surely. The only Africans in sight were waiters and bartenders. Klein ordered Mombasa oysters, steak, and a carafe of red wine, and found the food unexpectedly good, but left most of it on his plate. It was late evening in Tanzania, but for him it was ten o'clock in the morning, and his body was confused. He tumbled into bed, meditated vaguely on the probable presence of Sybille just a few air-minutes away in Zanzibar, and dropped into a sound sleep from which he awakened, what seemed like many hours later, to discover that it was still well before dawn.

He dawdled away the morning sightseeing in the old native quarter, hot and dusty, with unpaved streets and rows of tin shacks, and at midday returned to his hotel for a shower and lunch. Much the same national distribution in the restaurant—British, Japanese, Israeli—though the faces seemed different. He was on his second beer when Anthony Gracchus came in. The white hunter, broad-shouldered, pale, densely bearded, clad in khaki shorts, khaki shirt, seemed almost to have stepped out of the picture-cube Jijibhoi had once shown him. Instinctively Klein shrank back, turning toward the window, but too late: Gracchus had seen him. All chatter came to a halt in the restaurant as the dead man strode to Klein's table, pulled out a chair unasked, and seated himself; then, as though a motion-picture projector had been halted and started again, the British engineers resumed their shouting, sounding somewhat strained now. "Small world," Gracchus said. "Crowded one, anyway. On your way to Zanzibar, are you, Klein?"

"In a day or so. Did you know I was here?"

"Of course not." Gracchus' harsh eyes twinkled slyly. "Sheer coincidence is what this is. She's there already."

"She is?"

"She and Zacharias and Mortimer. I hear you wiggled your way into Zion."

"Briefly," Klein said. "I saw Sybille. Briefly."

"Unsatisfactorily. So once again you've followed her here. Give it up, man. Give it up."

"I can't."

"Can't!" Gracchus scowled. "A neurotic's word, can't. What you mean is *won't*. A mature man can do anything he wants to that isn't a physical impossibility. Forget her. You're only annoying her, this way, interfering with her work, interfering with her—" Gracchus smiled. "With her life. She's been dead almost three years, hasn't she? Forget her. The world's full of other women. You're still young, you have money, you aren't ugly, you have professional standing—"

"Is this what you were sent here to tell me?"

"I wasn't sent here to tell you anything, friend. I'm only trying to save you from yourself. Don't go to Zanzibar. Go home and start your life again."

"When I saw her at Zion," Klein said, "she treated me with contempt. She amused herself at my expense. I want to ask her why she did that."

"Because you're a warm and she's a dead. To her you're a clown. To all of us you're a clown. It's nothing personal, Klein. There's simply a gulf in attitudes, a gulf too wide for you to cross. You went to Zion drugged up like a Treasury man, didn't you? Pale face, bulgy eyes? You didn't fool anyone. You certainly didn't fool *her*. The game she played with you was her way of telling you that. Don't you know that?"

"I know it, yes."

"What more do you want, then? More humiliation?"

Klein shook his head wearily and stared at the tablecloth. After a moment he looked up, and his eyes met those of Gracchus, and he was astounded to realize that he trusted the hunter, that for the first time in his dealings with the deads he felt he was being met with sincerity. He said in a low voice, "We were very close, Sybille and I, and then she died, and now I'm nothing to her. I haven't been able to come to terms with that. I need her, still. I want to share my life with her, even now."

"But you can't."

"I know that. And still I can't help doing what I've been doing."

"There's only one thing you *can* share with her," Gracchus said. "That's your death. She won't descend to your level: you have to climb to hers."

"Don't be absurd."

"Who's absurd, me or you? Listen to me, Klein. I think you're a fool, I think you're a weakling, but I don't dislike you, I don't hold you to blame for your own foolishness. And so I'll help you, if you'll allow me." He reached into his breast pocket and withdrew a tiny metal tube with a safety catch at one end. "Do you know what this is?" Gracchus asked. "It's a self-defense dart, the kind all the women in New York carry. A good many deads carry them, too, because we never know when the reaction will start, when the mobs will turn against us. Only we don't use anesthetic drugs in ours. Listen, we can walk into any tavern in the native quarter and have a decent brawl going in five minutes, and in the confusion I'll put one of these darts into you, and we'll have you in Dar General Hospital fifteen minutes after that, crammed into a deep-freeze unit, and for a few thousand dollars we can ship you unthawed to California, and this time Friday night you'll be undergoing rekindling in, say, San Diego Cold Town. And when you come out of it you and Sybille will be on the same side of the gulf, do you see? If you're destined to get back together with her, ever, that's the only way. That way you have a chance. This way you have none."

"It's unthinkable," Klein said.

"Unacceptable, maybe. But not unthinkable. Nothing's unthinkable once somebody's thought it. You think it some more. Will you promise me that? Think about it before you get aboard that plane for Zanzibar. I'll be staying here tonight and tomorrow, and then I'm going out to Arusha to meet some deads coming in for the hunting, and any time before then I'll do it for you if you say the word. Think about it. Will you think about it? Promise me that you'll think about it."

"I'll think about it," Klein said.

"Good. Good. Thank you. Now let's have lunch and change the subject. Do you like eating here?"

"One thing puzzles me. Why does this place have a clientele that's exclusively non-African? Does it dare to discriminate against blacks in a black republic?"

Gracchus laughed. "It's the blacks who discriminate, friend. This is considered a second-class hotel. All the blacks are at the Kilimanjaro or the Nyerere. Still, it's not such a bad place. I recommend the fish dishes, if you haven't tried them, and there's a decent white wine from Israel that—"

Eight

O Lord, methought what pain it was to drown!
What dreadful noise of water in mine ears!
What sights of ugly death within mine eyes!
Methoughts I saw a thousand fearful wracks;
A thousand men that fishes gnawed upon;
Wedges of gold, great anchors, heaps of pearl,
Inestimable stones, unvalued jewels,
All scatt'red in the bottom of the sea.
Some lay in dead men's skulls, and in the holes

Where eyes did once inhabit there were crept,
As 'twere in scorn of eyes, reflecting gems
That wooed the slimy bottom of the deep
And mocked the dead bones that lay scatt'red by.

Shakespeare: *Richard III*

"—Israeli wine," Mick Dongan was saying. "Well, I'll try anything once, especially if there's some neat little irony attached to it. I mean, there we were in Egypt, in Egypt, at this fabulous dinner party in the hills at Luxor, and our host is a Saudi prince, no less, in full tribal costume right down to the sunglasses, and when they bring out the roast lamb he grins devilishly and says, 'Of course we could always drink Mouton-Rothschild, but I do happen to have a small stock of select Israeli wines in my cellar, and because I think you are, like myself, a connoisseur of small incongruities, I've asked my steward to open a bottle or two of'—Klein, do you see that girl who just came in?" It is January, 1981, early afternoon, a fine drizzle in the air. Klein is lunching with six colleagues from the history department at the Hanging Gardens atop the Westwood Plaza. The hotel is a huge ziggurat on stilts; the Hanging Gardens is a rooftop restaurant, ninety stories up, in freaky neo-Babylonian décor, all winged bulls and snorting dragons of blue and yellow tile, waiters with long curly beards and scimitars at their hips—gaudy nightclub by dark, campy faculty hangout by day. Klein looks to his left. Yes, a handsome woman, mid-twenties, coolly beautiful, serious-looking, taking a seat by herself, putting a stack of books and cassettes down on the table before her. Klein does not pick up strange girls: a matter of moral policy, and also a matter of innate shyness. Dongan teases him. "Go on over, will you? She's your type, I swear. Her eyes are the right color for you, aren't they?"

Klein has been complaining, lately, that there are too many blue-eyed gals in southern California. Blue eyes are disturbing to him, somehow, even menacing. His own eyes are brown. So are hers: dark, warm, sparkling. He thinks he has seen her occasionally in the library. Perhaps they have even exchanged brief glances. "Go on," Dongan says. "Go on, Jorge. Go." Klein glares at him. He will not go. How can he intrude on this woman's privacy? To force himself on her—it would almost be like rape. Dongan smiles complacently; his bland grin is a merciless prod. Klein refuses to be stampeded. But then, as he hesitates, the girl smiles too, a quick shy smile, gone so soon he is not altogether sure it happened at all, but he is sure enough, and he finds himself rising, crossing the alabaster floor, hovering awkwardly over her, searching for some inspired words with which to make contact, and no words come, but still they make contact the old-fashioned way, eye to eye, and he is stunned by the intensity of what passes between them in that first implausible moment.

"Are you waiting for someone?" he mutters, shaken.

"No." The smile again, far less tentative. "Would you like to join me?"

She is a graduate student, he discovers quickly. Just got her master's, beginning now on her doctorate—the nineteenth-century East African slave trade, particular emphasis on Zanzibar. "How romantic," he says. "Zanzibar! Have you been there?"

"Never. I hope to go some day. Have you?"

"Not ever. But it always interested me, ever since I was a small boy collecting stamps. It was the last country in my album."

"Not in mine," she says. "Zululand was."

She knows him by name, it turns out. She had even been thinking of enrolling in his course on Nazism and Its Offspring. "Are you South American?" she asks.

"Born there. Raised here. My grandparents escaped to Buenos Aires in '37."

"Why Argentina? I thought that was a hotbed of Nazis."

"Was. Also full of German-speaking refugees, though. All their friends went there. But it was too unstable. My parents got out in '55, just before one of the big revolutions, and came to California. What about you?"

"British family. I was born in Seattle. My father's in the consular service. He—"

A waiter looms. They order sandwiches offhandedly. Lunch seems very unimportant now. The contact still holds. He sees Conrad's *Nostromo* in her stack of books; she is halfway through it, and he has just finished it, and the coincidence amuses them. Conrad is one of her favorites, she says. One of his, too. What about Faulkner? Yes, and Mann, and Virginia Woolf, and they share even a fondness for Hermann Broch, and a dislike for Hesse. How odd. Operas? *Freischütz, Holländer, Fidelio,* yes. "We have very Teutonic tastes," she observes.

"We have very similar tastes," he adds. He finds himself holding her hand.

"Amazingly similar," she says.

Mick Dongan leers at him from the far side of the room; Klein gives him a terrible scowl. Dongan winks. "Let's get out of here," Klein says, just as she starts to say the same thing.

They talk half the night and make love until dawn. "You ought to know," he tells her solemnly over breakfast, "that I decided long ago never to get married and certainly never to have a child."

"So did I," she says. "When I was fifteen."

They were married four months later. Mick Dongan was his best man.

⁂

Gracchus said, as they left the restaurant, "You will think things over, won't you?"

"I will," Klein said. "I promised you that."

He went to his room, packed his suitcase, checked out, and took a cab to the airport, arriving in plenty of time for the afternoon flight to Zanzibar. The same melancholy little man was on duty as health officer when he landed, Barwani. "Sir, you have come back," Barwani said. "I thought you might. The other people have been here several days already."

"The other people?"

"When you were here last, sir, you kindly offered me a retainer in order that you might be informed when a certain person reached this island." Barwani's eyes gleamed. "That person, with two of her former companions, is here now."

Klein carefully placed a twenty-shilling note on the health officer's desk. "At which hotel?"

Barwani's lips quirked. Evidently twenty shillings fell short of expectations. But Klein did not take out another banknote, and after a moment Barwani said, "As before. The Zanzibar House. And you, sir?"

"As before," Klein said. "I'll be staying at the Shirazi."

⁂

Sybille was in the garden of the hotel, going over that day's research notes, when the telephone call came from Barwani. "Don't let my papers blow away," she said to Zacharias, and went inside.

When she returned, looking bothered, Zacharias said, "is there trouble?"

She sighed. "Jorge. He's on his way to his hotel now."

"What a bore," Mortimer murmured. "I thought Gracchus might have brought him to his senses."

"Evidently not," Sybille said. "What are we going to do?"

"What would you like to do?" Zacharias asked.

She shook her head. "We can't allow this to go on, can we?"

✹

The evening air was humid and fragrant. The long rains had come and gone, and the island was in the grip of the new season's lunatic fertility: outside the window of Klein's hotel room some vast twining vine was putting forth monstrous trumpet-shaped yellow flowers, and all about the hotel grounds everything was in blossom, everything was in a frenzy of moist young leaves. Klein's sensibility reverberated to that feeling of universal vigorous thrusting newness; he paced the room, full of energy, trying to devise some feasible stratagem. Go immediately to see Sybille? Force his way in, if necessary, with shouts and alarums, and demand to know why she had told him that fantastic tale of imaginary sultans? No. No. He would do no more confronting, no more lamenting; now that he was here, now that he was close by her, he would seek her out calmly, he would talk quietly, he would invoke memories of their old love, he would speak of Rilke and Woolf and Broch, of afternoons in Puerto Vallarta and nights in Santa Fe, of music heard and caresses shared, he would rekindle not their marriage, for that was impossible, but merely the remembrance of the bond that once had existed, he would win from her some acknowledgment of what had been, and then he would soberly and quietly exorcise that bond, he and she together, they would work to free him by speaking softly of the change that had come over their lives, until, after three hours or four or five, he had brought himself with her help to an acceptance of the unacceptable. That was all. He would demand nothing, he would beg for nothing, except only that she assist him for one evening in ridding his soul of this useless, destructive obsession. Even a dead, even a capricious, wayward, volatile, whimsical, wanton dead, would surely see the desirability of that, and would freely give him her cooperation. Surely. And then home, and then new beginnings, too long postponed.

He made ready to go out.

There was a soft knock at the door. "Sir? Sir? You have visitors downstairs."

"Who?" Klein asked, though he knew the answer.

"A lady and two gentlemen," the bellhop replied. "The taxi has brought them from the Zanzibar House. They wait for you in the bar."

"Tell them I'll be down in a moment."

He went to the iced pitcher on the dresser, drank a glass of cold water mechanically, unthinkingly, poured himself a second, drained that too. This visit was unexpected; and why had she brought her entourage along? He had to struggle to regain that centeredness, that sense of purpose understood, which he thought he had attained before the knock. Eventually he left the room.

They were dressed crisply and impeccably this damp night, Zacharias in a tawny frock coat and pale-green trousers, Mortimer in a belted white caftan trimmed with intricate brocade, Sybille in a simple lavender tunic. Their pale faces were unmarred by perspiration; they seemed perfectly composed, models of poise. No one sat near them in the bar. As Klein entered, they stood to greet him, but their smiles appeared sinister, having nothing of friendliness in them. Klein clung tight to his intended calmness. He said quietly, "It was kind of you to come. May I buy drinks for you?"

"We have ours already," Zacharias pointed out. "Let us be your hosts. What will you have?"

"Pimm's Number Six," Klein said. He tried to match their frosty smiles. "I admire your tunic, Sybille. You all look so debonair tonight that I feel shamed."

"You never were famous for your clothes," she said.

Zacharias returned from the counter with Klein's drink. He took it and toasted them gravely.

After a short while Klein said, "Do you think I could talk privately with you, Sybille?"

"There's nothing we have to say to one another that can't be said in front of Kent and Laurence."

"Nevertheless."

"I prefer not to, Jorge."

"As you wish." Klein peered straight into her eyes and saw nothing there, nothing, and flinched. All that he had meant to say fled his mind. Only churning fragments danced there: Rilke, Broch, Puerto Vallarta. He gulped at his drink.

Zacharias said, "We have a problem to discuss, Klein."

"Go on."

"The problem is you. You're causing great distress to Sybille. This is the second time, now, that you've followed her to Zanzibar, to the literal end of the earth, Klein, and you've made several attempts besides to enter a closed sanctuary in Utah under false pretenses, and this is interfering with Sybille's freedom, Klein, it's an impossible, intolerable interference."

"The deads are dead," Mortimer said. "We understand the depths of your feelings for your late wife, but this compulsive pursuit of her must be brought to an end."

"It will be," Klein said, staring at a point on the stucco wall midway between Zacharias and Sybille. "I want only an hour or two of private conversation with my—with Sybille, and then I promise you that there will be no further—"

"Just as you promised Anthony Gracchus," Mortimer said, "not to go to Zanzibar."

"I wanted—"

"We have our rights," said Zacharias. "We've gone through hell, literally through hell, to get where we are. You've infringed on our right to be left alone. You bother us. You bore us. You annoy us. We hate to be annoyed." He looked toward Sybille. She nodded. Zacharias' hand vanished into the breast pocket of his coat. Mortimer seized Klein's wrist with astonishing suddenness and jerked his arm forward. A minute metal tube glistened in Zacharias' huge fist. Klein had seen such a tube in the hand of Anthony Gracchus only the day before.

"No," Klein gasped. "I don't believe—*no*!"

Zacharias plunged the cold tip of the tube quickly into Klein's forearm.

"The freezer unit is coming," Mortimer said. "It'll be here in five minutes or less."

"What if it's late?" Sybille asked anxiously. "What if something irreversible happens to his brain before it gets here?"

"He's not even entirely dead yet," Zacharias reminded her. "There's time. There's ample time. I spoke to the doctor myself, a very intelligent Chinese, flawless command of English. He was most sympathetic. They'll have him frozen within a couple minutes of death. We'll book cargo passage aboard the morning plane for Dar. He'll be in the United

States within twenty-four hours, I guarantee that. San Diego will be notified. Everything will be all right, Sybille!"

Jorge Klein lay slumped across the table. The bar had emptied the moment he had cried out and lurched forward: the half-dozen customers had fled, not caring to mar their holidays by sharing an evening with the presence of death, and the waiters and bartenders, big-eyed, terrified, lurked in the hallway. A heart attack, Zacharias had announced, some kind of sudden attack, maybe a stroke, where's the telephone? No one had seen the tiny tube do its work.

Sybille trembled. "If anything goes wrong—"

"I hear the sirens now," Zacharias said.

From his desk at the airport Daud Mahmoud Barwani watched the bulky refrigerated coffin being loaded by grunting porters aboard the morning plane for Dar. And then, and then, and then? They would ship the dead man to the far side of the world, to America, and breathe new life into him, and he would go once more among men. Barwani shook his head. These people! The man who was alive is now dead, and these dead ones, who knows what they are? Who knows? Best that the dead remain dead, as was intended in the time of first things. Who could have foreseen a day when the dead returned from the grave? Not I. And who can foresee what we will all become, a hundred years from now? Not I. Not I. A hundred years from now I will sleep, Barwani thought. I will sleep, and it will not matter to me at all what sort of creatures walk the earth.

Nine

We die with the dying:
See, they depart, and we go with them.
We are born with the dead:
See, they return, and bring us with them.

T.S. Eliot: *Little Gidding*

On the day of his awakening he saw no one except the attendants at the rekindling house, who bathed him and fed him and helped him to walk slowly around his room. They said nothing to him, nor he to them; words seemed irrelevant. He felt strange in his skin, too snugly contained, as though all his life he had worn ill-fitting clothes and now had for the first time encountered a competent tailor. The images that his eyes brought him were sharp, unnaturally clear, and faintly haloed by prismatic colors, an effect that imperceptibly vanished as the day passed. On the second day he was visited by the San Diego Guidefather, not at all the formidable patriarch he had imagined, but rather a cool, efficient executive, about fifty years old, who greeted him cordially and told him briefly of the disciplines and routines he must master before he could leave the Cold Town. "What month is this?" Klein asked, and Guidefather told him it was June, the seventeenth of June, 1993. He had slept four weeks.

Now it is the morning of the third day after his awakening, and he has guests: Sybille, Nerita, Zacharias, Mortimer, Gracchus. They file into his room and stand in an arc at the foot of his bed, radiant in the glow of light that pierces the narrow windows. Like demigods, like angels, glittering with a dazzling inward brilliance, and now he is of their company. Formally they embrace him, first Gracchus, then Nerita, then Mortimer. Zacharias advances next to his bedside, Zacharias who sent him into death, and he smiles at Klein and Klein returns the smile, and they embrace. Then it is Sybille's turn: she slips her hand between his, he draws her close, her lips brush his cheek, his touch hers, his arm encircles her shoulders.

"Hello," she whispers.

"Hello," he says.

They ask him how he feels, how quickly his strength is returning, whether he has been out of bed yet, how soon he will commence his drying-off. The style of their conversation is the oblique, elliptical style favored by the deads, but not nearly so clipped and cryptic as the way of speech they normally would use among themselves; they are favoring him, leading him inch by inch into their customs. Within five minutes he thinks he is getting the knack.

He says, using their verbal shorthand, "I must have been a great burden to you."

"You were, you were," Zacharias agrees. "But all that is done with now."

"We forgive you," Mortimer says.

"We welcome you among us," declares Sybille.

They talk about their plans for the months ahead. Sybille is nearly finished with her work on Zanzibar; she will retreat to Zion Cold Town for the summer months to write her thesis. Mortimer and Nerita are off to Mexico to tour the ancient temples and pyramids; Zacharias is going to Ohio, to his beloved mounds. In the autumn they will reassemble at Zion and plan the winter's amusement: a tour of Egypt, perhaps, or Peru, the heights of Machu Picchu. Ruins, archeological sites, delight them; in the places where death has been busiest, their joy is most intense. They are flushed, excited, verbose—virtually chattering, now. Away we will go, to Zimbabwe, to Palenque, to Angkor, to Knossos, to Uxmal, to Nineveh, to Mohenjo-daro. And as they go on and on, talking with hands and eyes and smiles and even words, even words, torrents of words, they blur and become unreal to him, they are mere dancing puppets perking about a badly painted stage, they are droning insects, wasps or bees or mosquitoes, with all their talk of travels and festivals, of Boghazköy and Babylon, of Megiddo and Masada, and he ceases to hear them, he tunes them out, he lies there smiling, eyes glazed, mind adrift. It perplexes him that he has so little interest in them. But then he realizes that it is a mark of his liberation. He is freed of old chains now. Will he join their set? Why should he? Perhaps he will travel with them, perhaps not, as the whim takes him. More likely not. Almost certainly not. He does not need their company. He has his own interests. He will follow Sybille about no longer. He does not need, he does not want, he will not seek. Why should he become one of them, rootless, an amoral wanderer, a ghost made flesh? Why should he embrace the values and customs of these people who had given him to death as dispassionately as they might swat an insect, only because he had bored them, because he had annoyed them? He does not hate them for what they did to him, he feels no resentment that he can identify, he merely chooses to detach himself from them. Let them float on from ruin to ruin, let them pursue death from continent to continent; he will go his own way. Now that he has crossed the interface, he finds that Sybille no longer matters to him.

—Oh, sir, things change—

"We'll go now," Sybille says softly.

He nods. He makes no other reply.

"We'll see you after your drying-off," Zacharias tells him, and touches him lightly with his knuckles, a farewell gesture used only by the deads.

"See you," Mortimer says.

"See you," says Gracchus.

"Soon," Nerita says.

Never, Klein says, saying it without words, but so they will understand. Never. Never. Never. I will never see any of you. I will never see you, Sybille. The syllables echo through his brain, and the word, *never, never, never,* rolls over him like the breaking surf, cleansing him, purifying him, healing him. He is free. He is alone.

"Goodbye," Sybille calls from the hallway.

"Goodbye," he says.

It was years before he saw her again. But they spent the last days of '99 together, shooting dodos under the shadow of mighty Kilimanjaro.

SCHWARTZ BETWEEN THE GALAXIES

In the two years following the completion of the novel Dying Inside *in the fall of 1971, I wrote nothing but short stories and the novella "Born with the Dead." Despite the struggle that those stories, and "Born with the Dead" in particular had been, I allowed myself to take on commitments to write two more novels, which would eventually become* The Stochastic Man *and* Shadrach in the Furnace. *I also let two friends talk me into writing short stories for publications they were editing. But, even as I locked myself into these four projects, I felt an increasing certainty that I was going to give up writing science fiction once those jobs were done.*

My own personal fatigue was only one factor in that decision. Another was my sense of having been on the losing side in a literary revolution.

Among the many revolutions that went on in the era known as the Sixties (which actually ran from about 1967 to 1972) there was one in science fiction. A host of gifted new writers, both in England and the United States, brought all manner of advanced literary techniques to bear on the traditional matter of s-f, producing stories that were more deeply indebted to Joyce, Kafka, Faulkner, Mann, and even e.e. cummings than they were to Heinlein, Asimov, and Clarke. This period of stylistic and structural innovation, which reached its highest pitch of activity between 1966 and 1969, was a heady, exciting time for science-fiction writers, especially newer ones such as Thomas Disch, Samuel R. Delany, R.A. Lafferty, and Barry Malzberg, although some relatively well-established people like John Brunner, Harlan Ellison, and, yes, Robert Silverberg, joined in the fun. My stories grew more and more experimental in mode—you can see it beginning to happen in

"Sundance" and "Good News from the Vatican"—and most of them were published, now, in anthologies of original stories rather than in the conventional s-f magazines.

What was fun for the writers, though, turned out to be not so much fun for the majority of the readers, who quite reasonably complained that if they wanted to read Joyce and Kafka, they'd go and read Joyce and Kafka. They didn't want their s-f to be Joycified and Kafkaized. So they stayed away from the new fiction in droves, and by 1972 the revolution was pretty much over. We were heading into the era of Star Wars, *the trilogy craze, and the return of literarily conservative action-based science fiction to the center of the stage.*

One of the most powerful figures in the commercialization of science fiction at that time was the diminutive Judy-Lynn del Rey, a charming and ferociously determined woman whose private reading tastes inclined toward Ulysses *but who knew, perhaps better than anyone else ever had, what the majority of s-f readers wanted to buy. As a kind of side enterprise during her dynamic remaking of the field, she started a paperback anthology series called* Stellar, *and—despite my recent identification with the experimental side of science fiction—asked me, in May, 1973, to do a story for it.*

Her stated policy was to bring back the good old kind of s-f storytelling, as exemplified in the magazines of the 1950s, a golden age for readers like me. "I don't want mood pieces without plots," she warned. "I don't want vignettes; I don't want character sketches; and I don't want obvious extrapolations of current fads and newspaper stories. These yarns should have beginnings, middles, and ends. I want the writers to solve the problems they postulate...."

Since most of what I had been writing recently embodied most of the characteristics she thus decried, there was a certain incompatibility between Judy-Lynn's strongly voiced requirements and her equally strong insistence on having a Silverberg story for her first issue. And yet I had no real problem with her stated policy. My own tastes in s-f had been formed largely in the early 1950s, when such writers as C.M. Kornbluth, Alfred Bester, James Blish, Theodore Sturgeon, and Fritz Leiber had been at the top of their form. I had always felt more comfortable with their kind of fiction than with the wilder stuff of fifteen years later; I thought myself rather a reactionary writer alongside people like Disch, Lafferty, Malzberg, or J.G. Ballard. And I thought "Schwartz Between the Galaxies," which I wrote in October, 1973, was a reasonably conservative story, too—definitely a story of the 1970s but not particularly experimental in form or tone.

Judy-Lynn bought it—it would have been discourteous not to, after urging me so strenuously to write something for her—but she obviously felt let down, even betrayed. Here she was putting together her theme-setting first issue, and here I was still trying to write literature. *To her surprise and chagrin, though, the story was extremely popular—one of the five contenders for the Hugo award for best short story the following year—and was fairly widely anthologized afterward.*

I won the skirmish, yes; but Judy-Lynn, bless her, won the war. Our little literary revolution ended in total rout, with the space sagas and fantasy trilogies that she published sweeping the more highbrow kind of science fiction into oblivion, and many of the literary-minded writers left science fiction, never to return.

I was among those who left, although, as you will note, I did come back after a while. But it seemed certain to me as 1974 began that my days as a science-fiction writer were over forever. For one thing, the work had become terribly hard: my work-sheets indicate that "Schwartz Between the Galaxies" took me close to three weeks to write. In happier days I could have written a whole novel, *and a good one, in that time. Then, too, despite that Hugo nomination, I felt that the readers were turning away from my work. I was still getting on the awards ballots as frequently as ever, but I wasn't winning anything. That seemed symptomatic. The readers no longer understood me, and I felt I understood them all too well.*

So in late 1973 I wrote one more short story—"In the House of Double Minds"—because I had promised it to an editor, and then I swore a mighty oath that I would never write short s-f again. In the spring of 1974 I wrote the first of my two promised novels, The Stochastic Man. *About six months later I launched into the second one,* Shadrach in the Furnace *and finished it in the spring of 1975 after a horrendous battle to get the words down on paper.*

That was it. I had spent two decades as a science-fiction writer, and had emerged out of my early hackwork to win a considerable reputation among connoisseurs, and now it was all over. I would never write again, I told myself. (And told anyone else who would listen, too.)

And I didn't. For a while, anyway.

This much is reality: Schwartz sits comfortably cocooned—passive, suspended—in a first-class passenger rack aboard a Japan Air Lines rocket, nine kilometers above the Coral Sea. And this much is fantasy: the same Schwartz has passage on a shining starship gliding silkily through the interstellar depths, en route at nine times the velocity of light from Betelgeuse IX to Rigel XXI, or maybe from Andromeda to the Lesser Magellanic.

There are no starships. Probably there never will be any. Here we are, a dozen decades after the flight of Apollo 11, and no human being goes anywhere except back and forth across the face of the little O, the Earth, for the planets are barren and the stars are beyond reach. That little O is too small for Schwartz. Too often it glazes for him; it turns to a nugget of dead porcelain; and lately he has formed the habit, when the world glazes, of taking refuge aboard that interstellar ship. So what JAL Flight 411 holds is merely his physical self, his shell, occupying a costly private cubicle on a slender 200-passenger vessel which, leaving Buenos Aires shortly after breakfast, has sliced westward along the Tropic of Capricorn for a couple of hours and will soon be landing at Papua's Torres Skyport. But his consciousness, his *anima,* the essential Schwartzness of him, soars between the galaxies.

What a starship it is! How marvelous its myriad passengers! Down its crowded corridors swarms a vast gaudy heterogeny of galactic creatures, natives of the worlds of Capella, Arcturus, Altair, Canopus, Polaris, Antares, beings both intelligent and articulate, methane-breathing or nitrogen-breathing or argon breathing, spiny-skinned or skinless, many-armed or many-headed or altogether incorporeal, each a product of a distinct and distinctly unique and alien cultural heritage. Among these varied folk moves Schwartz, that superstar of anthropologists, that true heir to Kroeber and Morgan and Malinowski and Mead, delightedly devouring their delicious diversity. Whereas aboard this prosaic rocket, this planet-locked stratosphere needle, one cannot tell the Canadians from the Portuguese, the Portuguese from the Romanians, the Romanians from the Irish, unless they open their mouths, and sometimes not always then.

In his reveries he confers with creatures from the Fomalhaut system about digital circumcision; he tapes the melodies of the Achernarnian eye-flute; he learns of the sneeze-magic of Acrux, the sleep-ecstasies of Aldebaran, the asteroid-sculptors of Thuban. Then a smiling JAL stewardess parts the curtain of his cubicle and peers in at him, jolting him from one reality to another. She is blue-eyed, frizzy-haired, straight-nosed, thin-lipped, bronze-skinned, a genetic mishmash, your standard twenty-first-century-model mongrel human, perhaps Melanesian-Swedish-Turkish-Bolivian, perhaps Polish-Berber-Tatar-Welsh. Cheap intercontinental transit has done its deadly work: all Earth is a crucible, all the gene pools have melted into one indistinguishable fluid. Schwartz wonders about the recessivity of those blue eyes and arrives at no satisfactory solution. She is beautiful, at any rate. Her name is Dawn—O sweet neutral nonculture-bound cognomen!—and they have played at a flirtation, he and she, Dawn and Schwartz, at occasional moments of this short flight. Twinkling, she says softly, "We're getting ready for our landing, Dr. Schwartz. Are your restrictors in polarity?"

"I never unfastened them."

"Good." The blue eyes, warm, interested, meet his. "I have a layover in Papua tonight," she says.

"That's nice."

"Let's have a drink while we're waiting for them to unload the baggage," she suggests with cheerful bluntness. "All right?"

"I suppose," he says casually. "Why not?" Her availability bores him: somehow he enjoys the obsolete pleasures of the chase. Once such easiness in a woman like this would have excited him, but no longer. Schwartz is forty years old, tall, square-shouldered, sturdy, a showcase for the peasant genes of his rugged Irish mother. His close-cropped black hair is flecked with gray; many women find that interesting. One rarely sees gray hair now. He dresses simply but well, in sandals and Socratic tunic. Predictably, his physical attractiveness, both within his domestic sixness and without, has increased with his professional success. He is confident, sure of his powers, and he radiates an infectious assurance. This month alone eighty million people have heard his lectures.

She picks up the faint weariness in his voice. "You don't sound eager. Not interested?"

"Hardly that."

"What's wrong, then? Feeling sub, Professor?"

Schwartz shrugs. "Dreadfully sub. Body like dry bone. Mind like dead ashes." He smiles, full force depriving his words of all their weight.

She registers mock anguish. "That sounds bad," she says. "That sounds awful!"

"I'm only quoting Chuang Tzu. Pay no attention to me. Actually, I feel fine, just a little stale."

"Too many skyports?"

He nods. "Too much of a sameness wherever I go." He thinks of a star-bright, top-deck bubble dome where three boneless Spicans do a twining dance of propitiation to while away the slow hours of nine-light travel. "I'll be all right," he tells her. "It's a date."

Her hybrid face flows with relief and anticipation. "See you in Papua," she tells him, and winks, and moves jauntily down the aisle.

Papua. By cocktail time Schwartz will be in Port Moresby. Tonight he lectures at the University of Papua; yesterday it was Montevideo; the day after tomorrow it will be Bangkok. He is making the grand academic circuit. This is his year: he is very big, suddenly, in anthropological circles, since the publication of *The Mask Beneath the Skin*. From continent to continent he flashes, sharing his wisdom, Monday in Montreal, Tuesday Veracruz, Wednesday Montevideo, Thursday—Thursday? He crossed the international date line this morning, and he does not remember whether he has entered Thursday or Tuesday, though yesterday was surely Wednesday. Schwartz is certain only that this is July and the year is 2083, and there are moments when he is not even sure of that.

The JAL rocket enters the final phase of its landward plunge. Papua waits, sleek, vitrescent. The world has a glassy sheen again. He lets his spirit drift happily back to the gleaming starship making its swift way across the whirling constellations.

He found himself in the starship's busy lower-deck lounge, having a drink with his traveling companion, Pitkin, the Yale economist. Why Pitkin, that coarse, florid little man? With all of real and imaginary humanity to choose from, why had his unconscious elected to make him share this fantasy with such a boor?

"Look," Pitkin said, winking and leering. "There's your girlfriend."

The entry-iris had opened and the Antarean not-male had come in.

"Quit it," Schwartz snapped. "You know there's no such thing going on."

"Haven't you been chasing her for days?"

"She's not a 'her'," Schwartz said.

Pitkin guffawed. "Such precision! Such scholarship! *She's* not a *her,* he says!" He gave Schwartz a broad nudge. "To you she's a she, friend, and don't try to kid me."

Schwartz had to admit there was some justice to Pitkin's vulgar innuendos. He did find the Antarean—a slim yellow-eyed ebony-skinned upright humanoid, sinuous and glossy, with tapering elongated limbs and a seal's fluid grace—powerfully attractive. Nor could he help thinking of the Antarean as feminine. That attitude was hopelessly culture-bound and species-bound, he knew; in fact the alien had cautioned him that terrestrial sexual distinctions were irrelevant in the Antares system, that if Schwartz insisted on thinking of "her" in genders, "she" could be considered only the negative of male, with no implication of biological femaleness.

He said patiently, "I've told you. The Antarean's neither male nor female as we understand those concepts. If we happen to perceive the Antarean as feminine, that's the result of our own cultural conditioning. If you want to believe that my interest in this being is sexual, go ahead, but I assure you that it's purely professional."

"Sure. You're only studying her."

"In a sense I am. And she's studying me. On her native world she has the status-frame of 'watcher-of-life,' which seems to translate into the Antarean equivalent of an anthropologist."

"How lovely for you both. She's your first alien and you're her first Jew."

"Stop calling her *her*," Schwartz hissed.

"But you've been doing it!"

Schwartz closed his eyes. "My grandmother told me never to get mixed up with economists. Their thinking is muddy and their breath is bad, she said. She also warned me against Yale men. Perverts of the intellect, she called them. So here I am cooped up on an interstellar ship with five hundred alien creatures and one fellow human, and he has to be an economist from Yale."

"Next trip travel with your grandmother instead."

"Go away," Schwartz said. "Stop lousing up my fantasies. Go peddle your dismal science somewhere else. You see those Delta Aurigans over there? Climb into their bottle and tell them all about the Gross Global Product." Schwartz smiled at the Antarean, who had purchased a drink, something that glittered an iridescent blue, and was approaching them. "Go *on*," Schwartz murmured.

"Don't worry," Pitkin said. "I wouldn't want to crowd you." He vanished into the motley crowd

The Antarean said, "The Capellans are dancing, Schwartz."

"I"d like to see that. Too damned noisy in here anyway." Schwartz stared into the alien's vertical-slitted citreous eyes. Cat's eyes, he thought. Panther's eyes. The Antarean's gaze was focused, as usual, on Schwartz's mouth: other worlds, other customs. He felt a strange, unsettling tremor of desire. Desire for what, though? It was a sensation of pure need, nonspecific, certainly nonsexual. "I think I'll take a look. Will you come with me?"

The Papua rocket has landed. Schwartz, leaning across the narrow table in the skyport's lounge, says to the stewardess in a low, intense tone, "My life was in crisis. All my values were becoming meaningless. I was discovering that my chosen profession was empty, foolish, as useless as—playing chess."

"How awful," Dawn whispers gently.

"You can see why. You go all over the world, you see a thousand skyports a year. Everything the same everywhere. The same clothes, the same slang, the same magazines, the same styles of architecture and décor."

"Yes."

"International homogeneity. Worldwide uniformity. Can you understand what it's like to be an anthropologist in a world where there are no primitives left, Dawn? Here we sit on the island of Papua—you know, headhunters, animism, body-paint, the drums at sunset, the bone through the nose—and look at the Papuans in their business robes all around us. Listen to them exchanging stock-market tips, talking baseball, recommending restaurants in Paris and barbers in Johannesburg. It's no different anywhere else. In a single century we've transformed the planet into one huge sophisticated plastic western industrial state. The TV relay satellites, the two-hour intercontinental rockets, the breakdown of religious exclusivism and genetic taboo have mongrelized every culture, don't you see? You visit the Zuni and they have plastic African masks on the wall. You visit the Bushmen and they have Japanese-made Hopi-motif ashtrays. It's all just so much interior decoration, and underneath the carefully selected primitive motifs there's the same universal pseudo-American sensibility, whether you're in the

Kalahari or the Amazon rain forest. Do you comprehend what's happened, Dawn?"

"It's such a terrible loss," she says sadly. She is trying very hard to be sympathetic, but he senses she is waiting for him to finish his sermon and invite her to share his hotel room. He will invite her, but there is no stopping him once he has launched into his one great theme.

"Cultural diversity is gone from the world," he says. "Religion is dead; true poetry is dead; inventiveness is dead; individuality is dead. Poetry. Listen to this." In a high monotone he chants:

In beauty I walk
With beauty before me I walk
With beauty behind me I walk
With beauty above me I walk
With beauty above and about me I walk
It is finished in beauty
It is finished in beauty

He has begun to perspire heavily. His chanting has created an odd sphere of silence in his immediate vicinity; heads are turning, eyes are squinting. "Navaho," he says. "The Night Way, a nine-day chant, a vision, a spell. Where are the Navaho now? Go to Arizona and they'll chant for you, yes, for a price, but they don't know what the words mean, and chances are the singers are only one-fourth Navaho, or one-eighth, or maybe just Hopi hired to dress in Navaho costumes, because the real Navaho, if any are left, are off in Mexico City hired to be Aztecs. So much is gone. Listen." He chants again, more piercingly even than before:

The animal runs, it passes, it dies. And it is the great cold.
It is the great cold of the night, it is the dark.
The bird flies, it passes, it dies. And it is—

"JAL FLIGHT 411 BAGGAGE IS NOW UNLOADING ON CONCOURSE FOUR," a mighty mechanical voice cries.

—the great cold.
It is the great cold of the night, it is the dark.

"JAL FLIGHT 411 BAGGAGE..."

The fish flees, it passes, it dies. And—

"People are staring," Dawn says uncomfortably.

"—ON CONCOURSE FOUR."

"Let them stare. Do them some good. That's a Pygmy chant, from Gabon, in equatorial Africa. Pygmies? There are no more Pygmies. Everybody's two meters tall. And what do we sing? Listen. Listen." He gestures fiercely at the cloud of tiny golden loudspeakers floating near the ceiling. A mush of music comes from them: the current popular favorite. Savagely he mouths words: *"Star...far...here...near.* Playing in every skyport right now, all over the world." She smiles thinly. Her hand reaches toward his, covers it, presses against the knuckles. He is dizzy. The crowd, the eyes, the music, the drink. The plastic. Everything shines. Porcelain. Porcelain. The planet vitrifies. "Tom?" she asks uneasily. "Is anything the matter?" He laughs, blinks, coughs, shivers. He hears her calling for help, and then he feels his soul swooping outward, toward the galactic blackness.

With the Antarean not-male beside him, Schwartz peered through the viewport, staring in awe and fascination at the seductive vision of the Capellans coiling and recoiling outside the ship. Not all the passengers on this voyage had cozy staterooms like his. The Capellans were too big to come on board, and in any case they preferred never to let themselves be enclosed inside metal walls. They traveled just alongside the starship, basking like slippery whales in the piquant radiations of space. So long as they kept within twenty meters of the hull they would be inside the effective field of the Rabinowitz Drive, which swept ship and contents and associated fellow travellers toward Rigel, or the Lesser Magellanic, or was it one of the Pleiades toward which they were bound at a cool nine lights?

He watched the Capellans moving beyond the shadow of the ship in tracks of shining white. Blue, glossy green, and velvet black, they coiled and swam, and every track was a flash of golden fire. "They have a dangerous beauty," Schwartz whispered. "Do you hear them calling? I do."

"What do they say?"

"They say, *'Come to me, come to me, come to me!'* "

"Go to them, then," said the Antarean simply. "Step through the hatch."

"And perish?"

"And enter into your next transition. Poor Schwartz! Do you love your present body so?"

"My present body isn't so bad. Do you think I'm likely to get another one some day?"

"No?"

"No," Schwartz said. "This one is all I get. Isn't it that way with you?"

"At the Time of Openings I receive my next housing. That will be fifty years from now. What you see is the fifth form I have been given to wear."

"Will the next be as beautiful as this?"

"All forms are beautiful," the Antarean said. "You find me attractive?"

"Of course."

A slitted wink. A bobbing nod toward the viewport. "As attractive as *those*?"

Schwartz laughed. "Yes. In a different way."

Coquettishly the Antarean said, "If I were out there, you would walk through the hatch into space?"

"I might. If they gave me a spacesuit and taught me how to use it."

"But not otherwise? Suppose I were out there right now. I could live in space five, ten, maybe fifteen minutes. I am there and I say, *'Come to me, Schwartz, come to me!'* What do you do?"

"I don't think I'm all that much self-destructive."

"To die for love, though! To make a transition for the sake of beauty."

"No. Sorry."

The Antarean pointed toward the undulating Capellans. "If they asked you, you would go."

"They are asking me," he said.

"And you refuse the invitation?"

"So far. So far."

The Antarean laughed an Antarean laugh, a thick silvery snort. "Our voyage will last many weeks more. One of these days, I think, you will go to them."

✹

"You were unconscious at least five minutes," Dawn says. "You gave everyone a scare. Are you sure you ought to go through with tonight's lecture?"

Nodding, Schwartz says, "I'll be all right. I'm a little tired, is all. Too many time zones this week." They stand on the terrace of his hotel room. Night is coming on, already, here in late afternoon: it is midwinter in the Southern Hemisphere, though the fragrance of tropic blossoms perfumes the air. The first few stars have appeared. He has never really known which star is which. That bright one, he thinks, could be Rigel, and that one Sirius, and perhaps this is Deneb over there. And this? Can this be red Antares, in the heart of the Scorpion, or is it only Mars? Because of his collapse at the skyport he has been able to beg off the customary faculty reception and the formal dinner; pleading the need for rest, he has arranged to have a simple snack at his hotel room, *a deux*. In two hours they will come for him and take him to the University to speak. Dawn watches him closely. Perhaps she is worried about his health, perhaps she is only waiting for him to make his move toward her. There's time for all that later, he figures. He would rather talk now. Warming up for the audience he seizes his earlier thread:

"For a long time I didn't understand what had taken place. I grew up insular, cut off from reality, a New York boy, bright mind and a library card. I read all the anthropological classics, *Patterns of Culture* and *Coming of Age in Samoa* and *Life of a South African Tribe* and the rest, and I dreamed of field trips, collecting myths and grammars and folkways and artefacts and all that, until when I was twenty-five I finally got out into the field and started to discover I had gone into a dead science. We have only one worldwide culture now, with local variants but no basic divergences—there's nothing primitive left on Earth, *and there are no other planets*. Not inhabited ones. I can't go to Mars or Venus or Saturn and study the natives. What natives? And we can't reach the stars. All I have to work with is Earth. I was thirty years old when the whole thing clicked together for me and I knew I had wasted my life."

She says, "But surely there was something for you to study on Earth."

"One culture, rootless and homogeneous. That's work for a sociologist, not for me. I'm a romantic, I'm an exotic, I want strangeness, difference. Look, we can never have any real perspective on our own time and lives. The sociologists try to attain it, but all they get is a mound of raw indigestible data. Insight comes later—two, five, ten generations later. But one way we've always been able to learn about ourselves is by studying alien cultures, studying them *completely,* and defining ourselves by measuring what they are that we aren't. The cultures have to be isolated, though. The anthropologist himself corrupts that isolation in the Heisenberg sense when he comes around with his camera and scanners and starts asking questions, but we can compensate more or less, for the inevitable damage a lone observer causes. We can't compensate when our whole culture collides with another and absorbs and obliterates it. Which we technological-mechanical people now have done everywhere. One day I woke up and saw there were no alien cultures left. Hah! Crushing revelation! Schwartz's occupation is gone!"

"What did you do?"

"For years I was in an absolute funk. I taught, I studied, I went through the motions, knowing it was all meaningless. All I was doing was looking at records of vanished cultures left by earlier observers and trying to cudgel new meanings. Secondary sources, stale findings: I was an evaluator of dry bones, not a gatherer of evidence. Paleontology. Dinosaurs are interesting, but what do they tell you about the contemporary world and the meaning of its patterns? Dry bones, Dawn, dry bones. Despair. And then a clue. I had this Nigerian student, this Ibo—well, basically an Ibo, but she's got some Israeli in her and I think Chinese—and we grew very close, she was as close to me as anybody in my own sixness, and I told her my troubles. I'm going to give it all up, I said, because it isn't what I expected it to be. She laughed at me and said, What right do you have to be upset because the world doesn't live up to your expectations? Reshape your life, Tom; you can't reshape the world. I said, But how? And she said, Look inward, find the primitive in yourself, see what made you what you are, what made today's culture what it is, see how these alien streams have flowed together. Nothing's been lost here, only merged. Which made me think. Which gave me a new way of looking at things. Which sent me on an inward quest. It took me three years to grasp the patterns, to come to an understanding of what our planet has become, and only after I accepted the planet—"

It seems to him that he has been talking forever. Talking. Talking. But he can no longer hear his own voice. There is only a distant buzz.

"After I accepted—"

A distant buzz.

"What was I saying?" he asks.

"After you accepted the planet—"

"After I accepted the planet," he says, "that I could begin—" *Buzz. Buzz.* "That I could begin to accept myself."

He was drawn toward the Spicans too, not so much for themselves—they were oblique, elliptical characters, self-contained and self-satisfied, hard to approach—as for the apparently psychedelic drug they took in some sacramental way before the beginning of each of their interminable ritual dances. Each time he had watched them take the drug, they had seemingly made a point of extending it toward him, as if inviting him, as if tempting him, before popping it into their mouths. He felt baited; he felt pulled.

There were three Spicans on board, slender creatures two and a half meters long, with flexible cylindrical bodies and small stubby limbs. Their skins were reptilian, dry and smooth, deep green with yellow bands, but their eyes were weirdly human, large liquid-brown eyes, sad Levantine eyes, the eyes of unfortunate medieval travelers transformed by enchantment into serpents. Schwartz had spoken with them several times. They understood English well enough—all galactic races did; Schwartz imagined it would become the interstellar *lingua franca* as it had on Earth—but the construction of their vocal organs was such that they had no way of speaking it, and they relied instead on small translating machines hung around their necks that converted their soft whispered hisses into amber words pulsing across a screen.

Cautiously, the third or fourth time he spoke with them, he expressed polite interest in their drug. They told him it enabled them to make contact with the central forces of the universe. He replied that there were such drugs on Earth, too, and that he used them frequently, that they gave him great insight into the workings of the cosmos. They showed some curiosity, perhaps even intense curiosity: reading their eyes was difficult and the tone of their voices gave no clues. He took his elegant leather-bound drug case from his pouch and showed them what he had: learitonin, psilocerebrin, siddharthin, and acid-57. He described the effects of each and suggested an exchange, any of his for an equivalent dose of the shriveled orange fungoid they nibbled. They conferred. Yes, they said, we will do this. But not now. Not until the proper moment. Schwartz knew better than to ask them when that would be. He thanked them and put his drugs away.

Pitkin, who had watched the interchange from the far side of the lounge, came striding fiercely toward him as the Spicans glided off. "What are you up to now?" he demanded.

"How about minding your own business?" Schwartz said amiably.

"You're trading pills with those snakes, aren't you?"

"Let's call it field research."

"Research? Research? What are you going to do, trip on that orange stuff of theirs?"

"I might," Schwartz said.

"How do you know what its effects on the human metabolism might be? You could end up blind or paralyzed or crazy or—"

"—or illuminated," Schwartz said. "Those are the risks one takes in the field. The early anthropologists who unhesitatingly sampled peyote and yage and ololiuqui accepted those risks, and—"

"But those were drugs that *humans* were using. You have no way of telling how—oh, what's the use, Schwartz? Research, he calls it. Research." Pitkin sneered. *"Junkie!"*

Schwartz matched him sneer for sneer. *"Economist!"*

The house is a decent one tonight, close to three thousand, every seat in the University's great horseshoe-shaped auditorium taken, and a video relay besides, beaming his lecture to all Papua and half of Indonesia. Schwartz stands on the dais like a demigod under a brilliant no-glare spotlight. Despite his earlier weariness he is in good form now, gestures broad and forceful, eyes commanding, voice deep and resonant, words flowing freely. "Only one planet," he says, "one small and crowded planet, on which all cultures converge to a drab and depressing sameness. How sad that is! How tiny we make ourselves, when we make ourselves to resemble one another!" He flings his arms upward. "Look to the stars, the unattainable stars! Imagine, if you can, the millions of worlds that orbit those blazing suns beyond the night's darkness! Speculate with me on other peoples, other ways, other gods. Beings of every imaginable form, alien in appearance but not grotesque, not hideous, for all life is beautiful—beings that breathe gases strange to us, beings of immense size, beings of many limbs or of none, beings to whom death is a divine culmination of existence, beings who never die, beings who bring forth their young a thousand at a time, beings who do not reproduce—all the infinite possibilities of the infinite universe!

"Perhaps on each of those worlds it is as it has become here. One intelligent species, one culture, the eternal convergence. But the many worlds together offer a vast spectrum of variety. And now, share this vision with me! I see a ship voyaging from star to star, a spaceliner of the future, and aboard that ship is a sampling of many species, many cultures, a random scoop out of the galaxy's fantastic diversity. That ship is like a little cosmos, a small world, enclosed, sealed. How exciting to be aboard it, to encounter in that little compass such richness of cultural variation! Now our own world was once like that starship, a little cosmos, bearing with it all the thousands of Earthborn cultures. Hopi and Eskimo and Aztec and Kwakiutl and Arapesh and Orokolo and all the rest. In the course of our voyage we have come to resemble one another too much, and it has impoverished the lives of all of us, because—" He falters suddenly. He feels faint, and grasps the sides of the lectern. "Because—" The spotlight, he thinks. In my eyes. Not supposed to glare like that, but it's blinding. Got to have them move it. "In the course—the course of our voyage—" What's happening? Breaking into a sweat, now. Pain in my chest. My heart? Wait, slow up, catch your breath. That light in my eyes—

"Tell me," Schwartz said earnestly, "what it's like to know you'll have ten successive bodies and live more than a thousand years."

"First tell me," said the Antarean, "what it's like to know you'll live ninety years or less and perish forever."

Somehow he continues. The pain in his chest grows more intense, he cannot focus his eyes; he believes he will lose consciousness at any moment and may even have lost it already at least once, and yet he continues. Clinging to the lectern, he outlines the program he developed in *The Mask Beneath the Skin.* A rebirth of tribalism without a revival of ugly nationalism. The quest for a renewed sense of kinship with the past. A sharp reduction in nonessential travel, especially tourism. Heavy taxation of exported artefacts, including films and video shows.

An attempt to create independent cultural units on Earth once again while maintaining present levels of economic and political interdependence. Relinquishment of materialistic technological-industrial values. New searches for fundamental meanings. An ethnic revival, before it is too late, among those cultures of mankind that have only recently shed their traditional folkways. (He repeats and embellishes this point particularly, for the benefit of the Papuans before him, the great-grandchildren of cannibals.)

The discomfort and confusion come and go as he unreels his themes. He builds and builds, crying out passionately for an end to the homogenization of Earth, and gradually the physical symptoms leave him, all but a faint vertigo. But a different malaise seizes him as he nears his peroration. His voice becomes, to him, a far-off quacking, meaningless and foolish. He has said all this a thousand times, always to great ovations, but who listens? Who listens? Everything seems hollow tonight, mechanical, absurd. An ethnic revival? Shall these people before him revert to their loincloths and their pig roasts? His starship is a fantasy; his dream of a diverse Earth is mere silliness. What is, will be. And yet he pushes on toward his conclusion. He takes his audience back to that starship, he creates a horde of fanciful beings for them. He completes the metaphor by sketching the structures of half a dozen vanished "primitive" cultures of Earth, he chants the chants of the Navaho, the Gabon Pygmies, the Ashanti, the Mundugumor. It is over. Cascades of applause engulf him. He holds his place until members of the sponsoring committee come to him and help him down: they have perceived his distress. "It's nothing," he gasps. "The lights—too bright—" Dawn is at his side. She hands him a drink, something cool. Two of the sponsors begin to speak of a reception for him in the Green Room. "Fine," Schwartz says. "Glad to." Dawn murmurs a protest. He shakes her off. "My obligation," he tells her. "Meet community leaders. Faculty people. I'm feeling better now. Honestly." Swaying, trembling, he lets them lead him away.

"A Jew," the Antarean said. "You call yourself a Jew, but what is this exactly? A clan, a sept, a moiety, a tribe, a nation, what? Can you explain?"

"You understand what a religion is?"

"Of course."

"Judaism—Jewishness—it's one of Earth's major religions."

"You are therefore a priest?"

"Not at all. I don't even practice Judaism. But my ancestors did, and therefore I consider myself Jewish, even though—"

"It is an hereditary religion, then," the Antarean said, "that does not require its members to observe its rites?"

"In a sense," said Schwartz desperately. "More an hereditary cultural subgroup, actually, evolving out of a common religious outlook no longer relevant."

"Ah. And the cultural traits of Jewishness that define it and separate you from the majority of humankind are—?"

"Well—" Schwartz hesitated. "There's a complicated dietary code, a rite of circumcision for newborn males, a rite of passage for male adolescents, a language of scripture, a vernacular language that Jews all around the world more or less understand, and plenty more, including a certain intangible sense of clannishness and certain attitudes, such as a peculiar self-deprecating style of humor—"

"You observe the dietary code? You understand the language of scripture?"

"Not exactly," Schwartz admitted. "In fact I don't do anything that's specifically Jewish except think of myself as a Jew and adopt many of the characteristically Jewish personality modes, which however are not uniquely Jewish any longer—they can be traced among Italians, for example, and to some extent among Greeks. I'm speaking of Italians and Greeks of the late twentieth century, of course. Nowadays—" It was all becoming a terrible muddle. "Nowadays—"

"It would seem," said the Antarean, "that you are a Jew only because your maternal and paternal gene-givers were Jews, and they—"

"No, not quite. Not my mother, just my father, and he was Jewish only on his father's side, but even my grandfather never observed the customs, and—"

"I think this has grown too confusing," said the Antarean. "I withdraw the entire inquiry. Let us speak instead of my own traditions. The Time of Openings, for example, may be understood as—"

In the Green Room some eighty or a hundred distinguished Papuans press toward him, offering congratulations. "Absolutely right," they say. "A global catastrophe." "Our last chance to save our culture." Their skins are chocolate-tinted but their faces betray the genetic mishmash that is their ancestry: perhaps they call themselves Arapesh, Mundugumor, Tchambuli, Mafulu, in the way that he calls himself a Jew, but they have been liberally larded with chromosomes contributed by Chinese, Japanese, Europeans, Africans, everything. They dress in International Contemporary. They speak slangy, lively English. Schwartz feels seasick. "You look dazed," Dawn whispers. He smiles bravely. Body like dry bone. Mind like dead ashes. He is introduced to a tribal chieftain, tall, gray-haired, who looks and speaks like a professor, a lawyer, a banker. What, will these people return to the hills for the ceremony of the yam harvest? Will newborn girl-children be abandoned, cords uncut, skins unwashed, if their fathers do not need more girls? Will boys entering manhood submit to the expensive services of the initiator who scarifies them with the teeth of crocodiles? The crocodiles are gone. The shamans have become stockbrokers.

Suddenly he cannot breathe.

"Get me out of here," Schwartz mutters hoarsely, choking.

Dawn, with stewardess efficiency, chops a path for him through the mob. The sponsors, concerned, rush to his aid. He is floated swiftly back to the hotel in a glistening little bubble-car. Dawn helps him to bed. Reviving, he reaches for her.

"You don't have to," she says. "You've had a rough day."

He persists. He embraces her and takes her, quickly, fiercely, and they move together for a few minutes and it ends and he sinks back, exhausted, stupefied. She gets a cool cloth and pats his forehead and urges him to rest. "Bring me my drugs," he says. He wants siddharthin, but she misunderstands, probably deliberately, and offers him something blue and bulky, a sleeping pill, and, too weary to object, he takes it. Even so, it seems to be hours before sleep comes.

He dreams he is at the skyport, boarding the rocket for Bangkok, and instantly he is debarking at Bangkok—just like Port Moresby, only more humid—and he delivers his speech to a horde of enthusiastic Thais, while rockets flicker about him carrying him to skyport after skyport, and the Thais blur and become Japanese, who are transformed into Mongols, who become Uighurs, who become Iranians, who become Sudanese, who become Zambians, who become Chileans, and all look alike, all look alike, all look alike.

The Spicans hovered above him, weaving, bobbing, swaying like cobras about to strike. But their eyes, warm and liquid, were sympathetic: loving, even. He felt the flow of their compassion. If they had had the sort of musculature that enabled them to smile, they would be smiling tenderly, he knew.

One of the aliens leaned close. The little translating device dangled toward Schwartz like a holy medallion. He narrowed his eyes, concentrating as intently as he could on the amber words flashing quickly across the screen.

"...has come. We shall..."

"Again, please," Schwartz said. "I missed some of what you were saying."

"The moment...has come. We shall...make the exchange of sacraments now."

"Sacraments?"

"Drugs."

"Drugs, yes. Yes. Of course." Schwartz groped in his pouch. He felt the cool, smooth leather skin of his drug case. Leather? Snakeskin, maybe. Anyway. He drew it forth. "Here," he said. "Siddharthin, learitonin, psilocerebrin, acid-57. Take your pick." The Spicans selected three small blue siddharthins. "Very good," Schwartz said. "The most transcendental of all. And now—"

The longest of the aliens proffered a ball of dried orange fungus the size of Schwartz's thumbnail.

"It is an equivalent dose. We give it to you."

"Equivalent to all three of my tablets, or to one?"

"Equivalent. It will give you peace."

Schwartz smiled. There was a time for asking questions and a time for unhesitating action. He took the fungus and reached for a glass of water.

"Wait!" Pitkin cried, appearing suddenly. "What are you—"

"Too late," Schwartz said serenely, and swallowed the Spican drug in one joyous gulp.

The nightmares go on and on. He circles the Earth like the Flying Dutchman, like the Wandering Jew, skyport to skyport to skyport, an unending voyage from nowhere to nowhere. Obliging committees meet him and convey him to his hotel. Sometimes the committee members are contemporary types, indistinguishable from one another, with standard faces, standard clothing, the all-purpose new-model hybrid unihuman, and sometimes they are consciously ethnic, elaborately decked out in feathers and paint and tribal emblems, but their faces, too, are standard behind the gaudy regalia, their slang is the slang of Uganda and Tierra del Fuego and Nepal, and it seems to Schwartz that these masqueraders are, if anything, less authentic, less honest, than the other sort, who at least are true representatives of their era. So it is hopeless either way. He lashes at his pillow, he groans, he wakens. Instantly Dawn's arms enfold him. He sobs incoherent phrases into her clavicle and she murmurs soothing sounds against his forehead. He is having some sort of breakdown, he realizes: a new crisis of values, a shattering of the philosophical synthesis that has allowed him to get through the last few years. He is bound to the wheel; he spins, he spins, he spins, traversing the continents, getting nowhere. There is no place to go. No. There is one, just one, a place where he will find peace, where the universe will be as he needs it to be. Go there, Schwartz. Go and stay as long as you can. "Is there anything I can *do*?" Dawn asks. He shivers and shakes his head. "Take this," she says, and gives him some sort of pill. Another tranquilizer. All right. All right. The world has turned to porcelain. His skin feels like a plastic coating. Away, away, to the ship. To the ship! "So long," Schwartz says.

Outside the ship the Capellans twist and spin in their ritual dance as, weightless and without mass, they are swept toward the rim of the galaxy at nine times the velocity of light. They move with a grace that is astonishing for creatures of such tremendous bulk. A dazzling light that emanates from the center of the universe strikes their glossy skin and, rebounding, resonates all up and down the spectrum, splintering into brilliant streamers of ultrared, infraviolet, exoyellow. All the cosmos glows and shimmers. A single perfect note of music comes out of the remote distance and, growing closer, swells in an infinite crescendo. Schwartz trembles at the beauty of all he perceives.

Beside him stands the seal-slick Antarean. She—definitely *she,* no doubt of it, *she*—plucks at his arm and whispers, "Will you go to them?"

"Yes. Yes, of course."

"So will I. Wherever you go."

"Now," Schwartz says. He reaches for the lever that opens the hatch. He pulls down. The side of the starship swings open.

The Antarean looks deep into his eyes and says blissfully, "I never told you my name. My name is Dawn."

Together they float through the hatch into space.

The blackness receives them gently. There is no chill, no pressure at the lungs, no discomfort at all. He is surrounded by luminous surges, by throbbing mantles of pure color, as though he has entered the heart of an aurora. He and Dawn swim toward the Capellans, and the huge beings welcome them with deep, glad, booming cries. Dawn joins the dance at once, moving her sinuous limbs with extravagant ease; Schwartz will do the same in a moment, but first he turns to face the starship, hanging in space close by him like a vast coppery needle, and in a voice that could shake universes he calls, "Come, friends! Come, all of you! Come dance with us!" And they come, pouring through the hatch, the Spicans first, then all the rest, the infinite multitude of beings, the travelers from Fomalhaut and Achernar and Acrux and Aldebaran, from Thuban and Arcturus and Altair, from Polaris and Canopus and Sirius and Rigel, hundreds of star-creatures spilling happily out of the vessel, bursting forth, all of them, even Pitkin, poor little Pitkin, everyone joining hands and tentacles and tendrils and whatever, forming a great ring of light across space, everyone locked in a cosmic harmony, everyone dancing. Dancing. Dancing.

IN THE HOUSE OF DOUBLE MINDS

After 1970, which had been a year of relatively high output for me, each successive year of the 1970s saw my productivity steadily decreasing, and, as I indicated in the introduction to the previous story, by 1973 I found myself unable, or unwilling, to write very much at all. My records for that year show no novels, five short stories and novellas (including the major story "Born with the Dead") and one short magazine article—a paltry total of 81,000 words, less by far than I had produced in any single year since I began writing. (I had written more than that in a good many months *when I was younger.) Blame it on the chaotic* Zeitgeist, *blame it on an increasingly centrifugal private life, blame it on any number of things: the fact at the bottom of all the rationalizations was that after twenty years of steady production I was weary of writing and wanted desperately to escape from the profession I had so eagerly chosen for myself two decades before.*

Not that I see any sign of that fatigue in that year's work, meager though it was. "Born with the Dead," I still think, represents me at the top of my form, and the other four stories of 1973—"This is the Road," "Trips," ""Schwartz Between the Galaxies," and the present "In the House of Double Minds"—are included in this volume also, so you can judge their quality for yourself, but you will agree, I think, that they maintain the level I had set for myself in the years just preceding.

I wrote "In the House of Double Minds" in November, 1973, right after "Schwartz." Don Pfeil, the editor of the short-lived Los Angeles-based magazine Vertex, *asked me to write it, and perhaps even suggested the theme, for split-brain research was very much in the scientific news at that time.*

I had a difficult time doing it, as I did with everything I wrote then, and I think Pfeil, whose taste in fiction, like Judy-Lynn del Rey's, ran to the conservative side (literarily speaking), was no more happy about publishing it than Judy-Lynn was with "Schwartz," though he used it anyway, in the June, 1974 issue. My mood after turning the piece in was a distinctly to-hell-with-everything one. Writing short stories, I decided, had become an impossibly difficult ordeal, and I resolved then and there to abandon doing them forever, though I intended to continue writing novels.

*As you saw in the introduction to "Schwartz," I did indeed manage two more novels—*The Stochastic Man *in 1974 and* Shadrach in the Furnace *in 1965—and then, suffering from terminal burnout, I gave up writing books also, and let it be known that I was retiring forever from the profession of writing. My retirement lasted about four years, which was about three and a half years longer than anyone who knew me had predicted; but even after I went back to writing again late in 1978 with the novel* Lord Valentine's Castle, *I kept in mind how much trouble I had had five years earlier with short stories, and I stayed away from them. It wasn't until 1981 that Ben Bova, the fiction editor of* Omni, *coaxed me into trying my hand at one again, and I produced the first of what turned out to be a spate of short stories that I wrote all through the decade that followed. But that's a story to tell in the next volume.*

Now they bring in the new ones, this spring's crop of ten-year-olds—six boys, six girls—and leave them with me in the dormitory room that will be their home for the next dozen years. The room is bare, austere, with black slate floors and rough brick walls, furnished for the time being with cots and clothes-cabinets and little more. The air is chill, and the children, who are naked, huddle in discomfort.

"I am Sister Mimise," I tell them. "I will be your guide and counselor in the first twelve months of your new life in the House of Double Minds."

I have lived in this place for eight years, since I was fourteen, and this is the fifth year that I have had charge of the new children. If I had not been disqualified by my left-handedness, this is the year I would have been graduated into full oraclehood, but I try not to dwell on that. Caring for the children is a rewarding task in itself. They arrive scrawny and frightened, and slowly they unfold: they blossom, they ripen, they grow toward their destinies. Each year there is some special one for me, some favorite, in whom I take particular joy. In my first group, four years ago, it was long-legged laughing Jen, she who is now my lover. A year later it was soft beautiful Jalil, and then Timas, who I thought would become one of the greatest of all oracles; but after two years of training Timas cracked and was culled. And last year bright-eyed Runild, impish Runild, my pet, my darling boy, more gifted even than Timas and, I fear, even less stable. I look at the new ones, wondering who will be special among them for me this year.

The children are pale, slender, uneasy; their thin nude bodies look more than naked because of their shaven skulls. As a result of what has been done to their brains they move clumsily today. Their left arms often dangle as though they have entirely forgotten them, and they tend to walk in a shuffling sidewise motion, dragging their left legs a little. These problems soon will disappear. The last of the operations in this group was performed only two days ago, on the short wide-shouldered girl whose breasts have already begun to grow. I can see the narrow red line marking the place where the surgeon's beam sliced through her scalp to sever the hemispheres of her brain.

"You have been selected," I say in a resonant formal tone, "for the highest and most sacred office in our society. From this moment until you reach adulthood your lives and energies will be consecrated to the purpose of attaining the skills and wisdom an oracle must have. I congratulate you on having come so far."

And I envy you.

I do not say that part aloud.

I feel envy and pity both. I have seen the children come and go, come and go. Out of each year's dozen, one or two usually die along the way of natural causes or accidents. At least three go insane under the terrible pressure of the disciplines and have to be culled. So only about half the group is likely to complete the twelve years of training, and most of those will prove to have little value as oracles. The useless ones will be allowed to remain, of course, but their lives will be meaningless. The House of Double Minds has been in existence for more than a century; there are at present just one hundred forty-two oracles in residence—seventy-seven women and sixty-five men—of whom all but about forty are mere drones. A thin harvest out of some twelve hundred novices since the beginning.

These children have never met before. I call upon them to introduce themselves. They give their names in low self-conscious voices, eyes downcast.

A boy named Divvan asks, "Will we wear clothes soon?"

Their nakedness disturbs them. They hold their thighs together and stand at odd stork-like angles, keeping apart from one another, trying to conceal their undeveloped loins. They do this because they are strangers. They will forget their shame before long. As the months pass they will become closer than brothers and sisters.

"Robes will be issued this afternoon," I tell him. "But clothing ought not to be important here, and you need have no reason to wish to hide your bodies." Last year when this same point arose—it always does—the mischievous boy Runild suggested that I remove my own robe as a gesture of solidarity. Of course I did, but it was a mistake: the sight of a mature woman's body was more troubling to them than even their own bareness.

Now it is the time for the first exercises, so that they may learn the ways in which the brain operation has altered the responses of their bodies. At random I choose a girl named Hirole and ask her to step forward, while the rest form a circle around her. She is tall and fragile-looking and it must be torment to her to be aware of the eyes of all the others upon her.

Smiling, I say gently, "Raise your hand, Hirole."

She raises one hand.

"Bend your knee."

As she flexes her knee, there is an interruption. A wiry naked boy scrambles into the room, fast as a spider, wild as a monkey, and bursts into the middle of the circle, shouldering Hirole aside. Runild again! He is a strange and moody and extraordinarily intelligent child, who, now that he is in his second year at the House, has lately been behaving in a reckless, unpredictable way. He runs around the circle, seizing several of the new children briefly, putting his face close to theirs, staring with crazy intensity into their eyes. They are terrified of him. For a moment I am too astonished to move. Then I go to him and seize him.

He struggles ferociously. He spits at me, hisses, claws my arms, makes thick wordless grunting sounds. Gradually I get control of him. In a low voice I say, "What's wrong with you, Runild? You know you aren't supposed to be in here!"

"Let me go."

"Do you want me to report this to Brother Sleel?"

"I just want to see the new ones."

"You're frightening them. You'll be able to meet them in a few days, but you're not allowed to upset them now." I pull him toward the door. He continues to resist and nearly breaks free. Eleven-year-old boys are amazingly strong, sometimes. He kicks my thigh savagely: I will have purple bruises tonight. He tries to bite my arm. Somehow I get him out of the room, and in the corridor he suddenly goes slack and begins to tremble, as though he has had a fit that now is over. I am trembling too. Hoarsely I say, "What's happening to you, Runild? Do you want to be culled the way Timas and Jurda were? You can't keep doing things like this! You—"

He looks up at me, wild-eyed, and starts to say something, and stifles it, and turns and bolts. In a moment he is gone, a brown naked streak vanishing down the hallway. I feel a great sadness: Runild was a favorite of mine, and now he is going insane, and they will have to cull him. I should report the incident immediately, but I am unable to bring myself to do it, and, telling myself that my responsibility lies with the new ones, I return to the dorm room.

"Well!" I say briskly, as if nothing unusual has happened. "He's certainly playful today, isn't he! That was Runild. He's a year ahead of you. You'll meet him and the rest of his group a little later. Now, Hirole—"

The children, preoccupied with their own altered state, quickly grow calm; they seem much less distressed by Runild's intrusion than I am. Shakily I begin again, asking Hirole to raise a hand, to flex a knee, to close an eye. I thank her and call a boy named Mulliam into the centre of the circle. I ask him to raise one shoulder above the other, to touch his hand to his cheek, to make a fist. Then I pick a girl named Fyme and instruct her to hop on one foot, to put an arm behind her back, to kick one leg in the air.

I say, "Who can tell me one thing that was true of every response?"

Several of them answer at once. "It was always the right side! The right eye, the right hand, the right leg—"

"Correct." I turn to a small dark-visaged boy named Bloss and ask, "Why is that? Do you think it's just coincidence?"

"Well," he says. "Everybody here is right-handed, because left-handers aren't allowed to become oracles, and so everybody tended to use the side that he—"

Bloss falters, seeing heads shaking all around the circle.

Galaine, the girl whose breasts have begun to sprout, says "It's because of the operation! The right side of our brains doesn't understand words very well, and it's the Right that controls the left side of the body, so when you tell us in words to do something, only our Left understands and moves the muscles it controls. It gets the jump on the Right because the Right can't speak or be spoken to."

"Very good, Galaine. That's it exactly."

I let it sink in. Now that the connections between the two halves of their brains have been cut, the Rights of these children are isolated, unable to draw on the skills of the language centre in the Left. They are only now realizing what it means to have half a brain rendered illiterate and inarticulate, to have their Left respond as though it is the entire brain, activating only the muscles it controls most directly.

Fyme says, "Does that mean we won't ever be able to use our left sides again?"

"Not at all. Your Right isn't paralyzed or helpless. It just isn't very good at using words. So your Left is quicker to react when I give a verbal instruction. But if the instruction isn't phrased in words, the Right will be able to take control and respond."

"How can you give an instruction that isn't in words?" Mulliam asks.

"In many ways," I say. "I could draw a picture, or make a gesture, or use some sort of symbol. I'll show you what I mean by going through the exercises again. Sometimes I'll give the instructions in words, and sometimes by acting them out. When I do that, imitate what you see. Is that clear?"

I wait a moment to allow the sluggish word-skills of their Rights to grasp the scheme.

Then I say, "Raise a hand."

They lift their right arms. When I tell them to bend a knee, they bend their right knees. But when I wordlessly close my left eye, they imitate me and close their left eyes. Their Rights are able to exert muscular control in a normal way when the instructions are delivered nonverbally; but when I use words, the Left alone perceives and acts.

I test the ability of their Lefts to override the normal motor functions of their Rights by instructing them verbally to raise their left shoulders. Their Rights, baffled by my words, take no action, forcing their Lefts to reach beyond a Left's usual sphere of dominance. Slowly, with great difficulty, a few of the children manage to raise their left shoulders. Some can manage only a mere twitch. Fyme, Bloss, and Mulliam, with signs of struggle evident on their faces, are unable to budge their left shoulders at all. I tell the entire group to relax, and the children collapse in relief, sprawling on their cots. There is nothing to worry about, I say. In time they will all regain full motor functions in both halves of their bodies. Unless they are driven insane by the split-brain phenomena, that is, but no need to tell them that.

"One more demonstration for today," I announce. This one will show them in another way how thoroughly the separation of the hemispheres affect the mental processes. I ask Gybold, the smallest of the boys, to seat himself at the testing table at the far end of the room. There is a screen mounted on the table: I tell Gybold to fix his eyes on the center of the screen, and I flash a picture of a banana on the left side of the screen for a fraction of a second.

"What do you see, Gybold?"

"I don't see anything, Sister Mimise," he replies, and the other children gasp. But the "I" that is speaking is merely Gybold's Left, which gets its visual information through his right eye; that eye did indeed see nothing. Meanwhile Gybold's Right is answering my question in the only way it can: the boy's left hand gropes among several objects lying on the table hidden behind the screen, finds the banana that is there, and triumphantly holds it up. Through sight and touch Gybold's Right has prevailed over its wordlessness.

"Excellent," I say. I take the banana from him and, drawing his left hand behind the screen where he is unable to see it, I put a drinking glass into it. I ask him to name the object in his hand.

"An apple?" he ventures. I frown, and quickly he says, "An egg? A pencil?"

The children laugh. Mulliam says, "He's just guessing!"

"Yes, he is. But which part of Gybold's brain is making the guesses?"

"His Left," Galaine cries. "But it's the Right that knows it's holding a glass."

They all shush her for giving away the secret. Gybold pulls his hand out from under the screen and stares at the glass, silently forming its name with his lips.

I put Herik, Chith, Simi, and Clane through related experiments. Always the results are the same. If I flash a picture to the right eye or put an object in the right hand, the children respond normally, correctly naming it. But if I transmit information only to the left eye or the left hand, they are unable to use words to describe the objects their Rights see or feel.

It is enough for now. The children are silent and have withdrawn into individual spheres of privacy. I know that they are working things out within their minds, performing small self-devised experiments, testing themselves, trying to learn the full extent of the changes the operation has brought about. They glance from one hand to another, flex fingers, whisper little calculations. They should not be allowed to look inward so much, not at the beginning. I take them to the storeroom to receive their new clothing, the simple gray monastic robes that we wear to set us apart from the ordinary people of the city. Then I turn them free, sending them romping into the broad fields of soft green grass behind the dormitory, to relax and play. They may be oracles in the making; but they are also, after all, ten-year-old children.

It is my afternoon rest period. On my way through the dark cool corridors to my chamber I am stopped by Brother Sleel, one of the senior oracles. He is a white-haired man, tall and of powerful build, and his blue eyes work almost independently of one another, constantly scanning his surroundings in restless separate searches. Sleel has never been anything but warm and kind to me, and yet I have always been afraid of him, I suppose more out of awe for his office than out of fear for the man himself. Really I feel timid with all the oracles, knowing that their minds work differently from mine and that they see things in me that I may not see myself. Sleel says, "I saw you having difficulties with Runild in the hall this morning. What was happening?"

"He wandered into my orientation meeting. I asked him to leave."

"What was he doing?"

"He said he wanted to see the new children. But of course I couldn't let him bother them."

"And he started to fight with you?"

"He made some trouble. Nothing much."

"He was fighting with you, Mimise."

"He was rather unruly," I admit.

Sleel's left eye stares into mine. I feel a chill. It is the oracle-eye, the all-seeing one. Quietly he says, "I saw you fighting with him."

I look away from him. I study my bare feet. "He wouldn't leave. He was frightening the new ones. When I tried to lead him from the room he jumped at me, yes. But he didn't hurt me and it was all over in a moment. Runild is high-spirited, Brother."

"Runild is a troubled child," Sleel says heavily. "He is disturbed. He is becoming wild, like a beast."

"No, Brother Sleel." How can I face that terrible eye? "He has extraordinary gifts. You know—surely *you* must know—that it takes time for one like him to settle down, to come to terms with—"

"I've had complaints from his counselor, Voree. She says she hardly knows how to handle him."

"It's only a phase. Voree's had responsibility for him only a couple of weeks. As soon as she—"

"I know you want to protect him, Mimise. But don't let your love for the boy cloud your judgement. I think this is Timas happening all over again. It's an old, old pattern here, the brilliant novice who is unable to cope with his changes, who—"

"Are you going to cull him?" I blurt.

Sleel smiles. He takes both my hands in his. I am engulfed by his strength, by his wisdom, by his power. I sense the unfathomable flow of perception from his mystic Right to his calm, analytic Left. He says, "If Runild gets any worse, I'll have to. But I want to save him. I like the boy. I respect his potential. What do you suggest we do, Mimise?"

"What do *I*—"

"Tell me. Advise me."

The senior oracle is playing a little game with me, I suppose. Shrugging, I say, "Obviously Runild's trying to gain attention through all these crazy pranks. Let's try to reach him and find out what he really wants, and perhaps there'll be some way we can give it to him. I'll speak to Voree. I'll talk to his sister, Kitrin. And tomorrow I'll talk to Runild. I think he trusts me. We were very close last year, Runild and I."

"I know," Sleel says gently. "Very well, see what you can do."

Still later that afternoon, as I cross the central courtyard, Runild erupts from the second-year house and rushes up to me. His face is flushed; his bare chest is shiny with sweat. He clings to me, pulls me down to his height, looks me in the eye. His eyes have already begun to stray a little; one day they may be like Sleel's.

I think he wants to apologize for his invasion of my group. But all he manages to say is: "I am sorry for you. You wanted so much to be one of us." And he runs off.

To be one of them. Yes. Who does not long to dwell in the House of Double Minds, living apart from the noise and chaos of the world, devoting oneself to oracular contemplation and the service of mankind? My mother's father's sister was of that high company, and in early girlhood I was taken to visit her. How awesome it was to stand in the presence of her all-knowing Right, to feel the flood of warmth and understanding that emanated from her wise eyes. It was my dream to join her here, a dream doubly thwarted, for she died when I was eight, and by then the fact of my left-handedness was irremediably established.

Left-handers are never selected to undergo the oracle-making operation. The two halves of our brains are too symmetrical, too ambidextrous: we have speech centers on both sides, most of us left-handers, and so we are not likely to develop those imbalances of cerebral powers that oracles must have. Right-handers, too, are born with symmetrically functioning brains, each hemisphere developing independently and duplicating the operations of the other. But by the time they are two years old, their Lefts and Rights are linked in a way that gives them a shared pool of skills, and therefore each half is free to develop its own special capabilities, since the gifts of one half are instantly available to the other.

At the age of ten this specializing process is complete. Language, sequential thought, all the analytic and rational functions, center in the Left. Spacial perception, artistic vision, musical skill, emotional insight, centre in the Right. The brain's left side is the scientist, the architect, the general, the mathematician. The brain's right side is the minstrel, the sculptor, the visionary, the dreamer. Normally the two halves operate as one. The Right experiences a flash of poetic intuition, the Left clothes it in words. The Right sees a pattern of fundamental connections, the Left expresses it in a sequence of theorems. The Right conceives the shape of a symphony, the Left sets the notes down on paper. Where there is true harmony between the hemispheres of the brain, works of genius are created.

Too often, though, one side seizes command. Perhaps the Right becomes dominant, and we have a dancer, an athlete, an artist, who has trouble with words, who is inexpressive and inarticulate except through some nonverbal medium. More often, because we are a word-worshipping people, it is the Left that rules, choking the subordinate Right in a welter of verbal analysis and commentary, slowing and hindering the spontaneous intuitive perceptions of the mind. What society gains in orderliness and rationality it loses in vision and grace. We can do nothing about these imbalances—except to take advantage of their existence by accentuating and exploiting them.

And so the children come here, a dozen of our best each year, and our surgeons sever the isthmus of neural tissue that links Left and Right. Some kind of communication between the hemispheres continues to operate, since each half remains aware of what the other is immediately experiencing, if not of its accumulated memories and skills. But the Right is cut free from the tyranny of the word-intoxicated Left. The Left continues to operate its normal routines of reading and writing and conversation and computation, while the Right, now its own master, observes and registers and analyses in a way that has no need for words. Because its verbal skills are so feeble, the newly independent Right must find some other means of expression if it is to make its perceptions known: and, through the dozen years of training in the House of Double Minds, some of the children succeed in achieving this. They are able—I do not know how, no one who is not an oracle can ever know how—to transmit the unique insights of fully mature and wholly independent Rights to their Lefts, which can transmit them to the rest of us. It is a difficult and imperfect process, but it gives us access to levels of knowledge that few have ever reached before our time. Those who master that skill are our functional oracles. They dwell in realms of beauty and wisdom that, in the past, only saints and prophets and the greatest artists and a few madmen have reached.

I would, if I could, have entered those realms. But I came forth left-handed from the womb and my brain, though it is a decent one, therefore lacked the required asymmetry of function. If I could not be an oracle I could at least serve them, I decided. And thus I came here as a girl, and asked to be of use, and in time was given the important task of easing the new children into their new lives. So I have come to know Jen and Timas and Jalil and Runild and the others, some of whom will live to be among the most famous of oracles, and so now I welcome Hirole and Mulliam and Gybold and Galaine and their companions. And I am content, I think. I am content.

We gather in the main hall for the evening meal. My new group has not come before the older novices until now, and so my twelve undergo close scrutiny, which they find embarrassing, as I lead them to their place. Each year-group sits together at its own circular table. My dozen dine with me; at the table to my left is my group of last year, now in Voree's charge. Runild sits there with his back to me, and his mere presence creates a tension in me as if he is giving off an electric radiation. To my right is the third-year group, reduced now to nine by the culling of Timas and two deaths; the fourth-year children are just in front of me and the fifth-year ones, my darling Jen among them, at my rear. The older children are in the center of the hall. Along the sides of the great room are the tables of the instructors, those who have daily care of the ordinary education of the twelve groups of novices, and the senior oracles occupy long tables at the hall's far end, beneath a panoply of gay red and green banners.

Sleel makes a brief speech of welcome for my twelve, and the meal is served.

I send Galaine to Voree's table with a note: "*See me on the porch after dinner.*"

My appetite is poor. I finish quickly, but I stay with my group until it is time to dismiss them. All the children troop off to the auditorium for a show. A warm drizzle is falling; Voree and I stand in the shelter of the eaves. She is much older than I am, a stocky woman with kinky orange hair. Year after year I pass my fledglings on to her. She is strong, efficient, stolid, insensitive. Runild baffles her. "He's like a monkey," she says. "Running around naked, chattering to himself, singing crazy songs, playing pranks. He isn't doing his lessons. He isn't even doing his disciplines, half the time. I've warned him he'll be culled, but he doesn't seem to care."

"What do you think he wants?"

"To have everyone notice him."

"Yes, surely, but *why?*"

"Because he's a naturally mischievous boy," Voree says, scowling. "I've seen many of his sort before. They think rules are for other people. Two more weeks of this and I'll recommend a cull."

"He's too brilliant to waste like that, Voree."

"He's wasting himself. Without the disciplines how can he become an oracle? And he's upsetting all the others. My group's a shambles. Now he's bothering yours. He won't leave his sister alone either. Culling, Mimise, that's where he's heading. Culling."

There is nothing to be gained from talking to Voree. I join my group in the auditorium.

Bedtime for the younger ones comes early. I see my children to their room; then I am free until midnight. I return to the auditorium, where the older children and the off-duty staff are relaxing, playing games, dancing, drifting off in couples. Kitrin, Runild's sister, is still there. I draw her aside. She is a slender, delicate girl of fourteen, a fifth-year novice. I am fond of her because she was in my very first group, but I have always found her shy, elusive, opaque. She is more so than ever now: I question her about her brother's behavior and she answers me with shrugs, vague unfinished sentences, and artful evasions. Runild is wild? Well, of course, many boys are wild, she says, especially the bright ones. The disciplines seem to bore him. He's far ahead of his group—you know that, Mimise. And so on. I get nothing from her except the strong feeling that she is hiding something about her brother. My attempts to probe fail; Kitrin is still a child, but she is halfway to oraclehood, nearly, and that gives her an advantage over me in any duel of wits. Only when I suggest that Runild is in immediate peril of culling do I break through her defences.

"No!" she gasps, eyes widening in fear, cheeks turning pale. "They mustn't! He has to stay! He's going to be greater than any of them!"

"He's causing too much trouble."

"It's just a thing he's going through. He'll settle down, I promise you that."

"Voree doesn't think so. She's going to request a cull."

"No. No. What will happen to him if he's culled? He was *meant* to be an oracle. His whole life will have been thrown away. We have to save him, Mimise."

"We can do that only if he can control himself."

"I'll talk to him in the morning," Kitrin says.

I wonder what she knows about Runild that she does not want to tell me.

❦

At the evening's end I bring Jen to my chamber, as I do three or four nights a week. She is tall and supple and looks more than her fourteen years. Her counselor tells me she is moving well through her mid-novitiate and will be a splendid oracle. We lie together, lips to lips, breasts against breasts, and we stroke and caress and tickle one another, we smile with our eyes, we enter into all the rituals of love. Afterward, in the stillness that follows passion, she finds the bruise of this morning's struggle on my thigh and questions me with a frown. "Runild," I say. I tell her about his erratic behaviour, about Sleel's uneasiness, about my conversation with Voree.

"They mustn't cull him," Jen says solemnly. "I know he's troublesome. But the path he's taking is so important for all of us."

"Path? What path is that?"

"You don't know?"

"I know nothing, Jen."

She catches her breath, rolls away, studies me a moment. At length she says, "Runild sees into minds. When he puts his head very close to people, there's transmission. Without using words. It's—it's a kind of broadcast. His Right can read the Rights of other oracles, the way you'd open a book and read it. If he could get close enough to Sleel, say, or any of them, he could read what's in their Rights."

"What?"

"More, Mimise. His own Right talks to his Left the same way. He can transmit messages completely, quickly, making better contact between the halves than any of the oracles can do. He hasn't had the disciplines, even, and he has full access to his Right's perceptions. So whatever his Right sees, including what it gets from the Rights of others, can be transmitted to his Left and expressed in words more clearly even than Sleel himself can do it!"

"I don't believe this," I say, barely comprehending.

"It's true! It's true, Mimise! He's only just learning how, and it gets him terribly excited, it makes him wild, don't you see, when all that contact comes flooding in? He can't quite handle it yet, which is why he acts so strange. But once he gets his power under control—"

"How do you know anything about this, Jen?"

"Why, Kitrin told me."

"Kitrin? I spoke to Kitrin and she never even hinted that—"

"Oh," Jen says, looking pained. "Oh, I guess I wasn't supposed to say. Not even to you, I guess. Oh, now I'll be in trouble with Kitrin, and—"

"You won't be. She doesn't need to know how I found out. But—Jen, Jen, can this be? Can anyone have such powers?"

"Runild does."

"So he claims. Or Kitrin claims on his behalf."

"No," Jen says firmly."He does. They showed me, he and Kitrin. I felt him touch my mind. I felt him read me. He can read anyone. He can read *you*, Mimise."

*

I must speak with Runild. But carefully, carefully, everything in its proper moment. In the morning I must first meet with my group and take them through the second-day exercises. These are designed to demonstrate that their Rights, although mute and presently isolated, are by no means inferior, and have perceptions and capabilities which in some ways are superior to those of their Lefts.

"Never think of your Right as a cripple," I warn them. "See it, rather, as some kind of extremely intelligent animal—an animal that is sharp-witted, quick to respond, imaginative, with only one flaw, that it has no vocabulary and is never going to be able to acquire more than a few simple words at best. Nobody pities a tiger or an eagle because it doesn't know how to speak. And there are ways of training tigers and eagles so that we can communicate with them without using words."

I flash a picture of a house on the screen and ask the children to copy it, first using their left hands, then the right. Although they are all right-handed, they are unable to draw anything better than simple, crude two-dimensional representations with their right hands. Their left-handed drawings, while shakily drawn because of their left arms' relatively backward muscular development and motor control, show a full understanding of the techniques of perspective. The right hand has the physical skill, but it is the left, drawing on the vision of the brain's right hemisphere, that has the artistic ability.

I ask them to arrange colored plastic cubes to match an intricate pattern on the screen. Left-handed, they carry out the exercise swiftly and expertly. Right-handed, they become confused, frown and bite their lips, hold the cubes long moments without knowing where to put them down, eventually array the cubes in chaotic mazes. Clane and Bloss give up entirely in a minute or two; Mulliam perseveres grimly like one who is determined to climb a mountain too steep for his strength, but he accomplishes little; Luabet's left hand keeps darting across to do the task that is beyond the right's powers, as if she is at war with herself. She must keep the impatient left hand behind her back in order to proceed at all. No one can complete the block design correctly with the right hand, and when I allow the children to work with both hands the hands fight for control, the formerly dominant right one unable to accept its new inferiority and angrily slapping at the cubes the left one tries to put in place.

We go on to the split-screen exercises in facial recognition and pattern analysis, to the musical exercises and the rest of the usual second-day routine. The children are fascinated by the ease with which their Rights function in all but word-linked operations. Ordinarily I am delighted, too, to watch the newly liberated Rights come to life and assert their powers. But today I am impatient to be off to Runild and I give only perfunctory attention to my proper work.

At last the session ends. The children move off to the classroom where they will receive regular school-subject instruction. Runild's group, too, should be at school until noon. Possibly I can draw him aside after lunch. But, as though I have conjured him with a wish, I see him now, tumbling by himself in the meadow of crimson flowers by the auditorium. He sees me, too: halts in his gambol, winks, smiles, does a handspring, blows me a kiss. I go to him.

"Are you excused from classes this morning?" I ask, mock-stern.

"The flowers are so pretty," he replies.

"The flowers will be just as pretty after school."

"Oh, don't be so stuffy, Mimise! I know my lessons. I'm a clever boy."

"Perhaps too clever, Runild."

He grins. I do not frighten him. He seems to be patronizing me; he appears to be at once very much younger and very much wiser than his years. I take him gently by the wrist and draw him down, easily, until we are sprawled side by side in the grass. He plucks a flower for me. His look is flirtatious. I accept both the flower and the look and respond with a warm smile; I am flirtatious myself. No doubt of his charm; and I can never win him by acting as an authority figure, only as a co-conspirator. There was always an underlying sexuality in our relationship, incestuous, as if I were an older sister.

We talk in banter, teasing each other. Then I say, "Something mysterious has been happening to you lately, Runild. I know that. Share your mystery with me."

At first he denies all. He pretends innocence, but lets me know it is only pretence. His sly smile betrays him. He speaks in cryptic ellipses, hinting at arcane knowledge and defying me to pry details from him. I play his game, acting now intrigued, now eager, now sceptical, now wholly uninterested: we are stalking one another, and both of us know it. His oracle-eye pierces me. He toys with me with such subtlety that I must remind myself with a glance at his slim hairless body, that I am dealing with a child. I ought never forget that he is only eleven. Finally I press directly once more, asking him outright what strange new gift he is cultivating.

"Wouldn't you like to know!" he cries, and pulls an outrageous face, and dashes away.

But he comes back. We talk on a more serious level. He admits that he has discovered, these past few months, that he is different from the other children and from the senior oracles, that he has a talent, a power. It disturbs and exalts him both. He is still exploring the scope of it. He will not describe the power in any specific way. Of course I know from Jen its nature, but I prefer not to reveal that. "Will you ever tell me?" I ask.

"Not today," he says.

Gradually I win his trust. We meet casually, in corridors or courtyards, and exchange easy pleasantries, the sort I might trade with any of my former charges. He is testing me, seeing whether I am a friend or simply Sleel's spy. I let him know of my concern for him. I let him know that his eccentric behaviour has placed him in jeopardy of culling.

"I suppose so," he says gloomily. "But what can I do? I'm not like the others. I can't sit still for long. Things are jumping inside my head all the time. Why should I bother with arithmetic when I can—"

He halts, suddenly guarded again.

"When you can what, Runild?"

"*You* know."

"I don't."

"You will, soon enough."

There are days when he seems calm. But his pranks have not ended. He finds poor Sister Sestoine, one of the oldest and dimmest of the oracles, and puts his forehead against hers and does something to her that sends her into an hour's tears. Sestoine will not say what took place during that moment of contact, and after a while she seems to forget the episode. Sleel's face is dark. He looks warningly at me as if to say, *Time's running short; the boy must go.*

On a day of driving rain I am in my chamber in midafternoon when Runild unexpectedly enters, soaked, hair plastered to his scalp. Puddles drip from him. He strips and I rub him with a towel and stand him before the fire. He says nothing all this while; he is tense, taut, as if a mighty pressure is building within him and the time has not yet come for its release. Abruptly he turns to me. His eyes are strange: they wander, they quiver, they glow. "Come close!" he whispers hoarsely, like a man calling a woman to his bed. He grasps my shoulders, he pulls me down to his height, he pushes his blazing forehead roughly against mine. And the world changes. I see tongues of purple flame. I see crevasses opening in the earth. I see the oceans engulfing the shore. I am flooded with contact; I am swept with wild energies.

I know what it is to be an oracle.

My Right and my Left are asunder. It is not like having one brain cleft in two; it is like having two brains, independent, equal. I feel them ticking like two clocks, with separate beats; and the Left goes tick-tock-tick-tock, machine-dreary, while the Right leaps and dances and soars and sings in lunatic rhythms. But they are not lunatic rhythms, for their frantic pulses have a regularity of irregularity, a pattern of patternlessness. I grow used to the strangeness; I become comfortable within both brains, the Left which I think of as "me," and the Right which is "me" too, but an altered and unfamiliar self without a name. My earliest memories lie open to me in my Right. I see into a realm of shadows. I am an infant again; I have access to the first hours of my life, to all my first years, those years in which words meant nothing to me. The preverbal data all rests within my Right, shapes and textures and odors and sounds, and I do not need to give names to anything, I do not need to denote or analyze, I need only feel, experience, relive. All that is there is clear and sharp. I see how it has always been with me, how that set of recorded experiences had directed my behavior even as the experiences of later years have done so. I can reach that hidden realm now, and understand it, and use it.

I feel the flow of data from Right to Left—the wordless responses, the intuitive reactions, the quick spontaneous awareness of structures. The world holds new meanings for me. I think, but not in words, and I tell myself things, but not in words, and my Left, groping and fumbling (for it has not had the disciplines) seeks words, sometimes finding them, to express what I am giving it. So this is what oracles do. This is what they feel. This is the knowledge they have. I am transfigured. It is my fantasy come true: they have snipped that rubbery band of connective tissue; they have set free my Right; they have made me one of them. And I will never again be what once I was. I will think in tones and colors now. I will explore kingdoms unknown to the wordbound ones. I will live in a land of music. I will not merely speak and write: I will feel and know.

Only it is fading now.

The power is leaving me. I had it only a moment; and was it my own power or only a glimpse of Runild's? I cling, I grapple, and yet it goes, it goes, it goes, and I am left with shreds and bits, and then not even those, only an aftertaste, an echo of an echo, a diminishing shaft of feeble light. My eyes open. I am on my knees; sweat covers my body; my heart is pounding. Runild stands above me. "You see now?" he says. "You see? This is what it's like for me all the time. I can connect minds. *I can make connections, Mimise.*"

"Do it again," I beg.

He shakes his head. "Too much will hurt you," he says. And goes from me.

I have told Sleel what I have learned. Now they have the boy with them in the inner oracle-house, nine of them, the highest oracles, questioning him, testing him. I do not see how they can fail to welcome his gift, to give him special honor, to help him through his turbulent boyhood so that he can take his place supreme among oracles. But Jen thinks otherwise. She thinks he distresses them by scrabbling their minds in his still unfocused attempts at making contact, and that they will fear him once they have had an explicit demonstration of what he can do; she thinks, too, that he is a threat to their authority, of his way of joining the perceptions of his Right to the analytic powers of his Left by a direct mental flow is far superior to their own laborious method of symbolic translation. Jen thinks they will surely cull him and may even put him to death. How can I believe such things? She is not yet an oracle herself; she is still a girl; she may be wrong. The conference continues hour after hour, and no one emerges from the oracle-house.

In the evening they come forth. The rain has stopped. I see the senior oracles march across the courtyard. Runild is among them, very small at Sleel's side. There are no expressions on any faces. Runild's eyes meet mine: his look is blank, unreadable. Have I somehow betrayed him in trying to save him? What will happen to him? The procession reaches the far side of the quadrangle. A car is waiting. Runild and two of the senior oracles get into it.

After dinner Sleel calls me aside, thanks me for my help, tells me that Runild is to undergo study by experts at an institute far away. His power of mind-contact is so remarkable, says Sleel, that it requires prolonged analysis.

Mildly I ask whether it would not have been better to keep him here, among the surroundings that have become home to him, and let the experts come to the House of Double Minds to examine him. Sleel shakes his head. There are many experts, the testing equipment is not portable, the tests will be lengthy.

I wonder if I will ever see Runild again.

In the morning I meet with my group at the usual time. They have lived here several weeks now, and their early fears are gone from them. Already I see the destinies unfolding: Galaine is fast-witted but shallow, Mulliam and Chith are plodders, Fyme and Hirole and Divvan may have the stuff of oracles, the rest are mediocrities. An average group. Hirole, perhaps, is becoming my favorite. There are no Jens among them, no Runilds.

"Today we start to examine the idea of nonverbal words," I begin. "For example, if we say, Let this green ball stand for the word 'same,' and this blue box stand for the word 'different,' then we can..."

My voice drones on. The children listen placidly. So the training proceeds in the House of Double Minds. Beneath the vault of my skull my dreaming Right throbs a bit, as though reliving its moment of freedom. Through the corridors outside the room the oracles move, deep in contemplation, shrouded in impenetrable wisdom, and we who serve them go obediently about our tasks.